The Funkyhiphoopnautic
21 HUSTLE

Melki JK Russell

Anuword Media

The Funkyhiphoopnautic
21 HUSTLE

ISBN-13:978-0692570166
(Anuword Media)
ISBN-10:0692570160

Printed in the United States of America

THE RETURN OF ANU

The half-wise, recognizing the comparative unreality of the Universe, imagine that they may defy its Laws. Such are vain and presumptuous fools, and they are broken against the rocks and torn asunder by the elements by reason of their folly.

The truly wise, knowing the nature of the Universe, use Law against laws; the higher against the lower; and by the Art of Alchemy, transmute that which is undesirable into that which is worthy, and thus triumph.

Mastery consists not in abnormal dreams, visions and fantastic imaginings or living, but in using the higher forces against the lower— escaping the pains of the lower planes by vibrating on the higher. Transmutation, not presumptuous denial, is the weapon of the Master.

--From **The Kyballion**

PROJECT MARS, 2015 A.D.

Plop, plop, plop, *plink!*

Water continued to drop onto the cover of the latest edition of *2Grand*, the nation's newest hiphop magazine. The magazine was the shit-seller's dream; it was baby testosterone maturing into adolescence, and now all grown up. Unattainable whips that wore sparkling chrome-covered dubs. Beyond Mad Max electronic shit. Glossed-out thoroughbred bronze-skinned Honeyz with ass so thick you could see it from the front. Pheromone senses so acute that they could smell a true balla 2.5 blocks away. All the hook-or-crook-shit that Negus 'n' Whiggas loved and kept souls stuck on the planet for eon upon eon. Its cover story was headlined "Chinese Rapper Big Tao Explains Why He's 'Thugging for Buddha.'"

Moving slowly like the burgeoning puddle forming on the magazine cover, gradually diluting the copper-laced Platinum jewelry of hiphop's latest icon, a crowd began to form at the main viewing gallery on Reagun II. The Reagun was some real off-the-wall shit. NASA's engineers took this space station where none had gone before. It was as if they stole the design for the Lexus GS440 and upped it one or two. It only took 10 years of intense cooperation among world's elite, better known as the Ten Percent, that kept the 85 Percent, death, dumb, and blind and $660 billion in matching funds. Built with the purpose of serving as the staging point for the eventual colonization of Mars, it had a Herculean shine, and floated like some escaped Cadillac grill through the dense gooey darkness of outer space.

Most humans would not argue the fact that human beings were a funny sort—that if they were locked up in a cave for three weeks, pretty soon someone would find an area where the fireflies danced, and set up a bar there, where they'd sell overpriced, watered-down…water. Then, pretty soon, some brilliant muthafuka'd get the idea to create a VIP Section.

Deep in the middle of space, trapped on this expensive floating canister, the crew members on Xerxes aided of course by the ever flowing hard liquor, exacerbated by a less than normal oxygen level, got shit mo'popping than an uncut Lil' Jon video. Excitement buzzed throughout the space station quicker than news of the latest water cooler gossip. It was prime time for kit 'n' kin as the ship's orbit brought it closer to Phobus, one of the two moons orbiting the Red Planet. Gigantic reddish-brown dunes rose gracefully miles above the landscape to form pyramids of sand. Some saw faces, or shadows, and other undefined forms. The general consensus saw nothing but a dead moon and, of course, the next drink. Through the windows on the opposite side of the gallery lay a distant blue dot that they knew as home.

Surreal.

As the Xerxes space station passed Phobus, eyes glimmered, wondering when they'd be able to setup shop. Who'd get the prime plots? Already neo-scientific minds theorized that life on Mars—due to its rotation around the Sun, gravity, and possible unpolluted subterranean water supply—could serve as the fountain of youth that Ponce De Leon believed lay hidden in Florida's Everglades.

Scientists had theorized that by exploding tiny hydrogen bombs within the interior of the planet's core, they could reach the desired level of atmospheric transmutation necessary for human life. After they got the frozen oceans flowing again, they'd inhabit them with genetically altered supergrowth aquaflora.

The secondary aspect of the colonization project would create blocks of sustainable land that would be eligible for purchase by settlers within a few years. Those on the optimistic end of the spectrum believed that if things went well, they'd see the first interstellar fast food chain within a decade. To quote Jim Protek, the curly-haired, pseudo-Don King, proto-obnoxious head of NASA's Osiris Programs, the orbiting Xerxes space station "was state-of-the-art, squared."

About the size of Washington, DC, it glistened with acres of beautifully sculpted land, including white-sandy beaches, farms, shopping centers, stocked ponds, basketball courts, and 10 state of the art fitness centers. It was the crowning achievement of modern technology and international cooperation between the corporate sector and government. It was perfect, except for one slight problem—the smell.

Despite investing $3 billion in the latest high tech KAN Sewer System, continual malfunctions in the delivery system allowed the heavy odor of shit to stick in the atmosphere like flypaper. It wasn't too long before it earned the dubious or dookious distinction as "The Last Wrath of KAN."

Besides planning the eventual colonization of Mars, the Reagun served an immediate and highly profitable mission: providing its investors with an immediate return through monitoring activity on Earth using solar-powered satellites that tracked energy sources beneath the Earth and ocean surfaces. Once these energy sources were found, the corporate sector stacked chips for the list.

Dr. Soo Chen stood to the right of an overly gregarious group of onlookers, who barely acknowledged her as they stared at they hypnotic orbs. They weren't being malicious; they just didn't give a damn. All living beings produce an electromagnetic energy field, often called an aura. Some people attracted attention before they walked into the room, and some barely registered on the scale. For all intense purposes, Soo was damn near invisible.

In the midst of a crowd, she was still lonely glancing at the moons. For her, looking at Mars' moons only reminded her of her own deep loneliness and, for some strange reason, Pamela Anderson. She wondered if she could get an extension on her vacation long enough to visit the Beverly Hills plastic surgeon who'd done a job for her sister. She was a Noble Prize laureate. But she knew that that meant shit to the opposite sex, particularly when compared to twin 36-Ds staring them in the face. Tired of being ignored, Soo escaped into her huge antiseptic office, where she could fantasize and communicate with her online friends.

Daydreaming was the major aspect of Soo's existence.

She viewed life from a distance and avoided direct participation as if the Federation had given her a prime directive. Her title, Assistant Director of Strategic Utilization of Underground Resources on Earth (better known as the acronym SOURCE), meant nothing. *Big breasts, big breasts—if I think it, they'll grow, if I think it, they'll grow.*

A graduate of MIT's advanced School of Aerodynamic Physics, Soo later studied Geo-physical Detection and Environmental Engineering at Rochester Tech before earning her 4th doctorate in Solar Elemental Physics at Princeton. Smart and hard-driven, her intelligence was only exceeded by her goofiness.

Prior to the Reagun, Soo had served as a research assistant on the Hoffmeyer Project, which had perfected the SOURCE technology. Originally SOURCE was designed to track the levels of organic carbon found in grassroots. This was done to combat global warming after they had found out that huge levels of carbon dioxide produced by burning fossil fuels, rather than making their way to the atmosphere and increasing the greenhouse effect of CO, could be naturally absorbed by certain grasses particular to Africa. While utilizing SOURCE for this original environmental purpose, they accidentally came upon a more profitable way of using SOURCE—detection of underground energy sources. That was when the government took over the project and Soo ended up as the assistant director of SOURCE on the Reagun II.

If it wasn't for the money they were paying her, she was sure she'd be diagnosed with clinical depression. She rationalized that as long as she made this type of money she had no right to be depressed. So what if no one had hit on her in 487 days, and once in three years? She was sure that the sour milk smelling-ratchet-faced trash guy in the cafeteria winked at her yesterday. She loved the scar that passed up his neck over his right eye—that meant he either had character or had come up short one too often in his overzealous gambling. She wasn't bad-looking herself; she had deep soft eyes with long lashes that hid behind her glasses. She worked out every day and had beautifully smooth skin, athletic thighs and a flat stomach that regularly disappeared underneath a long white smock. *"Oh my God, 487 days,"* she thought. *Big breasts, big breasts, if I think it, they'll grow…*

Today something good was sure to happen—she deserved it. Plus, according to her online personal psychic, "Mars was in the aura of Venus Williams and the house music would be pumping." *That had to mean something good, right?* Never a slouch, she'd guaranteed that things would get moving today by adding a touch of horseradish to her normally bland soyburger. If that didn't spark some shit, she'd just have to dye her hair yellow with purple highlights, put in her nipple rings, and streak through the Reagun again. *Somebody'd look.* She'd just have to make sure that Jenny, the big boobed blond, wasn't planning the same thing on the same day again.

While Soo got her grub on, occasionally taking sips of Ginseng soda and glancing at her door-sized beefcake calendar, she began noticing a weird reading popping-up on her latest SOURCE-SCAN printout. The computer printout whirled and bucked from the printer into a box on the floor. To decrease the smell she constantly burned Nag Champa a cauky, orange incense that was a favorite of Buddhist, and so strong it drowned the funk from the entire wing of the space station. She peeked at a picture of her parents that sat in a dusty rectangular frame that slightly cut off her do everything sista with the big breasts. Normally, she'd get readings from newly detected sources that chirped loudly and quickly died out after a few seconds. She grew nervous, running her fingers through her long black hair, as this printout kept coming; prompting her to drop her sandwich and take a closer look. From what she could see, it appeared to be some undefined energy source emanating from an area in the Horn of Africa.

Soo slid over closer and put on her bifocals.

"Uummm…this is interesting."

She ran the same numbers through the computers and got the same reading. By the time the printout slid out of the computer, she was halfway down the hall yelling out the voice of her superior.

"Doc! Doc! You've got to see this! You've got to see this!"

Dr. Gergan Hoffmeyer was considered one of the most brilliant minds in science, yet he was still a man who congratulated himself each time he completed his 1040 correctly. He sat head buried into the photo of his ex-wife and two kidz. He still couldn't believe that she had left him, after seven excruciatingly long years of marriage. Not that he ever loved his wife; he barely *liked* her. But he still couldn't believe she left him. Hoffmeyer never really liked science either. But for the sake of his then-dying 179-year-old mother—kept alive through a genetic experiment, using Tortoise Growth Hormone—he married a wife and pursued a scientific career.

As he stared at the photo, the glint from his lamp reflected his face in the glass frame. He looked closer. His hairline had moved back another inch.

I'm going bald.

As he increased his stare, it seemed his left eye was shrinking. He yawned; in doing so, noticed two of his upper molars could easily been mistaken for Columbian coffee beans.

I need a dentist.

Hoffmeyer's office was filled with incense, the majority of them stashed in porcelain bowl resting neatly on the corner of his desk. His favorite was Blue Nile. He had air freshener of every kind—pop-ups, plug-ins, candles, and a miniature fan, strategically angled to deflect the funk off his right wall, through the door, and down the hallway. He'd consulted with a few astrophysicists to ensure that his calculations would appropriately deflect the funk in a cohesive manner. Not that it helped a whole lot, but a man needed to find peace wherever he could.

He hated the Reagun; the smell was drove him crazy. It seemed that fate plain didn't like him. As a youth growing up in North Carolina, his father had owned a chicken farm—in fact, several of them. The farm's runoff of chicken waste literally clogged up the local river, killing off the fish. He'd tried to force his father to simply use a mushroom based mulch that would have saved the ecosystem but his father was an uneducated disciplinarian, who lived life without planning on thinking too much and thought it won't nothing wrong with a little shit in the river. Besides, the smell made sure the tourists and developers would stay away. After being forced to learn the business by working his summers on the farms until he graduated from high school, he swore that if he didn't do anything else in life he would leave that shit-smelling place and never eat chicken again.

Now, here he was trapped again, where the aroma of shit smothered him like a shadow. The stress was slowly eating him away. He was fighting the idea that, despite his best efforts, he was still surrounded by shit. He'd already developed a nervous twitch in his shrinking left eye and now one had formed in his right cheek.

That's it. That's it, thought Hoffmeyer. *When the Shuttle docks in two weeks, I'm hijacking the bitch!*

Soo stumbled into his office, awakening him out of his pitiful state.

"Doc! Doc!" yelled Soo, huffing as she finally arrived at the end of the mile long corridor to the office of her mentor. Hoffmeyer figured that because of the distance between their offices, he wouldn't see her so much. He was only half-right.

As Soo dashed in with printout in hand, she accidentally knocked over his incense bowl, nearly setting the place aflame and inadvertently attempted to spray it out with Lysol.

"Excuse me."

"What is it?" Hoffmeyer snapped.

"I ran several tests, but nothing matches," said Soo as she handed the sheet to him.

"Hummm, did you run this through our HAL Computer?"

"Yes," replied a flustered Soo.

"And it still doesn't make sense?" frowned Hoffmeyer.

Hoffmeyer slowly put on his glasses and noticed that the undefined energy source found by SOURCE hadn't shown up in earlier scans.

Was the African Union doing underground nuclear testing?
Couldn't be, we had stockpiled the world's uranium supply.
Maybe some former KGB, or Chinese are helping them go nuclear.

Naw, we've been monitoring both of them, too.

He couldn't understand it. Something was causing tremendous energy bursts in the area of Northeast Sudan.

"Don't worry, Soo. We'll inform headquarters about this. Maybe they can track it from the ground," said Hoffmeyer, attempting more to calm his own nerves as opposed to Soo's.

Nervously, Hoffmeyer wrote down communication instructions and prepared to send his findings to Strategic Control via InstellarFax.

STRATEGIC CONTROL

Buried six miles beneath the Arizona Desert, Strategic Control was off-limits to the public since the Fifties, when locals began harping about UFOs. Commonly referred to as SC, it extended five by six miles and was ultra-modern. Word had it that security clearance was so tight at SC that every time somebody dug up his nose, someone 2000 miles away in the Pentagon was placing a booger on the wall.

It was a $4 billion facility that, in Pentagon dollars, cost the taxpayers $20 billion to build. It had been expanded twice. The first time was during the early Hanger 51 incidents, after insiders leaked U.S. military involvement with extraterrestrials or ETs who had been delivering increasing levels of high technology to the military. Only insiders were aware of the Timberlake Project begun in 1987 where the ETs provided the military with a device that allowed whitefolks to have rhythm. The Timberlake project was an advanced follow-up to the Denny Terrio project. After an executive at MTV paid some folks off to get the technology, the rest was history. The facility was remodeled again, after the Select Intelligence Committee found out about the Stepford Project involving the Reagan Droid.

The key group of ETs involved in the Earth Project— called Greys—weren't giving the military technology because they loved the U.S.; they were providing it to the Russians, Chinese, Iraqis, North Koreans, the Neo-Cons, Martha Stewart and anyone else they assumed willing to blow up the planet, except the French. Not that they couldn't find enough French willing to destroy the world for a belief. It was just that for some strange reason they wasn't feeling the anti-deodorant-slash-mayonnaise and French fries shit. Not that they hated the French, they just felt that anyone who smelled that bad, had no right to charge that much money for cognac. Now the Americans they hated, but they could deal with them since they were the most anal-retentive grooming product

Nazis in the entire Universe. At the rate they were killing off good bacteria, it was only a matter of time before some new plague emerged to wipe off the majority of humanity. At least they'd die well groomed.

The ETs own Holy Books found in the Askashic Records—called by some "Books of Destinies"—had determined that unless the former Godz of the planet awoke, man would eventually transport war and bloodshed to other parts of the Universe and initiate a star-holocaust that would take them a billion years to recover from. The ETs were crazy advanced, but won't no punks. They had two choices: either awake the sleeping Godz of the planet or allow the humans to destroy themselves.

It was predicted that once or if the Godz regained control of time and moved out of the dimension of CP Time, they'd awake. But after the Bling Bling era, few left even believed the old prophecies were relevant. Rather than depend on the former Godz waking up, the ETs took a surer bet, and began feeding more and more technology to the most ignorant, fearful and judgmental humans they could find. It was a really easy choice. Humans were already slowly murdering themselves and destroying the environment at a rate which evolutionary physical mutations were unable to match. And besides, they argued, the old Godz, whom they referred to as "Negus"—an Ethiopic derivative for "King"— were considered death, dumb, and blind, and in ever-increasing numbers had become worshippers of the one-dimensional vampire god Manna-Blingus. This evil deity Manna-Blingus fed on the intense energies generated by ignorance, fear, violence and materialism. He was a descendant of the red beast, which the ancients called Apopis, Set, Satan, or the Devil. The former Godz of the planet converted to the worship of Blingus. This created a tear in the Universal Balance and weakened the power of Right forces to intervene. Due to the limited amount of teachers left among the Negus, the majority of Godz had lost their mission, and few even realized the role that Negus were supposed to play on this planet. Negus were now pursuing materialism like there was no tomorrow. In a sense, with the speed at which the planet was losing its vital energies, they were right.

Despite the decision of certain ETs to speed up the destruction of Earth, they were not all malicious—they, like everyone else in the Universe, had a sense of humor, too. They never missed a chance to fuck with whitefolks, whom they blamed for creating "progress" and nearly depleting the Earth of its life's blood in only a matter of a few centuries. Every once in a while they'd get high off some Yak and hydro and buzz past the White House. They'd normally wait until the president had to take a shit or when the batteries on the vice president's heart monitor were low. Or if they were horny just kidnap a blonde coed. They'd seen those "Gone Wild," videos and couldn't help themselves. The horniest, and most barbaric of the alien races in the known Universe were the Greys. Greys even had an inter-universal pool going on how long it would take for mankind to blow itself up. Humans were dumb, they thought, especially Americans—they actually believed that democracy meant they all had a say in what their government did.

SC MAIN VIEWING ROOM

Strategic Control's main viewing room was jam packed with basketball junkies. A row of black kegs lined the back wall and the stench of cold pizza, mumbo sauce and hot-wings transformed the normally staid antiseptic air into frat house quality. On any normal day, the screen would be filled with SOURCE energy destinations, regional conflicts and Black Operation sites.

Today, the three-dimensional 88-foot Plasma flat-screen served as a huge teleprompter for game seven of the NBA Finals. These military men and women were the backbone of the nation's defense system. There job was to nip in the bud, any potential military strike by the enemies of freedom. They were committed to the protection of the Free World on guard 24-7. But everybody slacked off now and then, even them.

Of course a war could be starting somewhere in the world. Al Qaeda might be planning its next Jihad. Or Russian extremists could've hijacked the Soviet government and launched a first strike nuclear assault. If so, they'd get to it tomorrow. Today, they'd just have to take their chances—this was Game 7, Lakers versus Wizards, and America had its priorities.

Colonel Token Blackmann sat in the biggest chair in the room grimacing about the incredible dunk by the Wizard's 7-foot forward, Kendell Brown.

"He traveled. Traaaavel! Brown dragged his foot. Nobody that big can move like that without traveling."

Token was the first African American officer to command a Black Operations. He never really liked Hoop, but it was forced on him since he was normally the only brotha around, and stood six foot seven, once he got over drooping his shoulders.

Nevertheless, he was proud of the fact that two weeks ago, on his 38th birthday, he could finally complete a crossover dribble with out falling. AI didn't have shit on him; *I'da shut that little quick bastard down.* Next year, he was planning to dunk, and if things worked real well, maybe tryout for the local YMCA team. You know—keep his options open. Hence was the unspoken lure of basketball that few would openly discuss or admit. The fact that on any given Sunday, some fat, slow bastard with bladder control problems and a career scoring average of 2.3 points per game for his church League (and who wasn't above scheduling a few games with mentally challenged facilities to up their record) would now—in-between six-packs of beer and nachos, of course—be talking about how in his prime he could've dunked on Jordan, blocked T-Mac's shot, boxed out Shaq, and kept Ben Wallace off the boards. Talking shit wasn't in itself dangerous as long as you realized that you were talking shit.

None of this mattered to Token; he had skillz. In the spirit of keeping his options open, a year ago he began taking modified synthetic growth hormone. His vertical jump had increased by almost an inch, but his penis had shriveled up to the size of an acorn.

That's growing too, he thought.

Token leaned back in his brown leather executive chair with automated Reiki Therapy mode, and took a sip of beer. Commercials for cars, alcohol, and pizza flooded the screen during the timeout, while the military personnel at Strategic Control intoxicated and stuffed became engrossed in Madison

Ave.'s subliminal projection of needs, desires, and wants. Token scanned the room looking at his backstabbing colleagues, thinking Brutus didn't have shit on these bastards.

"General Token! Sir!

Oh no, thought Token, feeling a tap on his shoulder. *I know, I know. I paid in the pool already.*

As he whirled around-he noticed Major Innis Schitt. *Mr. Never-Saw-An-Ass-He-Wouldn't-Kiss.* Or his favorite term of endearment, *Sir Brownnose.* If there was one thing that irritated the hell out of Token, it was Schitt. Maybe it was the fact that he was short, greasy, sinister and had a bad haircut? Maybe it was the fact that despite being a lower rank, he always carried this smarter-than-thou attitude and condescending mannerisms while dealing with lifelong military? Maybe it was because he had an Ivy League degree? Or was it because he never saw him with a woman? Or maybe it was the fact he was from New England but passed himself off as a Texan? Whatever it was, Token despised him.

"What the hell! This shit better be important," Token shrilled at Schitt. "You are fucken' with my R& R big time, Major Pain- In-The-Ass."

Nervously flicking his pen off and on, Schitt smiled deviously:

"Sir, this is important. Sir, I think you better come with me to the conference room. General Brighton is already there. "

"What!" snapped Token, truly amazed that this talking fungal toenail had the audacity to pull him away from Game Seven of the NBA Finals for some bullshit.

"Why in the hell did you bring Brighton's old ass in on this? He's only monitoring SC for the Pentagon; he'll be gone next week."

"Yes, Sir," responded Schitt. "But according to section Four, Paragraph H, Subsection Twelve, we are required to infor—"

"God-dammnit, Schitt, I know the rulebook," grumbled Token, who got up from his favorite chair and headed to the conference room.

As Token and Schitt entered the burgundy colored conference room that was about the length of a football field;

16

General Stonewall Brighton, stood with his back to the door, puffing on his favorite Cuban Cohiba Robusto cigar. He was engulfed in "Axis of Evil," the latest virtually reality game. Brighton was a pot-bellied, pickled nose, Old School, cigar-smoking, Southern redneck. His family had been in the military since the Confederacy. He was well-connected and flouted all the rules and regulations whenever he felt like it. Shit, His great-great-great grandfather gave the Union Army its worst ass- kicking during the Civil War. He was a military blueblood and all these peons could do for him was to shine his shoes.

The Dominican cigars were good, Cubans better, thought Brighton as he decided to nuke Cuba anyway. The object of the game was to maintain your nuclear arsenal while causing the other nuclear states to use up their stockpile on lesser threats.

Hearing the arrival of Token and Schitt, Brighton pointed with his left arm to the recent Instellarfax from the Reagun Space station now rolled up on the conference table.

"Read that shit, Token." Brighton barked in his nasal driven Tennessee drawl.

"Tell me what you think, Boy."

As Token deciphered the report, Brighton continued "Axis of Evil" with his back turned to the officers now gathered at the conference table. He had just caused China to exhaust a third of its arsenal by moving a small amount of nuclear warheads to Japan, despite the wishing of the Japanese government. General Motors should love him. The Koreas would neutralize each other, and Israel would engulf the Middle East threats—Iraq, Iran and Egypt.

"So, I'm outside of the club and you think I'm a punk….
"So I go to my loaded tech-9 and popped the trunk….
"I ain't neva scured, what! I ain't never scured…"

Brighton hummed to himself as he racked up mega points.

While Brighton demolished the world, Token stood opened-jawed. He couldn't believe what he was reading, it seemed that the Osiris process had begun in the Horn of Africa. Well, actually, the readings pointed to some area in northeastern Sudan. The Osiris process was a top-secret theory developed by the Pentagon in conjunction with NASA. They discovered a process for revitalizing the dead parts of the Earth contaminated by war, pollution, or harsh weather patterns. All this was just theory, since the scientists were unable to find the proper energy source to make Osiris work. Token was responsible for the SET Project, which, unlike Osiris, was a long-active operational program that by any means necessary coordinated covert military operations designed to produce zero growth in Africa. This included crop destabilization as well as climate manipulation to create widespread famine in the Horn of Africa region. Famine was a main aspect for destabilizing the region. The unwritten colonial and Western foreign policy rule was that Africans should never be allowed to control their mineral resources. These minerals and elements were crucial to maintaining Western military technology. To allow Africans control of these strategic natural resources would basically signal the end of the Western Power hegemony. Token had followed General Benjamin Templeton as the key man in charge of making sure that the African continent was kept dangerously busy. During the Eighties, Templeton served as the key Economic Hit Man (EHM) for TAINT Consultancies, which played a hand in the overthrow of at least 11 elected African governments in the past two decades.

Token angrily looked at Captain Kelso Clark, also reluctantly called into the meeting.

"Clark, what's this?"

Brushing mumbo sauce off his fingers, Clark took the fax from Token.

"Well, Sir, you know our efforts in the region and calculations were based on the manipulation of water supply and environment via RNA destabilization of key crops in order to induce zero-growth by 2045."

"I know that, already. Tell me something else, stupid," growled Token.

"Well," said Clark, "the latest HAL projections for zero-growth were projected at 2055 two months ago. And according to the latest estimations, zero-growth has been pushed back to 2075. In other words, the SET Project is being reversed, Sir! The African continent is repairing its ability to sustain new growth at an incredible evolutionary level and there doesn't seem to be anything that we can do about it, Sir."

Clark sat down and dug into his wings again like he was

gonna re-kill the bird.

"They are implementing the Osiris project. No, this shit is impossible," declared Token. "General Brighton," he asked, "do you think it's possible to give us a little time to figure this out before passing it on to your people at the Pentagon?"

Still consumed by his reality game, Brighton, spewing smoke everywhere, paused for a second.

"Well, it looks like we've got ourselves a problem, boys. And I hate to be the bearer of bad news, but I got to take this little problem back to the Pentagon. I guess we'll do something," said Brighton in an *I-could-give-a-shit* manner.

"But, but…." stuttered Token, "they can't be reversing the process. They don't have the technology to do that; we don't even have that technology yet. They don't even have the technology to figure out what the hell were doing, much less reverse it!"

Token, flabbergasted, jetted out the conference room in need of comfort like a girl told she wasn't going to the prom. In times of crisis, only one thing gave him what he needed and he sought her out with a vengeance.

"Vivi, Vivi," he muttered to himself. "Daddy needs you. Come to Daddy, baby."

Brighton, fresh off a successful first-strike against the North Koreans, conveniently put out his cigar on the game screen and then politely asked Schitt, "Who is Vivi, son? That the boy's wife?"

"No, Sir," said Schitt, smirking like the kid who just released a silent but nasty smelling poot. "She's…It's his EMC. I mean, Electronic Massage Chair. He calls it Vivi, Sir."

Brighton finally turns around with a smoked-pork look on his face, dropped jaw. "Huh!"

As he returned to his "Axis of Evil" screen, Brighton noticed that he's now the only survivor of a thermo-nuclear war. *What! I ain't neva scured, what…I ain't neva scured…"*

"I love that song," laughed Brighton.

FORT MEADLE, MARYLAND

"General Wilson, please," requested John Shadow in a serene but soft voice into the VoiceScan biometric security system.

As the huge imposing door slid open, Shadow began his walk down the dimly lit corridor filled with framed photos of former distinguished officers, and stepped briskly towards the office of Major Averil Wilson, head of the Federal Bureau of Drug Intelligence, and Espionage or FBDIE. Glistening specks of sweat began to trickle down the angular slope of his forehead and Shadow's perfectly-fitted suit seemed to collapse like shrink wrap around his frame. He was nervous and knew that the Major General was not kind to disappointment or failure, especially when it involved his type. The only way a brotha like him made his way into the upper echelon of the intelligence game was by being two to three, aw fuck it, four to five times better than the whiteboyz. Despite this, he knew he'd always be on a precipitous edge. One fucken mistake and that was all she wrote. When it came to dealing with the folks he dealt with, he'd better have the answers before they did. Others might have time to contemplate an answer, but Shadow knew he wasn't afforded that luxury.

As Shadow reached the office, the receptionist, already standing, brushed back her wavy blonde hair and motioned for him to have a seat. Her desk was immaculate, neatly stacked rows of paper, color-coded files, and some expensive looking paper-weight Either she was more than efficient, or she had very little actual work to do. She couldn't have been more than 22 and wore a tight fitting blouse that exposed breasts that could have fed an entire nation. Her skirt fit even tighter. Shadow was pissed that he didn't put mirrors on his shoes anymore.

"He's expecting you," she said in manner slightly arrogant for someone of her age and position.

"Did you get caught up in traffic?"

"Naw, I was at your Mom's house," mumbled Shadow under his breath while ignoring her. He hated being questioned by anyone who could not legally have him assassinated.

Five minutes later a tall man with very bad acne greeted Shadow and escorted him back to the top secret meeting room, where the Major and others sat waiting.

"Welcome to Fort Meade. The meeting is ready to begin. Dr. Weismiller, your report, please," said the Major

General.

Shadow quickly sat down and opened his briefcase. He didn't think twice about being the only brotha in the room; Hell, he had gone to college in Boston.

The table consisted of many notables from various aspects of intelligence, covert operations, and government agencies, a group that made the staff at Abu Ghraib prison look like protégé's of Mother Theresa. Short, with pudgy unclean hands, bespectacled, bald and ugly, Dr. Weismiller was far from imposing, yet he was the leading expert on bio-genetic surgery and second in command of the successful Genome Project which had mapped out and categorized the total human genetic sequence and won the Nobel Prize. In his world he was king; on the street, he was normally mistaken for an Italian Icy vendor at Yankee Stadium.

"Gentlemen," said Weismiller, completely disregarding the presence of Sheila Moran, head of NAHM. "The initial experiments of the Omega Project were successful. We were able to replicate the original creation of genetically superior humanoids. However, it appears that the Chinese have gained progress also."

"More importantly," added Weismiller, "is the fact that some of the experiments—uh, excuse me, a few of the Noids—seems to have escaped the training facility and had to be shot. Unfortunately, there seems to be one still unaccounted for."

"Uggrhm," clearing his throat, Weismiller wiped the sweat from his brow. "We're still tracking the Noid, however, let me make this clear, there's no truth to the rumor that he's at Yale and was just initiated as a Bonesman."

This was a top-secret project where even the roaches needed clearance. Most insiders knew that the Pentagon was working on developing the new humanoids in order to create a super army. It was similar to the idea that the German scientists had worked on in the Thirties—creating a super race. The only difference was that up until now, no one knew how to do it, and no one had any idea about completing the genetic sequencing map. So they stole the patent from the French for creating artificial DNA. Weismiller's team, in conjunction with MACROSUN Technology, developed the "Shark Software" which brought supercomputers to another level by perfecting the use of thousands of parallel processors into actual thinking machines based on a scaled down decipherization of the neural code. These machines were then able to create new software in order to solve the unsolvable and thus re-create itself—a practical artificial life form.

The Shark Technology led to additional advances in nanotechnology, where atom sized molecular machines were created and used to build physical structures from the atomic level up.

These humanoid lifeforms were implanted with cerebral expansion slots, which allowed interface with the "thinking computers," A cyborg, basically. However, creating artificial thinking machines would not be enough; Weismiller and the military had another agenda. For one, the creation of actual super-humanoid lifeforms—or Metanoids, as they were now being called—had been banned by Presidential Memo No. 314. Yet, in secret meetings with the Joint Chiefs, President Thorn had given the approval after stressing plausible denial as his out should anything go wrong. They had laid some of the preliminary work out during the Persian War and now wanted to test these Metanoids out in Africa, if possible.

If they could restart tensions among the northern and southern Sudanese, they might be able to prompt a split in the African Union. They'd use protection of U.S. interests in Uganda, as the pretext for military involvement, or, quite possibly, if push came to shove, they could implement a terrorist attack and blame it on Khartoum. However, the major purpose was not really military conflict or having Sudan serve as a testing ground for the Noids; they could have used the War Against Terrorism's (WAG) South American front for that. They in actuality wanted to find the energy deposits located by SOURCE technology. Under Code name Project SET, they'd been destabilizing the environment in the Horn of Africa region to engineer zero-population growth. They eventually wanted to use to creation of disaster to send in relief teams as the covert front to regain a foothold in the region. But, for some reason, the zero-growth had been reversed slowly and the land was being rejuvenated.

The recent data from the Reagun had shown that the Horn of Africa was sitting on some new unbelievable energy source. Government scientists theorized that these energy deposits on the surface when broken down to molecular form had a stability and pliability necessary for total and full-fledged expansion of nanotechnology. One of the main features necessary for optimization of nanotechnology was creating a molecular grid that would allow molecules for any object to be laid out in a design on the grid. They needed a substance that would hold the molecules together. Many believed that the substance in Sudan was the missing link—ironically, they called it "Ether2." Whatever it was, they knew it was potent enough to have begun the Osiris process. This alone had everybody both scared and excited.

If the African Union—or possibly the Chinese, who had excellent relations with them—could exploit these energy sources, and commercialize it, then it meant the end of the neo-petroleum era-and Western geo-political dominance. Something this important could not be left to chance. America was prepared to maintain its hegemony and avoid the fate predestined for all great world empires—eventual destruction.

In analyzing the search for "Ether2," the group came across some mythical legends that were being resuscitated among the Ethiopians, and Sudanese. They traced these myths back to the time before the pharaohs, and it served as reason why they were speculating on this substance called "Ether2."

According to scrolls predating the Pyramid Texts, the term Ether, which most took to mean "heavenly," was an adaptation of the true name of Blacks. This was why all of Africa, was called Ethiopia. All those of Black skin—not just today's residents of that country—were Ethiopians, or the "Heavenly People."

The old scribes of Greece, including the famous storyteller Homer, knew this as in the first chapter of "The Iliad"; he called them "the blameless Ethiopians." The Greeks believed that there were no people more holy or beautiful. According to legend, these people were descended from the Godz and created civilization. This wasn't any different than most cultures, each of whom claimed that they were descended from Higher beings. However, there was still another aspect of the myth that few—including the most devoted researchers—were aware of. It dealt directly to the unbelievable transformation of the exhausted and polluted areas of the African continent into a previously unthinkable oasis of intense vegetation and growth. Responsible for the research on these myths was General M.M. Banes. Looking around the room, Weismiller nodded to General Banes, who then briskly rose from his seat with a huge white- tooth smile.

"As we have heard, we are continuing to analyze the possibilities of intervention via Project SET. No one knows for sure what this energy source is. The most we can ascertain is from some pagan myths about this magical staff or septre. According to our experts this staff of—er—Ptah, was the signal of the resurrection of the land and the rebirth of the chosen ones. However, according to other interpretations of this legend—er, myth—rather than causing the rebirth of the land, it will instead cause the reawaking of the sleeping Godz— the descendents of the Neterwu."

"What's a Neterwu?" loudly asked a confounded Shelia Moran, index finger brushing an ever-growing mustache.

Banes stared at Moran and smiled without blinking; thinking, *She'll have a full beard soon.* He paused in frustration, and then continued.

"Well, evidently, some people didn't take the time to read their briefing materials, that took quite an arduous, long time putting together. Nevertheless, Neterwu is the name for the Godz of Egypt, or Kemet, meaning the land of the Blacks— it's a term for the ancient Godz," said the General.

Before he began speaking again, Moran interrupted him once more. "Who are the sleeping Godz?"

Ignoring Moran, the General continued. "Where was I?"

"Er, um, now, we have been in contact with the opposition in Sudan and they report that this individual, Musa, is a key player in this whole myth crap. Now Musa is responsible for the Nigroes—excuse me, uh, Blacks, uh, sorry, Aaahfreekins Aaaamirikhans, I mean, Negus—leaving various countries to return to Africa. Musa and his wife are the leaders of this 'Return to Africa' movement," continued the general in his heavy Bostonian accent. "Now, the only problem with us dealing with Musa in the way we'd normally rid ourselves of his type, is that he's looked upon as if he is the return of Deng Majok—look into your notes for that backgrounder. Musa appears to be fulfilling some rare Dinka prophecy and seems to have been given unheard-of approval from a coalition of apparently powerful spiritual leaders from the Nuer, Dinka, and Shilluk uniting Sudanese across ethnic groups. On top of that, the spiritual leaders from Khartoum are in Musa's pocket as well. Not that he's paying them, but they won't take anything to go against him."

As if by command, Banes stopped suddenly, utilizing a pregnant pause to the maximum, and lit his cigarette. "Aaah, Shadow, you can pick it up from here."

John Shadow stood up quickly. Sweat beaded upon his forehead like little atoms of nervousness. He pulled out a handkerchief and wiped gently. He shuffled his papers and spoke.

"Thank you, general…I—I mean to say, we—we have made contact with our link in New York and it looks good. He is a son of Musa and attends Columbia. As a matter of fact," declared Shadow, loosening up quickly, "he considers me a friend of his. This guy really hates his parents and what they stand for. He's really jealous of his brother and would do practically anything to get back at his parents.

And get this: His uncle is the coach of the Kings," harped an excited Shadow. "And he basically hangs around with a bunch of losers. This kid is into everything—orgies, drugs, alcohol, partying until he drops. He's out there more than an Amish teenager—*loves* American culture. I mean, he's still doing the cabbage patch!" remarked Shadow, before bursting into his sickening laugh— "*heh, heh, a heh-aheh.*"

The silence stuck him like a brick wall. He realized that, as usual, he's the only one laughing at his jokes. Tightening up again, in mumblemania mannerisms that only Brian Gumble could be proud of, Shadow continued, speaking twice as fast.

"We are in touch and will be able to use him, whenever the opportunity presents itself. Thank you," said Shadow.

He slinked down into his chair, only to notice Sheila

Moran winking at him.

WORDS....

In times of peril hiphop is my rescue
Bloodlines flow from the Nile into my Nephews
Is it coincidence?
That my vernaculars hyped?
I rip the mike with pure knowledge
but can't read left to right

2018: JAY DA HUSTLER

As the Sky began dripping silky drops of moisture onto a thirsty planet, Jay "Sky" Walker stood in a corner phone booth up off the Ave, elbow leaning on an aluminum slab, phone stuck in the nook between his shoulder and cranium. Tenement buildings stared at him and rose into the dark sky like giant Legos blocks. Jay peeked up the street, back and forth, as the rain cathartically washed the smell off of New York for a quick second. The dredged buildings, cracked sidewalks, and slick streets soaked up the rain like a thirsty baby crying for its mother's milk. It was as if it needed the rain, as if only a good rain was a prerequisite for the city to cleanse itself from the negative emotion and violence that occurred regularly in its streets. Jay da Hustler, dressed in a black leather straddler, black Adidas and wool skullcap, took a deep breath, like a kid who'd got five of the six Lotto numbers, wondering if this was it—if the barely scraping by era was finally over.

Sweat trickled down his forehead, nose, and eventually dripping onto the pavement, meshing with puddles as they crept underneath the phone booth, like the sweat knew Jay was heading for a severe ass kicking and wanted no part of it. Water dripped onto the crumpled, tightly gripped piece of paper with several phone numbers on it, gradually and slightly blurring the ink. Glancing once more, Jay dialed the digits slowly with one hand; the other hand tightly gripped a black leather attaché case.

Fate had its moments. There were times when it was a little tired, when it slipped up and granted Negus that wasn't supposed to come up their moment. But Fate didn't make mistakes, though—well, mistakes that it didn't eventually square when no one was looking. As Fate would have it, Jay and a few kidz had been running several of a variety of them regular airport hustles and they finally lucked up big-time.

After securing access to the airport hotel, Jay and his associates, vicked some young well-dressed Negus for his briefcase. After unlocking the case, what they found was a caseload of top-secret documents and a listing of what author John Perkins called "Economic Hit Men" or EHMs. These were the worst sort of intelligence agents. Those who, under the guise of international corporations attempting to rebuild or modernize the so-called Third World, burdened them with immense debt. All they while, they destabilized any real progress towards independence through covert military actions, assassinations, and war, if necessary. The whole scheme for Africa and the Caribbean was all mapped out through a connecting web of multinational corporations, government agencies, think-tanks, politicians, and intelligence agents. It seemed everybody who was on the take was in those files. Figuring the information had to have some value, Jay and his peeps unanimously decided to try to sell it back to the folks they stole it from. They coulda done the right thing, and been celebrated on somebody's next album, maybe met Mandela's daughters or been given a plaque with red-black-and-green flags attached to it. But for kidz trying to come up, a few pats on the back and nods from the conscious crowd didn't seem worth it, especially when your kidz needed the new Airs or latest overpriced hiphop fashion-accessorized bag of self esteem. Jay hated these sellouts, and didn't have nuthing against other Blackfolks, but it was all about the Cream.

Phone snuggled between his ear and shoulder, sinuses sniffling; Jay had one simple intent—the specific goal that dominated his adult life: *to get paid*. If he could get paid, then his life would mean something. All the shit he'd been through and suffered would, might, make sense. Everything made sense when you were able to lay back on your deck overlooking the ocean, sipping Yak, right? Everything—all the hard times, days without—would have registered as just a few chin-checks, right?

The number began ringing.

Somewhere in-between the hypnotic rings, Jay's mind slipped into the zone. His mind transferred him back to an era when endorphins were plentiful, when life was a cornucopia of pleasure choices, when his upside as a human being shot through the stratosphere.

He thought about 8th grade when he was the best player in the city. By age 13, he'd shot up to 6-2 with the ability to dunk anything in sight. In his mind he was the King of New York. He was Jesus Shuttlesworth—and four years younger. All the best high schools wanted him, and he was happy to choose Jackson. Him and his boy El both had game and their plan was simple: go to Jackson, crush the competition and then sign for major figgas, hopefully with the Knicks. The worst that could happen was they'd go D1, and after a year or two go pro. He would play two-guard and El at the point. *Shit, we wuz pure nasty together, like da Pearl and Clyde all over again. If we'd stuck with it, not got caught up, we could've went big time—been a Lottery pick. Then it was all fucked up! I wasn't trying to hurt him… why that mawfucka had to say something about my moms?"*

The phone answered in a feminine, computerized voice. "This is a Level Three access area. Please enter your six-digit code now." Jay slowly pressed the three numbers after glancing again at the crumpled paper he held tightly but gently as a Faberge egg.

The phone skipped, then transferred as a voice answered: "This is Babel-Center One. State your contact."

"The war has begun," Jay spoke nervously into the receiver.

Suddenly, someone picked up the other end. "You are unauthorized to proceed. This is an FBDIE unauthorized access code. Who are you?"

Jay breathed deeply, his heart pounding like a Neptune drumbeat.

"I need to talk to, er, 'Othello.'"

"Okay," said the voice on the other end, simultaneously pressing the trace option that would signal to agents the exact whereabouts of the caller within 30 seconds.

"What do you want?"

Smiling into the receiver, Jay responded immediately. "I got something of his. Something I know he wants back. All we need to discuss is how bad. I'll contact you again—later!"

Jay slammed down the receiver and scatted off down the block, up the alley. No sooner than 40 seconds later, three dark blue Ford Tasers flew up the street doing 70. They quickly screeched to a halt at the phone booth.

"Damn bastard," said one Fed. "We'll get him," said another. One just sat in the car, thinking and planning and wondering, *Who is this motherfucker?*

"Well, whoever the bastard is, he's going to pay and John Shadow is going to make sure of that shit," he said under his breath while staring at the wet Gotham skyline.

EL'S WORLD

Ellis "Sun" Rey arrived home exhausted with a bag of chicken from Popeye's. For some reason, he began thinking about what Uncle used to say: "You know why they call it Pop-eyes? 'Cause Negus eyes pop when they see that chicken." His favorite uncle called all Blackfolks Negus, an Ethiopian term for king. He said he didn't have to have a college degree to see that there was some connection between Nig, Nigga, Niggaz and Negus. Plus, an ex-girlfriend from Ethiopia schooled his uncle on the knowledge many moons back, while he schooled her on some carnal knowledge.

His uncle, whom he just called Unk Breeze, wuz king of urban folklore, and, according to Urban Legend 27b-paragraph H, the Klan or neo-Nazis were in control of all the fast-food chicken spots in the Hood. "They knew that the best way to mess up Negus was to put sompin' in da food."

To Ellis it seemed like a bunch of bullshit.

How in the hell they gonna fry up chicken in them hot-ass sheets? Besides, if the Klan was making chicken-shit, they was doing a helluva job. The only people cooking soul food for Negus was the Asians, who crushed the comp so bad they was now calling it "Seoul Food." And he knew the Klan wasn't having not part of them.

After polishing off the yardbird, Ellis had no sudden desire to change his name to Toby. But he did wonder what the hell was actually in the Colonel's secret recipe, and felt the tug of a slightly hypnotic urge to run fo' his freedoms 'n' take Kizzy long wit' 'em.

As he glanced around his apartment he realized his place was a mess. Shit everywhere. Half of his files were on the floor and CDs were spread out all over the joint.

I've got to do a better job, thought Ellis. *My mom always said a person's place is a reflection of their life. If this was true, I was surely in trouble.*

Hoping to avoid the obvious transition of thoughts mushrooming into Mount Everest of questions, doubt, and eventually self-pity, he quickly began to add some order to the place. He glanced down and saw his pearls cast among the swine. It was an old copy of *Emege* magazine with Clarence Thomas on the cover, passed down to him from his West Indian Aunt Eyanna. She left it with El, after spending nearly twenty years trying to work roots on Clarence to no avail. He scooped up the magazine and noticed underneath it lay another one of his prized treasures passed down to him from his father—Games Five through Seven of the '94 NBA Finals on DVD.

It was a good series, 'cept as usual the Knicks came up short in Game Seven. Starks was like 0 for 40. Probably ate at Popeye's that day. They had at least two players who scored over 50 points in a game on the bench they didn't go to. *Pat Riley was the only coach able to turn career 20-point-per-game scorers into scrubs who couldn't make a damn layup, but he also was the only coach to turn journeymen scrubs into All-Stars.*

Beginning to feel sweat soaking his back, Ellis tore off his tie and shirt and checked his messages.

"Beeeeeep!"

"Mr. Rey, this is Ben Steeling from the Federal Student Loan Collection Foundation's Delinquent Division. You have not contacted us about your latest earnings. If you fail to respond within 72 hours, I will be forced to access the federal databank and come after your ass. Thanks, Jerk!"

C'mon, you and the rest of them bastards, fumed Ellis.

"Beeeep!"

"Yo, El, this is Jay, give me a shout when you get in—on second thought, I 'll call you later."

Jay? Must need some dough.

"Beeeeep! "Ellis Rey," said a computerized voice.

"You are eligible for a vast array of quality merchandise from Fingahous Incorporated. "Remember in order to take advantage of our no payments until November you must respond "immediately."

Give me a break. Shit, I still got 130 more payments to make on that AM pocket radio. Now if they get those new Air 2000s, I'd jump right on it.

BEEEP!

"Ellis, it's me, Maya; I picked up some fresh salmon steaks and zinfandel I'd liked to share it with you. Call me later."

Guess she's not mad at me anymore.

Excited by the possibilities, Ellis threw in the Knicks/Rockets tape and reclined with an ice-cold Stout. After dozing off midway between the third quarter, Ellis is abruptly shakened awake by the doorbell. Three long rings and one short one.

It's Maya.

She rang the same way all the time. Excited Ellis switched on his PC to Security Optic-Link, giving him a full-frontal view of the building entrance. It was among the latest in new security features from Homeland Protection Systems, John Ashcrots' billion-dollar corporation. *It wasn't a bad way to scope women when bored, also. Never know when some fine young thing in a short skirt might have to pick up her keys or adjust something.*

Ellis peeked and stared at an impatient Maya.

Damn, she's fine.

Maya was mocha brown with reddish-brown color locks tied up in a ponytail. Slightly bowlegged, she wore an expensive linen pants suit that fit her like a glove. Her eyes— a mahogany-smoke color—slanted sharply. Her lips were like succulent slices of Georgia peach.

Damn, she looked good.

Ellis realized that he could watch her for a long time. *Maybe it was time for them to put that DVD camera to use? Maybe have her throw on some high boots, and an Afro wig? Maybe a maid's uniform? Okay, okay get your mind out the gutter and let the girl in.*

"Excuse me, Ma'am, what up?"

"You know somebody here?" Ellis joked via Optic-Link.

Maya glared into the monitor, looking more irritated

than a shopper in the 10-item line behind someone with 11 items getting a price check before letting somebody else cut in front of her. She could see her slight reflection in the camera lens. Forever adept at pushing the irritation level a touch higher, Ellis continued:

"You know I caught you digging up your nose. Thought no one was looking—right? Just remember thanks to Dubya, somebody's always looking."

Maya rolled her eyes.

"Ellis! Are you going to let me in or continue to act silly until I pee on myself?"

Seeing his humor unappreciated, Ellis reluctantly signaled access.

BEEEP…BEEP!

Maya emerged out of the elevator and sauntered down the hallway; all the while, Ellis, peeking through his peephole, waited silently, and just when she went to press the bell, quickly pulled open the door.

WHOOSH!

She stumbled slightly.

"Ellis! You damn fool. You're going to get me hurt one of these days, with that dumb-ass stunt. You going to make me break a heel and you know how expensive these shoes are? Everybody can't go to work in Value City shoes like your old girlfriend."

Ellis laughed hard.

"Aaah, you just mad that I still get you with the okiedoke—you got to get with the program, my sista. As a matter of fact, City Community College is now offering a course on 'Ghetto Hijinks.' Think about it, before it's too late."

Maya sucked her teeth, fake-smiled at Ellis, and kicked her shoes off. She walked into the kitchen grabbed a bottle of spring water and glanced back at Ellis. Seeing his favorite basketball tape on again, she struck quickly.

"Watching basketball? Oh, let me guess, the Knicks against Houston? When are you going to give it up? That's the closest the Knicks have come to the title in three decades. Get over it."

Ellis attempted to pay no attention, but couldn't resist. Growing up in the Projects he suffered through all night cutting sessions where Negus talked about everything from your alcoholic father to your hoe sister, and paraplegic young brotha and that sour smell on your thrift store clothes. And the fact, that despite being in the 10th grade, you couldn't read the damn sports page. He was trained for verbal war and felt empty if he let anyone get the last slice.

"You talking like you know something about Hoop. It ain't like shopping for Prada."

Maya took another sip, then, slipped out of her bra and into one of Ellis' wife beater T-shirts that fit her like a dress, while continuing her banter with Ellis.

"Well, the one thing I do know about basketball is that the Knicks got their ass kicked by the Houston Sonics in 1994."

Ellis laughed. "It's the Houston Rockets. The Sonics are in Seattle."

"Whatever," sneered Maya "The guys from Houston spanked that ass!"

"Well, I wasn't really watching the game, It was just research for this story I'm writing," responded Ellis, quickly turning off the TV. As Maya worked to hook up the Salmon steaks and salad, Ellis snuck in the old Ray Obiedo CD "Sticks and Stones."

Turning up the volume, he eased into the kitchen, anxious to be near Maya and brushed up against her, gently pecking on her nipples now seeping out of her T-shirt "is there anything you need me to do?"

"Yes," said Maya, slicing up onions.

"Anything," responded Ellis, speaking to her breasts.

"Marry me."

"Huh?" responded Ellis, avoiding eye contact. *Where the hell that came from?*

"I want to marry you," said Ellis. Bringing the words from what must have been the farthest point in his body to his lips with a major strain. "I want to marry you, I just don't know if I'm ready now. I mean, I love you. Ain't that enough?"

Maya continued cooking. He could notice the wetness forming in her eyes and wanted to comfort her, but couldn't. He wasn't ready for the emotionalism—*neva was*, and now he just wanted to keep things light. He hoped it was just from the onions. The tears began to form, encircling her jet-black eyes, which swam in pools of white-milk. For some reason, it seemed he appreciated her beauty, even moreso when she was upset. *What's wrong with me?* The pain of emotion shot through his stomach and zigzagged to his temple, causing a headache in one eye.

Ellis stood frozen. He wanted to embrace Maya, hold her, to tell her everything was going to be alright. Tell her that he loved her and that they would never be apart—all the things he knew she needed to hear. But he couldn't. He had spent his whole life detaching himself from things he valued. Proving to the world that nothing could ever fuck with him. Not allowing anyone to know how he really felt. Being invincible. Things he loved only served to make him vulnerable. Only found ways to hurt him. He learned this early, growing up in the Projects. If he valued nothing, then no one could take nothing from him that mattered, most of all, his emotions.

He'd fought committing to relationships all his life and when he finally gave to a relationship with his ex, he found out she was fucken' around on him. It destroyed him and pushed him even further into his shell. Even though Maya was twice the woman his ex was, he still couldn't buy into this full commitment idea, couldn't show himself weak; make another mistake. Ellis didn't want to be there, but didn't know how not to be where he was.

His philosophy on life had served him well. Shit up till now, he never allowed anyone to become irreplaceable-but with Maya it was different. She wasn't just his lady; Maya had become his best friend. Now he was trapped. He desired to go neither to nor fro. He simply wanted them to remain where they were—the place of no-pain, no demands for the future, no responsibility. If she didn't place any responsibility on him, then he couldn't disappoint. If he didn't disappoint her, she wouldn't have to endure the pain his mother saw when his dad just up and walked out of their lives. Or, when to spite his mother, his dad said he'd never hold down a job long enough to pay child-support. Ellis saw the hate grow as days of empty bellies and not-enoughs wrecked havoc in their lives. Ellis' thoughts drifted further into his Pops, what it felt like on that dreary day when he and a bunch of folks he didn't know carried his father to his final resting place. Sitting in the church pews with a bunch of strangers who knew his father, while he and his little brother and sisters didn't. Listening to their stories, anecdotes and memories only made Ellis realize how little he actually knew about the man who helped bring him to this planet. He—nor his sisters or his brother, all of whom he hadn't had a conversation with in 10 years—never *really* knew their father. No games in the park. No punishment. No nothing. Shit, his Mom's was the one who taught him how to knot a tie. Now despite personalities grown hard on the surface through living, they were still just a bunch of kidz who knew they needed something from Pops, but never quite knowing exactly what. *How in the fuck did time go by so fast and how in the hell did we get here?*

His mind turned to Maya again as he wondered with his heart's soft side. *Why wouldn't I be like his father? We have the same genes? Shit, he* had *no father,* he thought. *A father protects and loves his woman and takes care of his children. Had he a dad? Maybe? Damn, what is this shit that made brothas run? Not claim our own?* Maya was way too good of a girl to have to deal with a Negus like him, a Negus that'd might just step any day the thought arose or things got too boring. What if after they had kidz he couldn't take it no more and his father's genes kicked in?

"Ellis, you ready to eat? The food is ready," said Maya, now refreshed after a short trip to the bathroom.

She was beautiful, and when she really smiled her cheeks dimpled up and eyes sparkled. She could cook too. Probably one of the most intelligent women he'd ever met. In actuality he knew very few dumb women; they had figured out this shit way ahead of the brothas. *Maybe that was the problem: We didn't realize that they were smarter?*

"Ellis, we got two choices for Black History Month, on Black Entertainment Television they are showing 'Soul Plane,' 'New Jack City,' and 'Sprung' and on NIA TV, they're showing 'Sundiata,' starring Wesley Snipes, and get this— 'Sankofa' and 'Beyond the Door of No Return' back-to-back. I love all of Haile Gerima's movies," said Maya, excitement competing with forgiveness in her voice as she clearly expressed her choice.

Ellis, back in a jovial mood, acted the fool.

"I wanna see 'Soul Plane,'" smiled Ellis. "You know that shit is funny."

Maya smiled her real smile and slightly pushed one of

her breast out. "If we watch 'Sankofa,' you might get something special later. Plus, you might learn something."

"Okay, okay, you win," smiled Ellis.

"Ellis you know that movie is dumb," whispered Maya as she took a sip of wine.

"C'mon, now youse know I's just a dumb Negus."

Maya, looked up and giggled, "You just stupid. Pure stupid."

Attempting to exact as much as he can from the skit, Ellis continued.

"Wells, I's reckon I's whateber yous' said I be, Massa."
BOINK!

Maya threw a chopped carrot, catching Ellis smack in the back of his head. He picked it up, sniffed it, and took one bite.

"Member, snake 'gwon eat whatere in da belly of dem frog."

Hushing him, Maya motioned for Ellis to sit down.

"Okay, Okay, be quiet, the movie's coming on."

Ellis sat down finally becoming serious, unknowingly aided by the sound of African drums and the chants of "Return, return to your past."

After watching the movies, Maya exited to the bedroom, while Ellis turned to the all-day Sports Network to catch up on some scores and highlights. The first bit of news is almost shocking.

"Today the Board of Governors of the Church of Latter Saints announced that they have awarded grave plots in the Elders Section to former Utah Jazz players Karl Malone and John Stockton. According to the Church, Malone will be the first son of Ham—er, African American—to have been offered entombment there and he and Stockton will join Steve Young and Jim Mchanon as the only athletes to be so selected. Reportedly, there's no truth to the rumor of the same offer being made to former Chicago Bulls forward Dennis Rodman.

Around 2 a.m., Ellis finally caught up on all the necessary highlights and peeked in on Maya. *Damn, She's asleep—or at least faking sleep.* He lay down and slowly pulled the covers over to his side just to confirm whether she's knocked out or faking.

WHOOSH!

She snatched them back and it's *on*! They both begin wrestling, snatching covers, mushing faces with pillows, blows to private parts, until the phone rang.

BRRRING, BRRRINGG!

The WWF grudge match is now interrupted by a series of rings and the untimely response of the answering machine.

BEEP!

"You have reached the residence of Ellis Rey, home to Sal's Pizzeria where extra cheese is two-fiddy. Please leave a message at the beep!"

"Yo, El, this is Jay. I need to talk to you. Shit's real serious, bruh. Shit is 'bout to get crackin' and I need some backup. Call me back at 718-514-33..."

Ellis picked up the phone.

"Yo, Yo, what up?"

"Yo El, I thought you was out. Man, I need to hook up with you."

"No can do tonight, boss, I'm here chilling with Maya. Plus, can't this shit wait till tomorrow? Man it's—."

"—Two A.M," added Maya.

Unrelenting, Jay continued, "Yo, this shit is real, cuzin, I need you to meet me at the Shack in about an hour—cool?"

"Yo, Jay, this shit better be real or…or…" stuttered Ellis.

"Yo, El, good looking out. I knew you'd come through, man. Peace."

Ellis avoided Maya's burning glare and began getting dressed.

"I can't believe that you still running after Jay. You aren't kidz anymore, Ellis. You know Jay is no good. He's never there for you and you still always running to pull him out of his latest scheme. He's just using you; he's not your friend. Ellis?"

Ellis threw on his Knicks cap and hooded sweatshirt, grabbed his car keys and kissed Maya on the lips amidst her frown.

"I'm out. I'll be back in about two hours."

"Ellis, I won't be here when you get back. I won't keep waiting. I won't keep waiting for you to mature…I won't…"

promised Maya. But Ellis was already out the door. On his way to help one friend, not knowing that his future chances to chill with Maya would be less than he expected.

TO THE RESCUE

Ellis hopped into the hooptie like Tonto out to save the Lone Ranger's pale ass once again. He slammed in the old CD of Nasty-Nas live on Hot Ninety-Sumthing. He could tell by the tone in Jay's voice, it was some shit going down. Jay was not someone who voiced the hint of fear 'bout nothing. *Fuck it,* thought Ellis, *it wasn't going to be one of those bootstrapping nights—already was.*

Despite the relative calm embracing the Hood versus the old days, it still had its no fly zones, those places where the criminal element invaded like radical roaches who still snuck out of their holes in search of food despite the lingering smell of Raid in the air or like flies on rotting meat. Negus still hanging at the same spot, since they was kidz. Jay and Ellis always hit the shack after clubbing. Grab some chicken and scope the Honeyz. 'Cept now its main thing was illegal business. Chicken, however, was still a close second.

Driving down the Ghouliani Parkway, Ellis' mind crawled into the sullen space of his cerebellum as a darken sky hung like a huge 'Fro above the New York Skyline. Ellis pumped the volume on Nas, cruising in what Billy Joel called a New York state of mind.

As El pulled up to the Shack, he could see crazy heads still frequented the high-cholesterol capital of the city and girded himself for any of several possible negative outcomes. *The* smell of the Shack's fried chicken began to bring back grease-stained memories. He used to love the fried gizzards. *Shit, about two a.m.,* remembered El, *some fried gizzards and hot sauce was mo better than caviar, not that he'd know what caviar tasted like, probably tasted like chicken?*

The Shack had a special on wings this week and actually began printing nutritional information on boxes of chicken. They had to do something based on the crazy competition they was getting from the new chain that opened up in several cities called Checkin Chicken. You could get chicken while you got your check cashed, or bought money orders and phone cards. For each additional wing bought, they dropped half a point off the 45 percent fee for check cashing.

El cruised slowly and popped out the Nas disc and threw in something that these kidz might be into as to not look too conspicuous. He was getting to the age where style mattered less and less. Looking through his discs, El realized that all he's got is Clever Jeff, Showbiz and AG, Ghostface, PRT—old-school shit classics from the Nineties. His Uncle Breeze, who'd served as his hiphop mentor, had groomed him on all the late Eighties and Nineties shit. When forced to choose, he decided to slip in the "Atliens" shit. He began blasting his speakers.

"Me an you, yo' momma an yo' cousin too..."

Ellis thought, *If I'm gonna be sitting in the hooptie two in the morning, waiting for fucken Jay and his box of surprises, I might as well listen to da shit.* He eased back in his seat, careful to keep an eye out for unwelcomed intrusions. Before he could settle in, El is awakened out of his groove by two taps on the now-slightly fogged window. He quickly wiped down the driver's side with a grin of relief, seeing that it's Jay.

"Yo, open up, crack-patient," said a voice that El's subconscious mind and third-eye immediately associated with debt, trouble and a whole range of sordid activities including true friendship or loyalty, which in Ellis mind were both one and the same. Yeah, it was Jay.

"What up?" said Ellis, anxiously unlocking the door. "Nothing," said Jay, peeping the perimeter nervously. "What up, Sun, you got me out here in the middle of the night for nothing, or you back smoking that shit again?"

"Naw," whispers Jay.

Ellis stares at Jay. "What the hell you whispering fo'?"

"Yo, El, we need to move quick—this spot is getting kinda salty."

With the thought of living in mind, El quickly jets up the Betsy and pulled out the parking lot. They skate so quick that they almost run over this grizzled old lady in a raincoat pushing a grocery cart full of 70 oz. aluminum beer cans.

"Damn, Jay! I see ya Moms being phased off of Welfare opening up all type of opportunities for her."

Jay cracked a smirk, "Aw, c'mon, El, you know that's ya old girlfriend. I see the hussie finally put some dubs on her ride, them twenty fours?" Both laughed. More worried than they would near admit as they headed up the Ghouliani Parkway—not saying nuthing, just listening to Outkast blaring through the speakers.

"Just two dope boys in a Cadillac Cadillac—ooh-oooo.
Just two dope boys in a Cadillac—ooh-oooo!

WAKING UP

After Jay was dropped off at his baby's-mom's house in Queens. Well, after breaking up three fights between them in an hour, Ellis finally headed back to the crib. Dragging through the door at 5:54 a.m., he was a complete mess! *Let's see, maybe I can catch some zzzz's and get to work by ten*, thought Ellis heading into the bedroom. Like Maya said—she's gone. *At least she made up the bed.* Ellis laid down fully clothed and just straight up crashed out like a light.

Daylight crept in like a cat burglar.

The subconscious dimension existed as a universe unto itself and Ellis realized this as he crossed over from the land of Rapid-Eye-Movement, into the kingdom of Nocturnal Emissions. He stood there naked, surrounded by a trio of BET's "Comicview" dancers, all thick-legged, scantily -clad, and wiggling him into ecstasy. They moved closer, closer. *Oh yeah, closer baby, closer…*

NNNNNT! NNNNT! NNNNNNNNT!

"Damn!"

Ellis angrily looked over at the Playa-hating alarm clock like it was a Black person trying to win Amateur night at the Apollo against some white Wall Street banker with a faulty voice, and swiped at it, knocking it to the ground. Slowly he slid over the bed and looked at it-six-thirty?

"Shit, okay, give me 20 more minutes, and I can still get in early," he convinced himself and pressed the snooze button.

Ten minutes pass, 20 minutes, 30, one hour, two. He continued to lay in the bed, trying to both shake off last night's rescue mission and get back to his fantasy date with the dancers. Unfortunately, neither seemed to be working.

The majority of times the brain controls bodily functions, and other times the body aggressively takes what it needs to survive. This time both brain and body fresh off some

Tony Robbins-type motivational shit, for their own best interest decided to join forces.

Both brain and body knew. no wake up, no job. No Job, no rent. No rent, no apartment. No apartment, no food. No woman? No woman, no cry. Taking the hint, Ellis awoke crusty-eyed, and reluctantly looked at the clock—7:30. *Good, that extra did me good.* Twenty minutes felt like an hour. He graciously thanked the Godz of Sleep and sat up in the bed. Wiping the crust from his eyes, he now sees clearly the time—8:30.

"Shit! Late again."

Without thinking twice, Ellis hopped into the shower, grabbed yesterday's suit with the same coffee-stained shirt, jogged three blocks to the train pavilion, and then hopped on, barely squeezing in through the closing doors.

Whew, just made it, thought Ellis, knocking over this sista's steaming cup of coffee.

"I'm sorry, Lady, I didn't mean to..."

Was where he stopped after seeing her rise up into a cat-stance. It was then that he realized she was a T'tottler. She was one of the rising numbers of businesswomen taking testosterone as a means of enhancing work performance. A bunch of them had formed clubs where they'd compare facial hair, lift weights, and go wilding after a night of drinking. He'd once seen a gang of them beating the hell of a bike messenger as they left Macy's. The messenger had the nerve to cut them off on the sidewalk. It was then Ellis realized why he never wore biker shorts. It was a damn shame what they did to him with them expensive-ass shoes!

The way she looked at Ellis made it clear to him that someone in her office was going to catch hell today. In any case, he was now at the point of coordinating the stains on his suit. Ellis wisely distanced himself and hid behind a bag lady with a perimeter-defense of foul, eye-watering smell. She was devouring a candy bar some bleeding heart gave to her out of compassion. *He shoulda gave her a bath,* mused Ellis to himself as his eyes watered up from the intense smell.

The train ride ended quickly as Ellis spurted up the street, slowing down gradually as he reached the office. He quickly composed himself and gently eased into *The Nubian,* the sole remaining Black-owned newspaper in New York. He was half an hour late. He smelled like Egyptian musk and coffee, with a touch of subway funk. He knew he was going to hear it from his husky editor, Nicole, a woman whom he publicly and affectionately called "Foxy Cleopatra," but secretly re-named her "Bertha Butt Boogie." He could hear Nicole already:

"You only got one thing to do—cover the Knicks.

And one more thing—get here on time.

Is that too much to ask to keep a job, Blackman?"

According to the Book of Ellis, Nicole was always sweatin' him heavy-handed style, 'cause he wouldn't take her out and flip her on her back. Not that she was bad-looking; she wasn't. She was one of those strikingly beautiful butter-pecan-skinned sistas with exotic looking eyes, who adorned herself with only the most expensive of materials and perfumes. She was the type of woman that didn't need to try to be beautiful; she just was. She was also a missed Chitosan pill away from 300 pounds. Ellis always had severe issues with overweight people; plus big and beautiful were adjectives that Western societies couldn't process without a major quantity of alcohol in the system. He remembered someone mentioning that physical weight represented the burden one's soul carried. He just accepted it as a truth, regardless of the sense it made. It certainly didn't apply to all the crackheadz he knew.

Besides he knew reporting was a dangerous occupation when he chose this career. Everyday, journalists had to worry about organized crime figures, corrupt officials or weak athletes getting back at them for damaging stories. He only had to worry about the 300-pound Ebony World-a- Girl smashing him up against a copier. As usual, Ellis focused on his problems with Nicole rather than deal with his own issues. He once again was on the verge of missing his deadline. As Ellis eased into his desk, Nicole, with the timing of a cobra, noticed the faint scent of Egyptian musk and coffee. She called loudly:

"Ellis!"

"What?"

"I thought I heard you. Your copy ready?"

"Naw, but I'll have it ready for audio transcription around 2. I got an interview with Don Worthy, who's about to break the offensive rebound record set by Moses Malone and you know this is a major coup."

"Well, I'm not worried about that," she said in an almost shockingly polite tone. "But there is something else. I want to speak to you about in my office."

As they began the slow walk to her office, the theme from The Executioner's Song began playing in his head. He couldn't afford to lose another damn job. The dimly-lit office got darker, and he sensed that something otherworldly was 'bout to happen. He thought he could see from the mail clerk smirking and the arts editor grinning that something was up.

Hell, I ain't going out like that, Ellis thought to himself.

Ellis convinced himself while rehearsing a quick possible response.

"Well, you see—me and you, we like brother and sister—it ain't gonna work.

"I'm busy.

"You're too nice for me to mess with.

"I can't give you what you need (in your case a series of colonics).

"Okay, okay, but I want an editor's position...

Naw, it wasn't gonna work, I just gotta come out and tell her straight up—I ain't wit' this."

Nicole sat down and motioned for Ellis to do the same.

She smiled a real smile that showed her beautiful mouth. "Would you like some coffee?"

"Only if I can spill it on my suit," replied Ellis in his usual sarcastic tone, one that had engendered warm feelings for him from his landlord to waitresses and collection agents all around the country.

He really enjoyed being acknowledged as a Major League smart ass. It was also the reason why he went three weeks wearing the 50 Cent model bulletproofed vest: *It wasn't that he was just good, but PTP baby!* Yeah PTP, except it didn't rhyme with his name, maybe 'zealous?' *Naw.*

"Well, Ellis," said Nicole, jarring him from his sad mindstate. "How would you like to—"

Before she could finish Ellis spurted out:

"It ain't gonna work, you know I got an interview in 20 minutes, Nicole, you see we just don't—"

"What?" she responded with a confused look on her face, cutting off his stammering. "Are you telling me you don't want a raise? It's already been okay'd. I mean, Ellis, despite your chronic bouts with Colored Peoples Time, you've been doing a great job. The only thing we ask is that every now and then we things get tight, you do a few news stories and personality interviews for us. I thought you'd be jumping for joy, since you've been sweating me about it for a while now?"

"Um…um…uha…oh…Ay ya, ya, ya…" stuttered Ellis, reverting to the primordial sounds of ignorance with his own version of fried Ying Yang Twins scrambled with some Hooked On Phonics.

He finally squeezed out a somewhat coherent "Un huh."

Ellis, the King of Witdom and Quick Comebacks, was finally silenced. He was always ready to do battle, but had no comeback for a sincere compliment, fo' mo' dough for his pocket.

Nicole slid her hand along the side of her head, brushing back her thick natural crown. She glared at Ellis with almond-shaped eyes. For a quick moment, she wondered, *Is this Negus crazy?*

"Thanks. Good looking out baby girl," nodded an absurdly nonchalant Ellis, who immediately got to stepping before he did something dumb like smacked her on the ass saying, "Good play baby, good play," or proposed.

Or worst, finally laid to rest his image of aloof *"give-a-fuck-ness."* He was still new at handling good news-n-shit. Deep down, he always felt there was a trap-door beneath every prize. There won't no free lunch. People had their trap- doors too, and like playing poker Ellis learned real early to always keep ya game face on. 'Cause just when you turned your back, like snakes mawfukas strucked—and when you least expected it. But Ellis couldn't spin this shit into something negative. Despite Ellis' deep ingrained pessimism—layered under a double shot of sarcasm, topped off with a swig of detachment—nothing could fuck with his feel-good right now. Ellis sauntered up the street to grab the train downtown for his pre-game interview. He was in that rare state—he was smiling without joking.

Finally getting some justice, he told himself. *Finally, after all this work I have risen above the per-capita income of that snobbish coffee-*

bean picking Columbian, Juan Valdez. "Each bean is picked by hand…" Yeah, maawfuk, pick this! Who said you can't buy respect; I'm putting chrome on the Hyundai!

THE HOOP RITUAL

Ellis lay sitting up in his bed as the sky began its daily transformation. Sunlight eeked through his tightly closed blinds and gracefully anointed his Lauren Hill poster. It was a gift given to him by his Uncle when he was just 8-years-old. He'd been in love with Lauren ever since. Ellis stared at the poster, waiting for it to speak. To say the magic words, "Ellis, where have you been all my life?" It didn't and his mind began its normal drift that occurred whenever he was unable to sleep, but too tired to get up.

He wondered what would it like to be rich. Not wealthy, but stupid-dumb rich, Bill-Gates-shitting-dollars rich. Would he be the type to rock at the latest hiphop designer gear, along with iced-out appendages and throwbacks? Or would he rock the latest I-talian silks, sandals, and Versace shades? Maybe he'd just do the neo-bohemian thing and rock some raggedy-ass jeans, T-shirt and sandals?

Fuck it—I'd do it all. Maybe buy a house in the hills of St. Thomas?

Maybe just move south—fuck it, Brazil—*and have lots of kidz?*

Okay, but what type of car would I drive? Benz, Lex, or…?

*BEERRing… BERRing…Brrrring….*the phone rang abruptly.

"Damn! Who in the hell?"

I'm not answering this. I'll just let it ring and see who it is.

The answering machine turns on. "I'm not here right now, leave a message. Peace."

"Hullo?"

"Yo, Ak, what up? It's me, Jay. I know you up, Sun, don't try 'n' front. Pick up the damn phone!"

Only one fool would know the only thing that could get Ellis out of bed and up that early on a Saturday. Ellis quickly picked up the receiver.

"Yo, what up, Jay? You down to hit the gym, cuzin?"

"Of course, Sun. Why else would I be calling yo' ass dis early?

"I thought yo' broke-ass wanted to borrow some money," mumbled Ellis.

"What?"

"Nothing."

"Check it out, I'll meet you down there. Peace."

The quickening begins.

In the twinkling of an eye, Ellis felt a tremendous energy surging through his joints. It was as if he pulled out some crusty triple-X labeled bottle of snake oil elixir bought off the farm for two bits from a dust-covered, Cornel West-looking traveling salesman. That, or either he just sliced off the head of some Highlander. Within seconds, the type of energy that always seemed to be on the disabled list, especially on Monday mornings, had him juiced. It was if he was the damn Tin Man and somebody had sprinkled some pimp juice on his joints.

This was the weird thing about ballplayers. Ellis believed that either you were born to play Hoop or not. It wasn't nutting you could develop. It was a religious calling. If you wasn't one of the select called to this game, then you'd be the one getting dunked on. Or the one saying, "I prefer something more intellectual, like Chess." More than likely, you'd be that nameless mawfuka who had the misfortune of being immortalized in some poster hanging in somebody's room with another Negus foot on his neck, and his mouth screaming, *"NOOOOOO!!!!!"*

No ballplayer knew exactly when it would come, but eventually everybody got poster-ized. If you were lucky, nobody had a camera and you could always deny it ever happening to you. Some ball players would intentionally hurt somebody before letting them dunk on them. But that in itself wasn't enough to remove the grim specter of "poster-ization" that hung like a pair of dookey-stained draws over each players' rep.

Still, true ballplayers retained their own secret society. Across the Hood, grown men—putting off every important task known to mankind—would get up at the crack of dawn, ride several trains (and trek through knee-deep snow in the winter), all for the sake of Hoop. All done in the hope of *today*—yes, maybe *today* you'd have the game that would cement your status as one of the nastiest to ever set foot on the court. The shit was worse than the pipe. Hoop called and you answered—regardless of your bad ankle, Achilles, back injuries, ligament sprains, death threats from the local drug dealer, your pending eviction or worse. Very few had the strength to go cold turkey. Ellis had heard about some Hoop addict programs being run by a Jenny Craig Company that branched out into dependency programs. Reportedly it had a good success rate. But he also heard some bad stories too. Like the kid who left the program after a few days only to be found in 20-degree weather, half-naked with an And-1 DVD duct-taped to his head, shooting three-pointers in Rucker Park.

Ellis sat on the edge of the bed to begin the ritual. Slowly he applied sports cream to his ankles. He then wrapped them with ace bandages. His socks came next. All the while, he wondered how much longer could he do this. He didn't know how to play the game half-way. It was the only thing in life that he ever took seriously. Seriously enough to give it his all each time he stepped on the court. He didn't know why this simple damn game meant so much to him, and way more important shit so little. For years he used Hoop the way some used drugs—as a vehicle to escape shit gone wrong. It was his anti-drug; all he had to do was go down a few flights of stairs outside the building and it was his world. Twin full courts painted red and green with white trim, and towering owl-eyed lights that reached into the stratosphere and stayed on 'till two in the morn, and street lighting that could keep you there all night. For all the messed-up things existing in the Projects, whoever built those courts must have known something. *Was it their intent to create a sanctuary, or did we turn it into one?* The court was where he cleared his mind, built his resolve, thought. It was there that he learned the hard work necessary to perfect something as complex as George Gervin's baseline jumpshot off the backboard. Or how to take the ball to the rim with enough velocity to get the and-1 against guys twice his size. Despite the creeping age, El still had game. He was still nice, but not nice enough to consider going pro, not nice enough to take Hoop seriously anymore. It paid for schooling and got him out of the Projects. But now it was just for fun. But it wasn't. It was still serious—*too fucken serious*. It still meant too much.

A 20-minute drive later, Ellis entered the gym, game-faced. Immediately he noticed Jay talking shit as usual. *What else is new? Oh, damn! He got the new AIR 2000s. My Negus. No job and he always got the latest footgear. Shit, hopefully now he can pay me the money he owed me.*

Normally the gym rats gave some good run and once in a while a few of the local players from all over the city, or D-1 schools would show up and things would get to the Gatoraide level. Today was one of those days.

"Mine!" hollered Ellis. He went up intending to put the fear of God into the gym and snatch the rebound off the rim as a means of staking his claim to the court. He imitated a young roaring lion to let the wannabe Kings of the Jungle know that this was *his* territory. *Proceed at your own risk.*

"Whoosh!"

Was the sound heard as this kid from nowhere jumped over his head, caught the ball and dunked it in a millisecond, which included enough time for him to hang on the rim and scream:

"It's my world!"

Damn, thought Ellis, *hope nobody had a camera.* As he brushed his footprints off his neck, he looked at Jay and Jay looked back, as both said in unison:

"It's *on*, baby."

The rim was looking huge today and Ellis' jumper was dropping from the perimeter like crazy—nothing but the panties—and boarding like a monster. Yeah, at 29, he still had considerable game, but so did the college kidz who ran them off the court, despite the gold medal heroics.

Taking a seat on the bench, Ellis looked at Jay, who still looked the same, except for the grey hair, emerging wrinkles, and extra weight, then thought to himself, *I'm getting old.*

Black as night, Jay was about 6-4 and 235. He had a 41-inch vertical leap and a turn-around jumper that was deadly from anywhere around the basket. But he was putting on weight like a fighter after the weigh-in. It slowed him down, and along with the decreasing level of conditioning, aided by high alcohol and drug use, bolstered by old age, made him just a little better than average which was sad, since he was a beast when in shape.

Jay was a complex cat; either he ran off at the mouth, sparked by some assumed dis, or sat sullen and quiet. You never knew exactly which one you'd get, after awhile you simply accepted the fact that this mawfuka was a bi-polar manic-depressive with a nasty crossover and much hops. Loyal to a fault, he had a mean streak that could go the length at a moment's notice. Negus on the street simply knew it was better to avoid him than fuck with him. He was the kind of Negus that stayed constantly on the nihilistic edge of sanity. When he was focused and in-shape, him and El could *take over* a gym. Their games complimented each other like Jordan and Pippen—*we were that close to being good enuff for da next level. That close to the Big League*, they always assumed. They were 'posed to be the ones to change shit, but things don't always turn out the way youngins dream they supposed to. They didn't realize that there was 10,000 other kidz in the city thinking they, too, was gonna be the next King James or betta. The old headz realized, often much later, that talent was only about 20 percent of the formula for making it to Dreamville. Talent alone wasn't worth the paper it was printed on. Talent in itself was a gigantic bag of what-ifs and couldas. As a rule, Negus was crazy talented, and any Negus who went pro will tell you 'bout some kid way nicer than him who went nowhere.

Ellis and Jay went back to the old school—growing up in the Projects—and knew each other since 2nd grade. Fought the same people, almost as much as each other, and still owed each other money. They'd survived the Projects wars, had some of the same bruises, and still technically—well, moreso in Ellis case, according to three out of five mental health experts—had their sanity. Er, well, at least part of it. Neither of 'em were dumb, both smart as shit. Just never had the time to clear their heads, 'cause they were always on the hustle playing the angles.

The only difference was Ellis lucked up and found out he could do something else—write. He never realized that writing lyrics everyday actually honed his skills so nasty that he could pen anything as smooth as an Ivy League Lit major without understanding the smallest aspect of grammar. He looked at grammar as a prison, so he just focused on communicating his thoughts and what sounded right. That was his formula—sound, phonetics. After a while Ellis learned to bend, twist, and break language into a sound that worked so well that it superceded grammar. And most importantly, mawfukas never knew his hustle. He parlayed his skill into becoming a journalist and didn't look back.

Jay's talent took another direction. He had a talent for another genre of hustle. He could scheme anything and vick anyone; he was official street legend. Every illegal idea he mastered and then perfected. He never got caught for his street activities. But when he wasn't scheming, he lost focus and made mistakes. His thug-streak grew considerably and his Hoop declined exponentially after doing 18 months Upstate for, out of all things, failing to show up for some assault charges stemming from a fight he got into with this punk-ass security guard at the mall. The guard started talking about his mother, who was in the hospital. Bad timing. Jay beat him senseless. It was the wrong time to fuck with him—the wrong thing said at the wrong place at the wrong time.

Timing was the majority of almost everything in life. If Ellis didn't pay attention to too many things, he at least tried to know when to move. Timing separated the men from the boys, and the living from the dead. If he remembered nothing about his father, he remembered him dropping those gems.

"Know the time, youngsta," he'd always say.

"Know the time?"

Ellis be like, "It's time to eat. I'm hungry—you got any dough?"

Sitting on the bench, head down and towel-covered, Jay looked up at the rim as if he were looking for God or something.

"Yo, El," he said, "Give me a lift around the way. Got to pick up a few things."

"Bet."

Ellis quickly warmed up the Betsy, and Jay hopped in. Examining the car like a new owner, Jay exhibited a rare moment of contentment.

Jay pulled out a fully rolled pizza-flavored Philly, and sparked it.

"Yo, El, this shit's murder. You hitting it?"

Ellis rolled down the window, allowing the fresh breeze in. "Naw, Sun, I'm chilling."

"Oh, what, Negus, you too fly now to hit da cheeba? You rolled that shit, you smoke it. Besides, I like the old school regular Phillies. Or even taking a nice Cameroon wrapper and hooking it up cigar-style. I don't trust shit developed with us in mind. Plus I ain't feeling that flavored-cigar shit."

Shit, knowing yo' ass, ain't not telling what you done laced it with, thought Ellis. He never forgave Jay for that time when he handed him a fat spliff full of dust, and didn't tell him that it wasn't just weed. El was 15 years old and on his way to play ball across town. The dust had him so hyper that the basketball looked as big as the moon. Everytime somebody put the ball down to dribble, El was there to strip 'em, like he was Spider-Man. He must have had 30 steals in one game, but the shit threw him off-balance so bad he never smoked dust again.

Driving through the Hood was uplifting and depressing at the same time. It was like Buju Banton's song "Untold Stories," "*...I say who can afford to run will run/ But what about those who can't...they will have to stay. Opportunity's a scarce, scarce commodity...*" You thank the Creator that you wuz gone and remembered how you overcame those obstacles, but at the same time felt sad for the folks who still had to go through what you went through and worse. No matter what anyone might tell you, Hood-living is hellish. It's like the Devil takes something from you that you can never get back no matter how hard you try. Negus play like they've overcome, but it's akin to the soldiers returning from Vietnam or Iraq. Seeing the war-torn faces of Negus they grew up with was some humbling shit.

It was if some dark cloud full of mischief, envy, hate, frustration, jealously, and low-esteem hung above the Hood. As youths their lungs were strong enough to dispel that shit, but eventually it wore you down to the core. This cloud was even thicker after the rebellions. Ever since the rebellion— when the Hood exploded in flames, the ole Hood it was never the same.

You would have thought that they'd have enough sense not to burn down their neighborhoods again, but wasn't too much thinking going on. The rebellion was during the eighth year of the New Depression. Negus was broke, angry, and hot. When the mob made the mistake of cutting through the financial district as a shortcut to looter heaven—the mall— all hell broke loose. Thinking they was heading for the banks instead, the cops gunned them down like ducks; they wasn't having it. They shot this one kid 41 times. Co-lit him up like the damn Chinese New Year. Everybody was like, *Damn!*

Forty-One times?

Them mawfukas must've took cigarette breaks between shots. Stretched, did yoga. Breathe in, breathe out—41 times?

They was like, you Negus can burn down yo' shit, but you fuck with ours, and you really gonna have some problems.

"Jose!" screamed Jay, leaning out the window, "crazy-ass."

It seemed that Jose spotted them long before they spotted him. He ran toward the car, motioning for Ellis to roll down the window. Ellis complied, knowing he had no choice.

"What?" said Ellis, waiting for the inevitable.

"Yo, El—got something to throw at you!" said Jose in loud whisper.

"Hop in, crack patient," said Jay.

"Yo," said Jose, "check this out man, what up wit' yo' boy Wardell?"

"He ain't my boy," frowned Ellis, immediately putting street distance between him and Wardell.

"I thought you wuz tight?" questioned Jose, with a perplexed look that caused both of his eyebrows to unite.

"Yeah, we hung a few times, but we ain't like that," said Ellis, defensively stroking his goatee, something he'd always do when fidgety. All the while he wondered what the fuck Wardell done got into. He hated the fact that he and Jay engineered his street credibility and added them to their clique. All the rest of the cats were Negus they grew up wit.

"Whatever, Sun," smirked Jose.

"My peeps been seein' War-D round some shady Negus, baby."

"Like who?"

"Well, you know me, El, I ain't normally on the NegusNet, but you my man, so I gots to lookout," said Jose, sniffling like his habit was getting the best of him. "We was downtown running the usual scam, when he pulled up at the FBDIE building on Madison—with some flatfoots, Kid!"

"I don't know what's wrong with Wardell, fake-ass Imitation New Yorker," said Ellis with a nervous twinge in his voice.

"Then why you be rolling with him?" said Jay, who hated Wardell worst than killing roaches with matches and aerosol spray.

"Man, you know his uncle Yusef's my boy and I told him I'd look out a bit since he asked me to. We ain't really cool like that. I mean we tried to school him a bit, but Wardell dress too funny for me to be tight with him like that. Plus, Negus got a hygiene problem, Kid.

"I mean, only reason I even bother with the kid is because of his Uncle Yusef. We 'posed to hook up later, 'cause Yusef's in town and the Kings play the Knicks tonight."

"What up with tickets?" asked Jay.

Purposely ignoring Jay's request, Ellis kept driving, wondering *What the hell is this Negus problem? Last time I left him on the floor tickets for the playoffs, brotha didn't even show up—said his tooth was hurting.*

"Yo, El, turn quick, gotta go," said Jose, straight off his Potential Vick Scan or what El and Jay called PVS. This muthafucka could see around corners. Jose could spot a vick six blocks away when he wasn't high, which was about as rare as a red moon.

"You got a five-spot?" asked José as he leaned forward behind El. He knew better than asking Jay—that shit alone might be reason enough for Jay to commence with his version of the Timbaland-upped River Dance.

"I'm trying to get my nod on," smirked Jose. "They got the new 80 ounce shit called Narcolepsy. The bottle is heavy as hell, but that shit will get you *fuuuucked up, mann,* it's like you be sleepwalking," said Jose joyously. It was as if he'd somehow be remembered as that one brotha who got higher than any in the history of the Projects. As if somehow, they'd bronze his last Forty and place it in the African American museum as the highest Negus in American history. Or maybe immortalize him in a gigantic colorful mural on the backside of the building with him draped in a Puerto Rican flag, smoking a blunt, sitting on four cases of ice cold Ballentine with a brown bag of Henny on his lap giving the peace sign.

Ellis performed his charitable duty and for sake of keeping it real quick, quietly slid Jose a Bush six-spot and they peace out.

"*Daaamn*, Jay, Jose still drinking that shit? It was only three years ago that they fined Weedchem Breweries for creating a formula that incorporated the atomic make up for crack, ecstasy, speed, horse DNA, along with Ozzie Ozborne's socks. It was madd birth defects all over the Hood."

Jay quickly relit the blunt he'd conveniently hid till José left and took a long tote.

"Shit, Jose fine. His son seems to be doing okay with that elephantitis."

"Yeah, I heard that lucky bastard just got a six-figure job offer with UniverSoul," said Ellis sarcastically. They both cracked up.

THE OLD BUILDING

They pull up to 225, the old building that they were supposed to be replacing with low-rise units real soon. In this sense, "they" could be anybody but you. It was always used to denote some bastard that was supposed to do something that ain't got done yet, or normally served as a connation reflecting "the man," or those in control.

'The 225" was a classic, 14 stories of red bricks, rats and roaches. Archaic slang, age-old names that were "bad to the bone," "wuz here" and more scribbled in pen, magic-marker, and spray paint decorated the hallways like some old Egyptian tomb covered with hieroglyphs. As if we always knew that by writing our names on the walls, we'd be guaranteed to live on forever.

They briskly walked up the stairs to the fourth floor. In earlier days, they used to run up the stairs with leg weights on, in hopes of increasing their speed and jumping ability. Unfortunately, their age-related slower pace allowed both to inhale full blast the saturating stench of old piss, beer, and something else the neither Ellis nor Jay wanted to smell nor mention. In the Projects, they had developed their own Jedi mind-trick, based on the idea that *if I see it, smell it, or feel it, and you do too, and neither of us mention it, then it don't exist.* Negus that paid too much attention to all shit in the Projects never left the Projects—that was a general rule.

Things had gotten worse in the building. It wasn't like this when they was growing up, in fact until the University decided that the Projects were too close, it was fine. Janitors cleaned up, people took care of their hallways and got fined in a second, if their shit wasn't correct. Drugs were around, but weed didn't hurt us none. And only the Old Gangstas fucked with the needles and after they was done all they did was nod anyway. Everybody smoked, even the housing authority police assigned to the buildings—Shit, they the ones that had the best buds. After smoking weed, didn't nobody have the motivation to do shit. It took energy and motivation to do anything, especially crime. Yet there were a few hiphop artists and Jamaican gangstas who proved that theory wrong. Still things were manageable—until the new drug wars changed everything.

Soon, with everybody scrambling to get high, crime increased. All that selling and attempted buying. The average folks got caught in the middle, as well as the white students who had the misfortune of making a wrong turn somewhere that ended in the Hood. They all became victims of circumstance. After awhile, newspapers that never in their history reported on what went on in the Hood started reporting on shit as if they cared.

Eventually, funding was cut back on public housing, then on janitors, then on enforcement of the building codes. What was a struggling community holding on by a thread just fell apart, and housing authority ended up closing down all the buildings except this one. The families were moved to Brooklyn in some half-built apartments. They offered the families $600 in moving expenses, and mothers jumped at it like they was hitting the Lotto.

"Damn, Jay, when they gonna fix these lights?" asked Ellis as he stepped into what he optimistically hoped might be dogshit. *But I haven't seen no dogs, cats, nor rats, since that new carryout moved in across the street,* Ellis thought.

"Be quiet," whispered Jay, as they entered his apartment. "My moms still up."

As they eased through the small immaculate living room, buffered by a huge portrait of a charcoal-colored, dreaded Jesus. Jay's mom leaned back in her recliner, her favorite chair that she often fell asleep in while watching television after a 12-hour day. She was a hardworking Blackwoman who fought everyday to make ways for her and her kidz, most of the time alone. She was the essence of mothers who refused to give in, refused to give up, to be tired regardless of how tired she was. And she was tired.

"How are you doing, Miss Jones?"

Fine, Ellis, I mean, Handsome."

"Thanks," said Ellis, giving her a kiss and hug.

"I wish Jay would try to do something with himself, like you did, Ellis. He needs to get some education or at least a regular job, 'cause I'm getting tired," Miss Jones snapped with a frown on her face.

In her sixties, she was still a beautiful bronze-colored woman with skin like satin and rarely a wrinkle. Jay got into many a fight while young because Negus acknowledged too readily how fine his moms was.

"Yo, El, come back here," yelled Jay. Jay's room was painted dirt brown with several large plants that gave it the feel of a rain forest or jungle. In prominent position was a huge poster of Claudia Ortiz on the back wall. He had one other item on his wall—a news clipping of him and Ellis from the sports page after they won the 13 and under city Hoop championships. Sitting on some expensive Asian looking dresser that neither Ellis nor Jay knew the correct name for, Jay had the most expensive Nakamichi tape deck on the market, a Yamaha receiver, CD player and about 500 CDs immaculately stacked above them on three shelves.

Jay dug pensively into his closet and pulled out something. "Check it. In case something happens to me, I want you to hold on to this package," said Jay as he handed Ellis a black attaché case.

"Don't open it, unless sumpin' happens to me. And look out for moms."

"C'mon, now, Jay, I thought you was gonna stay out of trouble, man?" anguished Ellis. He never knew what the hell Jay was getting into. He'd done enough dirt with him to know the possibilities.

Shit was different now, though. Now, Ellis had a few things going right for him. He had an amazing, fine, intelligent, woman, a good job with career potential, and now a car. On top of that, he had moved his mind out of the what mighta been mentality and finally gotten over not becoming the next T'Mac or Kobe. He knew he couldn't go back to their Old School hustles—that wuz then, but not now. The person who Jay knew, the kid he grew up with, was, for all good intentions, dead—or at least in a coma or something.

"I'm not fucken' with this, man. I got a career 'n' shit. I can't be doing the shit we used to. I got important people, depending on me, trusting me and I can't fuck that up—fo' what?"

Ellis stared out the window as if he'd see something new in a view he'd seen a thousand times and repeated his verbal stance.

"We ain't kidz no more, man, kicking that ole petty shit. I ain't living like that no more," grimaced Ellis.

Jay frowned. "Fuck you El. Just 'cause you came up some don't mean that we all there."

"Man, fuck you," whispered Ellis, trying to keep it an A- and-B conversation. Last thing he wanted was to disrespect or worry Mrs. Jones. He was raised mo' better than that; plus she already had enough to worry about just keeping up with this crazy mutha.

"Man, I am just hanging in there, just like you. Just a paycheck away from the Projects, So what the fuck you talking 'bout?" retorted Ellis.

"Whatever," said Jay, "just letting you know that if anything happens to me, come up here and flip this. Just look out for moms."

If nothing else Ellis prided himself on, it was his recently ability to know when to just shut the fuck up or end a conversation. Ellis stared at the ceiling for a second. He was summoning his Jedi mind trick. This was something that he was going to forget. *It didn't happen, and if it didn't happen, then it didn't exist.*

"It's getting late. I got to cover the game tonight. Peace."

"Yeah, peace."

THE AAAHRENA

As Ellis entered the arena, he could hear a cascade of indefinable noise rumbling, building, and mushrooming into a loud chaotic chorus of boo's. Even infants, strapped to dizzy drunk parents were booing. At first Ellis thought they were crying, but them rough little bastards were booing too. Booing like they got some bad milk or something. It was pure MSG ugliness.

I guess people started booing in the ticket line and continued on their way to their seats. How bad could they be doing?

By the time the third quarter rolled around, the Knicks were down by 40, that's when the 2-for-1 beer offer abruptly ended. New York finally looked like they were making a run against the New Orleans third-string, when 5-10 Knick point guard Ill L. Payne, betta known as "Illy," began beefing with the referee Fred Siteoff. Illy was the "Rudy" of the League. He'd worked his way up to "Bigdogville" after spending eight years in the Development League and another five overseas playing for a semi-pro Corsican bakery team that supplemented his income with all the bagels he could carry home from work on Friday nights. He'd secured a spot on the Knicks after destroying compromising photos of Knick General Manager Bob Klepto frolicking on an all male nude Corsican beach in exchange for a one-year offer sheet. Ily always told folks he'd make it to the Big League. It didn't matter how.

Referee Siteoff called Illy for palming the ball 3 times in a row. After the third time, Illy held the ball like former Knick Sly Williams, walked down the opposite end of the floor and then sat the ball at the farthest end of the court. Illy, then walked straight to Siteoff and said, "What the fuck up? You got sumpin' 'gainst da Ill?"

Siteoff—a former division four college player himself who was a trailblazer in the area of refereeing in that 10 years ago—had become the first ref with Tourette's Syndrome in League history. He normally worked hard at controlling his Tourette's through yoga, meditation, and boxing. Being that his Tourette's curse word was "Black Nigga fuck," Siteoff was a ticking timebomb in a League that was 90 percent Black. Still no one could push him to that point, no one till he ran across Ill. L. Payne.

"You walked. You do it all the time."

Illy crouched and pleaded angrily.

"I ain't walk; Jordan used to do that shit all the time and nobody called nothing."

Siteoff frowned, his left eye twitched and became watery, blinking his eyes rapidly, he walked right up to Illy's face, looked him up and down.

"You ain't Jordan, Black Negus fuck!"

That's when Illy dug into his sock and shanked him.

Needless to say, at least he was as consistent as the Knicks—as the ref beat him down, like a fan caught in the wrong bleachers at a European soccer match. Not only could this team not win a game, they couldn't fight either. New Yorkers loved winning teams, but if they couldn't get a win, after a few beers they'd always settle for whipping somebody's ass. Now they couldn't even get that bit of satisfaction.

This was a bad time for New York, during the post-Ewing years. Shit, with Oakley, Mason and Ewing, or even LJ, the Knicks lead the NBA in per-capita bench press. During those years every one on the squad and most of the Knick dancers could bench at least 250 pounds. In the Pat Riley era they'd beat you by 20 and kick your ass for the hell of it. Now, the Garden was stinking. Stinking so bad that 70-year-old former Knick star Willis Reed sat behind the bench, cane in hand screaming.

"Coach, put me in. Put me in! I know I'm old, and the cartilage in my knee is about as thin as flypaper, my prostate's big as a cantaloupe, I got a groin itch that ain't going nowhere, but I still got one or two pump fakes left. C'mon, baby, put me in the game. Put me in!"

Ellis had grown immune to the losing. It was one long dark era, sorta like the early Millennium "reality" shows. You knew it was going to end sooner or later, the question being when would your ex-wife join the cast first?

Despite the dread associated with covering the League's doormat team, today Ellis had a sense that something was about to change. The Basketball Godz could only take so much of the wailing and crying of hardcore New York fans, tossed in with a few fuck-yous. They had to answer soon, and Ellis knew it. In addition to his gut feeling, Ellis had heard from his prime source that a major news conference was happening and there were going to be "madd shakeups."

"Thanks," said Ellis, as he slipped his contact aka "Deep Jumper," a Clinton fifty-cent piece.

He was reliable, thought Ellis. *Probably the most well connected towel boy I ever met. Not only could he get cigars from Cuba, this kid could even get bank loans for inner city businesses.*

An amped Ellis raced down to the press conference room, where Nation Of Islam's (NOI) Fruit Of Islam was once again conducting the security. Press conferences had become extremely dangerous affairs, especially if someone might be fired. He was only a freshman in college when Red Johnson barricaded himself in the locker room and held League Vice President Jefferson Karl, the owner's mistress and three cheerleaders hostage for two weeks before that SWAT team coaxed him out with a promise from the Commissioner of an investigation into that 24 second-shot clock violation, and a general managers position with an expansion team from Fiji. He's currently doing a 30-year bid up at the Federal Prison in Danbury, Connecticut. Word has it that he's still coaching and his team is undefeated. Who they're playing? Don't ask.

The line was long as hell, but hey—better to wait than end up as disgruntled coach's hostage.

"Okay, take everything out of your pockets," said John 2X. "Step up. Hold up your arms."

Ellis jokingly mentioned that he forgot his Uzi, prompting a harsh look from John 2X.

"Pick up your right foot and stamp it to the ground. Now, your left."

Ellis made it through just in time to see Kings coach Yusef Black go to the mic.

"I feel that New York is an excellent place to be a winner and I believe that the winning tradition in New York will return and stay," said Yusef Black, the newly announced Coach and General Manager of the New York Knicks.

Damn! Fucken' unbelievable, thought Ellis. *This was great, a story, a great story*, he mused as he motioned up towards the front of the room, tugging, pushing and elbowing his way to Yusef, who he always called U Black.

"Yo, U, I can't believe you're coming to New York. "Damn! How come you didn't tell me earlier?" asked Ellis excitedly.

Ellis was not one to do a whole lot of cheesing or getting emotional, 'cept for that one scene when the cops shot Cornbread in the back.

U smiled for the cameras, and reached out and gave Ellis a palm.

"Well, this was kinda a last-minute move," explained Ellis. "You knew the Knicks had been courting me for a while, and they finally decided to give me the G.M. spot. Also, plus I left a message on your mailbox."

"Gotta go," said U, now several millions richer, "but we'll still hook up later with my nephew.

"Peace."

"Aiight, peace."

Ellis broke and headed straight to the office to download his audio copy.

No need to having World-A-Girl sweating me on deadline.

The headline read "U Gotta Believe In New York: New Coach Promises A Return Of Winning Traditions."

It ran on the front page-not too shabby, even though his instant editor software, wrote the headline. After reviewing his voice messages, Ellis realized that U had indeed hooked him up. It seems he had already scheduled a one-on-one interview with Ellis, where he was prepared to talk about cleaning house. He was particularly ready to get rid of the Knicks point guard Il L. Payne. Any player who got dusted by a 5-8 referee did not deserve to wear the Orange and Blue, unless she was a cheerleader.

Ellis and U decided to meet later in the week, after the taping of his new Sports Show "Can U Kick It," where star players from opposing teams would have to face 10 minutes of insults from gray bearded filmmaker Spike Lee. It showed aired in a split-camera, while Coach Yusef Black talked about his new line of sports ware, and why he was such a great coach.

JUST HANGING

Later that week, Ellis met Yusef and his nephew Wardell outside WLIB radio in Manhattan, where he was just finishing an interview. The misty rain streamed down hard, as street vendors hawked umbrellas meshing their sound into a canopy of horns and yells for those unprepared for the downpour. The city bustled with noise and motion and the pitter pat of feet walking created its own harmony. Crowds walked quickly as if the normal Gestapo pace of Gotham dwellers wasn't fast enough. Each person frantically sought their own private space of air like mice swimming to stay afloat in a flooding basement.

It was El's brilliant idea to get Yusef to drive the Lex 450 Uptown, rather than take a chance with Betsy the Hun'die With An Attitude; she didn't like rain. Plus, U hated to drive, so Ellis excitedly volunteered to steer the chumpy uptown.

The Lex was Phatt! Burgundy with crème-colored leather interior, an 18-speaker DVRD with video-screen audio system complete with F.A.R.T. technology. FART was an acronym for Foul Air Removal Technology, available only in top shelf luxury vehicles that detected a person's gaseous emissions and immediately announced on the speaker system who dealt it. It was like, "Human emission emerging from passenger front seat," in a polite, sexy feminine voice. With one button you could immediately refresh the environment. It caught the funky air midstream and just whooshed that smell out into the ozone, or, if you was lucky, into the face of some unsuspecting passerby—hopefully Rush Limbaugh.

The trio decided to grab something to eat at Sylvia's, and later they'd check out the hiphop show at the Exchange. It turned out to be an interesting night for Wardell and Ellis while U turned in early since he had an interview on both "Today" and "The Daily Show." Ellis and Wardell taxied to the Exchange and U jetted back to the hotel to get some rest.

As Ellis and Wardell taxied to the Exchange, Ellis remembered that he needed to have to talk to U about his nephew. He glanced at Wardell busy sparking his Cohiba, despite the obvious red light no-smoking sign staring him directly in the face. He noticed the diamond studded Platinum Tag-Heuer on Wardell's wrist. He had an Italian gray linen suit on, one that he bragged to Ellis several times about its four-digit cost. He also had a pair of gray Bruno Magli suede slip-ons. Ellis knew this mawfukas parents had some dough, and his uncle was paid. But this kid was dressing like a balla himself with no visible income. This the same mawfuka only a few years ago that was going to the club in gear straight outta the clearance rack in the dollar store and shirts so bright that Negus was walking up to him in the club trying to light their cigarettes off his sleeve.

I know U won't taking care of him like that? Shit, U was one of them no-nonsense, pull-yaself-up-from-your-own-Tim's-type Negus, so how was Wardell stacking chips like that? He'd deal with Wardell when the time came; right now it was all about da Honeyz, da brew, da music, and da Honeyz.

The Exchange was a hyped up tight spot built specifically for the urban older hiphop crowd. They used a high-tech soundwave scan that bowled over any headz attempting to introduce weaponry to the club. Sometimes for no reason, if you was high on Viagra the scan deflated your party.

Ellis' Uncle Breeze worked at the club. You know Utility? Whatever they needed, he helped out. He was an O.G., ODJ-whatever you'd call an old school deejay. El and Jay would come by his house and he'd be down in the basement sipping Coronas with lime and cutting up the old breaks like Pussyfooter, Grand-Groove, or Apache. He'd been making the phatt old school mixed street tapes for decades and was a veritable walking, talking, and scratching encyclopedia. If they had a hiphop *Jeopardy*, Breeze'd probably win it hands down. On second thought, he'd probably lose, since he'd tell the real stories as opposed to what everybody knew as the public truth.

He used to tell Ellis-'n'-them stories about the old glory days of hiphop at the Latin Quarters, when everybody from the old school, KRS and Scott LaRock, UTFO, the Furious Five, Bismarkie and the Awesome Two used to hang out. According to Breeze there were a few spots that truly captured the essence of hiphop from back in tha day, and his favorites were the Disco Fever, The Roxy, and the Latin Quarters. There was nothing like the LQ according to Unk Breeze. It was a time before hiphop got pretentious. It was as raw as the young ice creamed flavored sistas with razor blades stuck under their tongues with huge Dumbo earrings, with phatt ghetto ass squeezed into tight-tight jeans. It was the era of colorful lee jeans, suede pumas, or thick-laced Filas and counterfeit Adidas T-shirts and Nike hats from the Chinese store. You could feel the life, sweat, and blood of hiphop back then. Back when emcees didn't have bodyguards or entourages in the hundreds that acted like bodyguards. Back then you'd be standing sipping your shit and notice that the Furious Five was to your left, Slick Rick, to ya right as the Awesome Two, Teddy Ted and Special K, ripped shit to shreds on the turntables like there wasn't going to be a tomorrow. When the IOU dancers would be up on the stage innovating new shit every other minute and anyone that could catch the groove would join them. When you could actually see the Negus in the VIP room, if they had one? When you'd be on the dance floor with this fine-ass Honey with a body banging like PSK, and you both unafraid of getting loose or sweatin', while you wopped, grinded, twisted the stress of the day off your back like it was your birthright. When it was just about having a good time, not what you did, or who you was? It was before Negus had to name the game, before shit had to be spoken, when each Negus was cooler than most. In Breeze's mind it was the Golden Era. That was before things got madd wild up at the Hiphop supermarket Union Square where Brooklynites would just fly knots like crazy for gold.

Fortunately a lot of the Hood violence was eliminated by the Urban Collective, a group of anonymous brothas and sistas—sorta like that Nineties Blaxplotation flick "Drop Squad." Early millennia they formed a covert militia to patrol the community. The Bush Crime Wars re-ushered in a genocidal period akin than the Crack era. Uncle Breeze's boy Triny was down with the Collective, but he'd never come right out and say it. But after a few drinks he'd start talking that shit—

"Man, I could tell you some stories, Sun—some real off-the-wall shit, Sun. But if I told you I'd have to kill you."

That's when Breeze would be like, "Then keep that shit to yo'-self, fool."

This was one brotha that he made sure, the bartender stopped serving. Know when to say when baby, when to say when.

The Exchange was the type of political hot spot where

you could hear speeches from the grassroots legends, or PhD's and street corners prophets mixed over hiphop and jazz in a style like FLUID and at the same time rub elbows with the Black Bourgeoisie elite. It was the only spot in the world that served chitlin's, tofu and caviar.

The crew walked in during a song by the Funkster's entitled "Crucial." Glasses clanged, wood paneled walls made the place seem like some upscaled cavern. Shit was slamming as Ellis squeezed his way through the mass of well-dressed, immaculate hygiened bodies spitting da shit like they all graduated cum laude from the school of heavy fronting. Ellis emerged unscathed at the bar and ordered a stout. Ellis glanced around with an air of contempt, then leaned on his elbow, whipped out his satellite phone and moved into full fronting-mode. He glanced at the mirror behind the bar and checked his steelo, then held up his elbow, slid back his sleeve to reveal a glistening platinum Rolex. Smoothly, he reached into his jacket and pulled out his silver cigar case. He opened it gracefully and snared a miniature Fuente cigar that he propped on his hanging lip in the corner of his mouth. Slipping the case back into his jacket, he reached to his lower pocket and pulled out his latest gift from Maya, a silver Opus lighter and flicked it once. The flame roared red and blue light bringing his cigar to life and seeping the smell of manicured tobacco into his immediate area. He took a whiff and held it, then exhaled, blowing smoke towards the thick Honey next to him. He exhaled as if he'd overcome. As if he was so high above the shit, nothing or no one really mattered 'cause his game was beyond thorough and he held the good life in the palm of his hand.

It was all a ruse.

He got the Rolex—er,. Rol-less—off the Ave for 10 bucks, and he never really inhaled on his cigars-too afraid of getting cancer, plus the shit might make his eyes water or even choke him. Couldn't be a player with you choking on fumes like a novice. He told everybody his cigar case was pure silver, but it wasn't, some electroplated shit that looked good. His satellite only had 40 minutes of go time left on it. Ellis was cool, but not as cool as his personal representative that was now playing him in the club. It was not humanly impossible for anyone to be as cool as he projected. Plus, Ellis didn't really feel that comfortable round other people. But he wanted to feel comfortable, be a cool suave people person. He was cool but not suave as he figured he'd be. Ellis actually like spending his time alone, but hated feeling alone and the only time he didn't feel alone was when he was around a crowd. Crowds were easier than having to deal with a person one on one, or a small crowd. As such, he did the club thing on a regular and as much as he liked it, he disliked the whole pompous bullshit sophistication, but he figured when in Rome, be a fucken Roman.

Ellis took another whiff and sipped his stout, but he didn't want to get too toasty. Maya always made such a big deal if he had one damn drink. Wasn't like he was drinking every day. But every now and then Negus needed to clear his mind. It was like Showbiz and AG dropped, "a beer will relax my mind, but I still pack my nine. So I'm woozy and my eyes red, better than an Uzi and another man dead."

As Ellis scoped the club in a near daydream, until he saw an open stool at the opposite end of the bar near the huge exotic fish tank, the best spot to scope Honeyz from. They loved watching the beautifully colored exotic fish swim. It was prime club real estate and glimmered like an oasis in the desert.

Out of the corner of his eye, he hawk-visioned this 370-pound brotha who also eyed the open barstool. He looked like at one time, maybe years ago, he might have been able to break through the offensive line and sack McNabb. Maybe. That didn't matter, 'cause now it was the universal struggle between good and evil, the have and the have-nots, those who grabbed a veggie burger and those who gorged out at the buffet. It was like the tortoise versus the hare, except this time the tortoise tripped and broke a table in half.

After a few stouts and surveying the nonstop parade of beautiful, scantily clad women with jobs, Ellis walked over to the DJ booth for a sec to check DJ Slipup, and Emcee Mistake, two old associates now deejaying at the Exchange. He used to be in a group with both of 'em but had to drop them Negus since they was always fucken' up. Everytime he got ready to rhyme, DJ Slipup would fuck up on the mix, and be like "my bad, my bad." Then if DJ Slipup was on, emcee

Mistake would always fuck up his lyrics. Between the both of them, it took about 20 minutes just to do their 30-second stage introduction. He had to drop them Negus, but was glad they stuck with it and finally got better.

Ellis once took emceeing seriously enough to trek through the concrete byways of the city, stalking record producers and label execs for a recording deal with his boy Chilly C. He still had skills on the wheels, and spit multi-verse style-Uncle Breeze made sure of that. Tonight his interest wasn't so much about getting a chance to spin some cuts as opposed to trying to collect on the 70 dollars them kidz owed him. After a little chitchat, and a few passes of the Cuban blunt, Ellis returned to the bar just in time to see Wardell cozying up with some Negus who was clearly FBDIE.

The FBDIE was the sort of idea that emerged during the Clinton era, when the intelligence community, (affectionately called spies by regular folks), decided having some new enemies would be nice. And after much deliberation and consternation, they chose poor people, especially those with darker skin, as the new enemy and true reason for a $900 trillion budget. They had initially decided to spy on the European Community's multi-national corporations, but, according to CIA head General Dickey Short who had lead the "Get Ron Brown" investigation, "It just wasn't as much fun as bringing down Black officials."

It even got worse after the Taliban blew up the World Trade Centers in 2001. During the Bush era especially after 911, basically all civil liberties went out the window in the name of "ending terrorism." It was actually worse than COINTELPRO, since everything the feds did was now above-board and legal.

This time around, the government didn't blackmail brothas and sistas into infiltrating community organizations and destroying them, or spying on activists; they just went after yo' ass and often, Blackfolks were gave the orders to do so. Shit reached its height around 2009, (that's the year Pimpin', Negus with perms, Industry Beefs, and Jherri Curls were officially banned in the continental states and Puerto Rico), but more importantly it was the year that certain high level officials with dark skin started waking up with limbs missing. Those responsible for the Underground couldn't get to the whitefolks or "untouchables," behind the scenes, but they could sure as hell make the Head Negus in charge pay. Blackfolks were never "untouchable," according to FBDIE agency directive 187.

Most thought Laurana Bobbit's old ass had flipped out on dust or Jeffrey Dahmer had come back to life. An arm here, nose there, nothing special. But it seemed that things cooled down on the sellout tip a little bit. I mean it had to be kinda hard to explain the your co-workers, unless you wuz Mike Jax, why you no longer had a nose or why you only had two fingers on each hand—after all, it would be hard to call it a fashion statement. If nothing else, a group of Black conservatives were still on the run. Last report was that they were hiding out somewhere in the Caucus mountains. It was beautiful there- white snow, white foxes, and white rabbits-pure undisturbed whiteness. Word had it they loved it so much, that they decided to stay.

Ellis snuck a glance at Wardell, wondering: *What was Wardell doing with this mark? Everybody knew FBDIE was on that ole ill shit and couldn't be trusted. Plus, Wardell knew that the FBDIE had been using any means at hand to take down his folks. He can't be that stupid or that fucken' trifling, could he?*

Ellis wondered and watched, making sure he didn't catch him watching.

The question that kept popping into Ellis head—in-between of thoughts of his next beer, and that Honey in the black dress, with seductive eyes, small waist, and ass so phatt you could sit your drink on it while she was standing—was, *What the hell was Wardell up to?*

His mind went back to the Honey in the black dress. She was the type of woman that most men would gladly give their paychecks to and say something like, "Er, just leave the stub; I need that for my taxes." Looking at her made him think of Maya, who on any given night was damn near close to check-stub privileged type fineness herself. *Maybe, he should just go head and settle down—do the marriage thing. Then he'd have to give it all up, emotionally, everything-wasn't no road back from that type of shit, especially if something went wrong. What would happen ten years late, if she stepped out on him? If he met someone else or she hated him? He'd lose it; somebody'd get hurt. Fuck it—maybe it's better to love and have lost, than never to have loved at all? Plus what was he really giving up? Fantasizing about women didn't exactly make you a playa?*

Ellis peeked back over and saw Wardell still chilling like a villain. His lower back started panging. Stress was getting to him. In times of stress, Ellis remained consistent. No, he didn't face down what was bothering him, or dig deep inside and overcome his fears; or step to Wardell and get to the bottom of shit. He did what most Negus did when faced with a stressful situation: he jetted.

The last thing Ellis wanted was to have FBDIE sweating him. Once they determined that you were some kind of threat or worse "un-American," they came after yo' ass like McCarthyism on speed. They locked up his cousin for 2 years with no explanation at all based on the fact that the guy he normally bought his incense and oils from-a street vendor-normally bought his stuff from a Muslim, who had cousins, who attended a mosque that a cousin of someone who was a childhood friend of a member of Al Qaeda frequented. It didn't matter that over 1,000 other people attended the mosque. Fuck six degrees of separation, they was settling for two-degrees and a hunch. Then his nephew from Guyana got locked up because of some petty crime he committed 15 years ago. They held him for over a year in New Jersey, then deported him. Not that Ellis believed for a minute that his own life was that great, but shit, he definitely hadn't planned on checking out this early—especially with several of the *For Blackmen Only* magazine Bikini models still single. There was much ass to be conquered-not that he didn't plan on settling down-but until that time-hey-it was on, even if only in his mind.

Peeping the situation, Ellis quickly put on his "oblivious Negro" look, and attempted to stay away from that rat bastard Wardell until he could skate. No matter how many beers he had, this shit was fucken' up his high.

What was Wardell up to?

Despite his previous gear-challenged proclivities, he didn't seem treacherous.

Me n Jay took him on a few runs round the city, to try to hip him up.

I mean he was the regular heavy drinking, pleasure seeking, extrovert-which only put him into the same population as 98 percent of all college students.

Ellis ordered another shot of VSOP, took one to the head, and made his way towards the glowing red EXIT sign, to catch a cab. He hoped that Wardell didn't spot him. After reaching the outside door, Ellis exhaled and took a deep breathe of the crisp nighttime air. He stared at the fuzzy neon signs and watched the rain trickle down like Duke Ellington were had somehow engineered a deal with Mother Nature to orchestrate the rain. He checked his pocket for his keys and checked his wallet for cash.

He was straight.

He nodded to the doorman and had him flag down a taxi.

Some things hadn't changed much—like Negus' inability to catch cabs at night. Luckily now they had these new mobile armored vehicles designed especially for this occasion. As usual Negus was able to create genius from what America threw away. And all the time those experts at the Pentagon kept saying the A-2 tank would never be worth the $12 billion price tag? Shit, for Negus trying to get home, the billions of dollars the government paid for faulty weaponry was quite alright…A tax dollar well spent.

As he motored home, Ellis continued to wonder what today's events meant.

What was Yusef going to do when he found out that his nephew was cozying up to the same folks who had me trying madd hard to squash his brother and sister-in-law? I wasn't going to be the one to tell him.

Maybe I'm overreacting. Maybe that damn stout was making me paranoid after all these years. That's the reason I gave up weed for a few months; I ain't trying to flip. Yeah, that's it- damn drugs making me paranoid, I'm giving up the get high for good, yeah tonight's the night. I gotta stop eating at that Chinese spot. There gotta be a law somewhere in the food bible that you can't serve plantains with beef fried rice?

"Yo! Can't you find an English-speaking station?" yelled Ellis banging on the bulletproof divider.

The cabbie looks at his rearview mirror

"Infidel."

"Huh? What?"

The Cabbie looked straight ahead, ignoring the inebriated alter ego of Ellis Rey.

"Yeah, yeah, thought so. Thought so," postured Ellis, as he reclined against the rugged cushion seats plastered with American flags.

MEANWHILE, BACK AT THE OFFICE...

Ellis sat in his window-less office surrounded by dim yellowish-orange colored lighting that conflicted with the bluish-gray glare emanating from the computer screen. It was something that could go unnoticed 'til a person spent several hours staring at a fluorescent screen. His eyes began to flicker, and strain. A line emerged in his forehead like he'd been sliced in his youth by a box cutter. His mother told him he worried too much, needed to learn how to relax. He thought he'd learn how to take it easy, become detached, not fret about every damn decision to the point where it immobilized him, but when it was something he was really hyped about, he could spend hours in front of a television, computer screen straining his eyes. He wondered, *why did they build this building with practically no windows?*

Why did they want us working in the dark?

He had no qualms believing it's a plot to ensure that 10 years from now he was legally blind. He knew the subtle manipulation of color schemes was a step away from mind control.

Yeah, Nicole wants me as her sex slave; don't give into the dark side. Either that, or these broke bastards still not paying bills on time.

In his spare time, which was rare, Ellis often hid in his bunker-slash-cubicle with walls and manipulated his computerized audio music software to sample old beats that he eventually laced with lyrics. He had a choice earlier in his life: *school, Hoop or hiphop.* He chose the former, only after he realized that he was never gonna be a draft pick. He never let go of his hiphop, but neva believed that it was anything more than an exercise for releasing stress. Plus, he hadn't accumulated enough felonies for record labels to take him seriously. He stopped emceeing about five years ago, but old emcees never die, they just get older and heavier. He was currently working on sampling Gangstarr's "Take It Personal" into a beat that he was going to rip with a flow so nasty, so devastating, that the hiphop masses would quickly anoint him as "The One."

Okay, "bent, bnt, ban, bnt, ban, bnt, bnt, bnt…'

Oh, yeah, I'm feeling this shit.

"Ellis!" yelled Sasha, the world's top-ranked receptionist, with a record of 23-3; with 20 by knockout.

"Pick up Line Two."

"Who is it?"

"I don't know, fool!" she snarled with a viciousness that relayed either she really thought she could fight. Or were the rumors true floating around the watercooler that she used to be a hitman for a group of Dominican Gambinos?

Let's see…Which part of this job do I love more? Ellis mused. *Getting screamed at by a receptionist or taking calls from somebody I probably didn't want to speak with…definitely, not more than laying these beats.*

Ellis knew he had little choice in the matter, and painfully closed out his audio mix program on the computer and picked up the phone all the while thinking of slapping Sasha up against the back of her head. He'd been doing 50 pushups every day for the past few weeks; he might be able to take her. After flipping a coin, Ellis took a deep breath through his nostrils and exhaled through his partially opened lips and decided to take the call.

"As salaam walaikum," said a voice aged and raspy.

"Walaikum salaam. How can I help you?" asked Ellis into the speakerphone.

Ellis was unable to see him, since the telex-link monitor on his screen was still broke. After a cascade of rough coughs, the voice finally uttered again.

"Sir, I have some information that you may be interested in."

"Yeah?"

"Yes sir. It pertains to a legend."

"Legend, who?" said Ellis in his *it's-too-goddamn-early-to-give-a-shit* demeanor.

"It is regarding the rebirth of the Godz of the planet. A legend in which you will play a key role."

Ellis grabbed his favorite ink pen off his desk and slid it in his ear. He began tapping on the desk with his index finger to the Gangstarr beat *"Tap, tap tap tap…Tap, tap tap tap…"*, all the while wondering, *What the hell was this Negus smoking?*

Ellis found himself in a conundrum. This was not his shit. He was a sportswriter and unless this story somehow was going to pick the next champion or rookie of the year, then my man was talking to the wrong cat. On the same hand, he knew that because of their small staff, and his raise in salary, he sometimes had to take stories that didn't have nothing to do with sports if no one else was around. Ellis slid his chair and peeked around the office. He saw nothing but empty chairs.

Damn!

"Your name is…?" strained Ellis, wishing this Negus would just disappear.

"My name is Rudell. Can we meet tomorrow?"

"Sure, yeah. Come by the office at 2 p.m.," groaned Ellis, wondering where the hell this story was going to take him. He wasn't religious, although he was exposed to enough of the varying strands of beliefs growing up. He had an uncle in the Nation, an Aunt Sharon, now named Nebila, who followed some variation of the ancient Egyptian religion based on what she called "the Laws of Ma'at," which had to do with truth, and justice. Nebila was his favorite aunt, a beautiful dark chocolate woman with a slight gap between her front teeth. Ellis remembered seeing her dressed up for some reenactment of an Egyptian festival in full garb and seeing his grandmother throw holy water on her, then chase her out of the house with a loaded forty-five calling her an "idolater." Funny, as strange as she dressed sometimes, Nebila was the only extended family he ever felt comfortable with, other than Unk Breeze, whose only religion was Hiphop, straight with no chaser. Nebila always seemed truly interested in where Ellis wanted to go with his life and never once judged him which was rare for the world where Ellis resided, when even the wino up the street, or Dave the dopefiend had sumpin' to say 'bout what a Negus should or should not be doing.

He had two cousins who were Sunni Muslim, whose parents were Baptist preachers. His oldest sister was a former Nation of Godz and Earths, now a Buddhist in training. He'd heard it all. He was the fucken Tiger Woods of Religion. For

Ellis what folks believed just didn't matter, 'cause most of the time when they called on God in whatever language name or philosophy they used-God wasn't listening. Whether fasting, burning incense, or burning a cow, people'd pray and pray, and pray some more and God was busy watching the World Series, or planning the next plague or sumpin'.

Ellis just hoped that this Negus he had to interview wasn't crazy. The only things that really scared Ellis, beyond commitment, was dealing with crazy people. He didn't like being harsh or having to hurt folks, but every time he came around somebody crazy, he worried about having to hurt them for fucken' with him.

Ellis, like a lot of Negus, always teetered on the edge of full-blown "Colin Ferg-bine-ism." There was a dark place within in him that had grown in the innermost parts of his heart. It was a place where cold replaced gold due to the ways of the world. This side of himself is what frightened him even more than having to hurt someone. He feared it like a demon that was called up from hell. He knew, and felt pity for the mawfuka responsible for bringing that part of him to the surface. That was a bridge of no return. The wise Negus in the Hood knew this about folks that didn't do a lot of talking. The Negus that talked shit a lot were much often luckier, they didn't let their shit build to a level that could explode like napalm burning everything in its path as the frustrations of life's sufferings and pangs poured out of your soul like an river unleashed by a dam of emotional detachment. Despite Ellis' apparent ability to talk shit, he never really said a lot about anything serious, except once in a while to Maya, otherwise he always carried himself like nothing could ever bother him, it was a front, he was an extremely sensitive and perceptive person who saw shit that many didn't, but who learned to keep it to himself—Jedi Mind Trick. This was a side of himself that Ellis refused to unleash, unless he was ready for war.

Yeah, I hope this Negus ain't crazy. Come up in here with an AK or Uzi and start spraying folks.

"Ellis! Pick up Line Three. It's Maya."

"Hey, what up, baby girl?"

"Nothing," responded Maya with a touch of skepticism in her voice.

"We still on for tonight—get something to eat and movie?"

"Of course," hummed Ellis, not responding to the pragmatism in her voice. "Check it out—I'll be by at 7, after I make this run around the way."

"Good," she said melodiously like a song lifting the depression out of her voice.

Maya had a unique way of speaking as if notes fluttered out her mouth as if instead of speaking she sang. Sometimes, Ellis just listened to her voice, not even paying attention to what she said, just vibing to the intonations and subtle vibrations of her words. Unless she was angry, then she was short and static.

Some men looked for the tits, others ass, some face. For Ellis, those all played an important role in getting his dick hard, but a woman's voice was important. Of course a nice ass, and beautiful hands and intelligence made Maya a coup d'etat. Now this formula for attraction could be altered by a number of factors, including days without sex, alcohol blood content level, and credit rating.

Maya was definitely gorgeous, plus she had good credit. She was about 5-3 brown silky skin with orange undertones and "phatt as all outdoors," as his boy Harry O used to say. She had almost Asian shaped eyes and thick supple lips that were as soft as cotton and pearly whites and walked slow and sexy like a Beres Hammond song. She had everything going for her; education, intelligence, money, looks. But the most important thing in her life were her relationships. Her energy went into her relationships—making other people happy, making them like her even at her own discomfort.

Ellis met her through a wrong number and taken by her voice he started up a conversation with her that led to a date. She was the first woman he had to complete his sentences before he finished—and get them right. She was the first woman that seemed to always climax at the exact same time as he did. They never made love for a long period—never needed to. Everything just came together in passionate rush that enveloped their whole body and souls like an ancient Kundalini life force that exploded into ecstasy.

Deep down he loved her, and every now and then he'd

even admit it to himself and maybe to Maya. She was a sincere challenge to his desire to live life dispassionately. He really cared about her and that bothered Ellis for one simple reason—the only things that can hurt you are the ones you really cared about.

CON-SPHERE-I-SEE

Twenty years into the Millennium and Negus have still found ways to throw a monkey wrench into the plans of the powerbrokers aka the Illuminati, aka the Ten Percent, aka mawfukas with money, power, but no respect for the planet. With a little hustle, they forestalled the emergence of the cashless society that former president Curious George, made such a priority some years back. The government kept saying that soon no one was going to be able to use cash, that those dead presidents would soon be buried. They frightened the American public by saying that terrorists had now developed a way to create counterfeit dollars indistinguishable from real dollars. The wealthy folks were the first in line to get rid of their cash, but Negus won't having it. In reality, it was an attempt to prevent African and Arab nations from exchanging their US owed monies into Euros, which would have instituted a major economic depression. The US hoped to keep the dollar as the major world currency by scaring folks while flouting their virtual and high tech security features as the only protection against cyber terrorists stealing their money, while promoting flaws of the European financial security system.

Many began trying to convince Negus to get with this new technology and let the old ways pass, but it wasn't that there was some type of digital-divide the way people tried to play it; shit, Negus was always up on new technology, and they just couldn't afford it without the CP deal. The problem was that with a cashless society, Negus with bad credit was up shit's creek-and most Negus—at least the ones we knew—had bad credit. The worst thing about living in a cashless society is that the creditors are the first ones with access to your money—no ands, ifs, or buts. As usual the only folks hyped about the system, was the folks that didn't use cash to begin with.

According to the no-brain media, Negus was just going to be walking around with this damn computer chip implanted in their head or hand or maybe a "smart card," that looked like a Visa or ATM card, except that it had your whole life story on it.

Fortunately, as usual, Blackfolks was slow to buy in. Negus didn't trust the government anyway and wasn't wit' the program from the getgo. Some thought "it the Book of Revelations." Others thought it was just the most recent revelation. So, about 2 months before the government was phasing out cash, that natural born Nubian ingenuity struck and Negus started spreading bootleg chips, quicker than street copies of the latest Black movie.

Several inside folks, reportedly called "Da Underground," had peeped and deciphered the whole Advanced Encryption Standard. They designed an Acrylonitrile Budtadiene Styrene (ABS) based card that utilized the body's own magnetic field in order to enact external and internal authentication. It was complicated, but certainly not as hard as finding an original tape of Kool Moe Dee's microphone battle with Busy B Starsky.

They traded microchips for all types of stuff. It started Uptown then spread to Chicago, Atlanta, L.A. and St. Louis. From there, it moved throughout Hoodville and Hoodburbia, quicker than a rumor of a Tupac sighting. As a matter of fact, it became the main business of the Blood-Crip-Latin King Alliance, which grew out of the 2011 Peace Conferences. The BCK Alliance began spreading the chips throughout the nation through their satellites gangs, who moved out of the dope game after the CIA came clean about "Project Windspitter."

The system was designed so that the chips would use Fourth Generation technology that combined multimedia, voice, and data systems into a high-speed WiFi broadband system to download and transfer funds electronically to offshore accounts prior to releasing an undetectable Enki technology-erasure virus, which removed any traces of the transactions.

Folks got paid.

It eventually broke down the HAL636 worldwide supercomputer located in Brussels, Belgium, where at least 10 pages of data was collected on every living person from all Northern-based industrialized nations.

After the mass bootlegging of smartcards caused worldwide market depreciations, and super-inflation, governments started printing money again. They even printed a Black face on the three-dollar bill-only some people were upset that they passed over MLK, and Malcolm for Carl Rowan.

All this meant little to Ellis. He was still a man that kept his extra change in a shoebox, and made pause-button mixed tapes. Driving into the ole Hood, Ellis crept like a villain, slowly checking for his peeps. First thing Negus wanted to say was that since he moved out, he was dissing kidz. Sometimes he inadvertently dissed Negus, but that was only because he refused to wear his glasses like he was supposed to, and he wasn't gon' tell Negus that he was half-blind, or drive around looking like a nerd, they could think what they wanted. Cautiously he glanced in the rear view mirror to make sure that Five-O won't trying to sweat him, particularly FBDIE.

There's Chill.

Ellis pulled over to the curb.

"Yo, what up, Chill. Seen Jay?"

"Nah man, he jetted out with madd heads earlier," remarked Chill, while polishing off his new suede Air 2000s with matching black velour sweatsuit. Chill was one of those mysterious icons from the Hood who always appeared unscathed by the continuous dramas of life. He had to be close to forty, but looked like he was in his twenties. Always immaculately dressed, he didn't eat particularly healthy or bad, never drank too much, but when he did, enough to consider A.A. as an option. He did smoke helluva weed when he smoked, but you never saw him smoke that much. His secret was that he was a taster, a nibbler of things as opposed to a gorger. That kept him looking like a ghetto celebrity.

Chill, reached into his pocket and pulled out some John Blaze and sparked it. It was if he was saving it for a special occasion and seeing Ellis was reason enough for today. He took a pull and then passed it to El. Ellis waved him off.

"Naw."

"Yo, Ak!" blurted Chill, in between puffs of his genetically altered marijuana that allowed one blunt to burn for 40 minutes

"Yo, Ak, you heard that new Biggie shit?"

"Nah," said Ellis, shaking his head.

Chill grinned, "Nah."

Chill had grown up with El n Jay from way back. These kidz fought like dogs growing up, but had built bonds that couldn't be broken. It was family ties that only Negus that been through the fire together could grasp. Only real Negus that been through the wars of Hoodism and poverty deserved to sit at the main table and break bread together. It was a rough fraternity that you earned your way in. It was a clique fo' life. It was a trust built on the fact that you really knew the good and bad of each other, it wasn't no secrets that one or the whole clique didn't know about each other. That was Hoodlife, if somebody was hittin' the pipe, trickin', an informant, child molester, Negus knew all about it, whether it was true or just rumor. If you were able to retain some veil of sanity and not be broken by everything that the Blackman faced and carried the burden of blame for in this society and not lose it or fall off; then all praise was due-'cause you knew you would get none from the world. These cats knew that every Negus deserved his praise, the right to be a man and some sense of relativity about who they really were, beyond the bullshit stereotypes that creators of illusions forced them to be. The fact that yesterday, one of them talked himself out of murdering this cat and instead talked himself into going back to work and coming home to his wife and son. Somebody had to acknowledge that shit, tell him he was right and a good man for doing so. Somebody had to tell him he won't no punk for trying to keep from killing a Negus who in his heart he felt really deserved to die.

This was the way they thought and saw the world

whether it made sense or not. They believed you knew a man's wars by a certain glint in his eyes. They say the eyes were the windows to the soul and it was so subtle that outsiders or wannabes might miss it. It won't no fag homo shit, but it was that look that death recognized as a one-way ticket to cross over at any time. It was a look that stared the world in the face and screamed, "Is that all ya got, bitch?" There was a certain brutal energy to these cats that could explode at any time and a courage that wasn't bolstered by arsenal or rolling with a thick posse. They weren't really gangstas, thugs, or killers; they were just Negus caught in situations where they might have to be a thug, even if just for a moment, day, week, year. No matter how far Negus got from the mind-state, they couldn't release it or let it go-not 'cause they didn't want to, they just didn't know how. They didn't know that they were the essence of the former Godz of the planets. Those who regardless of the hell they experienced refused to let the dyslexic world turn them into dogs-scarred but unbroken.

No matter what Negus spit on them discs, no one wanted to carry the nightmares of war forever. Everybody wanted to exorcise those demons, everybody wanted to sit back and smile at their kidz and wife. We all wanted the Bobby McFerrin; main problem was that we had no idea how to get there without assuming that we'd lose this burden of identity that we'd built a whole lifetime carving.

Chill took another deep pull. *"Phoooooooove."*

Then glanced at El and his car, then stared at him like he was a proud father or something. Like he'd see his son graduate from college. Chill leaned over through the passenger side window and looked the car up and down and smiled.

"Yo, El, that Biggie shit—that shit is straight up Taliban, Sun!" he yelled in Ellis' face, close enough for his breath to singe a few nose hairs.

"Yo Chill, check it out—if you see Jay, tell him I stopped through, aaiight?"

Chill stared disappointedly at Ellis.

"Yo, Kid, that Negus Jay," Chill paused and just shook his head as if Jay was shot dead or something worse.

"Yo, Kid, he running with dem crazy kidz from Up da Way—you know, Benni 'em dem. Them straight up den-ofthieves, eat-da-hole-outta-a-donut Negus.

"They still running dem hustles at the airport en shit. I told dem Negus to ice that shit, 'cause they bringing heat on my thing and I can't be going out like that El, these Negus fucken' up shit for all the legitimate street biz up this way. I'm try'na go WalMart up this mawfuka, El, expand my outlets and Jay en them kidz depreciatin' my net worth, nawmean? Shit, I'm even going a step betta than WalMart, 'cause m' peeps only need one job to live the shiny life.

"Yo, El, you ain't in on that shit, right? I mean you got educated an shit—got a real job, right? You graduated, right? You ain't one dem Negus with 30 grand in student loans, still two credits away from graduating, right?" laughed Chill as if he might be describing himself.

Ellis paused for a second, thinking, *How many times have I've gone through this conversation with Chill? Did Negus only hear shit like who got shot, who got locked up or who getting out of jail this week?*

"Yeah CP, I graduated and yeah I write for *The Nubian*—I thought you knew," said Ellis failing to mention how much he owed in student loans. Chill, seeing a spot on his Air Two Grands, quickly pulled out his brush and went to work.

"So, El, you work for who?"

Frustrated, Ellis mumbled, "Nobody, man, nobody."

Coming around the way always humbled El, because no matter what he thought he was doing, Negus never really gave a shit unless they thought he was coming out with an album. He'd always be that skinny kid from the 3rd floor to them.

El, seeing he's getting nowhere, put his car in drive and said peace. As Ellis began to pull off, Chill, after performing madd due-diligence on his kicks, looked up with a serious face, a face full of warning.

"Yo, El, be careful. I know Jay's ya boy, but it was only a few moons ago when FB was all up the block looking for him. So you know just watch yo'self. 'Cause man, a lot of these Negus around da way ain't 'bout shit. You made it up out of this nonsense, and Negus won't say it, but they respect dat shit."

Ellis acknowledged Chill, and begins to pull off when

suddenly what Chill was saying registered.

"Damn Chill, FBDIE on Jay? How come you didn't say that shit at first?" asked Ellis, always wondering why he was always the last Negus to know shit.

"I did," said Chill. "You won't listening; 'member El, I's never sleep 'cause sleep is the cuzin of death. Don't sleep, God."

"True, true dat," nodded Ellis while he sped off quickly on his way to Jersey, hoping that the hot water ain't out again.

Heading to the crib, he dialed Maya on the cellular.

"How you living?"

"Laaarge," she said slowly in her sweet voice, "Especially when you're buying."

"Aw, now, why you have to go there?"

They both chuckled.

"Check it out," said Ellis, "I'll be through in about three hours, be ready and make sure your bodyguard ain't round."

"Now, you know you wrong," chuckled Maya.

"Gail is good people—she just like eating. Just like you and Jay like smoking those semi-illegal substances, Ellis."

"Me and who…" fronted Ellis before continuing his verbal jabs.

"Don't get mad 'cause you hang with people who measure time in hair weaves," Ellis laughed.

Maya sucked her teeth.

"Ellis, if you and Gail don't get along, it's your fault. I mean that one spoon wedding gift was real, real bad."

Ellis raised his voice a little.

"See, you can't do nothing for some people! Ya girl just straight up Hoodburbia, she should have registered at a regular store! She went and registered at that expensive-ass store and the only thing I could afford was one spoon. I wanted to get the set, but I wanted to pay rent more," said Ellis.

"Ellis, you could have got her something else instead of one damn spoon? That's ghetto. I really think got a real problem with overweight people," she said. "I think it has something to do with your childhood. Probably got your lunch took by some fat kidz. You'd better check yourself. You know what they say, 'You become what you fear.' And you've been putting on a few pounds lately.”

"Hell naw, not the K-I-D,” responded Ellis as she touched a nerve. "Shit, you the one putting on pounds lately,” popped Ellis on the quick comeback. "Probably eating ice cream and chicken wings right now.”

Maya smiled through her voice. "Yeah, okay. As a matter of fact, I'm eating butter pecan and barbeque wings. See you later, chubby.”

UNKH BREEZE

Before shooting home to clean up and get ready for his love rendezvous with Maya, Ellis decided to stop by the fish market and get some of his favorite red snapper and tuna steaks. As he pulled into the wharf, he caught a deep whiff of fresh fish and glanced over the canopy of fish boats and stands into the bay. The sun shone brightly, its rays dancing off the top of the canopies of fishermen, and off the Hoods of shiny cars. It was Ellis' dream to one day, have a boat, a yacht to be exact. Something that he could take trips to the Caribbean or South America in; where Maya be laying half-naked on the deck and he'd be sipping a cold stout staring out into the ocean while listening to Miles Davis as he contemplated the meaning of life.

His daydreaming almost turned dangerous, as barely noticed this old brotha walking hard, who almost bopped himself directly into his front bumper.

Beeep!

What tha Hell?

The guy kept going as if he doesn't see or hear Ellis and Besty the Hyundie with an attitude?

"Beeeep Beeeep!"

Finally, the brotha turned around, raised his hands high, balled his fists and banged on his Hood.

"What the fucks yo' problem?” yelled Ellis before recognizing the face.

He was somewhat blinded by the sun beaming off the gold grill, but it could be no other than his Uncle Breeze, probably, the oldest B-Boy fanatic on the planet.

"Ellis, that you? Got damn sun, I was 'bout ready to fly that knot.

"You-you-you got to be more careful, Sun. You know

since that incident at Central Park with the faulty speaker wire, I can't half-hear in one ear."

Ellis smiled and turned down his music.

"I'm sorry, Uncle Breeze. Where you heading?"

"Nowhere but home. You think you could give me a ride?" asked Breeze, already headed to the passenger side.

"Sure, hop in."

After picking up his fish, Ellis revved up Betsy for what should have been a short ride-since Uncle Breeze lived three blocks away. Unk said the smartest thing he ever did was to decided to buy into the townhouse that he now owned. It was in a run-down section of the city before they redeveloped and re-assimilated it into Whiteworld. They offered a payout to the renters or they could use it as a down payment to purchase the property. He was the only one to use it as a down payment. The second smartest thing he did was to help recruit whitefolks to move into his neighborhood to facilitate an artificial increase in property values. Now it was worth 20 going on 40 times what he paid for it. Said, he was gonna leave it to Ellis, since "El was the only real family he had left."

No sooner than they got a block away from the Wharf, Uncle Breeze goes into his usual routine. "Ellis, Sun, I need to stop over on the Boulevard—you know, pick up my drink. I'll be right out."

"Okay," agreed Ellis already knowing the routine, and realizing that he had no choice.

Once Uncle Breeze went somewhere he's never right out. Brotha knew everybody in the city, or was it that everybody knew him? With Unk Breeze it was like the Twilight Zone. Somehow 10 minutes could fall into a time warp and quickly transform itself into an hour. This time, 10 minutes became two hours of driving to pick up this and that till they finally made it to his spot.

"Ellis, now you know I appreciate you taking me around. You know me once I get to yapping—I can't stop sometimes.

"I run into old friends and we reminisce about the days when we was gonna change it all. Everytime I run into my old partner ReK'less, it reminds me of the dayz when we was running things. Rek gonna try n tell me that The Real Roxanne and Roxanne Shante was the same person. I told that fool to stop sniffing gasoline 'cause glue is cheaper. It was about 20 Roxannes, and 4 of 'em lived right up the street from me, as a matter of fact, one of 'em, the one used to rock that lumberjack shirt, she invented the pogo stick. Then he gonna talk about how when me and Red Alert battled, that he thought Red won. Man, I almost took out my pint of Martels and smacked him with it. Instead I poured that fool a drink and he started remembering correctly. Couldn't nobody fuck wit' yo' Unk Breeze baby. None."

Breeze conveniently refueled on a sip of yak before he picked up the pace again.

"You know back in the day when I used to rock those parties-my mix tapes were the hottest shit on the street, man! I'm telling you I was a beast boy!

Unk Breeze starts humming *"...nnnn, nnn, dddda, bridge... ddda.the bridge.nnnna.na... nna.... nnnn...nnna...hiphop started out in the park."*

Then it hit Ellis he's going into his old story about his battle at New York's short-lived hiphop mega Castle-Union Square. Breeze done told Ellis this story at least 75 times complete with nearly 70 unedited DVD versions and before Ellis could react, his Uncle was there once again…Eyes spinning like albums under a strobe light…drifting, drifting. All he needed was a deep Barry White voice saying "we gonna go back, back into time…" Ellis sat back and made himself comfy.

"It was 1988, maybe 9, and me and yo aunt, Eyanna, was just chilling. We decided to go down to Union Square and check out my boys Masters of the Ceremony, with Don Baron, Grand Puba 'n' them. Right, So I'm Chilling, rocking the green suede Bally's, the Goose and sporting my gold three-finger ring with 'Breeze' on it. And your aunt got her matching goose on, looking good as shit! She had on them tight ass jeans-*Oooo*! She was looking sweet. That's the night we made your cousin James—his hardheaded ass, God bless the incarcerated. Okay, so we walk in shit was slamming, D.J. Clark Kent was tearing up the wheels-He was nice, but you know nobody couldn't touch my shit, right? So, it's madd heads in the spot, then all of a sudden, this rack of Negus from Brooklyn started running Negus shit. Just housing jewels. Taking chains, rings, everything.

"We were just chilling up on the second floor near the banister overlooking over the crowd on the dance floor. Clark Kent puts on our song "The Wop," so, I just whip out the ring-you know the engagement ring-and proposed to your aunt. So, we leaning over the banister admiring the jewel, right? And these Brooklyn thugs tossed some helpless kid into me knocking the ring out my hand onto the dance floor below. I was stunned, Kid—frantic. And you know I ain't frazzled easily, right?

"I had just sold some turntables to get that ring. Pissed off like a mother—and you know Uncle Breeze is nice with the hands, right? I turn around and it's about 10 of 'em, but I ain't one for fear so I just start flying notz...I don't even remember the rest, but Negus was telling me later that I co-wrecked shop. Set things straight."

Breeze paused for a second as if he'd lost his way, then continued. "My shit was like Jackie Chan, Jim Kelly, Jet Li, Smell Lee, Brew-Ski combined...So, just know Unk Breeze ain't no punk… I always handle mines Sun. Just remember El, you can't always run from shit, sometimes you can't even hide, sometimes in life, you just got to stand your ground and go for what you know. Everybody 'fraid of sumpin', but never let fear stop you from handling yo' business. Capiche."

Ellis could hear the music in his voice slowing to a halt, as the glassed over look disappeared from his Uncle's eyes, and was glad it was over. Uncle Breeze tells his version of the story all the time, but according to the real deal giving to Ellis years back by his late Aunt Eyanna, Breeze did fly some knots for a quick minute, then them Negus from Brooklyn threw him off the balcony onto the dance floor- while Clark Kent was cutting up Apache—that's when the music stopped in the club "and started in his head," she used to say. He was in traction for three weeks. But he went for his, and was my man—and won't no punk.

Ellis pulled up his driveway and Breeze slid out handing him a Bush $2 coin.

"Naw, naw, Unk, I'm cool."

"You sure, you sure?" he asked simultaneously slipping his bill back in the wallet before Ellis could change his mind. Wit' Uncle Breeze, it was a one-time only shot to get dough. He always figured that if somebody really needed money, you never had to mention it twice.

Uncle Breeze scooped up his bags nervously, making sure he didn't forget anything. Before his wife Eyanna passed, he never had to worry about these types of things. Eyanna was a big boned thick woman without an once of fat. She had the body that most video chicks would kill for and sly penetrating eyes that conveyed easier than spoken word her distaste for bullshit or her passions. Cinnamon brown with long beautiful hands, she was as thorough as they come and made sure Uncle Breeze, never lacked any of his favorites. He really loved her, although he wished he'd had expressed it a little more. He just always figured he'd have time for that. She was the type of woman who went the extra mile and made sure you knew you were special. She enjoyed making him happy and always saw through his hard exterior with a will-breaking smile. He never even thought about being with another woman, when she was around. You could feel the sadness in his voice every time he mentioned her. Not that he was that lonely; Not Playa playa— he still had women, even at his age. Still there was only one Eyanna.

Uncle Breeze pulled out a pint of Martels, took a sip and screwed the cap back on. Looking in the opposite direction he whispered rough voiced, "Yo, El, before I head up, hit me with one of them rhymes. I know you still writing. Once it's in ya blood, it never leaves."

Ellis grinned, and reminisced a little, thinking. *Shit it was Unk Breeze that put me on to hiphop. Showed me how to DJ, and got me writing lyrics. He was more a father to me than an uncle.*

"Yeah, Yeah, you right Unk, but now I'm writing news and sports," Ellis replied, knowing he's already running late.

Breeze took another sip. It was if he really needed this just to get by. Sometimes people just need the weirdest shit to make them feel like pushing on. Whatever it was, they just needed it. Sometimes it was alcohol, or some weed, or sex. For others it might be hiphop.

"C'mon, Ellis, I know you got something for me…"

It wasn't just that Uncle Breeze needed to hear Ellis spit; it was like he was trying to get El to give something back to himself-to remember a part of himself. Uncle Breeze understood that any true emcee never stopped writing lyrics—totally. Any true emcee only sought the right opportunity to drop lyrics. No true emcee could ever resist the right opportunity to drop lyrics. For Ellis, who rarely dropped lyrics anymore, it was the parable of "casting pearls among the swine." *If I knew they wuz real headz—real connoisseurs of hiphop—then it had to be done. That was one of the ten commandments of Emceeing.* "*Thou must never refuse a true hiphop headz request for lyrics.*"

"Alright, Alright," Ellis grunted, knowing deep down he really wanted to spit anyway.

"I just wrote this it ain't even memorized yet."

Breeze, grinned and continued to stare out the window, as El began nodding his head to some imaginary beat that only he could hear, but everybody could catch simply by his rhythm...

Grim
Metaphysical, Lyrical, I expound
Universally at an apex and will only come down
If Negus rain on me or corrupt this sound
The planet spins
While I snatch kingdoms like KG rebounds.
Prelude to something
avoid obvious clues.
Octaves build within this syntax to split the atom into
Elements of surprise
Indeed I am a teacher who has studied with Ghosts
Dialogue is not a contest and my thoughts cannot cease
Tidal wave full of emotion as my soul is released
Crushed are the foul and any caught in my wake
Am I real or antimatter
Instruments indicate
That this sound is profound
but whence it came unknown
Genesis of the omega
not some wanna be clone
El will extend, mental meridian
Max-Amun
Intact remains crux of attack
In fact
Black is Back in the sense that it never went
Am I a mortal or far beyond intelligent
Heaven sent, destruction bent this sign represents
I am
M-A -N
I fess
nonsense
Prior theories are replaced
And my thoughts take precedence

Squirming all over, Breeze is ecstatic.

"Yo, Sun, you deep man—deep! Just like your Pops. I forget how deep you are until you drop them lyrics. Don't be afraid to be wise Sun. You know we still ain't too old to do an album. I just heard De La was coming back."

"Just like your Pops?" I hope not? thought Ellis, cringing in fear. *Then again, I never really knew my father. He was just a ghost I'd been trying to avoid my whole life. If nothing else, I damn sure didn't want to be anything like him. That's why I ain't got no kidz now. Shit, if you ain't gonna take care of 'em, strap yo' shit up and leave it be.*

Ellis acknowledged mentally, as he moves further and further away from the Now.

"El, El."

"Huh."

"You be easy now, aaiight?"

"Yeah Unk. Peace."

Ellis didn't like thinking bad about his father, but whenever he put his mind on thinking about him, bad appeared out of nowhere, like Five-O, whenever you skipped that stop sign at 2 in the morning with your Osama T-shirt, a Guiness stout sitting between your legs, some chick you met at the club that barely looked 18, a Nine in the arm rest, a half a pound of weed in the trunk and no video camera in sight.

Not only didn't Ellis really know his father, he didn't even have someone around who could tell him, or would tell him, about the man. Surely he had to get *some* of who he was from his father? I mean, he knew his moms and could see part of who he was that was here. But his pops….that was just a guessing game. If nothing else, he'd like to at least be able to blame some of his quirkiness and idiosyncrasies on his father. *That's what parents were for anyway—for their kidz to blame them for whatever shortcomings they had.*

It only made Ellis wonder more.

"Did pops have my sense of humor?

Or am I the only muthafuka running around with this sick mind?"

"Yeah, Unk. Peace."

MAYA'S BUILDING

As Ellis pulled up to Maya's building, he began his ritual odyssey of finding a parking space. Her community was a pre-fabricated (and incorporated) community, and parking was controlled by a slew of private companies. If you didn't have a local zoning sticker, the companies had the right to charge you an arm and leg for parking. Her parking company was HIJAK, which had the worst reputation in the city for not simply booting cars, but providing beat-downs to protesting owners.

It didn't hurt their task that the company's owner, Jim Hijak, ran a prison-release program that staffed HIJAK with only the most violent criminals they could find. Word had it that you didn't fill out an application; you just brought your rap sheet. The most gruesome bunch worked the nightshift and reportedly made up of former ENRON executives.

Most of the time, Ellis had to park in the business district about three blocks away and foot it up to her place. The nearest place other than that was near Newt's, the organizing site for the Neo-Con Republican Convention during the day and a gay bar at night. El wasn't trying to park there. One time he parked across the street and had to sprint three blocks to her complex, with three guys literally on his ass. Them bastards were mad 'cause he beat this drag queen to a parking space and she—er, he—wanted to beef. So, Ellis sucker-punched her—er—him. Before he could blink, three of her—his steroid-enhanced friends, looking like a combination of Hulk Hogan meets Madonna, gonna raise up and try a brotha.

Yeah, punks jump up to get beat down was Ellis' motto.

But avoid getting yo' ass kicked was another motto that he saved for a rainy day. Any reports of getting beat down by a drag queen could be grounds for getting your Hood Card revoked and being banished to the sucker emcee zone forever. Fortunately, the Godz of 'save face' had mercy on Ellis, when after running for a block and a half-one of them broke a heel. Tonight, he'd have to park at least three blocks away. That night he had on his Sean Carters.

Upstairs in apartment 19B, Maya continued to wait for her man to show up. As she listened to her favorite Gangstarr CD "Step Inside the Arena," she moused her fingers through her thick labyrinth of wooly locks, wondering if Ellis really understood how bad she hated waiting. It really made her angry. Not so much the waiting, just the inconsideration involved in it. She stared at her Romere Bearden clone nestled on the wall above her fireplace hoping that he didn't take it personally when she made him wait.

Sometimes she despised Ellis—well, maybe not him, but some of his antics. He seemed to think the whole world revolved around him. His world was supposed to revolve around her, her needs and what she wanted. Instead it seemed to her he only turned her way for a little entertainment and some pounanny.

She wondered how he would feel if she told him how many times she got hit on today by guys as good-looking as him—well, maybe not as good-looking, but certainly with more in their bank accounts and a lot more education. How many times she'd been asked on trips? She didn't have to put up with him. She hated the fact that she wanted him so bad— bad enough to deal with his bullshit. She was sure she loved him deeply and he said he loved her. Why couldn't he seem to act right? According to that best selling book on how to snag a man, he should have proposed 2.4 years ago. They had been together for four years and three months and two days; so why weren't they married yet? What was he waiting for? She followed Chapter Six exactly, and even did that unmentionable thing with her tongue, the jelly donuts and that mask. She wanted to settle down and have kidz, be normal, not this single or shacking-up ghetto shit.

I need to get my act together, she thought. *Later for Ellis; if the firm is going to jump my salary 35 percent and handle living expenses in order to move me to the corporate headquarters in DC then I've got to move on. I love Ellis, but I'm not going through what my mother did. Waiting around for some man for ten years then he goes off and marries a twenty-year old floozy with a push up bra, and a big ass. If he's not going to do right, I've got to move on. My old college roommate keeps telling me it's nice down in DC Maybe I'll just leave him be, and find me a husband and home in Prince George's County.* she thought in between sips of merlot, knowing all the while she'd never be happy unless he was with her.

While Maya contemplated her future with Ellis, he was busy jogging three blocks to her building in a downpour with newspaper and her favorite white lilies in hand. It took him twenty minutes to park and activate his Boot-Theft-prevention device car alarm. The boot device was the main protection against theft in the 21st century. At the same time, the parking companies used their own boot-devices to incapacitate illegal parkers. So, if you wuz real lucky, you could come back to your car on lock down, with boots on every wheel.

By the time he got half a block, the rain began coming down. A block later it was pouring! Ellis arrived at her building, just as someone was leaving out-he dashed and caught the door before it closed only to be met by Tito, the 300 pound 6'5" security guard-who liked Maya but, for some ugly reason, hated his guts, worse than Donald Trump hated barbershops.

"I'm sorry, Sir, but I have to ask you to leave the building."

Ellis looked up disdainfully as if he could take out his dick and smack Tito silly.

"Mannnn…you must be crazy."

Tito cleared his throat, "No one, I mean no one, comes into this building unless let in by a resident-company policy!" He said with a slightly raised voice while grimacing at Ellis like he was the neighborhood enforcer and Ellis was short on his protection money.

"Well, shit, I was just let in by a resident," snapped Ellis shaking the rain off his clothes as if by doing so, he had established the fact that he by no means planned on getting wet again.

Tito snarled, drawing the various lines in his forehead together like a leafless branch.

"Running into the building when a resident is leaving is not how it works. They must buzz you in."

Brushing the water off his head, Ellis pleaded. "C'mon, now, brother, you know me—I've been in this building a thousand times. What's the problem?

"I know you know, my lady. What's up?"

Tito grinned as if someone just told him that the Colonel was extending their dollar days sale another week. "That may be the case, Sir, but rules are rules are rules.

"You wouldn't want someone like me to lose my job, now, would you?" he asked sarcastically.

"Fuck you and your job," mumbled Ellis.

"Okay, Sir, you have been warned," said Tito, placing his swimsuit edition of *For Blackmen Only* face down on the desk. The only thing he liked better than staring at pussy was beating the hell out of somebody he just didn't like fo' no particular reason. It relaxed him in a way that Yoga did for some folks. He particularly enjoyed his post-beatdown chats with his former cellmates over a glass of chilled St. Ides, where he'd describe the blow-by-blow with the precision of a CIS medical coroner detailing the way a serial murderer tortured his victims.

Tito smacked his lips, and punched several numbers into walkie-talkie until connected with the emergency channel. It was a safe guard that would keep his ass outta trouble should he have to use force on an individual illegally entering the building.

"I am reporting a possible Code 4. We have a Code 4 possible combatant."

Tito moved slowly as if he were remember each proper step or procedure. He then detached his Lazer 4000—a 350,000-volt Stun Baton and walked slowly towards Ellis.

"Sir, I repeat, you must leave the building now."

As much as Ellis wanted to make a run for the elevator, or pick up the steel chair and crack it over Tito's tree-stump shaped noggin, he quickly realized that Tito 'the fat-bastard' knew full well what he was doing. Tito knew that he was soaking wet. If this Negus had the audacity to stun him with his baton, the fat lady might as well start singing-'cause it's over. *Ain't that some shit? He'd be dead before marrying Maya, having kidz, seeing the Knicks win the damn title? Ain't life a bitch? Hell no, not today.*

Ellis slowly began to step backwards, leaving his flowers on the floor.

"Okay, Okay, I'm leaving. But you'll be hearing from my attorney, you oversized thug-Barney."

He moved quickly out of range and returned outside to dial up Maya on the Optim-link Security system.

Without mercy, the rain increased its intensity. *Hope she ain't on the toilet.*

"Who is it?"

"It's me—I know you can see me, let me in."

"Wooah! Just one-minute, Sir, you were supposed to be here an hour ago. What happened?" asked Maya in a frustrated, teasing tone.

"I'll explain when I get upstairs."

Maya took a sip of wine. "What makes you think you are coming up here? As a matter of fact, I need to see some identification, Sir. You might me some rapist or some overzealous Jehovah Witness." She giggled.

Ellis strained at the monitor and spoke in a very low voice, trying his hardest not to yell.

"Hey, I'm not in the mood, can you just let me in. I ain't got time for all these damn games. Shit."

"Oh," said Maya. "So, you got time to mess with me when I visit you, but can't take it huh, Mr. Tough guy. You outta get that new book on Ghetto Hijinks, it's really good." Maya giggled.

Ellis looked up at the monitor as if he could strangle her. Yeah right after he smoked fat ass Tito.

Buzzzzzzzz.

Buzzzzzzzz.

Ellis walked back in briskly with anger that only a broke, unemployed Blackman, 20 cents short of bus fare could understand. As he arrived at the front desk and Tito now smiling sadistically took the pen out of his shirt pocket.

"You'll have to sign in, sir-company policy."

Ellis doesn't say anything; he just took the pen and signed in before catching the glass elevator to the ninth floor. As the elevator floated up into the heart of the lobby, Tito read the sign-in sheet and saw that Ellis had scribbled "Ya mother."

As another visitor walked in, he smiled and pointed to the guard's ink-stained shirt pocket, and asked the security guard if he had an accident. Tito stared at him confused without answering and then pulled out his pen and noticed that the ball-tip had been removed. He glanced at the rising glass elevator and saw Ellis' with a subtle smirk on his face.

"Damn punk!"

As Maya opened the door, she planned to let Ellis Rey have it. The bell rang and she opened the door ready to spit fire, but instead burst into laughter upon seeing the pitiful rain-soaked mess Ellis had become.

"Oh I didn't mean to," said Maya.

"Well I'm glad somebody finds this shit funny," fumed Ellis, whose mood had improved considerably after his recent stunt on Tito.

"Come on in," she motioned, feeling him up as he passed by.

"Hey, hey! Jumped Ellis, "I don't know what you heard, but I'm not that easy. Give me a drink or piece of chicken first," he smirked. Disarmed by his humor, Maya smiled.

"Let me get you out those wet clothes."

She took off his shoes and socks and walked him over in front of the fireplace. There, dressed barefoot in a white camisole, she began to slowly undress Ellis, while drying him off with a towel. She stared into his eyes pleading for love, melting him with sleepy seductive eyes colored deep-deep chocolate, matching her beautiful mahogany skin that glistened in the candle lit room. Her slanted eyes fluttered slightly, as she spoke gently into his ear.

"How my baby get so wet?"

Her supple wet lips gently sucked on his neck, bringing chills throughout his body. She whispered into his ear as she undressed him, her nipples slightly brushing against his back, exciting him. His breathing became slower more intense. "Ellis you came in wet; now I'm so wet," she whispered.

Her perfumed body resonated throughout his senses. Like the sound of the ocean, her smell took his mind off his daily mishaps. Her brown thick thighs curved in slightly at tender knees extending down to thick calves. Ellis turned around slowly and dipped to his knees, be began kissing her legs, her knees, then turned her slightly and stared for a second at her plump sweet ass. He began kissing her inner thighs working his way up to her chocolate behind. Gripping her thighs he spread them slightly and began kissing her slowly standing and gently sucking on her back finally reaching behind her neck. Maya turned and kissed him passionately, while reaching down with her right hand slowly rubbing Ellis into full mast. She backed him onto a large beach towel on the futon and laid him on it. Then she placed her favorite Fertile Ground CD in the continuous play mode and climbed on him, easing into the right position. They began making love with their bodies blending with the music. The bodies curved and twisted till their souls were passionately intertwined, until they both climaxed and collapsed simultaneously. There were no legible words to be uttered.

After taking a shower together, they propped up the couch and turned on the television. Ellis had wanted to catch some of the Spurs versus the Suns game, which had started around 10:30. But Maya had wanted to talk. Being that it was her house and she held the home court advantage. They talked.

Turning down the television, she said, "Ellis, what are we going to do?"

"Huh?" Ellis remarked, as if she was crazy.

"You know, are we going to get married and settle down? I'm turning 29 next month."

"Yeah, Yeah, I'm getting up there myself," remarked Ellis, knowing where this was going but hoping that just maybe he was wrong. Maybe there was some huge rock in the living room that he could quickly hide behind. Maybe some alien tractor beam would pull him through the window to a spaceship of onion-ass-shaped women who would use him for sexual purposes only but refuse to talk to him. Maybe an earthquake would hit?

Maya patiently asked again. "When are we getting married?"

"I don't know," responded Ellis, thinking more about the game than the discussion.

"I mean, I want us to be together, but I just want to be able to do this thing right."

"Right?" repeated Maya, confused. "What's not 'right'? You do love me, don't you?" purred Maya as Ellis continued to watch the game.

"I don't know—I mean, I do," murmured Ellis, "but it's just that my pops got married at an early age, had a bunch of kidz and then jetted off. I don't want to repeat that pattern. I just want to be sure. What happens if I can't live up to your standards?"

"Standards? What standards!" asked Maya in an exasperated tone.

"Ellis, I chose you, evidently I got no standards," chuckled Maya.

"Oh you got jokes, huh?"

"I mean, seriously, Ellis, what are you talking about?"

"Well, just look at this place—Hell, I can't even afford to park in your neighborhood—much less provide for you."

Standing up, Maya leaned bowlegged, hand on hip. "Who said you have to provide for me? I do a pretty good job of providing for myself and together we'd do all right," affirmed Maya, bending to rub her hand in Ellis hand.

"I do feel that you're the one for me," said Ellis turning to face Maya for a split second, hoping that his sincere look could convey something beyond words. "It's good, our relationship, but I don't want to have a kid and then start flaking out. You know how I am, I've been fired from three 3 jobs—two of them good ones—for talking shit. You know me; I tend to get into trouble quick. How are we going to raise a family and all that and you might not be able to depend on me?"

Maya grabbed the remote from Ellis and turned off the television.

"We love each other. Isn't that enough? Isn't that enough, Ellis?"

Silence filled in the gap, where, according to Hollywood and romance novels with colorful themes and bright book covers, the man is supposedly able to stumble upon the right words and express himself fully to his woman, ultimately sweeping her off her feet and carrying her into the sunset—fade to black.

But this is real life and Ellis—groomed on a lifetime diet of non-emotionalism, non-intimacy, and non-affection—doesn't answer. In reality, he doesn't even know how to answer. Instead, he continues to stare out into the space formerly occupied by a basketball game.

"Well, Ellis, I can't wait forever. I can't live on the faith that we'll get married after ten years, only to see you decide that you want someone else. My company has offered me a huge salary increase if I move to DC to an upper management position at our corporate headquarters. These chances don't come around daily for a sista. I believe that I'm going to take up their offer. I can't turn down money like that. I figured we could get married, buy a house in P.G. County—it's nice down there and there's lots of newspapers in that area. Plus, with my increase, I'll be able to carry the load for awhile."

Ellis, now angry, looked at Maya. Ellis hated the fact that he was unable to make any real commitment to people or ideas. This motif served him well growing up in the Projects; it allowed him to distance himself from things, survive. But it had now become a liability in a world where people were beyond the survival phase—where people had something to lose, or, worse, were trying to build a future together. Despite his inability to make decisions at times, he hated even more for someone to make a decision for him. It was his to make, even if he never made one. Unable to respond in intimate moments, he sure as hell knew, if nothing else, how to fight. Now fighting was something that he was not only experienced at, but and good at. When it came to anger and grudges, shit, he'd take on the whole fucken' world; just back him into a corner and give him a boxcutter. Hell, in his mind, he was still undefeated.

"What about me? What about my career? It's taken me years to carve out relationships with folks in the city. Shit, who can I work for in DC, "the last damn colony"—The fucken *Washington Piss*? They want you to kiss ass for years before they give you respect? They don't even look at the Black media as legitimate and want you to spend five years in some damn training program, even though you out-scooped their top reporters everyday. Or maybe I can make 20 grand a year working for a Black newspaper if I'm real lucky? It ain't that many good jobs with the Black papers down there. Usually you end up working harder than an illegal immigrant, and get paid three steps below minimum wage, then they fire yo' ass rather than promote you. Then after you give your all and have a heart attack at age 35, they'll call you a bum and piss on your grave.

"My boy from school is in DC working for the

government and just filed a lawsuit for racial discrimination and it's damn 2018. That shit was 'sposed to be over in the Sixties. I ain't the most conscious barley-grass-and-tofu-eating Negus out there, but even I know that working for them folks would just make me part of the problem," steamed Ellis, preparing to go into second and third gear.

He looked up and downshifted as he saw the tears forming in Maya's eyes.

"Why do you always do that, Ellis?" cried Maya. "Why do you have to tear down everything that conflicts with your view?"

"Well, you don't have to work for anybody."

"I just want us to be together, but you seem like you've got a problem with that. By the way, lock the door when you leave," said Maya, teary eyed in a huff headed to the bedroom, slamming then locking the door.

Ellis just sat there, frustrated and agitated. He wondered why he always felt like the villain when she got upset. *Maybe she's right. Maybe non-commitment was in his blood— just like his pops. Yeah, I mean it's in our blood. We just don't commit to anything or anybody. "cause once you do, they got you and then that's when the pissing starts."* Ellis grabbed the remote and turned back on the TV, *Damn! Game over.*

MOURNING

BZZZZZZ!!!!! BZZZZZ!!!

Ellis awoke, spun around like Akeem on one of those turnaround jumpers and slapped the alarm clock.

Shit. Late again!

Hopping out of the bed, he felt a deep pain in the back of his thigh. *Maybe I twisted something on my dash to Maya's building. Yeah, probably.* Other than that, for some reason, he felt good, although unable to remember why this should be a good day.

Yes! Yes, Ya'll, to da beat ya'll, you don't stop dat body rock.

As Ellis arrived at the office from a drama-free commute, he could see from a distance that there's a ton of paper on his desk. He can also see that Ebony World-a-Girl was making her way towards him. Coffee in one hand, donut-box in the other; eyes squinted, nostrils flared. It was like 4th and goal and Ellis had the ball-as an icy fog covered the gridiron and the only thing between you and the goal line was linebacker Ray Lewis, and for some strange reason he had on a Philly-green jersey-numba Eight One.

"So Ellis, what you got for me? I know you're supposed to have a major scoop on the way, correct?" remarked Nicole in a manner that in some fringe dictatorships might actually be considered pleasant. While she said this, she gave Ellis the one-eyed up and down.

Quickly thinking of a way to change the subject, Ellis perused the idea of asking for a jelly donut. After weighing the options of being embarrassed about not having his story done compared to a possible deathmatch, he quickly reconsidered.

"Yeah Nicole, I'm supposed to meet this kid a little later, for a potential off da planet story," paused Ellis decisively before deciding to go in for kill. "You've been looking good lately, Nicole. Been working out?" he asked, hoping to hook the big one.

"Oooh, you noticed?" Nicole blushed in between slurps, cheesing from ear to ear. "I'm preparing to go on a fast."

Yeah, and I'm running for Mayor, Ellis wanted to add badly, yet not as badly as he wanted to continue paying rent.

Smiling, Nicole proudly blurted out, "my wholistic doctor gave me a colonic and bunch of stuff like acidophilus and Pau' D'arco, Cascara Sagrada, and Black Walnut to clean out my colon. They say most people carry from seven to thirty pounds of waste in their colon, especially people who eat a lot of meat, sweets, and don't drink any water. And you know that's me, child. I usually wash my meals down with Krispy Krème. The doctor said I could have parasites or tapeworms or something."

"I had a relapse today with these donuts, but I'll tell you Ellis, this is the last run for me. I'm phasing out all red meat and dairy products. I didn't even know that most Black people are lactose-intolerant. Shoot, you can get Vitamin D from green vegetables and just getting out in the sun a little every day. But really, Ellis, that colonic made me think about some things; you know, my whole family's diabetic and all my girlfriends got fibroids. Ellis, I'm just starting to make a little dough—I don't want to be over the hill at 40. You looking at a changed person, so remember this big boned girl, because she's gone," said Nicole, quickly turning and sashaying off.

Damn, that was easy, thought Ellis.

After hearing her talk about having a colonic, Ellis then decided it was time to sacrifice an ox as a burnt offering to the Creator. Amen, time to thank God that at least he wasn't in the room with her when stuff started dropping. *No telling what they might have found up there—some of the missing Zapruder tapes? Dade County ballots from Election 2000, Tupac's and Biggie's murderers, Osama, or John Kerry's heart?*

"Ellis! Your one o'clock appointment is here," screamed Sasha on the intercom at a decibel slightly below her average daily shrill.

"I'll be out in a second. Okay?"

Even Sasha is somewhat pleasant today. What's going on? wondered Ellis. *Wasn't today the day predicted by Nostradomus for that major earthquake to hit New York or was it actually that day that a brotha like me was going to snatch that Pulitzer? Yeah, now that I think about it, he did say something about that in one of his quatrains. "On the day of the jelly donut, El of the New City shall gain the prize Litzer..." or something like that? Better get my speech ready. "I would just like to thank the Academy, the School of Hard Knocks and special shouts to the posse at 225 Ashmun Street, and my deejay Expired Buspass..."*

"Ellis, your one O'clock is waiting," spouted Sasha, messing up Ellis' journalistic wet dream.

"Okay, okay. I'll be out in a second."

"I-Salaam Wa Laikum."

"Wa Laikum Salaam," responded Ellis.

"Did you have any trouble finding our office?" he asked, attempting to make his interviewee feel more comfortable.

"No, Sir, it wasn't too bad at all," said Rudell X, an ancient brotha whose gaze instantly relayed ages upon ages of experience. He was light brown skinned, slim, about 5-9 with grayish-blue eyes that matched the gray in his beard. He still had his hair. *No way this guy is 90,* thought Ellis.

"Have a seat, Sir," said Ellis as he excitedly rustled out his notepad and recorder. "You don't mind if I record this?"

Rudell blinked and glanced militarily around the office. "No Sir," he replied calmly.

"Would you like some coffee?" asked Ellis.

"No sir."

"Okay, then let us get started."

"Yes sir.

"I first joined the nation in the Forties and helped to set up the Temple in Washington DC., Temple Number 3. I knew the Honorable Elijah Muhammad and was trained under him. I also knew Brother Malcolm. We met first in Chicago and shortly after he joined the Nation. I also knew Wilfred and his other brotha, what's his name…? Well, I knew them all," he said, gazing at Ellis with a sympathetic eye, as if Ellis could help him out.

"I'm sorry," Ellis disappointedly spit out, "I read 'The Autobiography' in 5th grade, and saw the movie, but don't remember a whole lot. I did drop some lyrics over 'Funkin' Lesson' by X-Clan, but I was never really interested in all the Black stuff."

Rudell grinned and anxiously cleared his voice with this horrible phlegm loosening *'grrrrrrrrrrrrr,'* before continuing with his story.

"You see," he said, nervously leaning closer to Ellis, "My father was a key member of the UNIA and he told me some stories growing up."

"You mean the Marcus Garvey movement?" asked Ellis, attempting to mask his ignorance about Black history. He was trying not to reveal that the only reason he recognized the UNIA was because it was a "Jeopardy" question last week. Ellis felt shame starting to kick in; he knew a little somethin' about Kwaanza and the candles but Rudell was going beyond that ole superficial Korean made Kente cloth shit.

"Yes Sir, the United Negro Improvement Association, one of the greatest organizations created by the Asiatic Blackman in this wilderness of North America," boasted Rudell. "Brother Garvey, you see, was a short, proud, and powerful Blackman, Du Bois and them integrationists didn't like him at all, and they used to call him all types of names. But Mosiah was the man. As a matter of fact, I always carry around this Garvey quote as a talisman." He pulls out an old folded slip of paper from an aging leather pouch worn around his neck and begins reading.

"What do I care about death in the cause of the redemption of Africa ... I could die anywhere in the cause of liberty: A real man dies but once; a coward dies a thousand times before his real death. So we want you to realize that life is not worth its salt except you can live it for some purpose. And the noblest purpose for which to live is the emancipation of a race and the emancipation of posterity."

He puts the paper away and cleared his throat again like an aged Master P ... *"Uuuuggggggggh, uh, hum."*

Ellis offered Rudell water, but he declined and continued like a man who knew his time and memory were waning. If he didn't get his point out when it arose, he might not remember it again.

"Garvey's paper, *The Negro World*, was read across the entire planet.

"Sir, do you know that in 1926 there were over 1,100 branches of the UNIA and over 200 of them were outside the U.S.? They were in Cuba, Panama, South Africa, Nicaragua, Brazil, Australia, Nigeria, Puerto Rico, Southwest Africa (Namibia) and Canada.

"In Louisiana alone they had over 74 branches, and in Virginia 48. They even had branches in Utah and Oregon. And that was in *1926!* " exclaimed Rudell.

"Wait a minute," said Ellis, hoping to slow down Rudell's monologue and check his recorder.

Suddenly, the old man began to laugh, a sinister type laugh, almost uncontrollable leading into a rambling monologue on 90 years worth of living, in a manner that Ellis intuitively knew that even Rudell had trouble believing.

"Um, could you hold on a second," asked Ellis, scrambling to take notes just in case his recorder turned faulty. He hated this old shit; everyone else had the hip jammys that digitally recorded interviews and actually read them back to you and allowed you to voice edit them on your computer.

"Okay, you can continue," said Ellis, pushing the recording closer to his face.

As he spoke, Ellis began to notice Rudell wore a lot of jewelry—not the expensive platinum kind, but lots of silver and turquoise, bracelets.

"Yes, I got these while living in Pakistan," he said,

practically reading Ellis thoughts. "I spent several years in Pakistan studying Sufism and the Holy Scriptures. Sufism is a highly spiritual form of Islam. I even met Jinns.

"Jinns?"

"Yes, Jinns. These are beings, some with great powers, which often manifest as humans. Many are quite evil. As a matter of fact, King Solomon had been given power over these beings. We have books on all of this information in our library and secret study group. We call it 'Babylon in the Wilderness.' You see, the ancient Babylonians actually borrowed from our ancestors—the Sumerians, who were among the first peoples—the Black people. They used to call Sumerians the 'Blackheads.'"

He continued: "In actuality, the whole planet Earth was known as Ki—where you get the term Geo—was Black at one time. Everybody on the planet, all of the races, are descended from the often-despised Black race. The first dynasties in China were Black. Many of the ancient Greeks and Romans were Black. I bet you didn't know that Rome had several Black Popes and even emperors. Have you heard of Septimus Serverus?"

"Didn't he choreograph that Ur Kelly video?" quipped Ellis. Immediately seeing by the bland look on Rudell's face, it was clear that it was one joke he didn't get.

"No, brother," he responded in a voice pleading for a mental breakthrough, as if he was trying to teach whitefolks the latest dance.

"He was the emperor of Rome during the early Christian era. He also conquered England. In fact, during a later period, many of us were in the eastern Roman Empire of Byzantium; if you were barely touched by a person from a lower-caste, you'd have to purify yourself for weeks. We were very pompous then."

Ellis is looking at this man and listening, thinking *information-overload*. All of this information is just too much to handle at once as he felt his brain was about to burst. Rudell knew a lot, and much more than most people on the planet. He knew that most people in America thought from two reference points, The Bible, and the Dictionary. In the case of Ellis, he had three reference points-Points, Rebounds, and

Assists. *Black Romans, Sumerians—where is this guy getting this shit from? I mean, he sounds like he knows a lot, but I ain't never heard of no shit like that before. I know Cleopatra was Black or something like that, and I knew George Washington Carver—or was it Booker T. Washington?—that made peanut butter, right? Shit, I need a sub— Coach, get me some air, an icepack, something!*

"Okay, okay," said Ellis, "I'm getting a little lost here. What is it that you are trying to tell me? I mean, what is the story that you want to get out?" said Ellis, becoming borderline rude.

Rudell stood up quickly and at attention. "Yes, Sir, I'll get straight to the point, you seem to be a very busy man and an old man like me just enjoys telling stories about things that seemed important in my life," Rudell said. He calmly rubbed his silver bracelet and glanced away from Ellis like he was a lost cause.

Rudell stood up, and gave Ellis the most intense stare that he'd ever seen and whispered.

"Sir, just consider me a warning."

Ellis began tapping his index finger on his desk, and lines appeared on his forehead, the same ones that appeared any time he got defensive.

"Warning? Warning for what?" remarked Ellis.

Rudell smiled slyly.

"Sir, if you don't pay attention to too much, always heed the warnings of an old man. It's us that are close to passing on and the newborn that speak to you all, all the time."

Ellis leaned back in the chair readying himself to attack whatever it was that Rudell was planning on dropping on him. He didn't like threats, warnings or none of that shit. This cat Rudell was 'bout borderline kooky, and Ellis could smell the craziness rising to the surface.

"Sir, I'm going to have to ask you to leave. I got work to do and you ain't saying nothing to put bread on my table. I mean you just came in here off the street, so I'll take ya word, you ain't crazy. I ain't trying to be rude, but I can't deal with this mythical stuff, for real man, I got things to do."

Rudell smiled, "I am only here to tell you to be careful. You have been selected for a mission that will affect everybody on the planet. But it really isn't about you; it's about everybody and you. You'll be traveling farther than you ever traveled physically and mentally. Just understand that no matter how low things may appear, you are not alone. Just remember you—we—are never alone." Rudell looked at Ellis as if he were a father attempting to tell his son why getting a college degree is important. He gracefully stood up and walked out of Ellis' cubicle down the dark hallway to the stairwell.

Ellis sat dazed and stared at his screen, wondering *What the hell that was about?*

He then quickly dialed the front office on the instellcom.

"Sasha, I'll be out for a few, but I'm expecting to get a call from the Knicks front office about the interview with Yusef. Transfer the call to my mobile phone if they call."

"Is that it?" asked Sasha in a tone that struck fear into the heart of every living being—including Jocko, the undefeated champion Pitt Bull, who deep down knew there was always somebody bigger and badder quietly waiting in the wings.

"Bye."

THE AIR OUTSIDE

Ellis stepped outside into the cool breeze and looked past the traffic and noise directly into the sun. Still reeling from his conversation with Rudell, he conversated with himself.

I need a good walk, maybe I'll head downtown to Munchies to grab a cup of coffee; they really make some good coffee. Ellis felt a little ill, a little sick in the stomach. Now, to top it off, rain began to trample onto his skull like a thousand microscopic headaches.

The walk to Munchies normally helped Ellis to clear his head. Munchies did have the best coffee in the tri-state area. But Ellis knew to stay away from the food; unlike most fast food joints, Munchies' management decided not to sign the genetic non-proliferation treaty. So they used that juicier and softer form of beef created by combining feline and pig DNA with bovine DNA. As a result, it inadvertently transferred a few of the subtle animalistic traits to people— hence the name Munchies.

Damn, this line is long.

"May I take your orda?"

"Yeah, just a cup of coffee."

"Is dat it?"

"Yeah, that's it."

After picking up his caffeine, Ellis strolled over to Stein's Deli to pick up a soy Reuben, and glance through the paper and read the sportspage. His mind drifted to the most important subject on his horizon—the upcoming INBA draft.

I wonder who Yusef is going to take with the first pick. I think he should go with that brotha out of Kenya, Ugonna Git'dunkedon. Git'dunkedon was a 7-3 point forward, who was a combo of Jason Kidd and Amarie Stoudamire. As a matter of fact coaches were now teaching his cross over dunk in basketball camps on every continent.

Everybody was wondering whether Gitdunkedon would pass up the draft and sign with his national team. Each nation had first signing opportunities with homegrown talent. The Kenyans did not plan on letting this brotha get away—at least not without a serious Mau-Mau type beat down. In basic terms, Ugonna meant billions to the Kenyan economy. They figured if Michael Jordan generated over $10 billion for the US economy during his career; Ugonna could do the same for Kenya; Shit, in the country's mind, he was both the MVP and GNP. Ugonna did have an affinity with African Americans; his descendents had come from Mississippi in the 19th century with other Blacks from this country to pick cotton in Sudan before they ended up in Kenya.

After munching out, Ellis glanced at the television screen and noticed that they getting ready to try O.J. Simpson again. It'll be pay-per-view this time. During his fourth civil suit, despite the fact that the prosecutors decided to drop the charges, the media decided to go ahead and hold the trial anyway at Haroldo's CBBNC studio. After his latest conviction by the media, the judges—all Nielsen families—determined that his parts in the "Police Story" movies and that first episode "Roots" would be deleted, with Marcus Allen digitally inserted into O.J.'s roles.

Noticing that time is flying, Ellis called down to the office to check his messages.

"Hello, Sasha, this is Ellis. Did I get any calls?"

"Yeah."

"Is there some law against you telling me who?"

"The Knicks."

"Thank you…" *and may you get hit by a schoolbus as you step out the door.*

"I'm heading down to the Garden. Try to take legible messages, okay?" grumbled Ellis.

"Bye!" said Sasha, slamming the receiver.

THE WAITING GAME

Shocking himself and the Godz of journalism, Ellis arrived at the Garden a few minutes early.

"Excuse me, do you have a pass?" asked this farsighted 120-pound security guard with a 10-pound Glock-22 with laser scope, sitting like a spinal extension on his hip.

"Yeah, I'm Ellis Rey from *The Nubian.* I have a four o'clock with Yusef Black."

"Is your name on the list?"

"Should be?"

"Well, I don't see it," smiled the security guard with a look that said *Nice try, bastard,* and the world was gonna pay for the abusive wedgies he experience as an adolescent. Today, he'd exercise his demons on Ellis with glee.

Ellis frowned and gritted his teeth. Clearly he saw the symptoms of BMSS, aka "Blackman In America Stress Syndrome." BMSS was something that was discovered during the case of New York City shooter Colin Ferguson. According to experts, it normally attacked middle-aged Blackmen. Symptoms normally included: twitching and nervous ticks upon noticing a police cruiser behind you in the slow lane; anxiety while trying to cash a check drawn on your bank with only three I.D.'s; inability to wave down a taxi despite flashing Benjamins and wearing a suit more expensive than the cab; or sweaty palms and eye ticks whenever alone in a room full of white people upon hearing a *"yahoo"* type sound.

"I should be on the list. They confirmed it two days ago," said Ellis as his blood pressure slowly rose from irritated to crazy Negus level. "They told me they wanted to do the interview after taping the show. "I wouldn't be down here if I didn't have an interview," snapped Ellis while pulling his press credentials out in a manner akin to the way a wino might sneak out his brown bag of MD2020.

"Well, I don't see you down here."

After the security guard repeats himself again, Ellis is now positive that he's speaking to a fucken' robot.

The guard looked down then up without blinking.

"I'll have to make a call to confirm. You understand, right?"

Ellis just looked at him and nodded.

"Have a seat. Coffee is on the table over there," he said.

After ten minutes went by, Ellis started to get a little steamed and the more he thought about this shit, the madder he got. The madder he got, the more he began to think.

If they don't let me in soon, I'll have to pull my Eddie Murphy-"Beverly Hills Cop 5" routine.... "What you mean is that you don't want a Blackman to interview the new Black coach. Is that it, huh?"

Or, thought Ellis, *I could do my Al Pacino blind man act... "If I was half the man I was five years ago, I would've taken a torch to this place!"*

Naw, okay, maybe my Scharzanegger Terminator move: "I'll be back,"—and then come back with two Uzis and a streetsweeper.

Okay, maybe I'll just rip my shirt off and do some DMX-type shit, singing "They Don't Know?"

Naw, I could just leave. I mean, my plan might work or I might just get shot. But if I got shot, then I could write a book and call it "I Got Shot Waiting To Interview Yusef Black."

But what if they shot me in both hands?

"Mr. Rey. Mr. Rey, Sir?"

"Huh? You talking to me?"

"Yes, Sir," responded the security guard, startling Ellis out of his multi-dimensional revenge fantasy.

"Sir, you've been confirmed. I'm sorry about the wait."

"Oh, it wasn't that bad. I mean, I got a chance to memorize the last five episodes of 'Road Rules Versus Real World,' which I had been planning to do for quite some time now. It's a shame what they did to that Black girl; maybe the show will help with funeral expenses. Oh yeah, but I'd like to thank the New York Knicks organization for providing me with the opportunity," said Ellis in his 25-cents-of-sarcasm voice.

"You can head up, Jerk," mumbled the guard, finger

inching towards his holster.

"I heard that punk, I heard that," Ellis mumbled in response as he headed upstairs to the Orange Room where they just finished taping the final segment of this week's show. The show was nationally syndicated but now they were filming in New York, as opposed to Sacramento.

"Have a seat, Ellis," said this fine sista in a dark blue suit, sporting natural twists. "Mr. Black will be with you in a short while, as soon as taping is over. Can I get you anything in the meantime?" She smiled at Ellis in a smooth inviting-type voice that prompted Ellis to begin licking his lips like Cool J in search of chapstick.

Nothing other than your phone number and a quick massage, thought Ellis, but the only thing he uttered was a nonchalant "Naw, I'm okay."

"Enjoy the show," she said.

"Thank you," said Ellis, considering the single life again—if only for a second.

THE SHOW

There was U, comfortable—seemingly moreso in front of the camera than on the bench. He was definitely an interesting character. He was sort of a true-life hero to Ellis. He was probably the only person, other than Unk Breeze, that Ellis even contemplated looking at in a fatherly sense. U demanded that type of respect—not verbally or intentionally, it was just in his aura. The energy he gave off called you to attention. People realized real quick upon meeting him that this was someone to be respected. He projected a type of regal authority that was his naturally; what the French call "de Jour." He took Sacramento from post-"C.Web scrubs" to the hypest club in the League, then left in the middle of the season to take the Knicks job.

Ellis amusingly glanced at the action ongoing in Studio B—officially the "Spiked Seat," after Mr. 40 Acres and a Mule himself, and numba one Knick-stunna Spike Lee. Ellis sat in amazement as Spike verbally assaulted Pacer guard Pop Beattoe.

It was incredibly hilarious. The producers liked to impose the "Spiked Seat" on anyone who scored over 30 points against the Knicks. This time they brought in Pop

Beattoe, a nasty 6-3 guard from Papua New Guinea, with a silky smooth jumper, who lead his national team to a 20-point pre-season thumping of the Knicks at the Garden. On the other half of the split-screen, U talked about basketball, the Knicks and his sporting goods line. In studio B, things were heating up, as Spike called Beattoe every name in the book, and talked about his moms and her bad leg. But Beattoe kept calm—practically motionless, except for a few smiled. Ellis couldn't figure out why there was no reaction from Beattoe?

Then it came to him; the producers fucked up. It seems that no one knew that Beattoe was deaf and never learned sign language. Fortunately he could read lips, but he didn't speak English. The only thing they taught him at the French missionary school in New Guinea was the crossover, proper way to use a napkin, and how to rebound on an empty stomach.

After about ten minutes they finally brought in a French translator and the whole joint got wild. Good thing Beattoe missed on that chair throw.

Meanwhile, on the Studio A side of the split-screen, U was taking phone calls from Knicks fans interested in the upcoming draft and season.

"Okay, Bill from Manhattan."

"Yeah, Coach Black, do you plan on implementing the 2-2-1 full court press that you deployed with Sacramento? I hope not because it looks like a sorry excuse for a zone."

"Well," said Black, "As you know, the League no longer allows zone defense, so we'll first have to check our personnel to analyze whether or not we have the players to handle the 22 full-court. And as for it being a zone—Bill, you must have me confused with Jerry Sloan.

"Next caller, Sandra from Queens."

"Yo, Black, when you gonna get rid of that soft-ass point guard Illy Payne?"

U chuckled. "We already spoke with Illy about his future with the organization and he understands. Now, I have heard reports that the New York Liberty maybe interested, but after speaking to coach Witherspoon, Illy's best opportunity may be abroad. We have received interest from the Swiss national team, which offered him a good deal as an enforcer-I hope he takes it."

"Hi, this is Jim from Jersey. Um, Coach Black, are you making any trades for Jumbo Parkson? You know he's one of the best power forwards in the game."

"We haven't made any offers to anybody yet, but we know of a few free agents that we're interested in, including Parkson. Our only problem with Parkson is that he refuses to sign that non-eating clause with his last team. Call me old fashioned, but I just don't feel comfortable with a player of mine taking time out in the fourth quarter to nibble on a cheese-steak between foul shots. I mean I love Parkson—and a Philly cheesesteak even more—but the owners know that if we do sign him, our insurance rates on the team jet will shoot through the roof.."

"Mike from Brooklyn, you're on."

"Black, love your show. Who are you going to take as your first pick in this year's draft? It's no surprise that everyone wants to take the Kenyan fellow; that crossover dunk is straight up porno. But the Kenyans get first shot, that's the League rules, but some of our lawyers are negotiating a possible deal with the Kenyans to allow us to draft the guy in return for removing for export tariffs against them. We also like a few players such as King out of UConn, who reminds me of a young Vin Baker. Terell from Pepperdine, probably the best defensive guard in the draft, Johnson of Syracuse and Grant at Carolina are all possibilities-it depends on our position in the Lottery. We have to fill some holes up front and need a point guard who might make the 22 work," said U.

"So you are going to use the 2-2-1?"

"Like I said before, if we have the personnel."

We'll be right back after this short commercial break."

THE T-BOK II SWERVES

"Before the Swerve, I was just a regular scrub with no game and when it came to getting run at the park, they'd pickup the pudgy chain smoking guy with goggles before me. Well, that was until I skipped my rent and shelled out $750 for a pair of T-BOK II Swerves. Now, I got hops. Plus, apartments are overrated, by living at the park, I always get first game, plus-I can dunk! Well, almost. Call 1-800-CAN-DUNK to take your game to where it needs to be. It's time for you to get yo' swerve

on? Yo! Who got next?

Visa, Mastercard, Medicaid, Food Stamps and Iraqi Trading Cards accepted.

The "crawl" at the bottom of the screen read: *"The Yusef Black Show is not responsible for the claims made by this product or liable for any accidental deaths due to bad coordination."*

After seeing someone increase his vertical jump by half an inch, Ellis began salivating over the Swerves. *Damn! Those shoes look phatt! I might have to pick me up some. Seven hundred and fifty balls ain't too much to spend to prolong my skills. I already got the nice vertical, stupid handle, dime drops skillznaps. Maybe I should just try out for the Knicks? I mean, I used to handle those kidz from St. John's well and U is now coaching? Yeah, maybe it ain't too late. One year in the CBA. I could start getting in shape tomorrow…*

"Mr. Rey, Mr. Rey!"

Huh, oh.

"Are you okay, Sir?"

Ellis returned to Earth.

"Yeah, just thinking, just thinking."

"Well, Mr. Black is waiting for you in his dressing room."

"Cool."

El walked briskly into the room.

"Yo, Black! The show was fly. You were great, man."

U smiled. "Well, you know, what can I say? I got skillz, baby. Yo, I'm hungry."

"Yeah, me too," agreed Ellis.

Yusef checked his watch and slipped on his coat. "What about Imani's on 123rd?

"You buying?"

"Don't I always?" said U with a *"Now, you-know-betta-Negus"* straight face.

"Then I'm down," said Ellis proudly.

"Bet. Let's go."

IMANI's

Ellis and Yusef entered Imani's immediately greeted with a "Peace and Blessings," from this baad Pam Grier-looking sista. She had eyes as old as the Orishas that pleasantly tore into your soul. "The special today is grilled Angolan Trout with brown rice. We also have an excellent band," she said in her smooth nonchalant voice to Yusef, with a twinkle in her eye-practically ignoring Ellis' "right-guy-for-you-look" that all women loved...especially after a few Long Island Ice Teas.

They sat down quickly and ordered a round of stout.

"U, What's up? You know that dime?"

U grinned. '"She's from the Old school."

"Old School?"

"Yeah. I went to elementary school with her."

"U, you sick."

"Yusef, blank faced, looked at Ellis.

"No, seriously. We went to elementary school together."

Ellis chuckled. "So you wuz a pimp back then?"

U stared straight-faced. "From da cradle to the stable."

Never to be one upped, Ellis leaned back, extending his right hand into the air to maximize the flash from his silver and onyx pinky ring. Then sucking on a toothpick, he pulled out his silky slim voice.

"Well, you ain't said nothing, I was a pimp back in nursery school. All my teachers wanted to bone me. They wuz bringing me extra cartons of chocolate milk and crayolas—just straight-up macking."

U took a sip of water. "Oh, that explains why you fucked up now—lactose intolerant Negus like you drinking all that milk in the formative years. I bet you got all your vaccinations too—probably even the non-mandatory ones."

Ellis started to laugh, then realized that U won't laughing, but unfortunately made sense. Since U rarely smiled, Ellis never totally knew when U was serious or just joking.

The waitress returned just in time with their drinks, as the band increased its funky level to near Bootszilla proportions. Imani's was ultra posh African-centered thing that was slowly becoming fashionable upon the children of the conscious movement now spending the cheddar their parents made. There were now over 20,000 multimillionaires in Harlem alone. Their thirst for culture inadvertently ushered in a Harlematic renaissance. Imani's dining area was oval-shaped with a spiral staircase leading to a glass enclosed office area adjoined to the dance floor. Both the dinning and dance area had stages. The whole aura was brown, green and soft white and Egyptian musk filled the air.

There were huge wooden carvings from Benin on both sides of the entrance, which gave the place a sense of royalty. The ceilings were powerful, designed to mimic a map of our galaxy highlighting the Sirius and star constellation as detailed by the Dogon peoples of Mali. It was an impressive bit of architecture.

After sipping on South African stout and getting their eat on, both U and Ellis leaned back and enjoy the music. The band gradually evolved the funk into a fusion jazz beat with hiphop drums tracks. It was sorta like Miles Davis's "Shh/Peaceful" meets Bob James "Mardi Gras." Within a minute of making the transition, some kid no more than 19 climbed onto the stage and began to spit lyrics into the ionosphere.

Within a twinkling of an eye my words build fire
Enemies proceed within an inkling of a sigh
I flow higher
My thoughts leave yesterday without goodbye
We fly
Like pimps in colored furs
Negus exist before Christ and Ben Hur
No slur
Before the race began
We exist
Before Time Spans
My hands
Built worlds based on thoughts
Never fought
To make it happen just did
Contract clauses come guaranteed in modern slave bids
Proceed
Like the Roots
Get Pus
Like boots
Reflecting intellect in metallic suits
I weather storms lounging
Born to rebel
Pounding

Mental drumbeats for incomplete
Idiosyncric idiots
Yeah I did it
 Shot the sheriff
Then pissed on his grave
Muthafuka had the nerve to call me a slave
Forgave
But never forgot
I keep the spot hot like Glocks
In cops' hands
Metaphysical angles develop hypotenuse styles
I cream
 While others dream of being top of the pile
Blackchild
First sun
Like Jimmy Castor
It's just begun/

"Yo, U, them lyrics are hitting, huh?"

"Oh yeah, he's ripped it," nodded U, sounding about as interested as mud. Evidently he had something else on his mind.

Then, out of nowhere, he mumbled:

"Ellis, I like your work. You're a good *writer*, not just a reporter—and believe me, there's a big difference. Plus, you know the game, because you played ball and are a pretty decent player. I'll make you famous if you don't flip on me with the bullshit you sportswriters come with," said U taking another sip of stout.

Yeah, evidently I ain't the only one that stout is working on, thought Ellis. *U musta seen one of those Hallmark commercials earlier.*

Yusef continued his groove.

"I mean, how these bastards at *The Pest* gonna write that I was a scrub, 'cause I didn't carry my team to the title? I mean some punk that ain't never even played ball gonna tell me *I* was a scrub? Shit, El, I averaged 20 points a game and seven assists for three straight years, till I blew my knee out. These guys think it that easy? Scoring 20 a game against the best of the best? Shit, even Shaq didn't win nothing without Kobe, Oscar without Kareem, Wilt without West. I mean you sportswriters are crazy. You muthafukas ain't got nobody looking at your bullshit predictions and half-ass writing skills at the end of the year. What you know about pressure? You bastards ain't being judged; all you do is siphon a living off people that got the talent. They don't pay to see some wannabe proving their manhood by talking about what I should be doing. They pay to see the players. Man, if I see that writer from *The Pest* on the street, I'mma break his jaw. Then let him write about that. El, you think I was a scrub?"

Surprised by U's onslaught of words, Ellis was sure that this was the longest diatribe ever uttered by Yusef Black in all the years that he has known him.

He took a sip and responds carefully.

"Naw, U, you were the man. What can I say? You right. If you ain't played the game, if you ain't carried a team, won the title, what the hell do you know about it? I mean, I at least carried my team to the 15 and under title and got MVP during the summer League once. I mean, me and Jay, wuz real nice at one time. We shoulda went D-1. But, really, to really respect the game, you got to know the game, and if you ain't really played the game-shit U, what can I say? That's like a virgin trying to tell a playa like me about sex. No matter how many books he read, it ain't gonna work, nawmean?"

U took another sip, as if to wash the bitter taste out of his mouth. He hated hating anything, but he hated the way these sportswriters treated him. U glanced at Ellis.

"El, to top shit off, you know what has bothered me for 20 years, for 20 fucken years?"

Before Ellis could attempt to respond, U did for him.

"Basketball I.Q."

"U, what you talking about?"

Yusef frowned, like, *C'mon, Negus.*

"Basketball IQ El! Fucken basketball I.Q.! These mawfukas don't even want to give players credit for being intelligent enough to figure out a complex game, so instead of calling us smart, they just started saying I had a 'high basketball IQ.' C'mon El, do you ever hear somebody say a lawyer has a high legal IQ, a doctor a high medical IQ, a sportscaster a high sports I.Q.? Naw, just us, like when some guy with a 'education' gets outsmarted by some high school dropout, they call it street-smart. What the fuck up with that?" spewed U as if he didn't already know. "If a mawfuka is smart, give 'em credit for it, instead bastards always want to quantify shit. You know when mawfukas quantify shit all they doing is playing a damn game, and the damn game is 'fuck you,' said U with an angry voice, but a barely changed, almost-blank facial expression that sought some kind of validation of saneness.

U stared into space, as if he'd stepped into another dimension.

"You Ellis, to this day. Me and Hook—you remember Hook, we played together my first two years in the League. Man, because I responded to some misquote by the media to something he supposedly said, but never did—we don't even speak anymore. Man, I was 22-years-old, and some reporter asked me to respond to Hook saying I was overpaid and overrated. Come to find out, he didn't even say that shit. Man, you thought I'da known better from the Kobe-and-Shaq shit to simply just shut the fuck up. I got respect for you, El, but I got no love for you fucken journalists."

Not really ready to deal with a whole lot of shit that was going to fuck up his high, Ellis never liked being around pissed- off Negus. He saw too much of that shit growing up and learned to simply keep shit to himself. He realized that most Negus didn't have the answers to their problems and could go on a venting tirade that might last into next week, so he'd mastered the art of ending conversations with "angry Negus" with his Bobby McFerrin version of kill that noise by giving U a hint that he'd had his fill for the evening.

"Yo, U, it's crazy. But that's just how it is, man."

With that comment, U sucked his teeth, and both men drifted off like clouds on a rainy day into the music as well as into their private thoughts. Good music tended to take you away from the daily grind. Ellis' mind traveled back in time to when he first met Yusef Black.

In some funky type ghetto way, U's life was like a fairy tale, practically. He grew up in Building 360 at the Villa Housing projects and attended Ronald McNair Science High School. He was one of the few from his Hood to escape to college.

Yusef was what teachers would call "off the scale" intellectually. Everyone knew about his ball skills, but most slept on the intellect. Not that he'd readily reveal himself. That type of shit, everybody knew, got you a rep you didn't want. You couldn't be too smart without being a punk. If you showed skillz in the class in any overt way, you had to be ready to get tested physically. It ain't had shit to do with "acting white"; acting white and acting like a punk won't necessarily the same things. Being smart was fine; it was not being cool that got you tested on a regular.

Yusef realized that shit early on, and early on chose what most Negus in his position choose—their peers as opposed what older headz think is more important U, like most kidz stuck in his situation, knew that street knowledge was what moved in the Hood.

So as the street moved, he moved. By 4th grade, he as caught up in all the criminal antics of his peers, 'cept while they was getting sent upstate with other juveniles, he was sidestepping every possible landmine while scoring off da record on standardized tests. For U, it was the simple fact that he read everything he could get his hands on. Simultaneously, he also boosted everything he could get his hands on, too busy to be idle. The contradictions were the type that gave his teachers heart attacks.

His story veered from the norm after taking an aptitude test in the 4th grade. He scored so high that teachers started taking a special interest in him and referred him to this elite program for "talented-and-gifted minority" students. He never liked that "talented and gifted" tag, 'cause what did it mean? That all the other students were "mediocre and ignorant?" And his neighborhood was practically all Black and Spanish, so why was they calling him a "minority?" It was all a plan: If they only had to provide opportunity for the talented and gifted, then whatever happened to the rest of the Negus could simply be written off like fate.

The aptitude test was developed by the Federal Science Administration (FSA) as part of the now-defunct Black, Indian, and Asian Studies (BIAS) program, specifically designed to gauge the math, perceptions and logic skills of African American and Latino children, while at the same time measure their vertical jump. It was similar to some of the psychological experiments conducted at major New York City universities.

At the time, no one knew why or what study FSA was conducting, except that Yusef was invited, along with a group of 28 other young brothas and sistas from all over the country, to attend a summer program ran by the FSA on the campus of Maryland State University.

The ringleader of the whole program was Dr. Carl Kleinden. He appointed by President Thorn and allowed to run the FSA Space Logic program, despite opposition from many African American groups. His critics accused him of using false data to promote a theory. The theory called for altering the cerebral-genetic makeup of Black kidz to increase their ability to compete with whitefolks, while decreasing their alleged genetic predisposition towards crime and delinquency. They never explained how they were supposed to measure *intelligence*, since standardized tests like the SAT were only designed to gage the first-year grades of elite prep school graduates in their first Ivy League year.

They used data from Dr. Kornstain and Charles Blurray's propagandist masterpiece "The Bull Curve," funded by the AMM Enterprise Foundation. As a matter of fact, the National Association for the Advancement of Black People (NAABP) voted Kleinden "Racist Of The Year" after his early fiasco at NIH.

Kleinden had organized an NIH-funded experiment to find a link between race and a genetic predisposition to crime. Of course, his test population was incarcerated African Americans, since, according to him, they were "more likely" to commit crimes. He theorized that since prison normally provided African Americans with a more stable environment than the outside society, they sub-consciously acted in a manner to get arrested. "They couldn't help themselves," he truly believed, and actually felt sorry for them.

Kleinden, just like most others, actually bought into the myth that more Negus were locked up because they committed more crime, which was pure bullshit. Every study done showed that Whites committed just as much crimes as anybody else, but were arrested, prosecuted, and penalized less than Negus.

After the controversy died down, funding continued at several sites, including the University of Miami-State, Kell-Radcliffe, Berkeley Institute, and Maryland West-Shore. All Yusef would say about the whole experience was this: "Shit was wild, man. Shit was wild." Of course, Ellis would get him a few beers and hope that he would open up a little, but he never did. Except once, until Ellis mistakenly called him an old man, to which he responded by promising to rearrange Ellis' dental work, to which Ellis considered, upon realizing the bullshit he normally went through with his dental DMO plan. Of course, unlike his DMO, he could pay Yusef for the work by ordering him another round of stout.

Wardell was Yusef's nephew through his brother Musa, whom Ellis never met but heard a ton about. Musa had a JD/MBA from Stanford and worked for the Clinton Administration's USAID program as a researcher and consultant and started his own non-profit organization. His job took him all around the globe, but most important to Malakal, Sudan, where he met his wife Dinkaa.

Unlike Yusef, Musa spent a good part of his childhood growing up in Sudan. Evidently, due to Musa's problems with the law at an early age, their mother allowed him to join an organization of American expatriates that moved to Sudan in the 90's.

Musa and Dinkaa had two sons, Wardell, and Menelik, and one daughter Tye. Wardell's first name was Ali. But he never liked it, so he went by his middle name. After marrying his wife in Sudan, Musa decided to return to America with Dinkaa and formed the "BlackStar Line," a Back-to-Africa movement which brought about 150,000 Brothas and Sistas out of the cities back to the Motherland to build new communities for themselves. A good majority of them settled in Sudan, Tanzania, Ghana, and Mozambique. They picked up where the Garvey movement left off about a century ago.

It took some effort to get the movement off the ground, especially since Sudan's North and South's reconciliation plan implanted by the African Union was still being completed and many critics still felt the Arabic-dominated Blacks of the North owed a lot in blood for allowing what happened to millions of Blacks in western Sudan, Dafur, Nuba Mountains, and the South. All of the northerners were not involved in the murder and war, but their failure to stop it left tons of bad blood that would take generations to heal. There was still a lot of bitterness between the various peoples of Sudan. Foreign involvement worked hard to keep the negative shit going. However, everything dramatically changed across the face of the continent with the Pax-Africa Movement that swept across Africa in the wake of the nightmarish "Occidental Plague."

The Occidental Plague was worse than AIDS. Around 2011, a cure for AIDS was found by an African scientist with a background as a herbalist. Just as the world began celebrating the end of AIDS, the Occidental Plague emerged. It killed millions, but struck especially hard among the European Elite, African leaders and military juntas. No one could totally explain it, not even the World Health Organization (WHO), which quickly suspended all Africa operations.

No European, except the most truly pious, would even set foot on the continent since they were among the first to die, by the thousands. The "Afropeans" were also hit hard, which meant that the majority of bureaucrats and military leaders died quickfast. No one had ever come across a virus that seemed to murder based someone based on a state of mind or mentality. Some said that a genetic sequence predominate to left-brained thinkers somehow triggered certain amino acids in the body and produced chemicals that the virus responded to.

The ruling classes of Africa, including Americans, Europeans, and Arabs who indirectly or directly participated in the countless oppression and genocide were brutally wiped off the map, virtually removing a parasite from Africa's stomach without forcing the new generation to shed blood. A new cadre of young Africans took over all of the leadership positions and established the basis for a Union of United Africa. Sudan joined Ethiopia, Eritrea, Somolia, Chad, and Kenya to form the New Kemet Region.

The old oppressors simply died away or moved to the United States and Europe, but the plague followed killing millions in many of the European cities and had recently shown its ugly face in America. The Occidental Plague's brutal attack on the wealthy and corrupt so threatened the elites that it ushered in a powerful atonement movement that began reducing worldwide poverty.

The Occidental Plague first turned a person's eyes blood- red, and their throat swelled to twice its normal size. Its victims were constantly hungry and thirsty but couldn't swallow any food. Eventually they died of starvation. It was sickenly, since unlike the previous generations suffering from famine, these suffering from the plague actually had access to food but could not use it.

Some people said that the Angel of Death had lost a hand of poker to the Archangel Gabriel. Rather than simply blowing his horn announcing the Day of Judgment, the legend goes, Gabriel merely had the Angel of Death remove those in Africa whose hands were soiled with exploitation, oppression, and bloodshed. The Plague struck with the mysteriousness of some old mummy's curse. No one knew for sure how many Africans died during the half a century prior to the plague. Estimates in the Congo region alone ran into the tens of millions.

Yusef's brother Musa first left Sudan when USAID pulled out, and began organizing the Exodus Movement with his wife Dinkaa. After receiving calls from friends, he began returning to Sudan with other Negus from America to help rebuild a region that was miraculously freed from its oppressive leadership and foreign covert intervention. Even the land had forgiven the people as the Sahara began transforming from a barren wasteland of sand into a lush tropic paradise with underground streams of water popping up every day to first form streams then rivers. It coincided with climatical changes in Europe. It was utterly amazing and scary.

The Exodus movement was hugely successful, except that Musa and Dinkaa ended up losing Wardell to the bright lights of the big city. He decided to school at Columbia, although his parents were dying for him to attend Howard. Always eager to disappoint his parents, he quickly chose to attend Columbia.

In any case, Dinkaa and Musa returned to Sudan with about 150,000 folks, short of one son—Wardell. Quietly,

Dinkaa was a little happy that Wardell stayed. He was too full of the Western ways and left-brain thinking; she was worried that if he did return with them, the plague would kill him. Like most mothers, she simply held out hope that one day he would wake up.

Wardell was the type of kid that would cause the average parents to catch a case. He was a pure problem child.

He loved New York and immediately picked up on all the styles, and lingo during his transformation from Sudanese to a strait up M.O., aka Imitation New Yorker. He loved New York because for once in his life, there wasn't anybody there to keep track of him. His uncle Yusef was on the other side of the country and could check on "little Mack," short for Machiavelli, only so often. Despite his trying, the only thing that Wardell couldn't figure out was gear. You know—how to match his shit. He'd be wearing Honda-Honda colors, plaids and stripes, and think he was fly. But lately, he seemed to had gotten to the point of near fly.

Yusef was loved by everybody—everybody except sportswriters. But he didn't have too many friends. It seemed that solitude was his choice. Most Negus had issues with trust; U was no different, just a little more distrustful. If he kept folks at a distance, they couldn't fuck him around and he'd done put himself out there too many times to let that happen again. He was mad cool with Ellis, at least most of the time. They clicked for the simple reason that they both had some sort of noble integrity and never asked each other for too much or got too personal; they followed some modern "Rat Pack" style and just kepted it simple. Their relationship was sort of uncle/nephew or mortal enemies, depending on what Ellis wrote in the newspaper that week. Since U was 20 years older, Ellis taught him what he thought and Yusef in return taught Ellis what he knew.

Ellis and U first met in New York, after Ellis was hired to cover sports for *The Nubian*, the city's last Black-owned newspaper. Fresh out of school, if he couldn't play pro ball, Ellis at least wanted some access to the game. His journey landed him at *The Nubian* working for wages any self-loving immigrant might turn his back on. "Don't blame me, blame NAFTA," was his slogan.

Ellis had a real simple job: cover the Knicks and St. John's. So in between squeezing time in for his masters in Web Communications Technology and Journalism at Big State University, he covered the Knicks and the RedStorm.

Covering the Knicks was sickening. During the 2010 season, New York proceeded to break the League record for least amount of wins in a season.

Nevertheless, the games were interesting and then some. Ellis remembered back in 2015, when the Kings came into town to mop up the Knicks. He had hooked up with Walt Skittles, the League's premier offensive player, Yusef, and Wardell.

Yusef's team at the time was Sacramento, who, behind Skittles, Mitch Grant and James, were the darlings of the League. After coming out of the University of Kentucky early and enduring drawn-out contract negotiation and injuries, Skittles became the only player to lead the League in points, assists, steals and endorsements.

Skittles credited his professional development, particularly his innate ability to endorse hundreds of products at the same time, to the Jordan's Rites of Passage Mentoring Program. He was recruited by the program while attending Five-Star basketball camp in his sophomore year of high school. It was Michael Jordan's way of giving back to the community. They never talked much about ball, but Damn! Those sessions on "Good Smile Versus Bad" and about "The Best Camera Angles" used to get intense!

According to Skittles, the Jordan Mentoring Program was amazing and had a tremendous impact on his development as a player and endorser.

"It was weird because we'd study all forms of political theory and history to be able to say, 'I'm sure the factory conditions aren't that bad, besides my signature sneaks only cost $450 dollars.' From there they'd move to his favorite workshop—'No comment. I'm just here to play ball.' It was my most amazing life experience. We'd sit for hours watching old 'Juice' commercials. Know when to say when, baby, just know when to say when—ha, ha."

In keeping with the tradition of Jerry West, whose image became the symbol for the NBA, and Michael Jordan, who sold his image to Nike, Skittles became the first player in professional sports history to sell his big toe to endorsers. But everything wasn't peachy-keen as one might think after getting such a deal. According to an interview on HBO's Real Sports, "The Big Toe was angry and wanted a higher percentage of the deal."

In an interview that left tears in the eyes of the "Real Sports" reporter and left the studio smelling like cheese for weeks, the Big Toe said that he felt he was being exploited and "wanted to take a stand for little Big Toes growing up so they wouldn't have to experience what he went through."

"Yo, patient!" Yusef tapped Ellis on his shoulder waking him out of a momentary relapse into reminiscent-land.

"You okay, El?"

"Chilling, but yo, check it. I need a few comments for my story."

"Cool," said Yusef, "but let's do it quick, 'cause I'm 'bout ready to jet."

Ellis passes a stout to Yusef, and hit him up on his top point guards.

"Give me your top ten."

"Top ten? Mine or the general consensus?" quipped Yusef.

"Yours, old man. Give me your top ten."

Okay, okay," said Yusef beginning to scratch his head.

"Just watch that old man shit. Now you know, I've got to go with my boy Magic, first. Uhm, the Big O—Oscar, of course. Clyde."

"Clyde? Wasn't he a two-guard?"

" Naw, he's point," said Yusef.

"Okay, you making me lose my train of thought, let me finish this...humm. Okay, I'll give you two, before the injuries who were pure nasty—Tiny Archibald and Hardaway-Penny? No, Tim. Now I'd might have to put Penny up there, but he switched to the two-guard. Damn! I almost forgot-Isaiah."

"Yeah, yeah, Isiah. How in the hell did Isaiah not make the Dream Team? There were only four players that lead their teams to titles and dominated that era, Bird, Jordan, Magic, and Isaiah. And Isaiah was the only one not on the team!

"That shit was fucked up…well, you know what happened. Remember when he said that shit about if Larry Bird was Black, the media wouldn't be talking about him being the G.O.A.T.?" said Yusef. "If he was Black—yeah, you right. But it was Dennis Rodman who said it and Isaiah agreed."

Yusef took a sip of beer.

"Whatever. All I know is he had to take a 15-hour taxi from Detroit to Boston to apologize for that shit. They never forgave him. Isaiah he went from being the darling of the League to a 'Spreewellian' malcontent."

Ellis laughed. "A 15-hour taxi? C'mon, man, you know he flew—"

"Whatever," interrupted Yusef.

Ellis took another sip.

"Well, actually I heard that it was Jordan who didn't want Isaiah on the squad?"

Yusef looked up from his beer surprised. "What…?"

Ellis lost concentration for a second as this tall sista walked by with a back-out shirt and jeans practically glued to her thighs, he looked down and saw her open-toed, high-heeled shoes and almost dropped his tongue to the floor. Ellis gathered himself and continued. "Yo, truthfully U, they told Isaiah that he could play on the Dream Team if he agreed to pose on *Sports Illustrated* with a chain and shackles around his neck, like an escaped Slave."

Yusef gave a sarcastic, "Really?"

Grinning, Ellis laughed. "Yeah Sun, that's where Charles Barkley first got the idea from."

"What? Naw El, you fucken' with me. You think I'm drunk, can't hold my liquor, you a damn idiot. Okay, U, don't get all touchy. Okay let's see, how many more?"

U continues his list. "Uhmm, Okay, the next few players were way underrated for their skills: and that's: K.J., Iverson, Mo Cheeks, and Rod Strick. Oh yeah, and let me add Michael Ray Richardson, before the drug problems…Yo, wait a minute, Yusef; how could you leave off Payton or the Pearl?

And Iverson was a two."

"The Pearl was really a two. I always saw him as a two. But, oh yeah I gotta throw Jason Kidd in there."

"What about Stockton?" pleaded Ellis.

"Good, but not top ten. Listen, youngin', you asked for Yusef Black's top ten, not *Sports Illustrated*'s or *Sporting News'* top ten, so that's what I gave you."

"Okay, old man I can deal with that. I can deal with that. But you know who you forgot to mention. Yeah, one of your former players."

"Who?" asked Yusef, anxiously angry.

"Illy," chuckled Ellis.

"Who?" asked Yusef.

"Ill L. Payne—yo' boy Illy Payne."

"Illy Payne," cackled Yusef, nearly falling to the floor with laughter.

"You had to go there on me, huh? Damn Illy. You sick, man, El."

Looking up from his stout, U stopped laughing.

"I'm getting ready to step," continued U, "my brother is coming to town with his wife and my other nephew, but we'll hook up later this week. Peace."

"Peace," said Ellis. *Damn, today turned out not so bad, this place is alright! Wait a minute. I forgot to ask him about the trade deadline and the mid-season free agent Lottery—shit!* The waitress returned and smiled slyly, at Ellis, handing him a piece of paper. *Oh, she must be trying to kick me the digits,* thought Ellis, for a second, until he realized that she just handed him the bill.

The bill? I knew that.

THE DAILY GRIND

For Ellis Rey, today is a day for the ages. He woke up early breathing fire and caught the train early, arriving at work without any mishaps, or coffee stains. And for some incomprehensible reason, his blue wool pinstriped suit that had suffered through the trenches of the daily grind, looked brand new. Five years of sweaty funk, mustard burns, and near brushes with the unwashed homeless, West Fourth Hoop junkies, and no deodorant-wearing adherents to the philosophy of "funky by any means necessary," and his suit had refused to bail out on him. It as a loyal as a battalion of brothas in Vietnam—not even so much as a loose thread could be seen.

He matched it with a sweet yellow tie with white stripes, and white shirt. To the average onlooker, Ellis actually looked as if he wuz somebody-had a good job. The universal axiom was always dress for your next job-never dress down. This wouldn't work for Ellis since in his case the only thing he'd be wearing would be raggedy boxers and a T-shirt, since he planned on retiring before his next job. Still hadn't figured out how he was gonna afford retirement yet. But that was just a small technicality in an otherwise beautiful plan

As he took his usual jaunt into the office building, Ellis casually glanced across the street and notice a black Lincoln Mark Six, parked in the tow zone. His mind immediately picked up the fumble and went the length of the field.

Let's see… two Caucasians dressed in black, no facial hair and shades and probably rubber wing-tips-eyeing me. Either they were Mafia, or more likely FBDIE. A distant third possibility was that they were extras for "Men In Black." Or perhaps the damn "Matrix" is real?

Probably FBDIE, thought Ellis. *FBDIE had made an attempt to shut down the Nubian several times using the IRS, an old trick. It always seemed every Black newspaper had problems with back taxes. Maybe problems were created for them. All these maafukas can't be that bad in accounting; anybody ever heard of Peachtree? Shit, all you got to do is put the numbers into the damn software, right?*

I hope they're not sweating me. Shit, I'm low man on the totem pole and I don't remember doing anything in about three years. My 6th grade teacher always said somebody was going to catch my smart-ass one day-just 'cause she couldn't. Yeah Miss Crabtree, I'm over 21 and I ain't behind bars or dead…yet.

"Ellis!" screamed a voice that sent shrills up his spine and caused involuntary convulsions down in his lower pelvic region, completely shutting down his root chakra, the one most important for sex and survival.

"Huh?"

"Ellis, I want you to get down to WTOM," said an excited Nicole. "There's supposed to be some riot going on at the radio station."

"Alright, but can I get some coffee first?"

"No! Get it on the way," said his favorite talking hero-sammich.

"Alright, I'm out!" groaned Ellis like a 4th grader with no recess.

Scrambling, he grabbed a piece of chewing gum, his note pad and mobile pc recorder. Heading down to WTOM 86 fm with him is photographer James Beammer, a brotha who always greeted you with a warm smile and the slightly warmer smell of fresh gin on his breath.

Ellis turned to Beammer to get the lowdown on the radio station. Beammer is only happy to give the full 411.

"Yo," smirked Beammer, "check it out, man. This shit is crazy with a capital K. Will Lye—you know, the Black conservative, who always talking about how affirmative action—"

"—You mean 'remedies to racism'," blurted Ellis, knowing Maya would be happy that he remembered her hour-long lecture on the topic several months ago.

"Yeah, 'remedies to racism'," chimed Beammer. "Y'know, he's always talkin' 'bout how it ain't necessary and how Blackfolks need to get off their lazy ass, get a job, in all that…"

Lighting a cigarette, Beammer continued:

"This motherfucker makes Ward Connerly look like Rap Brown. You know, I called that bastard up one time and he told me I was an underachieving alcoholic and a born loser. That's when I had to correct his ass on-air. Yeah, I'm a Grade-A alcoholic, but I sure as hell ain't no underachiever. Shit, not as many photography awards as I've won. Negus musta been sipping n slippin'. So the bastard hung up on me. Then he went on to quote that old rusty cracker, Senator Strom Thurrand and go into an hour-long monologue on how the Supreme Court was justified in the Dred Scott case saying 'the Blackman had no rights that the white man was bound to respect,' 'cause the Blackman ain't done nothing deserving of respect."

Sensing J.B. had probably been sipping a little hard this morning, Ellis tried to bring him back to Earth by asking about the riot.

"Huh? Er, Oh yeah, well, you know that today is

African Liberation Day and a group of folks, 'bout a thousand deep, left the park and marched on the radio station where Strong was delivering his most recent sermon on how Blacks were better off due to slavery and how European colonization was good for Africa, because it civilized us. He was on some wacked Zora Neale Hurston shit."

"Damn! He went there?"

"Yeah, man, this is what I been trying to tell you," said an excited Beammer. "But that's not all; folks have surrounded the radio station and are practically shaking it off its foundation. The thing is, Strong keeps going on and on and said that they'll have to burn him out, if they want him off the air. Yo, El! Hopefully I can catch them burning Strong alive. Shit, like that wins the Pulitzer."

"Yeah," said Ellis, praying for a cup of coffee as they pulled within a block of the station. Glancing into the park, Ellis saw what looked like Carnival in Trinidad. There are brothas hawking 'Burn Will' T-shirts, selling hotdogs, veggie patties, organic cotton candy, Blasting Gil Scott-Heron, African dancers on stilts, that brotha doing the robot from the Chapelle show—the whole nine. They reach the station and heard Lye's Ebonic-less milquetoast voice streaming over the outside loudspeaker.

"I am an American! An American! I'm not going back to a backwards continent like Africa. If you want me off the air, you'll have to burn me out!"

Then, as in unison, about 200 Negus screamed back, "You ain't no American! If you was an American, You wouldn't have no problem!"

It's total madness out here. Where's Beammer? wondered Ellis, scanning the place. Finally, he saw that Beammer was on his job like a madman, snapping up crazy shots of the entire scene. Seeing his intensity on playoff level, Ellis quickly figured he'd better get going and find out what's happening.

Ellis navigated his way through the zealously persistent T-shirt vendors, and saw that a makeshift stage had been set up using milk crates and Kente cloth. On top of the stage is community organizer Zulu Shakor. Ellis moved like a panther, and rapidly got comments from various people in the crowd, while circling the stage, to make it around the backstage, just in time for Bey's people to check him up for weapons. The way a few of their breaths' smelled, they shoulda been checking for mints. One too many root drinks without brushing.

"Yo, see the I.D.," said Ellis, holding up his tags like he's with the U.N. or something. "It's me, baby. Ellis Rey with *The Nubian.* C'mon, Omari—you know me, so stop faking."

Omari Senghor, Shakor's second-in-command, just looked at Ellis with the disdain normally reserved for the kid who took the prize out the Capt'N' Crunch box. He and Ellis go way back, but now he decided to play this superior-to-thou Black radical shit, which only pissed Ellis off more than anything. Especially when Ellis knew of a time in the not-so-recent-past when *The Nubian* was the only newsmedia covering their events.

Shakor finally came down off the stage. He tied his long dreadlocks into a bun and shook clean his brown dashiki. He was revolutionary Black Nationalist incarnate, 'cept for one slight proletarian mistake—he had on Air 2000s. Ellis looked at Shakor's sneaks and wondered, *Damn, am I the only person who can't afford the new Airs?* Then it hit him, why was Shakor rocking the Airs? *Ain't they got some Ashanti Airs? Garvey Airs? Hey that's an idea: a new brand of sneaks for the revolutionary Blackman. We could do a whole sporting line or something.*

"Yo, Shakor, what's up? It's Ellis Rey from *The Nubian.* What's going on?"

Shakor looked Ellis up and down, frowning. Then looked directly over Ellis shoulder to wink at this beautiful Nubian queen dressed in an extremely tight fitting Che T-shirt. Shakor then gritted back at Ellis again.

"Aren't you the sportswriter? This ain't no sporting event, my brotha."

"Well, I'm doing news now, so like I said, what's going on down here. You trying to burn Will Lye off the air?"

Shakor cleared his throat, removed his chew stick and paused like he's bearing sextuplets before speaking. "The same thing that is always going on, my brotha. Every time we get an institution in the community for the community, traitors—collaborators—in order to make money, allow infiltration by the enemy and the institution ostensibly for us no longer serves us."

Playing dumb reporter, Ellis then asked, "How is Will Lye the enemy simply 'cause he has a different view point?"

He hoped that Shakor and his folks were smart enough to take the sucker pitch and hit it out the park. Media savvy folks always knew that a reporter needed them to say something inflammatory or quotable, as opposed to a reporter saying it himself. If you did, it was called editorializing, which was sacrilege. So you always tossed a few obviously offensive questions at a speaker that made you sound like a dumb fuck. This was done in order to get them to respond. If they understood this, they'd know that this is a time to talk about whatever you wanted to for the ideal soundbyte. But, if they were so caught up in their own importance, they might not get it. If not, they might just call him a sellout and proceed to whip his ass.

Immediately, the barrage began from the entourage. 'Sellout, Uncle Tom, idiot, bomma clod!" Shakor calmed down his folks with a wave, and Ellis relaxed slipping his cargo knife back in his pocket. "My brotha Rey, you know very well that Lye is paid for, bought, and promoted by the Heritage Corporation. Therefore, my brotha, we cannot continue to allow this co-conspirator and member of the Boul'e to continue a rhetorical dialogue which takes our people back to first base when we are heading to third," said Shakor, while taking a second to pose for Beammer.

"We are prepared," Shakor continued. "Prepared to do what is necessary to remove any person from our community—Black or not—who is not willing to place our struggles, identity, and history first."

"What do you mean by 'remove'?"

"We mean remove from the air…that's all we're saying," smiled Shakor, finally overstanding what Ellis was trying to do.

"Amandla!" yelled Shakor his fist clenched raised high in the air. "Uhuru!" continued his entourage…beginning a chant… "Uhuru! Uhuru! Uhuru!"

As Shakor's supporters continued to chant Freedom in Kiswahili, the radio station interrupted Will Lye's squeaky voice for a message from one of its sponsors. *COSTLOT.*

"Forget about Baby Phat, Sean John, and Tommy Gear for

kidz. COSTLOT is now the new move in designer-wear for infants. Spark that Hiphop flavor before your child develops into a full fetus with our embryonic wave caps-guaranteed to keep baby hair on your head till 30. Also hot, are our Cristal milk bottles, and Roless Gucci-style thermometers. Any purchases made this week are eligible for a 25 percent discount on baby stroller hydraulic kits. Remember COSTLOT- 'cause it does! Go Coslot, Go Coslot, Get Coslot, get ya Costlot now!"

Damn, thought Ellis, if it was one thing he hated, it was hiphop designer infant wear. That shit caused him madd problems when he was an infant. It took him years to rebound from the blows to his self esteem when he spotted the other kidz with the latest gear on, bling-blinging, while breast feeding when his mom's couldn't afford the same. A lot of the poorer infants suffered the same fate as him, and were forced into a life of crime as early as two months old to get the gear they couldn't afford. Shit, there was no terror like getting rolled on by a nine-month-old, thugged-out infant in a dirty diaper slapping you silly with a Big Bird teething ring. *Didn't people see that infants would turn to crime if they couldn't get the latest phatt gear? Somebody has to stop it now, before any other infant's self-esteem is destroyed.*

"*Vrrrooom!*"

Suddenly, as if by cue, the door of the station went up in flames, snapping Ellis from memories of his tortured childhood. Fortunately, it was put out quickly by the then arriving firemen. No one knew where Lye was. No one, 'cept Beammer.

"I saw that sucker run out the side door like an escaped slave. He was willing to let them burn him out, but when they started feeding him P.E.'s "Shut 'Em Down," into the on-air room, he flipped! "Shut 'em down, Shut, shut 'em down—We shut 'em down, shut 'em down, shut, shut 'em down." We shut 'em down! The crowd chanted in unison. African drums reaching a fever pitch. "What a way to go out—like a sucker," sung Ellis to himself.

FORT TRICKNOLEDGE, MD

Deep within the dark caverns of the Earth, the major players of the Intelligence Community were all nervous. This was the second meeting in a week, following the previous meeting at Fort Meadle, to get a gauge on this whole Africa mess.

They sat in a dimly lit, oval shaped conference room with an oval shaped table. Although the secured room was a few miles beneath the Earth's surface, the virtually enhanced windows gave it the ambiance of a city beneath the sea or another planet. No one spoke-that is very loudly. The major sounds were the clicks from attaché' cases, papers ruffling, coughs, and gas. One of the twelve seated was FBDIE Black Operations chief, John Shadow.

The room came to attention quickly as NSA head Cecil Kraze entered the room and mumbled quickly, "Let's get this thing going." After sharing the recent holographic reports from the Reagun, Kraze scoured the cipher.

"We know that the Osiris process is taking place in the Horn of Africa. What we haven't fully figured out yet is how to get at it. Our Harmonic Resonance capacity has been neutralized and we are no longer able to effectively manipulate weather patterns in that region. Our scientists are working on a possible plan to detonate a few depleted uranium warheads in the North Pole to disrupt the oceans currents as a means of destabilizing the current weather patterns, only problem is that if they get it wrong we might be looking at another ice age. Which may not be such a good idea, especially since I bought that timeshare on the Jersey Shore. Er, there are some possible options that might involve creation some opposition groups to destabilize things. But, we can't find anyone over there willing to oppose anything—folks are doing quite well of late, and frankly don't need our help.

"Our military and space programs need those elements that Africa has in abundance if we are going to maintain strategic control on this planet. If we are denied access to these key minerals and elements, hell, we might as well acquiesce to being a second classed military power, like them pansies from Europe.

"The Ethiopians and the Somalians refused us entry. Now, we could possibly threaten the Eritreans with withdrawing aid, but it's such a measly amount, they'd probably laugh at us. Besides with the oil revenues being shared among the African Union of States, they're actually in a position to loan us some. One good thing is that the SOURCE crew has pinpointed the area, where this energy source seems to be spreading from. However, we need to make a move before the process becomes almost irreversible."

Kraze nodded and one by one the attendees began giving their components of data. First was CIA spokesman Claude Rhodes. "Sirs, we have narrowed down our best links to destabilizing the Osiris process. He appears to be a close relative of the leaders of the BlackStar Line movement and resides in New York. We should be able to use him as a pawn, or possibly remove some DNA to clone him," said Rhodes quickly sitting down. "Who's monitoring this guy?" Asked Kraze, eyes bulging.

"I thought the FBDIE had tabs on the bastard?"

"We do," said John Shadow, nervously raising his head from his briefing papers long enough to maintain a second of eye contact with Kraze.

Shadow looked up again, with the look that Ron Artest might have at hockey night in Auburn Hills, and hurriedly stated his case.

"We have been monitoring our subject and can reach him at anytime. Anytime we feel like it. For one, he really hates his folks and would do anything to bring their whole movement down. I don't even know if a clone is necessary. The last one we used was unstable. I'm sure we all remember the Cheney incident?"

Shadow paused for a second and gave a wary look at his co-conspirators. The Intelligence Community was a kindler and gentler acronym for these folks. This was some serious group of rat bastards, and not necessarily intelligent. They were extremely protective of their particular domains that had been somewhat forcefully integrated by Congressional reforms and watched each other like a first time exchange between a seller and buyer of crystal meth.

As predicted, Kraze abruptly interjected. "We don't want to blow this one on some sudden case of loyalty. We want to be sure. Shadow, it's your call—let's get it done. You know how to work with those people—I mean, your people. Um, you know what I mean?" asked Kraze.

As the other 12 got up from the table, John Shadow

remained, alone-lost in thought. His face was expressionless. Concealing his feelings had been something he'd mastered a long time ago as a kid growing up in East New York. His was the mind of a computer, a calculator, always eager to prove himself the *Man*. It wasn't that he hated his own people. Really, he didn't, he almost respected some of them. For him it was about survival. And to survive you had to be on the right side. Shit, if Black folk were serious about this thing—freedom, liberation, equal opportunity, or what ever it meant to them— he'd even consider switching sides. He was, above all, a winner. And deep down, he knew winners were about the business of winning-fuck emotions and loyalty. He had no permanent friends nor enemies-just one permanent interest…Self.

Shadow did economics at Yale, and then graduated from Harvard Law. Afterwards he matriculated to the neo-conservative THOM Institute and eventually made his way to the FBDIE Intelligence Inner Circle.

The line for Black Conservatives was short, and for those willing to enter the field of intelligence, quicker still. This was the quickest way to the top, for sure. But recently he had begun to question himself: *What the hell he was doing?* He called his philosophy "Machavellism." He had read Machiavelli in college. His treatises excited him, more than women. *Machiavelli was a genius, fucken Genius!*

"It was better for a ruler to be feared than loved."

This was why he was on the other side. Blackfolks definitely had love, hell! Enough love for the whole world. But the power structure was feared. And in this system fear certainly worked well, whereas love, shit, that was theory, and it sure as hell didn't help Blackfolks progress any—certainly not John D. Shadow, especially the many times he got his ass kicked by Negus in his neighborhood who didn't give a shit about love, or helping the next Negus trying to make something of himself. Part of what he did now was a payback of sorts. Not really against those kidz that beat him up every other day and called him "whiteboy," or "midnight" but against the world. He never wanted to feel helpless again and he'd make sure of that by gravitating to those capable of protecting him, even if it meant being considered a sellout or the fact that his family hadn't spoken to him since his mother died.

Still the speed of things began to frighten Shadow, just a little more than he'd ever admit. He was moving into the sphere of invisibility. Did he really exist beyond the evil he did? Shit, sometimes he wondered if he existed at all? The question of existence was not simply an idea argued by Descartes, but took its form in numerous ways. For some men, it was only through having sex that they verified their existence, others it was through violence, and for the lucky few through power. For Shadow, he defined his existence by the challenges he overcame. In ways he was the model of success, from the ghetto to Harvard and by the time he had graduated he had traded in Enyce, Kani and Lugz's for J Press, Brooks Brothers, wingtips and membership in the American Enterprise Foundation. He'd become the worst enemy of Black people and the wet dream of David Horowitz.

Shadow was not simply transformed by the mainstream value-spell; he was utterly fascinated by it. From his perspective this was normal, since he never felt natural in the Hood among his own folks, anyway. He hated being among his own people. Everybody made fun of him because of-his intelligence-book-smarts, and his lack of coolness. On top of that being dark-skinned didn't help him any. He got more attention from pink-toed Suzy, than the "around-da-way girls." It was garbage what people were saying about loving dark-skinned men; all he remembered was being called "midnight," "Blackie," "toast," and a few other less pleasant attributes. Shadow never really analyzed it, but Freud was right about some things. Deprive a person of being able to get a piece of all that phatt sweet honey brown-skinned ass walking around the Hood, could make a brotha a wee bit resentful. That was the thing about the Hood, it didn't matter how poor the neighborhood, the women grew up beautiful. In any city it was all the same. It was just too much ass to be seeing and not able to get some.

His failures in the Hood mattered little once exposed to life on a predominately white campus. The white women loved his intellectualism and dark-dark features. After his first nut, he forgot about sistas, bought some loafers, dockers, and joined IDI-OT Gamma Si Frat-those passing out the ghetto cards sent him an email to drop his off at the nearest liquor store, 'cause they knew it was over.

Now, thirteen years later, he was questioning his whole state of existence and actually beginning to yearn for the unthinkable. Something that he promised he'd never have again—No, not a date with a sista, Naw, not a gold tooth nor the first Eric B and Rakim album—he did: a fat, juicy, hot piece of hard fried chicken and some mumbo sauce.

11:11 AM WAKENING

Brrrrrrrrrrrrring,

Brrrrrrring!

"Hello, you have reached Ellis Rey, Home of the Seventies Salvation Society and Sal's Pizzeria. Extra Cheese two- fiddy…"

"Ellis! Ellis! Are you there? It's me, Nicole…"

Scrambling, Ellis picked up the phone. "Uh, huh, hullo…Nicole?"

"Yeah, Ellis it's me, your boss. Why you ain't here?"

Ellis wiped the crust out of his eye.

"Nicole, how many times do I have to tell you, it's 'Why *aren't* you here?' If you don't improve your grammar, you'll never succeed in the newspaper business, didn't you learn anything from Cosby?"

"Listen, you wannabe Chris Tucker. If you don't get your skinny behind down here immediately, you is gonna have some problems. We have the exclusive interview with Shango, the notorious gangsta rapper, and you the only one here that knows anything about that music. Therefore, Ellis, if you want to keep a job, I suggest you forget about the grammar and scraight-up flex. Peace, Audi, Chevy Camaro, Mitshubishi!"

Clunk!

Damn! They got Shango down there? Shit, I got all of his CDs: "Does Heaven Have A Section-8," "Pop, pop, pop, Goes My Glock Against Ya Knot," "Dead Po-lice Can't Frame You;" and my all time favorite "Hell Is When The Bailbondsman Got A Broken Pager."

Brrrrrrrrrrrrrring!

Ellis raced to the phone.

"Okay, Okay, Nicole, I'm on my way. Let me throw on some gear. Damn!"

"Excuse me? Excuse me? This is Abdul Haki of the Coalition of Black Advertising Executives, and were attempting to verify the existence of any 'Black Nielson families.' Are you one of them?"

"How'd you get my number?"

"From the Federal Database. Are you a Neilson family?"

"No!"

"Would you mind answering a small survey?"

"I've got to go. Call me later."

"Well, er, uh, um, do you know any Neilson families? Have any relatives who are Neilson families?"

"No! Man I've got to go. The only people I know who heard about any Black Neilson families live in Minnesota."

"Yeah, we spoke to them already."

"Now, if your looking for Nelsons, shit, I can give you a whole bunch of them."

"No, thanks. Thank you for your time."

"You're welcome."

Talk about a hard job.

After throwing on some gear madd quick, Ellis finally arrived an incredible 45 minutes later and not a minute too soon. The lobby is in total commotion. Shango's entourage is about twenty deep and not counting the four pitbulls. Ellis remembered reading Shango never traveled without his dawgs, but always thought he was just talking about his entourage.

Ellis anxiously walked towards the group to introduce himself to Shango when three of Shango's peeps promptly pull straps on him.

"Represent, fool!"

"Whoooa, partner, Whooa! I'm Ellis Rey. I work here." Looking frantically, he finds Sasha. "Sasha, tell them I work here." Sasha stared at Ellis, rolled her eyes, and turned her back and walked away smiling. Seeing the grimness of the situation, Ellis saw two possible realities occurring in the near future—one a real-bad beat down, including bullet wounds and dog bites-maybe some surgery, or him pulling one of Uncle Breeze's moves and Jackie Chan-ing the whole clique. *Naw, I don't think so*," figured Ellis, as he visualized the sand dripping from the top of the hourglass, then it finally hit him.

He quickly starts singing Shango's latest platinum hit, "I Wonder If Heaven Got A Section-8?"

Yo, Yo, Yo check it out, the pearly gates open wide/But how do a real Negus like me get inside?/ Can't afford the rent/madd cheddar is spent/Negus represent/ I be Heaven sent/Cut like Clark Kent/but still live in tenements/as my peoples gets bent/See, you got money, so you can't relate/can you tell me if Heaven has a section 8...

Suddenly, the room is grooving aided by the faulty blinking overhead lighting and El's co-rocking the crowd, girlies shaking, bubbly flowing—the whole nine. At any moment Free and AJ was gonna appear and announce the next video. Then, Shango rose off the sofa and joined in Chorus... *"Can't pay the rent, can't participate/I wonder if heaven has a section 8/ C'mon, can't pay the rent, can't participate/I wonder if heaven has a section 8."*

After that, it was like backstage at the Vibe Awards, all love, madd daps and instant respect. His Unk Breeze told him a long time ago the greatest compliment felt by any emcee is when they hear someone reciting their lyrics. They could be in the middle of busting a nut, and would stop cold to find out who's reciting they shit. As they make their way to the conference room for the interview, Ellis asked Shango to leave the pits outside. "As a matter of fact, there's a empty cubicle next to Sasha's desk. She loves dogs," he said gleefully.

Shango sat down and sparked up a fat Buddha spliff and kicked off his boots. Ellis was planning on objecting at first, but upon remembering the guns-and-dogs, and entourage, he decided to let this one pass. Besides, the weed was the only thing in the room, masking the smell emanating from Shango's feet. The combinations blended gently like skunkweed, roadkill, and nachos with just a pinch of sour cream 'n' onions.

"So, I'm glad you decided to give us the interview. Normally folks decide to talk to *The New York Pest* first, then drop us a little crumbs."

"Well, I ain't wit' dat, I just tries to keep it real," grinned Shango.

" Three years ago, I couldn't even get through the door

of The Pest without getting arrested, so fuck 'em."

"Yeah, Yeah, I feel the same way," agreed Ellis. "But tell me how did you get the idea for your latest album, 'American Gangsta-isms?'"

Shango cleared his voice and gently laid his spliff on the edge of the formika table.

"My album is all about America. Excuze me, Amerik-ka, ka, ka! You know—society. In this nation, everybody loves the gangsta. I got the whole 'Rambro' DVD series and all the 'Dirty Harry' movies, Scarface. And I just watched dem flicks and see how much money they made. I mean we love that shit here, watching a mawfuka get his brains splattered all over the screen is some real entertaining shit. Just look at the Godfather, Sopranos, Swarznegga, Vin Deisel, I mean, every show on television is about a cop, and eurybody got a gun. Shit, America ain't no joke, just ask Bin Laden and dem. El, you know we got troops in a hundred countries. We just straight up strong arming folks, knowwhatemsaying? American Gangsta is what I am, and I learned from the best, or at least the best movies."

"Yeah, I hear you," nodded Ellis. "But what do you think about the controversy surrounding your lyrics? Media was blaming you—your music—for creating violence? There were three kidz shot at your last show."

"So you trying to say *I'm* guilty for that shit?"

"Naw, I'm just…"

Shango cut him off, "I give the people what sells. What they want to hear."

"So you feel that you're being maligned?"

Shango leaned back, staring into the ceiling.

"When I say maligned, I was just talking about…" explained Ellis.

"I know what maligned means, mawfuka. Shit, you like the rest of them bastards. All you see is some dumb Negus. I'mma tell you a little something, that I don't tell them fools interviewing me. I was raised on politics, Kid. My grandmoms and grandpops were fighting with the Panthers back in the 70's. All of my uncles are in jail under COINTEL-PRO. Shit, I got books on Malcolm n Mao, and other shit by the time I was ten. But, all my peoples who wuz committed to that shit eventually broke down, after the Federals came down on them.

They ended up either selling drugs, cracked-out or in jail. Or, or just plain fucken bitter! They made sure Negus paid for they activism-pay hard. Meanwhile, my moms and me was starving. I mean Blackfolks don't remember shit. My grandpops and uncle was running breakfast programs feeding the whole neighborhood and shit. When the Federals came down on them—set them up—they just rotted in jail. Ain't nobody come to see them, even send them any money on they books. But when they was doing all this good shit, these folks in the Hood was up at six in the morning to make sure their kidz got a free breakfast.

So you talking to the wrong motherfucker about that shit. I ain't going out like that. Committing myself to some movement, so the FBDIE can come down on me like I'm the Black Messiah; and then have my Negus skate and leave me hanging like the disciples did. Then I'm locked up or strung out and my kidz are starving. Then I'm a have some Negus like you, tell them that if they work really hard they can get on the list of some government program. Shiiiit…I don't think so. You Negus are too funny."

Feeling the tone of the discussion beginning to shift into a downward spiral, Ellis, tried to reestablish a bond with Shango. *I mean, I wasn't the enemy*, thought Ellis to himself.

"Me? I'm down with hiphop," said Ellis.

"Yeah," said Shango. "What the fuck you talking 'bout? You Negus falling for the Okie-doke, Sun, talking that hiphop shit. What the fuck you think hiphop is? Let me ask you something: if some country music star go into the porn business, you think mawfukas gonna say he's down with porn or country music's down with porn? You think hiphop was dropped from Mount Sinai?"

Shango chuckled loudly to himself making Ellis feel like an idiot. Shango smiled like Negus please, and continued his attack.

"You down, alright. But let me ask you a question: Why is it you Black Bourgeois Negus always giving us grief-talking about the lyrics when it's you Negus that control and own the radio stations, the networks, and the newspapers, magazines and all that? Huh? I mean you Negus is crazy fucked up in the head. First you take hiphop and separate it from

Black people like it wasn't always a part of our culture. Like somehow we done did some shit we ain't neva done before, or been doing all along. You muthafuckas turned that shit that we created into something that could be sold. Fucken Hiphop. I mean, we created Jazz too, and them Negus was as revolutionary and more. Hey but since you bourgie Negus found a new way to use our culture to sell capitalism-don't hate on me, 'cause I'm trying to get paid. You Negus created the mechanism to allow a record label to spend 20 million for a video showing me gunning down some fools. Why they gonna spend 20 mil on a video, Mr. College educated Negus—'cause they like Shango? 'Cause they down wit' hiphop?"

Ellis taken aback by Shang's comments. Ellis is stunned and angry. He grits his teeth and looks Shango up then down.

Negus calling me *Bourgie?*

"I ain't one of them Bourgie Negus. Man, you rap artists think you the only Negus, holding it down! You think just 'cause you on TV presenting some image, you more real than the next man? Like to be real hiphop you 'posed to shoot somebody, drop out of school, sell crack, or not give a fuck 'bout shit? What the fuck that got to do with being able to spit lyrics? It used to be Negus in hiphop spoke for the Hood to the Hood, now you Negus speak at the Hood like you pissing on us. Like you Negus trying to get some childhood beefs off yo' chest and you grown men, talking 'bout this Negus and that one on some record when you could just pay for a psychiatrist. C'mon Shango, instead of talking to some writer 'bout yo' beef or putting it on a record, why don't you cats take a few years off and go finish yo' beef. Then the last one standing can make a record about sumpin' worthwhile. It's hard as hell fo' the average Negus to live up to the images you Negus be manufacturing. It's Negus like me looking at you cats like, I'd be happy with a piece of what you throw away. You Negus need to be real instead of keeping it real dumb as shit. Like, like Negus like me got to prove my Hoodthencity to you? I mean, where in the fuck are you rap artists when Negus like me trying to get an education and despite getting honors 'n' shit, can't get no money? Meanwhile you Negus flossin' like it going out of style, spittin' Cristal out in videos. What the fuck do Negus on the street know 'bout spending a thousand dollars on French grapes? Spending a quarter mil on some damn ice? It ain't like you Negus doing nothing for me or my fam, 'cept maybe toss a few free gifts out around Christmas time? Don't get me wrong, Shango, I love all you cats—Biggie, Pac—but you Negus get worshipped for *what?* Doing what for us?"

Shango softly patted his glistening gat tucked tightly in his waistband.

"O' Kid, you on point. Like Elijah say, 'Why Blackfolks love the devil, 'cause he give them nothing?' But, yo' my man, keep it civil, don't get too excited, cuzin, 'member who you talking to. Since you somewhat of a street cat, I know I don't need to take it there. But don't get shit twisted, Sun, I ain't create this matrix. I ain't the one teaching the children to worship a mawfucka 'cause he makes records or can dunk a ball. Not meeee!

"Shit, you can't give me responsibility for that," grinned Shango, as he leaned back and blew out circles of smoke.

"You just like the rest of them mawfukas. I mean you Negus take everything wrong in America, the world and blame that shit on a Blackman, the lowest mawfuka on the totem pole. Now, even the older cats wanna turn around and blame their children, when their children is they own product? Whatever path youngins following now, the older cats led us there. I mean I read all them Black magazines, all them bourgeoisie Black women, and Negus like you, Kid, that ain't down fo' the struggle no more 'cause they overcome and Negus like me can't even get in the door where they work less I'm delivering something. Then some Negus want to talk bad about me 'cause I don't speak like Negus with education and money who do a better job of imitating whitey. You Negus is fools, like, 'cause the system let yo' ass in, you holding it down, sucking up everything this society spit at you like Pavlov but always got time to piss on brothas like me. Then, soon as the same type a Negus like me get a record deal, now all you bourgie folks wanna get close, 'cause, 'cause now I'mma idol, famous. Then the media-you make the people worship us like American idols and then tear us down when you find we just human, making human mistakes. How Negus in hiphop gonna educate the kidz and put them on the right track, when they don't know how to put *themselves* on the right track? Negus come into the game fucked up, and now 'cause they getting checks they 'posed to act with some sense—Shit, it was them acting out that got them signed in the first place. You and Negus like you need to catch kidz while they young and teach them something that they can use before they become famous, 'cause then it's too late. You people teach a kid that all that is important is the dollars, blinging, and being a player, then get madd when the mawfuka grown up into somebody worshipping the shit you done weened them on. They, they end up like me, a Negus who don't give a fuck 'bout nothing, 'cause nobody gave a fuck about me. It's way too late for a Negus like me, I come up hard sun."

Ellis nods. "So you making points but okay, let me get this right, you just a victim with $100-grand worth of jewels on your arm, you done cut 3 models this week, and you travel by private jet? Damn, cuzin, I almost feel sorry for you, 'cept for the fact that I'm still trying to figure out how to pay off my fucken student loan. C'mon Kid, I remember when hiphop used to say something, Negus like PE, and everybody in the Hood was wit' dat. So, now, you modern emcees want us to believe that if you started kicking some knowledge that the whole Hood wouldn't follow the same way they following you Negus into 'Bling Bling Land'?"

Shango leaned back and took a long tote of his spliff, holding it. Then exhaling circles.

"Five companies, baby, five companies."

Ellis looked confused. "Five companies?"

"Yeah Mr. newspaperman, that's who controls all these so-called labels. Five major corporations and ain't none of them owned by us. They giving our own shit back to us adapted fo' television with commercial breaks already inserted It's show biz, my Mello."

Ellis just nodded, realizing that Shango is nothing but a certified teacher hid underneath layers of gangsta-isms.

Shango continued:

"I'm just making a way out. And since we know they paying us to paint a picture that entertains them, we gonna do what we got to, to get paid! But you funny-ass Negus, with your suit and tie and degrees from Howard, Yale and Harvard, what you doing for ya people? 'Cept trying to find a Negus like me to exploit enough to get yo' bling-bling on and get yo' playa dreams wet? What I'm supposed to do, stay broke while I wait for you pedigreed Negus to create some job-training program? What, um supposed to tell my girl when she say the baby needs pampers, or the lights are out—oh, 'I'm sorry baby, I'm know the label is gonna pay me 7 figgas to be ignant, but I got morals'? See how long morals last when you hungry and starving, when you feeling like less than a man 'cause you can't do shit for your family! You Negus got other options, but half of you trying to be what I am. But I can't be you; it's too late for that.

"Yo, the struggle over," chuckled Shango, as if El was a fool. "Ain't nobody fighting to do nothing no more but to get paid and get their 15 minutes of fame or shame. I mean, what you doing to get the Negus on the frontline out of jail? You know the same Negus who got you your jobs at *The New York Pest*, *The Washington Pest*? The Negus who was burning shit down so bad in the Sixties that the Whiteboyz was afraid to go into the Hood and they recruited the Negus to mop up for them. You think it wasn't a rack of Black journalists capable of working for *Time* magazine, ABC, back in the day? You never even heard of people like Sam Lacy, Louis Martin, or Ida B. Wells, probably. You think Sam Russwurm was working for *The Times*? Like like you the first generation of smart, qualified Negus? I'm real sure there was some Negus on the plantation able to write in Arabic and do Algebra. I know you ain't up on that yet, so I'm dropping you a jewel. Live and learn, baby. Shiiiiit," spouted Shango, nonchalantly.

Ellis just looked at Shango, perplexed, trying to understand why this rich-ass mawfuka still so angry. *Why? For what?* Shango was angrier than Ellis ever let himself get, and Ellis ain't had nothing his whole life. Ellis felt the guilt rising in his soul, inescapable like the tide on Goree Island, where Africans were packed like sardines and shipped off to da New World.

Seeking to gain some common ground, but unable to meet Shango's well-versed rapid attacks, as Ellis tried to figure out how somebody that knew this much could do so much crazy shit, he stuttered…"I. I...I hear what your saying, you got everybody else down pack. You know what's wrong with everybody else, but I guess yo' shit don't stink. You got these young Negus running round thinking they gonna be the next Shango. Thinking that they gonna be able to survive six shootouts to go on and sign some eight-figga jeweled-out contract and date the next Pussygalore. When you Negus gon' talk about the whole rack of Negus that don't make it back from the shootout, that's serving bank numbers with no hope of parole and no lyrical skill enough fo' a record label to exploit? What 'bout dem Negus? What they 'posed to do when the clips empty? What they gonna do, say, cut…take two? Your video is crazy, gunning down kidz like that.

Shango just laughs as if he wants the whole world to hear his laugh, but anybody listening close can feel the pain layered into his chuckle. Maybe it was a cry that sounding like a laugh?

"You know, El, I like you. You got some heart, Sun. Believe me on some bad days, I done took Negus off the planet for less than what you kicking. You want me to make better shit, positive shit? Then stop making it so damn easy fo' me to do what I do. We got two fo' one specials on inner city murders this week. Kill one Negus and nobody gives a fuck; kill another and get 10 percent off ya next Glock. Negus in conditions where we got to kill. Believe me, all I want is peace, I got a half a bill in the bank, and you know I can barely enjoy the shit. But, I refuse to be a punk, respect is worth more than life for me right now. I know it's wrong for me to smoke dem fools in the video, but if Negus ain't got no love for me, then I handles my beef the only way Negus on the street respects," said Shango pointing his hands like guns and clicking his fingers. "You need to listen to that old shit by the Getto Boys, ummm. 'The Point Of No Return,' 'cause that's where I'm at. If I got to blast my way out, instead of begging the same cops that gunning fo' me too, for help, well then fuck it—it's *on*, baby. Negus step to me betta come correct-or they gets wet."

"What about your career? Your last video was banned by BBN, the Black Booty Network, for being too violent."

"Fuck them, they sellouts anyway. BBN shows in yo'

face ass all day and they want to talk about violence. They just mad that I was below their required booty-shots per minute. Hah, hah…You probably didn't even know how John Career started BBN?"

Looking at his recorder, Ellis responds. "No, I know he was a smart businessman."

"Well," said Shango "let me tell you. The mawfucka probably spent less than 2G's of his own money. Why? 'Cause when the city council was looking to give the cable franchise to a Black-owned corporation, he got with his white benefactors and his peeps in City Hall and fronted for them."

"What do you mean, he 'fronted'?"

"Well, he misrepresented his company as Black-owned and beat out other Black companies to get the cable contract— pure capitalism or exploitation, whatever the fuck you want to call it. He sold us out like a two for one meal deal on the first of the month. And you know what, Mr. Journalist? This Negus will go down in history as somebody great, and all the successful Negus will sing his praise. Sing his praise while they tearing Negus like me down."

"I didn't know about that," replied Ellis.

"Of course you didn't, Boss. But I bet you know about every incident with the law I've been through. See, most of you 'educated folks' ain't really educated. You just brainwashed. At least I know why I'm considered a menace to society. And it ain't got nothing to do with my criminal mindedness. See the reason why I'm portrayed as a menace is because I get Negus thinking. Even if I get you thinking 'bout the wrong shit, mawfukas fear me 'cause tomorrow, I might just flip my shit into something that wakes Negus up. But most of you educated cats is just trained. Trained like my dawgs, and you know my dawgs, they love their master-they'll kill somebody who fucks wit' me.

Shango stood and checked his satellite skypager. "I got to step. But it's been real, El. You think about what I said and be real as opposed to keeping it real. I gotta respect the way you kick it, most of the Negus that interview me either act afraid or spend they time trying to prove they ain't afraid- which is worse."

Ellis stands up and daps up Shango, having new

respect for his intelligence. This Negus was brilliant like Malcolm he was a clear shinning brilliance, hidden underneath a basket case image. "Shango, before you jet, what up in your future? More albums, movies, lectures?"

Shango grinned before saying, "Well, eventually….death."

3 MONTHS LATER

I stand alone/ but with many
Any who step to me/ gets plenty
To deal with
I flip
Like narco-acrobatics
Tongue twist/ like cunniliguist
Quick to spit shit/ and stay fit
Like them aerobic chicks
Can I kick it?
Yes I can
Through Space and Time zones
Chew words and Choke metaphors
That break bones
Within the exact expectations of Visions untold
Moms n Pops broke the mold
Words age/ but never grew old
God Damn, it's cold!
When I rip the stix/ I gets outlandish
Like gold teeth/ bottles of Cris/ and club flicks
I ticks/ before dropping bombs
Quick
Propel your mind through a star trek
Negus you sick/ unequipped to deal with
My wit or grit
Aw fuck it/ yous a ditz
Chew bits then spit mo better shit
That makes women come fast and quick
Kem
Made like Kam
I be the All and All
An that's All I am

PRACTICE

The day's practice was intense. It was as if everybody received an epiphany on how good this team could be and flipped it into high gear. From the coaching staff down to the ball boys to the vendors, hope of quality Hoop in the city, a team that could compete for the ring was spilling its way into everything. Everybody was working extra hard, which was the way U liked it. They worked the 22-1 full court press to perfection. The only problem was that it was the second team working it.

Marshall, a mean-eyed journeyman forward who came out of Juco, worked through the developmental Leagues and played in Spain, was as intense a player you would see. As usual he was drenched in sweat, and always found a way to outwork the better skilled players with bigger contracts by a sheer determination to pay his rent. While the other players learned to pace themselves during long practices to save enough energy to do multiple stunts and groupies later that night courtesy of the VIP section, Marshall worked from whistle to whistle and then put in additional hours in the weight room.

Today, his victim was Will Johnson, who he was currently making look like a bum. Marshall stood outside the paint, seeing trigger happy Swipes up top with the ball. The same Swipes who never saw a contested three-pointer he didn't like; and prepared himself to secure rebounding position. He leaned on Johnson's back and nudged him with his shoulder out of rebounding position. Although Johnson was one of the most talented players in the League, he never produced in a way the franchise had expected when they drafted him number 3. Johnson didn't realize that everybody in the League was near as good as everybody else and most in their mind was better than everybody else. He thought the League would anoint him, but they only gave you what you took.

As expected Swipes pulled up at the top of the arc for a three, the ball rotated toward the rim, but Marshall knew it was off. Then holding Johnson down with the left hand on his shoulder. He leaped, catching the ball as it bounced off the rim— *whooosh*! Slamming it through with his right hand. *"Screeeeech!"* from the whistle is the only sound heard as U breaks up the two-hour practice session for a breather.

As the players headed towards the bench, U called over Marshall and patted him on the butt, "Good play, Marsh."

Marshall grinned knowing that he'll definitely be getting more court time in the playoffs and the extra minutes will allow him to qualify for a bonus hidden in his contract. U looked over at Johnson, like a disappointed father.

"C'mere." Johnson knows what's coming next and dragged his feet cautiously towards U.

" Now, listen, Sun. How many times do I have to show you how to box out your man?"

"Put your ass on him! Arright!"

"Unhuh." Johnson just keeps his head down, too embarrassed to say anything.

"Will J, if you're getting beat up by your own bench players, what the hell you gonna do when we play Jersey? You got to get hungry. Get hungry, baby. That's the only we win in this League-staying hungry."

Johnson, nods and walked away dejected.

The *Scrrreeeeech* from U's whistle interrupts the 10-minute break. "Arrright, lets go," yells U as he threw the ball to point guard Isaiah Wilson. "Let's get this shit going; we got New Jersey in the Finals and I'm sure you all remember how they waxed that ass during the regular season, so lets pick it up a little bit." After doing his motivational Speaking 101 thing, U jogged over to his assistant coach, Tim Chassell, and whispered "Johnson's guaranteed is up next year; we're going to have to let the boy go."

Smiling, U whispered:

"Have you seen Ugonna?"

Chassell frowned, "I haven't seen him or heard from him. I don't know what's wrong with that kid. You know he's been hanging around Timmy, a guy who can't remember his own play, but can give you intimate details of every bar in the city. This is not like Ugonna to miss practice though. I mean this is the playoffs n shit," added Chassell. U said nothing but continued to stare onto the court with a blank face.

The season thus far was like a new edition of the Bad News Bears, U had whipped the Knicks into playoff form. It was nothing short of a miracle. By becoming the general manager and coach, he reworked the salary cap and outmaneuvered Kenyan death threats to sign the top draft pick and the League's first $350 million player—the Kenyan Giant

Ugonna G'dunkedon. Next he traded seven players, signed free-agent shooting guard Donald Swipes and began building the attitude of winning for a franchise that'd seen much better days

After reworking the salary cap to sign Ugonna, the Triple Zero mill man, the team picked up Isaiah Wilson, who reminded folks of Gary Payton—tough, gritty in-your-face point. He made folks forget about Illy Payne real quick. It wasn't a dream world. During the first 30 games, the Knicks went 14-16 and the articles began appearing that maybe, U didn't have the answers. Things changed quickly after Ugonna, who had sat out the first 20 games due to contract negotiations, came aboard and Isaiah finally healed a preseason injury to his Achilles tendon. Ugonna—a 7-3 power forward-swing man who perfected the crossover dunk—was like, *Whooa*. He was like Kevin Garnett with Karl Malone's body and Dirk Nowitzki's jumpshot, and finished like Stoudamire. After struggling early in the season, Ugonna scored 46 points and grabbed 27 rebounds and 4 assists against I.C. Reid, the League's top power forward, but not the smartest guy in the League (Some thought I.C. stood for "I can't"). After that game, Ugonna was a beast. He ended the season as the League's top scorer, rebounder, shot blocker, was third in steals and 4th in assists.

Ugonna was the leading force in turning the Knicks around—well, along with U's 22-1 defense, which could be shifted to a pressure defense, with Isaiah at the front and Ugonna at the back. After the All-Star break, the Knicks went 45-15. Despite the winning, the New York fans got sicker—if that could be possible.

Word had it they were intent on keeping their reputation as the most ruthless and lawless fans this side of an English soccer team. According to unnamed sources, the fans from Philadelphia, and Detroit, were encroaching on their territory as the group of fans most likely to burn, loot, and pillage, after a defeat, victory, bad call, road rage or pink slip.

During the last game of the season after the Knicks lost a season-ender double overtime game to Orlando that determined the top seed in the Eastern Conference, the fans got as buck-wild as a cop from the 47th precinct. Referee Barry

Cecil called a goal tending on Ugonna with 0.9 left on the clock and the game tied. At the end of the second overtime, 200 fans rushed to the floor and grabbed Cecil.

No one ever saw him again—except in pieces—mailed to NBA commissioner Pat Ross inside boxes with "We Wuz Robbed" written on them. This pressure was taking its toll on U, who was turning gray faster than a London morning. The pressure only grew as U wondered, where the hell is Ugonna?

DA MAYOR

Today was an early day for Ellis. He arrived on time to work with no fanfare or threats of bodily or economic harm. He even had enough time to stop at Munchies to grab a cup of the new Tanzanian coffee and a slice of Cinnamon Raisin Ezekiel bread with soy butter. *The world is beautiful,* he thought.

Without warning, Ellis suddenly noticed someone standing in the doorway to his bunker-slash-cubicle with walls.

Despite Ellis' desire to have a hassle- free day; enjoy the fruits of freedom and justice for all, he could feel the heat of interposition and nullification breathing hard down on his neck and, unfortunately, it also smelled like Sasha.

"Ellis! Yo, boy! The editor wants to talk to you!" yelled the rudest mammal this side of Orca.

"Who the hell you calling a boy? Either call me 'Sir' or 'Daddy.' You keep playing games and we gonna box. Capiche?" asked Ellis.

Sasha smacked her teeth and slunk back to her lair where she kept all the press passes of devoured journalists.

Ellis sauntered down the hallway to see what Nicole wanted. As he rounded the stairs, he began thinking about jetting his job. Not that he didn't enjoy what he was doing, but the meager pay and stress from all aspects of his life was kicking his ass. Once Ellis reached a conclusion about stepping, he almost never retracted. Throughout life most folks responded to stress with a wish list—something, or maybe one thing that if they had it, their life's problems would be solved. Of course, it's merely a placebo, but simply thinking about it gave you the luxury of procrastinating towards that real issue that was making you miserable. For Ellis, rather than deal with what he was supposed to be doing or responsible for, he queried reasons why he didn't come through that normally led to someone else's fault.

I've been getting less and less non-sports stories—and less sports stories for that matter, since the radio station piece. Shit, I wasn't no bad writer. My skills are madd tight-everybody agrees with that. I ain't trying to get played; if she comes out her bag with some tricks, I'll just flip her desk over and go back to school. Get a PhD. or something. Yeah, that sounds good. I'll have my joint in 4 years and be able to teach or write or do something better than this drama. They just got issues with giving a brotha what he deserves. First Negus got to deal with a system run by someone who's afraid of them, and now we got to handle these hungry as sista's thinking that we just ain't progresses as fast as they are 'cause it's our fault. Shit just 'cause the system giving them breaks we don't get they wanna think we ain't pulling no weight. Shit, I pull my own weight, and had to fight for every inch of it.

As he entered Nicole's office ready to do battle with the system's appointed authority figure, he immediately became distracted by Nicole's jovial mood. This seems to be happening a lot lately. Ellis figures that on-line interactive dating software must be working wonders for her life.

"Ellis, Come here, and sit down."

"Come here? Damn, I ain't no tantric master, how about some foreplay first?" mumbled Ellis under his breath.

"Would you like some coffee?" smiled Nicole.

"Naw, I'm a recovering Caffineholic."

"Well Ellis, New Haven Mayor Imani Moore is in town. She's the hottest thing on 3 continents and we've got the exclusive. How would you like the interview?"

Ellis stared into oblivion and went into a trance. Suddenly he's on Broadway, top hat and cane, grinning harder than Ben Vereen...okay, okay, he's channeling now becoming one with the Force...it's not working, he's still in dream-lala land...*Imani Moore...Ookay, okay, I'm back, I'm back.*

"Ellis, you okay?"

"Yeah, yeah, unhun," said Ellis, remembering the deep crush he had on Imani, ever since he saw her feature story in *Essence* magazine. He'd have to wear the good cologne to this interview, maybe throw on some Egyptian musk.

"So, do you want the story or what?"

"Yeah...I...I want her, I mean it," spilled out like drool.

Ellis Felt woozy, blinded by the right jab, like "Rocky" in the 12th round against Apollo Creed, 'Cut me, cut me Jake.' *My mind playing tricks on me. Maybe it was somethin' in that coffee. Maybe Sasha dropped a Mickey in it. Whatever, I used my secret weapon. The little known secret that always sobered me up quick. In times of stress and trouble, I simply visualize of Condi Rice naked—spread eagle—and I'm back! Oh, shit, that ain't working no more—damn! Okay, Rosanne?*

Suddenly with a whiff of mental smelling salt, he was back to the real world.

THE AUDUBON

Ellis hopped into the hooptie and headed uptown to the new Audubon Hotel. An African businessman from Ghana spent $200 million to build the Audubon Unity Hotel. It was beautiful and immediately reminded you of the new Huey Newton building in Oakland.

White marble, limestone with columns arranged like the great temple at Abu Simbel, marked the entrance. A nine-foot fountain stretch of water went 90 feet to the front glass doors. Clear crystal windows shaped like triangles, interconnected and reached up and shook hands with the sky. As you walked through the automatic doors, you were greeted with smiled and a glass of pure spring water from the mountains of Uganda. The lobby's layout was plush and the dark royal blue and gold Kente contrasted heavily against the white marble walls and front desk.

Damn, life is good.

Ellis smiled to himself while sipping his spring water-pinky extended.

"Greetings, brotha, how can we help you?"

Asked a young front desk attendant with glossed lips and her hair pushed up into a bun.

"I'm Ellis Rey from *The Nubian*. I'm here to interview Mayor Moore."

The attendant fingers quickly flickered on the keyboard, her dusky eyes stared at the screen intently. "Yes, your interview is listed. She'll be down shortly and will meet you in the Patrice Lumumba room. I'll escort you."

The Lumumba Room possessed a rare view. A 70-foot circular fish tank served as the room's centerpiece. The fish seem to swim in unison to the beat of Roy Ayers "Third Eye."

Imani Moore was pure phattness in all sense of the word. She started an international student organization as a sophomore at Hampton University that grew to over 50,000 members. It was there that she wrote her theory on "Ujaama: Intra-African Collective Economics" She believed "that by forming international collective partnerships with our brothas and sistas overseas, we can create industries which feed each other, and serve as a basis for a federated African state."

In working with the Economic Collective of West African States (ECOWAS), she was able to create a regional convertible currency, which Africans in the Diaspora— particularly those in the U.S.—could exchange for U.S. dollars. They could also exchange the new currencies for their own at equal rates when buying industrial equipment from the West or which Africans in the Diaspora could exchange for their own currencies at rates equal to their own. The whole process was kept alive by a $100 billion floating fund, supported in part by the Black Athlete Investment fund.

The result was that money flowed, equipment was brought and West Africa entered a golden age of industrialization using indigenous African techniques, as opposed to Europeanized models. Eventually, this led to Africa gaining a major share of the processor chip market. West Africa was no longer called the "Gold Coast;" it was now known as the "Tech Coast."

Moore was keenly responsible for this whole economic and technology explosion. She later formed a Black/Latino alliance, then pulled from her college contacts and entered politics. She returned to her hometown of New Haven, Connecticut, and was elected mayor at age 28.

There she established an economic exchange program, and allowed public funds to be invested in job development in Ghana. In return, the Ghanaians invested in New Haven, moving it from the 7th poorest city in the country to the 7th wealthiest—even ahead of Fairfax, Virginia. For this she was loved by the Blacks and Latinos and hailed internationally as one of the most powerful and respected women in the world. Just recently, she presided over a deal in which Yale University separated itself from New Haven proper. They had just renamed the city New Heaven. Aside from all this drama, the sista was only 32; phatt as all outdoors and a brotha like Ellis Rey the lucky Negus who got the interview. Who woulda thunk it?

Beeeeep...Beeeeep...

Who's paging me now? wondered Ellis bending to check his video page. He simultaneously senses someone behind him and the strong scent of Dolce Gabbona.

"Peace, brotha," smiled a tall thick beauty dressed impeccably. Her deep eyes fluttered slightly. Her lips were thick and glossed well. Ellis eyes traveled the length of her body, taking in all the curves, and indentations causing cerebral malfunctions that curled his toes and temporarily took his ability to speak. Ellis stood there smiling until his cerebral cortex realized the tragedy it was causing.

"Uh Mayor Moore, I'm Ellis Rey from *The Nubian*. I'm a big fan of your work," he said worrying if his natural is still looking decent.

"I'm a big fan of yours, also. I've followed the Knicks from yay-high, and read your column a lot. Your style is fluid and powerful." Ellis said, "thanks" blushing enough to make her compliment feel appreciated.

"I thought that would we start with talking about politics. I mean your success in the arena of politics, to be specific," said Ellis in his smooth, but mellow voice, simultaneously motioning for the waiter to bring him a bottle of Zambezi sparkling water. "When or why did you feel the need to enter politics?"

"Well," she said, while unconsciously stirring her finger in her glass of water, "I've been involved in organizing since my collegiate days at Hampton. Besides that, as you know, my grand father before he was killed was one of the original organizers of the New Haven Panther chapter, and set the outline for the group's structure. Secondly, my parents were teachers and one of the major tools that they taught us growing up—"

"—Us?" interrupted Ellis.

"Yes, me and my brother Re. He died during the rebellions, shot down by the Police on his way home from work. They said they thought he was a looter. A looter in a two-grand suit?"

"I'm sorry."

"Yeah, well, as I was saying, or attempting to say, I believe that organizing is in my blood and my parents prepared me well to become a leader. We didn't just learn about Martin and Malcolm. I was learning Nkrumah's political theories, studying Cheik Anta Diop's work, and people like Noam Chomsky by the time I was twelve. And importantly, we didn't just study this material; we had to find ways to apply what we learned to current international, and national politics. My parents created a game which allowed us to do that, kind of like 'Monopoly' or 'Life', you know?" she said, taking a short break and sipping on her water.

"I'm impressed. How did you pull off the deal with the Ghanaians and the city of New Haven?"

"Well," laughs Imani, "actually I received some opposition from the state department, and federal officials who make it a policy to prevent any concrete interaction between the Africans here and those back home, unless it's co-opted and controlled by the multi-national corporations. However, through the work of former Virginia Governor Willdon, who established trade agencies for intercontinental commerce, I was able to utilize the resources of Africa and the technical know-how that Blackfolks over here have.

"Things had been extremely grim in New Haven, since the closure of Olin and the cut backs at Yale University, the only two major employers in the city. So, when I broached the idea of establishing a plant that would create 10,000 jobs within four years, the normally inactive Nubian population along with the Latinos decided that they would ensure that the city administrators who opposed the plan would do so at the cost of their elected seats.

"I had also gained some valuable support on the continent from Ghana's president and the cooperative support of Ecowas during the 54th Pan-Afrikan conference in Abuja," she said.

She continued, "as you know, brotha, when I became active in all this stuff, it was at a time when Black folk saw no other way but to come together. After the era of Radical

Republicanism, we all understood-finally, in clear and exact terms—that we had to do for self, here and back home. Any pretensions of mainstream assimilation, moved to the periphery. C'mon, you know that when they revoked Justice Tom from the High Court on charges that he lied during the confirmation hearings, after he did their dirty work for ten years; You knew what time it was? What I'm saying is nothing new. And certainly nothing that others didn't already state."

On his way back to the office, Ellis couldn't stop thinking about what homegirl was doing. She was the real deal. And she knew so much about us, and our history that he actually felt ashamed at his ignorance on the subject-which had to be a first. Not about his ignorance. Shit, he was proud to tell mawfukas he didn't know about something and didn't give a shit that he was ignorant—he actually took some pride in not knowing shit that didn't fit into his world. It fit into his image as an 'not-giving-a-shit Negus.' Not giving a shit had crazy currency in da Hood. However, after meeting Imani and seeing how she spit her facts and backed it up—this was the first time he actually cared about how ignorant he was. Luckily, he'd already read several articles on her, or he would have appeared a lot more dumber.

Ellis rushed back to the office to download his copy into his computer and finish his article with a flourish. Tomorrow was a sports day and he'd have to cover the Knicks playoff game against New Jersey. Jersey had been talking crazy shit in the press, especially their backup center and knowing the climate at the garden; he had a feeling that some extra-curricular festivities might be erupting in between the action on the hardwood.

THE GARDEN

Was jam-packed! Orange and Blue everywhere. The joint was humming like the excitement of a Tyson fight. Celebs began making their way into the prime real estate, courtside, while die hard Knick fans up in the nose bleeds began gargling with brew as they prepared to unleash their pent upped barrage of profanities at the opposing team, the Refs, and anyone in between. Somebody'd hear them.

The Knicks were expected to do work tonight and everybody kept saying that this might be their year. They had shocked the League during the regular season and the expectations, just like the fans…were high. Ellis made his way down to the floor level and while the players warmed up and chatted with assistant coach Tommy Davis.

"Yo, Tom, what up?"

"Winning baby, just winning," said Tommy, dapping Ellis up, giving his usual nonchalant reply. Ellis handed him a piece of chewing gum and gazed at New Jersey warming up. They had a good team, but according to Tommy, "New York was going to kill all that noise with some fundamental drama-ending kick-ass."

Ellis waved at U, as he chitchatted his way to the reporter's table, near the Nets basket. *U looked serious*, thought Ellis. *I mean, he was always serious, but tonight he looked it.* He did take some time out to stop by the table as Ellis attempted to gain some control on his interactive stat hook-up.

Things had changed a lot since Yusef joined the League nearly twenty years ago. Now each writer on the floor had an mini-palm with holographic video replay screens, set up on a Wifi system into the NBA Super-Computer, which allowed a megaton of info to be share, crossed-examined and head ached throughout the game. Every second, every shot, assist, steal, foul, three pointer was quantified in a statistical analysis that'd give a German physicist a nosebleed. Ellis tried to stay away from that crap. *I didn't feel the need to know a players', stat scores, favorite foods, and total career fouls committed during the first three minutes of the third quarter. Plus, the mouthpiece made him feel like a cyborg.* He rationalized.

"The usual, Mr. Rey?" said Renee, one of the Knick gals, who provided media with whatever they needed. "Yeah, Renee," nodded Ellis eagerly awaiting his ginseng soda and glazed cashews just as tip off was getting underway. What a lot of folks never understood about the media was the perks that the teams provided. You were like sports royalty. So many were out of shape due to all the free meals the teams provided.

U was starting the usual lineup, Isaiah Wilson at the point, Jones, Hardaway, Johnson and D. Marshall, who was normally the sixth man, 'cept that Ugonna G'dunkedon, the 'Triple Zero Mill-man, had missed the previous practice and showed up late for the game. So U decided to let him sit for a while. Everybody knew that Ugonna was gonna get beaucoup playing time, since U wasn't about to let the playoffs slip away due to the tardiness of his star player.

Tip-off started the momentum in the Nets favor. Despite all the hoopla, New Jersey always brought it, and were tough inside. New York was sorely missing Ugonna's rebounding and inside presence, plus Teller, New Jersey's 2-guard, was lighting up the three point and four point bonus areas. After the first quarter, New Jersey was ahead by seven. At the start of the second quarter, the chants of "Defense, Defense, Defense," spread through the crowd like mustard on rye. In the huddle, the Knicks got the hint. U looking around the huddle and glancing at his young center and said "Defense, Defense!"

The look made the third year player think twice about whether buying that house in Stamford was such a good idea.

"We've got to rebound better.

Box out! And lets kick it out quick to the guards on the outlet passes.

We're holding the rock to long and we need to get the fast break going.

Ugonna, you're in for Marshall and Akhmed, you're in for Hardaway—we're going big," said U. As the players joined hands in the huddle and said in unison "What's the word? Hard work!"

The second quarter began with a steal by Ugonna, who took it the length of the court and dished on a drive to the hole with his left to Johnson, who almost tore off the rim with a tongue-wagging, body-squirming, dunk! After that, New York went on a 20-4 run which broke the game wide open. After the second quarter, Jersey never recovered and got stomped. The Knicks ended up sweeping New Jersey 4-0 and went on to the conference Finals, where they almost pulled the upset of the century and took Orlando to seven games. If Ugonna, hadn't pulled his Achilles tendon in game four, who knows?

The following year was the Knicks year belonged to the Knicks, after U made room in the salary cap for Craig Moncrief, the all-League two-guard with the Cincinnati Police Department's "shoot-first-ask-questions-later" mentality.

After acquiring Moncrief, the Knicks crushed all competition and went on to win the title. At least that's what they told Ellis when he woke up.

WELCOME TO LA-LA LAND

After seeing the Knicks dust off New Jersey in Game One, Ellis decided to trek uptown to Imani's and catch a meal. U was too busy to hang, so Ellis jetted up there solo. It took him an hour to find a decent parking space and another twenty minutes to figure out what was wrong with his Boot-camp anti-theft device. He finally got the shit working correctly and quickstepped it up the block to Imani's.

Imani's had this shrimp with angel-hair pasta dish that had Ellis name written all over it. His mouth began watering as he began thinking about the sliced green peppers and mushrooms sautéed in butter and garlic sauce had him feigning for the dish in the way that he was feigning for Maya. But she was in DC and the dish was a lot closer—just a half a block away. *Oh, the things I'm gonna do to that shrimp were sicker than an R. Kelly lookalike video,* thought Ellis.

Ellis' cuisine-driven libido made him think. *Why, when you're by your damnsome, did eating seem so important—practically erotic? Wait a minute—do I really want to think about this shit while eating? I mean I never made love to a sammich before; would that be considered cheating?*

Seeing that traffic was backed up due to a show at the Apollo, Ellis decided to cross the street-Brooklyn zoo style. He cut through one car and stood on the median, looking for an opening. Only one line of traffic stood between him and his grub. As soon as a hole opened, he was going to hit it like Barry Sanders on crack. Ellis was far from a math major, or disciple of quantum physics, more physical ed., than quantum. But he had an uncanny ability to understand, time speed and space. He was able to cut angles on a court and beat a player to a spot, or surprise a defender with a sudden burst of quickness that would leave opposition as if their feet were stuck in cement. His timing was so acute that he often would catch the opposing players shot and tip it towards his basket like Bill Russell. The thing about athletes former or current is that they looked at every physical action as a challenge, a competition. Today it was him against the traffic and just like he did when he scored thirty against Tweak Williams, an all-American guard at Stevenson, he'd respond. The only problem was that Tweak was only about 165 pounds and a 4.2 sprinter-today the opposition was 5,000 pounds and a step or two quicker than a hungry cheetah.

Suddenly it was open, he made the dash....*Screeeeeeeeeeeeech!* One cabbie doing 90 came a foot away from sending Ellis to that old press box in the sky. Seeing him haggard, the cabbie leaned out and screamed, "Get fuck outta way, asshole!" He had some accent and although Ellis couldn't quite understand him, the sign language made it very clear.

Just being himself, Ellis returned the love by giving him the finger yelling "Fuck you, Osama—that's why I'm giving INS your license plate!"

This all happened in a matter of seconds, which gave him another five seconds to get across the street before this Hyundai doing sixty got too close. To his right he quick-peeked this brown-skinned bowlegged sista with a tiny T-shirt that cut off at her midriff and jeans that clung to her ass more vigorously than a breast-feeding baby to a nipple.

Damn!

The glance cost him another 2.5 seconds off his dash, which still gave him another 2.5 seconds to get across the street and pay his debt to his stomach. Unexpectedly or for some uncanny—no, for some sick reason—the car sped up... Ellis wasn't no Banneker, but he understood speed, time, and space, and for this reason he braced himself. It took Ellis 0.5 seconds, which is enough time to get off a three-pointer, to realize that he wasn't going to be having shrimp tonight. *Screeeeeeeeeeeeeech! Thud!*

"Ugh!"

The car reversed, then shifted back into drive and curled around Ellis who lay sprawled out legs twitching frantically. Slowly, he felt his consciousness leaving and wondered if he'd still be able to have kidz. If this was his last call, maybe he could scribble out on the sidewalk in his own blood for someone to run over to Imani's and grab him one 'scrimp.' At least that way if the afterlife had a long line, he wouldn't be hungry. He felt like Foreman in Round 8 during the Rumble in the Jungle. Bomay'e, Bomay'e—*Damn! Somebody don' hexed me.* Beyond woozy, wobbling, head spinning, going down, he was going down for the count. The last thing he remembered as the sped off, was a Cheney-Bush bumper sticker on his rear fender-*fucken loser.*

"Spell Iowa, mawfucker, IOWA."

THE C, THE O, THE M, THE A (THE MIDDLE PASSAGE)

Ellis was awake. Well, sort of. He was conscious, but in a floating in a dream-like state. It was as if his body and mind were blended into the same oneness. Everything was connected; everything was made of the same form. Inexplicable his mouth began to move and the words came out:

I am the Supreme Divinity
Soul is of Heaven, the body belongs to Earth
My mind has pure thoughts, so my soul and life force are pure
Behold I am the heir of eternity, everlastingness has been given to
me

I have gained power in the water as I conquered Set: Greed Lust and Ignorance
I know my heart, I have gained power over my heart
The power is within me to open all doors in Heaven and Earth
I am a spirit, with my soul

Although Ellis' mouth spoke the words it was more like the words spoke themselves. They were the ancient Nile valley term Hekau: words of power. Words that broached the space-time continuum and connected the souls of the Heavens with those existing in the physical world. Words that brought matter and form into existence. Ellis laid on his back-dressed in a white linen robe. Within a millisecond, a figure appeared-shining brightly, moving closer and closer. Weirdly, Ellis was moving too—but vertically. This shining figure appeared to float out of a portal of the nothingness that surrounded him. He wanted to be nervous, sought his adrenals to supply him with enough cortisol necessary to run for shelter-but he remained fearless, even against his own will in a supreme state of peace. Again Ellis tried to move, but couldn't. The figure got closer. Jesus? *Naw, it won't Jesus, was it? Was this Heaven? Judgment time? I hoped not*, thought Ellis, wondering if *bad breathe could send you to hell?*

Unable to speak or move, he could only think. The figure was directly in front of him. Instantly, he recognized him and knew who he was. He had no idea how or why he knew this, he just did. Ptah was short and brown little man with a sly smile. He held a staff with both hands that seemed taller than he was. He spoke, but did not move his lips. Ptah had existed before history and was considered a God by ancient Nile Valley civilizations He was of the ancient ones, the fashioner, and the developer-he who raised Kemet from the mud of the Nile into its foundation.

He was the builder of the city of AN, also called ON, later called Heliopolis by Greeks. And shockingly, he looked a lot like Ellis' grandfather Peter. Ellis had no idea, how he knew these things, but he did. His mind was plugged into some universal database, where everyone knew everything. There were no more secrets nor ignorance, nor separation. He had entered the subjective realm.

HEKA!

His voice began to resonate...
"Welcome, sleeping one."
Ellis said nothing.
Ptah smiles.
"Do not be afraid. I am of the ancient ones, the father of Ra, who was the father of Set, Auser, and Aset whom you call Osiris and Isis, who gave you the falcon Heru. Your blood flows back to us—it is we who have brought you forth. Ye are Godz—but alas, now you only sleep. It is time to reawaken the lost and found."

His words vibrated throughout Ellis soul and he

overstood everything that he meant. It was as if his brain had been awakened, given birth to. His mind had traveled through its own birth canal, simultaneously wiping away the sludge and phlegm of ignorance. It was as if for this moment in time his mind was at total peace. All the self-imposed, fear-driven barriers that he'd built up since he heard his first "No," had been washed away by the purest of life-giving water. He realized that all of the fears he'd given power to-had no power except what he gave them-all limitations were self-imposed. He felt as if he were in communion with the whole universe.

Yes, you are," says Ptah, instantly reading his thoughts.

"We have returned to awaken the sleeping Godz.

The universe pains at the horrors endured here.

Did we not leave you enough to remember the old ways by?

You have discarded your divinity for chariots of steel, sandals that do not allow the feet to breathe and painted papyrus that you value more than your life.

You have given value to that which neither creates nor destroys

That which neither has life nor can give it

You have fallen quickly.

How long did you think we'd be away?

Was one Sar too long!

3,600 years too long?

It was a mere pittance!

A mere grain in the vault of eternity-Worry no more, we are here. Here…we be…"

Suddenly Ellis was asleep again.

RESURRECTION

Ellis was instantly awakened while a tingling arose through his spine. A golden light emerged from his body's solar plexus region just above his navel, causing his body to glow like a miniature sun, spreading light everywhere. A throne appeared to him in a flash. The great Olive green God-Auser sat nobly, flask and flail with the white crown. The Neter or God of judgment, called Osiris by the Greeks, sat solemnly as a bird-headed man, an ibis, talked to him in some forgotten language.

The ibis-headed man was named Tehuti, also called

Thoth, the God of wisdom and the God of the scribes-the written word. Although they were "Godz," Ellis became immediately aware they these beings were still only an aspect of the ALL. That all-powerful force that collectively gave existence to these beings—those who were our ancestors and that we all were a part of.

Ellis gazed to his left and right and realized that he was not the only one there. There were hundreds, thousands, hundreds of thousands of awakened women, a lesser number of men, and more beautiful children than anything else, wondrously filling the space of several auditoriums. For whatever reason, they all had been pulled out of their daily consciousness; their daily lives to hear this message. Their minds were empty of the daily drizzle of questions and worries. What needed to be done at work? What was going on with their children? Were they getting fat? Was their mate cheating? Were they getting the latest XBOX for Christmas? It was a period of Tabla Rasa, and they had no choice, more importantly a no desire for anything but to listen.

Auser glances at the multitude and speaks:
"You are not the first or the last.
 We have sent many into the world.
Moses was one of our students, as you are, so too was he—skeptical.
Do not be amazed that I am reading your thoughts before they are complete.
I am the judge of those who live—so you'd best come correct," he said with a sly grin, which made the other Neteru (Godz) giggle.

What the hell was going on? Ellis began to wonder. *Was this a dream?* It didn't fit into anything that he knew about the afterlife. Where was the bearded old man sitting on a throne? The angels dressed in white or that red guy with a pitchfork?
None of this made sense.
Why me?
What do you want with me?
Am I dead?
Is this judgment for me?

174

Tehuti begins writing quicker than light with a reed and says,

"You are one of many pulled from this wicked time.
This time of hueman kind,
when Neters have descended into the depths of animal instinct.
Where you have forgotten the meaning of the Sphinx, where the righteous, the salt of the Earth have lost their savor.
Did you think we'd be gone so long?
Don't answer;
Although you could and should
We encoded our knowledge into your DNA and still you sleep
I'm sure it probably hurts your brain to think.
Where are your thinkers?
More importantly where are the knowers? Are there any left?
This is why we pulled you in—our descendents.
You to whom we left the pyramids and texts long enough to wrap around Ki-ten times—
Have you now forgotten who and what you are?
Still you all seek to be Osiris?
So full of yourselves you humans, so smug in your assumed righteousness.
All of you have become judges and in doing so have brought the judgments you issued upon yourselves.
Hah!
Has the nation taken on itself the role of Judgment?
You strain at a gnat, but remain blind to the elephant.
The nation of you sleep."

Auser grins.
"Tehuti, don't be too hard on them; they are just children.
Even your best students took some time to catch on.
Moses wasn't the best of students at first, now, was he?
He definitely had trouble expressing himself.
Everybody can't be like Enoch, or Siddharta."

Suddenly, Ellis was asleep, again.

THE MIDDLE PASSAGE

Ellis was moving, quick, quickly, quicker...than the speed of light. The various strands of light wizzed by him as if they were moving in slow motion, but they weren't. He wanted to reach out and touch it to feel it, but couldn't. He stood still. Arms crossed, right over left like a mummy. In fact, he wasn't really moving; it was as if time and space were moving past him. He was gradually surrounded by black gooey darkness that pulled at his soul. As if he were tossed through this gigantic black hole, traveling universes in milliseconds. Then through the denseness of space, he saw it: a gigantic star——no, a planet. A shining planet coming directly towards him, speeding, faster, faster, an intensely bright light. ...then sudden impact!

Aaaaaaaaaaaaah!

Ellis opened his eyes, what he saw was astonishing. He was in a room built of emerald and Lapis Lazuli. He laid silently in his pure white linen, surrounded by three similarly dressed brothas.

They spoke to each other telepathically, and Ellis was allowed to eavesdrop. Ellis heard their minds, and did, but did not understand them. They were soldiers-warriors. Not war-like, but soldiers of righteousness. Their mission was to maintain the balance in the Universe. Their power was in their minds. Those forces considered good never sought to conquer evil or negative forces. Their job was to ensure that neither side overpowered the other. Balance was the key to the Universe. If they eliminated all those forces considered evil, or negative, then it would merely manifest in another form. Energy cannot be destroyed, only its form altered.

Eons ago, at least billions of what we call years ago, these beings were able to master their physical selves. Since then they continued to evolved and now stood as the guardians of the Universe. The keeper of the ME's. They commanded the planet of the Crossing. It was a planet, and a spaceship, alive, and breathing, akin to something far beyond human understanding of technology. Astronomers called it the 10th planet and it traveled throughout our solar system on a path counter clockwise to the other 9 planets. It was the planet that crashed into the Earth-then called Tiamat, cleaving from it the Moon and Asteroid Belt, billions of years ago.

They walked over and smiled. For universal beings the smile was the inter-universal, inter-dimensional vow of peace and no harm. Only those beings at the lowest level of "intelligence" and neo-civilization would ever violate its contract. It was for that reason that many intelligent beings fled the Earth, since Earth Beings, humans alone, among 38 billion advanced civilizations were the only ones to violate this inter-universal contract. With humans a smile often preceded a negative action even the lowest action—murder.

One of these brown giants placed something on Ellis' head. It looked liked headphones. Ellis brain swirled like a reel-to-reel tape deck, playing back his every memory and thought into a database of the Akashic Records, the universal library where every thought, and deed was recorded.

Within a matter of milliseconds he was reliving his birth, speeding through his mothers canal into the world—*aaa aaaaaah! The light—it's bright.* Growing quickly, *there's dad, my brotha Greg playing ball and me, my mother crying, looking out the window as my father walked away, out of our lives. Moving faster, faster. My first day of high school, my shirt bloodied from a fight, there's Lester-fucken punk, I'm a kick his ass. Graduation, Moms smiling, waving, pictures-college. The images moved quicker, faster turning into blurs. There's Maya, she's crying in her apartment in DC There's Jay, and Nicole. The images move even faster, faster, faster, suddenly I'm at 125th crossing the street again. The taxi, ah ha you missed-bastard. No! Lookout, the car screeeeeeeeeeeeeeeeech!*

LIGHTS, CAMERAS, ACTION-AWAKE!

I'm awake. No, Not dreaming, I'm awake! I'm awake, thought Ellis ecstatically. He opened his mouth to speak, and it's like mumble mouth. His tongue is practically glued to his mouth. So what comes out is *"mmmrmrm, mrmrmmrm,"* something that only Frankenstein, the Incredible Hulk or maybe James Brown, or Jesse might understand. Finally, the nurse turned around and gaped, mouth wide open, at Ellis.

"You're talking? You're talking?"

Damn! Alzheimer's kicking in early, thought Ellis, but the only thing that comes out is *"mmmmmmrmrrmr, mmmrerrrea, rur, rura."*

She stared, at Ellis like was a ghost. Like she's angry that he had the nerve to wake up on her shift. She had gotten used to the daily routine over the past year, come in and clean up, check the IV, and fantasize about what she'd do to Ellis, if he were awake and her boyfriend out of town. She wasn't ready for this.

"You're not 'posed to be talking;
You haven't spoke in two years."
Ellis looks at her like she's nuts.
'Roo RREERS?
"Dmmmn, drue drereous? Roo Reers!"

BACK TO LIFE: 2020 A.D.

After running out of Ellis' hospital room like her panties were on fire, the nurse returned in two minutes with a bunch of smiling doctors, one with a camera. Ellis thought he'd won Family Publishers Clearinghouse or maybe Reader's Digest. *This is great! After all those guaranteed winner letters and 3,400 subscriptions it finally paid off. Finally.*

"Welcome back, Mr. Jackson," said the tall goofy one. Well, the tall goofier one. "You've been away for quite some time now; how does it feel?"

Ellis wanted to tell him that it felt like a Mack truck had hit him, but seeing his earlier success with words, he just decided to smile.

Just smile until they decide to leave me the hell alone.

Then suddenly, without the slightest warning or provocation, Ellis stomach began rumbling and immediately the big one erupted—Olde Yeller slipping through clenched butt cheeks, bringing forth the combined stench of hell and 20,000 episodes of Jerry Springer. A fart so monstrous that he felt the earth beneath him quiver, while his colon shifted into a 180-degree angle. A cloud of funk darkened the room and the bed shook like the Exorcist.

The smiled were now gone, replaced by watery eyes and squinted nostrils.

Damn, I guess I had been holding that one for a while. Ellis thought. He was pissed. In the nearly thirty years of playing the fart game for keeps, he had never been caught. Well, never in an official way that he'd ever admit to without some DNA samples and signed affidavits. He had blamed everyone from his 96-year old grandmother, to his nephew on Ritalin, to El Nino for his foul eruptions, but today was the day of reckoning. Alas, a Hiroshimic jammy and—yes, he alone—would have take responsibility for it. Alas, farting is such sweet sorrow.

With their marking boards held over their noses, the doctors whispered something and nodded their heads in unison and as quickly as they came, they left. Ellis sadly only had one question: *Where's Ed McMahon and Dick Clark?*

THREE DAYS HENCE

After three days of being alive again, Ellis had no desire to start from the beginning. He wanted to skip through all the remedial shit and go right back into being that old wise cracking individual, whom the world thought gone for good, after being struck in that hit and run.

All he could remember about the hit was the driver's face-ugly and the diplomatic license tags. For some reason, putting individuals with diplomatic immunity behind the wheel was a dangerous thing. It seemed that every time that London or Wall Street lowered the rate of exchange on their currencies, they'd even things up by taking out somebody on the street.

His body was sluggish and weak. His eyes reddish, easily irritated by the bright light, but his senses were sharp. Ellis could tell when someone was coming towards his room as soon as they left the elevator. He could even hear conversations halfway down the hall. *Them nurses talked too damn much. Homegirl knew she was wrong—makin' all them long distance phone calls to straighten out her credit, while she 'posed to be working.*

Ellis still couldn't believe that he was in a coma for two damn years.

What's Maya's doing right now, he wondered—*probably married with kidz to some wannabe Cosby-type. Shit, she betta not be married or it's gonna be Hell up in Harlem. Your woman couldn't step out on you when you was in a coma, right? That was like losing your starting position while on injured reserve-shit just wasn't Kosher. If she was dumping him, she'd have to do it when he was healthy, at least that way he'd be fully able to experience the humiliation aspect of it.*

Was The Nubian *still around? How did the Knicks do? Did they win the title? How was my family? Uncle Breeze? Did they even know what happened to me? What if no one knew where the hell I was? Where were the flowers, cards, the ice cream? I bet everybody else that come out of a coma have flowers, cards, ice creaaaam! But let a Negus go into a coma, when he wake up all he got is a damn docta bill. Damn, I woulda took a balloon with my name, even a get well yo' on it.*

Ellis' incessant worrying simply caused his body to overload and shut down. In his thirty years of existence, he rarely ever enjoyed a good sleep. Dealing with domestic violence, growing up in the noisy-ass Projects, where people sung and blasted music outside your window till about 2 am, caused him to be unable to ever simply fall asleep easily again. The only time this was not the case, was when he was just so dead tired that parasympathetic organs simply took over and took what they needed in order to rebuild his body. After fighting a good fight for 34 minutes, as usual sleep wins by TKO.

Three a.m. Ellis re-awoke, bored as hell, wondering if he can pull himself together enough to simply walk out of the hospital. He didn't trust doctors that much and wanted to find something familiar to touch base with—someone someone familiar.

Shit, it's 3 a.m., he thought. *Who the hell can I talk to? I know what I'll do, maybe I'll check my answering service. Let's see if I can remember the code. Okay, 1-800-343-Call.* Ellis excitedly dialed the number…. "Beep…*beep.* Please enter your password." *Okay, okay I remember. My password is "Duke sucks."*

After entering his password, the computerized voice took over. "You have accumulated 10,407 messages. Please enter your smart-card number, social security or national identification numbers now in order to access your messages."

Okay. He enters his social security; *What the hell is a 'smart card'? What about a dumb card? 'Cause anybody who gives me credit, expecting me to pay them back, is dumb as shit.*

Once again the computerized voice spoke: "I'm sorry, but you will be unable to access your messages until your account has been settled. Your current balance is $2,366.

Would you like to pay by smart-card deduction, account transfer or automated banking account debit? According to federal statute E-187D, we have the authority to withhold additional credit and garnish taxable assets. Statute E-187D The National Debt Personal Responsibility Act, established in June of 2006, provides that all personal credit information and financial obligations are now consolidated under the auspices of the I.R.S. and Treasury Department's Debt Reconciliation Bureau. As passed by Congress in order to conform to European Economic Union standards for fiscal responsibility each member country will not only decrease the national debt to GNP levels to less than 3 percent, but that each citizen shall participate in voluntary governmental debt reduction or be subject to wage garnishment, restriction of future credit and asset liquidation. Exemptions are available to selected individuals and or multi-national corporations involved in high-tech and national defense and any known relatives of Donald Rumsfield, George W. Bush, or Dick Cheney. Violations of this act are punishable by either a prison sentence of *10-15 years or 16 continuous hours of Vanilla Ice's return LP, "Who Stole the Hootie Mack?"*

"If you are a U.S. racial minority you may be eligible for a low-interest debt consolidation loan—available when you complete applications for your smart-card available at local banks. Please dial 1-976-333-1776 for further information. Each call costs $7.60 per minute and is recorded. Thank you."

By the time the phone message ended, Ellis was sound asleep and snoring harder than a 400-pound smoker with high cholesterol and arteries packed tighter than a cat suit on Serena's ass. Forty-eight hours later Ellis awoke to the sounds papers ruffling and whispering. "Why *I* got to always be the one working weekends? I got a life. If you paid me some real money, my weekends might improve."

Ellis slowly opened his eyes seeing this sexy, svelte ebony figure in a tight fitting nurses uniform bending over. Her perfume smelled so good it was intoxicating. It had been such a long time since he had some that anything with a twat, was looking like Halle. This girl was fine as shit. More though like a Teresa Randle type with a little more thickness to her. Ellis looked as she continued working. The way she moved, and held her arms—skin like silk, ass like whoa! He contemplated what he would do to her if given the right opportunity, along with a six-pack of herbal Viagra. Maybe lean her over the hospital bed, take a running start and….

Slowly the sheet located over his groin began to rise slowly, slowly, until at full mast. The nurse swirled around and suddenly and stood eyeball to sheet, she backed away for a quick sec, then stared at an embarrassed grinning Ellis who desperately wanted to say in his bad Scarface imitation, "say hullo to my little friend," but too embarrassed to say anything.

"Well, at least it's still working," she smiled; seductively rolling her eyes, and looking at the flag pole once more before she walked out shaking her head, wishing she was single. Ellis just lay there until his shame knocked the wind out of his sails.

I got to get out of here, Ellis thought to himself with anxiety based on experience. He never trusted hospitals. One of his professors called the majority of our health problems "iatrogenic." He never grasped the meaning, didn't care to so long as he was eligible to play Hoop. Still he knew it was something bad. In his opinion they treated Blackfolks like a conveyer belt—get 'em in and out, never really listening to us, nor figuring out what the hell was wrong. One of his biggest fears about hospitals was going in for a blood test, and ended up getting the operation that the guy in the next room was supposed to get. Come to think about it, he never had any health issues in his life until getting vaccinated for college. At that point, his anxiety pushed Maya's cell phone number out of his subconscious. He nervously dialed Maya's cell number.

"The number you dialed is no longer in service."

Shit, Uncle Breeze don't have a phone. Jay? Shit, that Negus got new digits every other week. I got to get out of this twilight zone. Then it hit him, *'I got an idea: why not call Nicole and find out if I still got a job at* The Nubian?*"*

Ellis anxiously dialed the number to *The Nubian* and grew excited as the phone began to ring. All types of thoughts ran through his head. Of course, they'd be excited to hear from him, right? He could just play it off with a mellow *"What's up? Naw.*

Guess who?

I'mmmm Baaack!

Whoop there it is!
Who's Bad?
Mamma say mamasa mamacusa…
Finally the phone stopped ringing…
"I'm sorry the number you dialed is no longer in service, please check again."
"Damn!"

Ellis slammed his head viciously against the pillow. His mind disoriented, he felt trapped like a caged pigeon. On someone else's schedule. He hated that shit.

My mind flashes like a neon sign/ No ones home
Words flutter out of the basement of my mouth
like some synthetic drone
they stare in amazement
That I haven't flipped
Or crossed-over
like Chris Smith
or
Skip-to-my-Lou
Do You
Emotions transform into words
now Blurred
but neva scured
We herd like Bills
Shatter domes on the Hill
As we trip and spill
knowledge

Words attempted to fly through Ellis head as he reverted back to his enclosed garden of thought. At times, his mind was his best friend. He could and normally did, create outrageous fictional moments when closed in or trapped by his often self-imposed negative circumstances.

Simultaneously his mind could be his worst enemy. He thought he thought too much sometimes. Today, he couldn't even get the lyrics together. All he could do was stare out his pigeon shit-filled window into the grayish sky.

Too much/ too many people/
A frown hung around his face like a crown to the

wooly headed ones called an afro. Ellis stared out the window feeling smaller than he'd ever felt until his blood red eyes begin to slowly droop as he transitions into the realm of Rapid Eye Movement. That's the thing about the body; it takes what it wants when it wants it. Right now it wanted rest.

ON THE ONE, TWOS….

At age 50 sumpin' or maybe 60, still got the madd skills on the set, he thought to himself in between sips of his favorite concoction—a 40-ounce of X ale mixed with lemons and one lime-shaken vigorously, but not stirred. In the basement of his spot was his personal Fort Knox that began with his three Numark TTX21 Limited Edition black and gold turntables with matching black and gold groovemaster limited edition cartridges. On a shelf above the turntables, lay the Akai MPC 12000, while his turntables were hooked up to either his Numark PDM22 or Tascam X-21 digital mixers with AKG K540-DF headphones and Crown power tech amp.

His system kicked with Cerwin Vega three way speakers. To top it off, he was one of the few individuals left with a Roland 808 drum machine. He had every Disco break beat in the world, in original copy, not the re-mastered ones. His walls were fireproofed and sprinkler system was intact. His whole setup was like something out of Conspiracy Theory. According to Unk Breeze, all he had to do was scratch "Great to be here," in a certain way and C90 plastic explosives would take up the whole block.

Right now, he was in the midst of cutting up "Last night changed it all," for probably the 12,000[th] time. Headphones, hanging between his shoulder and ear, he concentrated intensely as he put needle to the groove and made the wax spit back at him.

Hello, heh, heh, heh, heh, hello, wic, wick, wic, wic wick/ Hello, hey, hey, hey woman where was you at last night/ Hello, hey, hello, hey hey, hey.

"Damn! This mix so nice, I'mma put it on the market UB's, naw, UBBC, "Unk Breeze's Before Commercial? Yeah, B.C. School mixed tapes."

The thought excited him for a quick second until he realized 20 minutes into the mix that he forgot to turn the

PDL-247 CD recorder on. He was too old to cry, so instead he just took a sip. And another, and another and another, well, you get the idea, until he eventually stretched out lounging on his favorite household accessory-the velour couch.

Unk Breeze laid back and was glad this couch couldn't talk. If it could, he rationed, after a few drinks, it'd start spilling all the details of the stunt-ventures between he and his wife. *Well, hopefully, the couch would show some discretion. I mean, what type of couch would it be spilling all…all his bizness to folks it barely knew?*

He missed his late wife Eyanna with a sincere passion and every time he got too lonely he'd mix a tape of what were her favorite songs or the songs he knew she'd like, while talking to her about each song. " 'Member this? Oh, yeah, and 'member that time at the club when this came out?" Too bad she wasn't around to hear them, he'd only gotten better with age and not just on the turntables. He wished they had done more things together, spent more time with her and less time Deejaying. *Maybe if he'd gone with her to church more-she'd still be around. Yeah shoulda went with her to church more he thought. That's what God woulda wanted. Then why he put 'Soul Train' on Sunday mornings?*

Smiling, he thought of her oval-shaped chocolate eyes. That's what he called her Choc-late. She was a sweet honey dipped in chocolate and always late. The first date they went on she had him waiting two hours while he had to conversate with her mother about why Luke and Laura didn't stay together on General Hospital. He was pissed off, until he saw her, and she smiled—all she had to do was smile and he was in la la. His eyes became watery, thinking about her. She's gone now, no need to get depressed. Shit, he was too old to cry, or at least he told himself, so instead he just took a sip, and another, and another.

WAKENING (REFRAIN)

WAKEUP! This won't no Spike shit.

Ellis was trapped in the dimension that exists between sleep and consciousness-between the ancestors and those yet to be born. There, he heard the hope and pain of a million screaming souls on the verge of seeing their chance for existence being pushed off the ledge of possibilities. These were the ancestors to be and they weren't having it.

WAKE UP!

WAKE UP Negus!

Wake up!

Get Yo' Bitch-ass up!

Brrrrrrrrrrrrring! Brrrrrrrrrring! "Uh hullo, hullo."

"Ellis? Ellis, is that you? Oh my God—you woke up? You woke up-this is wonderful."

"Yeah, I took a little nap—"

"You took a long nap, baby. Almost two years long."

Suddenly Ellis realized who he was talking to. His eyes swelled up. Holding the tears in check, he cleared his throat.

"That you?"

"Of course it is. But I changed my name, I'm called Makeda now," she gleefully spurted. Plus, I got rid of my perm." "You mean your temporary," snapped Ellis.

Makeda giggled as Ellis felt the excitement in her voice, which got him excited in every way possible. "So, when you coming by to get me out of this place?" asked Ellis, trying to cover-up his nervousness. You *never* let your woman see you scared about anything, especially about being in a hospital.

"Well, lazy butt, I'll be in town tomorrow. I've been in Washington DC for two years and I just received a very good proposal from this software firm—they're talking big money, for me to do some consulting for a few months. So I'll be back in the city for a while-you woke up just in time. I can't wait to see you."

"Good," smiled Ellis, still trying to hold down his enthusiasm.

"As a matter of fact, I'll have a big bonus for you," smirked a mischievous Ellis.

Makeda giggled. "How big?"

"Oh, it's big, huge, and pretty hard, too."

"Yeah, well then you'd better save your energy. I'm going to get my legs waxed."

"Oh, you go head and wax them legs, 'cause I'm gonna wax that ass."

Makeda, anxious to get packing, said an elongated

"Byyyye, Ellis. Bye."

"Bye." Ellis hung up and lay there thinking about Maya, I mean, Makeda.

He tried to remember what her soft silky bronze skin felt like, her nipples, and her soft sweet lips. Ohhh, he was gonna do some work. Well, as much work as possible for someone backed up for two years. He began to wonder, wonder if a person in a coma, had nocturnal emissions. *I mean if the mind doesn't think about sex and isn't even conscious, does the body feel the need for sex?* Oh, well, this wasn't something he needed to worry about anymore.

AND IT FEELS SO GOOD/"CAUSE WE UNDERSTOOD....

The basement was thickly coated with darkness, 'cept for the glowing strobe light on the turntables. Unk Breeze lay, unconscious on the couch as his only copy of Chocolate Milk's "Action Speaks Louder Than Words" continued to spin round and round. Breeze hated leaving his set on—that was unprofessional. *Your equipment is an extension of the DJ's body,* he always said. His music was his religion and his religion was his music-'cause anytime "Ultramagnetic" came on, he caught the Holy Ghost.

Breeze stood about 6 feet tall with long plaits, sprinkled with gray always worn in a ponytail. At 50, he could still pass for his thirties, so long as it was a little dark and you was a little drunk. Didn't hurt if you was high, either. Really, it was whenever he was mixing. It was like the Philadelphia Experiment. Every time he got on the wheels, it was like he was transported through a wormhole to 1986 when he used to rock the blue Filas with the thick laces, his crack-buster T-shirt, and WBLS-FM biking cap.

Maya, now Makeda, stood anxiously outside the door leading to Unk Breeze's basement. She knocked. She knocked harder. She banged. Reaching inside herself she focused on the door, took a deep breath, slowly whipped her foot back and kicked the door with all her might.

"*Booom!*"

Quickly she heard Breeze's grizzled voice.

"What the Hell! Who is it?"

Makeda, grinned for a second, she knew those self-defense classes would eventually come in handy for something. She just hoped she didn't break her new $180 pumps.

"Uncle Breeze, she said in her sweet sexy voice.

It's me, Mak… Maya. Open up."

"Maya?"

"I ain't heard from you in two years," shouted Breeze, now scrambling for his sweats pants, wiping the crust from his face. "Just hold on, baby girl. You got to be careful about kicking my door back here; you know I got it hooked up c-o-n spiral Style. You could've set off my alarm and the whole block woulda went up in flames."

Makeda didn't say anything. She had to take a leak and needed to conserve energy. She waited patiently through four locks clicking, a four-digit combination lock and then a dead bolt. Finally the door squeaked open with a grinning Breeze standing there with his arms open. As her bladder began to explode she burst pass Breeze, practically knocking him down in a dash to the bathroom.

Makeda reemerged out the bathroom practically purring like a kitten and with the look on her face of somebody after dropping off their taxes at 12 midnight on Tax day. She hugged Breeze and sat down. Breeze just smiled and looks at her like a proud father. He always wanted a daughter, but all he and Eyanna had was his son James, and Ellis was like a son. But he wanted a little Eyanna, and Maya reminded him of her or at least if he had a daughter, he'd want her to be like her.

"So, what brings you up this way: Marion Barry got re-elected?"

"Naw, he lost in the primary," smirked Makeda.

"Actually," she hummed, "It's great news, Uncle Breeze."

"Yeah, what? You won Powerball?"

"No! It's Ellis, he's awake. That's why I'm back. Were going to go pick him up."

"We who?" asked Breeze.

"Me and you, dummy."

Tears begin to swell in Breeze's eyes. He wasn't one for emotions; that was a tradition passed down through the men in Ellis' family. The only time he'd cried in twenty years was two days after his wife's funeral and when Lauren Hill cut off her locks. Of course both those times, his was alone in his bathroom.

He had been praying for the longest for Ellis and would check in every now and then, but after awhile his hopes sorta dimmed into that ole New York pragmatism. He couldn't take getting his hopes up and being disappointed, so he just exorcised expectations from his life. But, now he was excited. *My boy's coming home, coming home*, he thought to himself. He wanted to tell the whole world. Call up everyone and probably would've—if he had a phone.

COMING HOME

Today was a good day for Ellis. How could it not be; *I'm going home*, he mused. He was elated. Not only was he going home, he hadn't farted in two days. It was a brand new day, fuck it, a new world. Even the pollution had a sort of weird beauty to it—*the way the orange colored PCBs melted onto the creamy clouds like orange sherbet spread thick in the sky. Oh Shit, da kid getting a little poetic*, thought Ellis. *I mean, I'm a sportswriter-slash-emcee with some lyrical skill-not no Saul Williams.*

Ellis hopped up and popped into the auto-shower. No soap needed; the shower provided you with a mix of the latest organic suds, mixed in with tea-tree oil and a touch of Aloe Vera. It then detected the amount of dirt left on your body and continued to pour suds before switching to pure oxygen coated water. The shit was wonderful; and you came out all shiny and moist—like when your moms cleaned you up for class photo day. Ellis was seeing his boo today. He wondered as he shaved around his goatee, whether she still looked as good as he remembered, thinking to himself, *I know that ass must've got phatter.*

As Ellis slipped into his hospital coat, Uncle Breeze and Makeda headed towards the hospital with eager anticipation. Makeda drove a spanking new 7 series with leather/wood kit and 20 speakers. Not that she needed that type of juice; she never really blasted her music.

On the other hand, Breeze couldn't wait to pop his latest mixed tape in the CD changer.

"Check this out. Maya, this here is da crushnazzy—you don't mind, do you?"

"No, Uncle Breeze, it's okay—just don't crank it too high."

Breeze nodded like a kid given the okay to have a party while the parents are out of town and slid in the disc while proceeding to increase the volume to head-banging level.

"Er, um, Maya, what you call yourself now—Mac Daddy? McDonald's?"

"No, it's Makeda. Candace, or Bilqis. You've heard of the Queen of Sheba? It's simply another name for her."

Slicing open his blunt, and neatly emptying out the filler tobacco, Breeze nodded his head on beat in agreement.

"Sure, sure I know. Kinda like Queen Latifah?"

"No Uncle," moaned Makeda, 'It's not Latifah, it's like the Queen of Sheba, Solomon and Sheba."

"Yeah, yeah, it's all the same," said Breeze.

"I mean, Sheba wuz a fine ass sista seeking wisdom and Queen Latifah dropped it on her albums. Right? Uncle Breeze ain't no dummy, girl. But why'd you drop your God- given name?" strained Breeze.

Looking straight ahead, Makeda explained like she explained to all of her family, friends, former teachers, etc… for the umpteenth time.

"Nothing, I was just tired of walking around with a name that didn't identify me. I know, I know, Maya is not exactly Jenny. I know about the Mayan people and it's Hindu meaning, but I really wanted to be able to define who I was. Nobody thought twice about a hiphop artist changing their name to something crazy, like "Signpost," or "Dum'azhel," but people felt like I did something to them personally by changing mine. It was about me finding and being me Uncle Breeze, that's all."

"Yeah, I gotcha, babygirl," smiled Breeze. "I can feel ya that's why I tell folks to call me Breeze—never did like Babatunde."

"What's Babatunde?"

"Oh, that's my real name…Yo, Maya, make this turn here on the left."

Makeda, a little worried, asked why, since the hospital is the other direction.

"Yeah, I know," said Breeze. "There's this little bodega right up the block, you know I gots to celebrate my boy—Ellis coming home and things—it'll be a minute."

Makeda pulled up in front of Hector's Bodega, a ramshackled red bricked joint with a huge yellow sign. Crates lined up in front of it and peeking in the window, Makeda saw items that looked as if they'd been there for decades. It was nothing like the hygienic 7-11's she'd grew up around.

"Lock your doors—I'll be right out."

Makeda quickly locked her doors. She didn't enjoy these Hood spots that Uncle Breeze always circulated at. Normally, she'd have Ellis there with her to lessen her fright. The Hood wasn't always a violent place, but violence always hung just beneath the surface, waiting for any opportunity to commence. If there was some grungy out of the way place, where they were either putting up or removing yellow police tape-it was likely that Breeze hung there.

He always knew somebody at a spot that used to be something else back in the day-most of these places now just looked like drug spots or condemned buildings. Makeda popped out the head-banging cassette, wondering how somebody Breeze's age still listened to that migraine shit. She threw in some Erykah Badu and leaned back gazing at the graffiti-laced wall of brightly colored towering X-Men that guarded an empty lot next to the bodega. Badu took her into a separate dimension while Breeze gabbed and sipped an hours' worth of liquor squeezed into fifteen minutes. She dozed off, not even realizing that she was tired. So tired she didn't realize that Unk Breeze had been banging on her window for 40 seconds before she awoke.

Ellis lay on the bed flipping channels awaiting the posse that *he 'spected to take him off dis here plantation.*

Shit! What could be taking them so long?

He wondered if Breeze was up to his usual habits—playing mayor of the city.

Damn! What was up with Jay?

Shit, as long as he didn't see Jay's mugshot posted on America's Most Wanted, he figured that Jay'd be okay. Ellis grew more antsy and frustrated each time the long hand of the clock moved an inch; he didn't want to lie down. Not again. Hell, he'd slept enough for a lifetime.

I got to stay awake.

He began scavenging through the magazine rack until he came across *BlackSportz* magazine. They had an article on the upcoming INBA Dream Team. This squad was supposed to put Team USA back on par with the international teams. *Interesting* thought Ellis as he flashed through the pages, page after page until sleep overtook him. As his eyes began to close, *I'm tired of sleeping* he thought. *Tired.*

HERE!

"Ellis? Ellis. Wake up, Hon. Wake up. It's me, Maya, and Uncle Breeze."

"Wake up, Sun. It's ya Uncle Breeze!" yelled Breeze, unintentionally filling the room with the scent of Tanqeuray and orange juice thinly coated by the smell of Doublemint.

Ellis rolled over.

'Yeah? Yeah? Give me a Caesar salad and two bus passes.
Huh…Maya? Uncle Breeze…" he slobbered before quickly wiping the moisture from his mouth.

"Yo! Yo! Yo! What up? What's up, my people?" screamed a teary-eyed Ellis, simultaneously group bear hugging his two favorite people.

"What up!"

Everyone was in tears, crying and smiling. Hugging and making so much noise that the comatose patient in the next room finally awoke after 2 months. It was the Million Man March—minus about nine hundred thousand and ninety-seven. Shit was like a hiphop concert with a decent sound system.

"You ready?" asked Breeze. Chill. "We come to take you home. You'll be staying with me for a while. We'll go by storage and pick up a few of ya things."

A MONTH LATER

"Who ate my last Fripat? Those shits are expensive. You folks know I've got to stay on a veggie diet…" grumbled Ellis on death ears.

Makeda was gone to work and Uncle Breeze was practically comatose after sipping heavily last night. Ellis just sat and stared at the wall, frustrated in ways he couldn't understand. Makeda and he decided to save the money that her company was using to put her in the city by taking the top floor of Uncle Breeze's townhouse. He spent all his time in the basement anyway, and the place was huge for one person. Still, Ellis despite his desire to get back to self, the process was tougher than he imagine. Even tougher than the summer when he nursed himself back into basketball shape after pulling a hamstring. Shit, that used to only took him four weeks to heal from.

How long was this gonna take?

He was a pure ritualist, religiously tied to his arcane habits. He viewed habits in the way that an addict viewed drugs—when he didn't get his fix, his whole world began to unravel. He looked in the mirror and didn't recognize himself. Bleariness filled his whole being and he needed to do something to get out of this situation, but what? He had awakened to a place that he didn't recognize, an environment he didn't have control over. He thirsted for familiarity. He needed to see someone, anyone who could remind him of who he used to be. And he needed them right at this second. Even he didn't recognize himself anymore.

Fuck it, I'll take a walk, he thought. *Nothing like the funk of New York to bring you back home. If Cleveland was the armpit of the world, New York was definitely the toejam.*

The city had the same feel that he remembered. Still getting used to his legs again, he walked drunken style along the Ave, realizing along the way that somebody must have cleaned up the city. Not Ghouliani style, but really cleaned up the city and the air. Traffic was deep but less noisy. A good amount of the new cars practically steered themselves. All the driver did was to type in the address and sit back and sip herbal tea or read the newspapers. Even the taxi's drove in a civilized manner. He definitely was not ready for this—a civilized New York? *Naw. Couldn't be, probably some shit out of the Stepford Wives and they replaced everybody with robots—yeah, that's it. Robots.*

The smell of java filtered through his nostrils and propelled him in the direction of the nearest coffee shop. He never drank anything other than organic coffee, but it's been a while and he needed to wake up from his nightmare.

Ellis walked in and sauntered drunkenly to the counter

like a soon to be a dead malcontent in an old Western movie.

"Can I help you?"

"Yeah, just a sec."

"El? Yo, El!"

Ellis turned slowly to see this tall brotha with dreads almost to his ankles. Staring, he didn't recognize him, but his voice felt familiar.

"Yo El, it's me, Jamal."

"Who?"

"Jamal, distribution manager from *The Nubian*. I know it's been awhile, but…"

Slowly Ellis began to remember.

"Jamal, Jamal, my man! Damn, you need a haircut, you hairy-ass bastard."

Jamal just laughed and hugged Ellis like he really missed him.

"What happened, man? We were worried about you."

Ellis frowned and questioned Jamal quickly.

"What happened to *The Nubian*?"

Smiling still, Jamal spurted out, "Oh, they still around."

"Oh, yeah?" asked Ellis. "What about Nicole?"

"She's publisher now. As a matter of fact they right up on Ossie and Rubie Ave, close to Lenox. You need to go by there; folks be happy to see you."

Suddenly, Ellis felt his soul returning to his body. Shit was beginning to make some type of sense now. Grinning, now comfortable that *The Nubian* is still around, Ellis asked Jamal, "So what you doing now?"

Jamal spread his arms wide.

"This is me, Kid. You know, I always wanted my own business and I opened this spot about a year and half ago—— it's doing me right, the ends keep coming."

"Oh, yeah," said Ellis face contorted between disbelief and relief.

"That means I can get the coffee for free, then, huh?"

Jamal smiled.

"See a bruh come out of a coma and still be begging."

Ellis laughed.

"You just mad 'cause you 6-foot-7 and can't dunk. I mean, don't blame me 'cause you got white man's disease. It's probably ya hair that's too heavy."

They both laugh.

THE NUBIAN

African cultures of antiquity as well as contemporary hold this principle (polarity) paramount in the formation and maintenance of creation and universal order. Nigerian born Dr. C. Kamalu defines life itself "with the duality of being and becoming…the product of being and becoming is the Life Force, that which gives rise to change and motion…. The Life Force is also the organizing power bringing order to the primeval chaos. This organizing power, this force of life and motion, is sometimes described as the first created [thing]."

--The Principle of Polarity, as according to Dr. Wayne B. Chandler in the book *African Presence in Early Asia*

The Nubian had progressed in the time Ellis was away. About 11 months after he went under, a rack of new technologies began sweeping across the planet. It was like someone opened Pandora's box and shit. WORLDGATE Technologies had come up with a new form of cerebral cellular microchips that allowed direct communication between the human brain and computers. Folks could process information a billion times faster than possible by the human brain. Some people even resorted to implanting the chips directly into the cerebral cortex, which resulted in a melee of lawsuits from headz getting fried during sunbursts or anytime someone in a 12-mile radius played a song where Lil' Jon said "yeeeah!"

This technology allowed *The Nubian* to create a 24-hour news channel that broadcasted news from all around the world in whatever format people wanted it. They even changed their name. It still pronounced "Nubian," but they now spelled it as *The New Being*.

Ellis was amazed at what he saw as he slowly walked through the huge glass front doors into a lobby with a circular leather sofa and circular receptionist desk that had to be mahogany or some type of expensive wood that *The Nubian* would have never spent money on before. Above the receptionist or behind her actually was a huge carving of an African face, the same used as the logo for *The New Being*. The reception lobby was sealed with glass doors that led to what appeared to be a massive newsroom filled with what looked like the hardest working Blackfolk, this side of Reconstruction. Ellis felt as if he had entered the command room of the Starship Enterprise without having to beam up.

Shit, maybe they put something in that coffee.

"Can I help you? Excuse me, can I help you?"

"Huh?"

"Can I help you?"

Must be some interstellar language, mused Ellis as he repeated these undecipherable words to himself.

Can Uh hulp U, Can I help U?

Can I elp yu? Oh, Can I help you?

Can I help you?

El was shocked he'd never heard those words coming from a *Nubian* receptionist at decibels that low.

The receptionist just stared at him with her finger on the red security button. Not a yeller, screamer or fighter, but she was famous for quick security actions. She'd call security in a second. And if they didn't come quick enough, she'd jab his eyes out with a mail opener, politely of course.

She waited as Ellis talked to himself, before asking: "Excuse me, Sir, are you on the phone? Can you hear me now?" She figured he had the audio chip implanted and was carrying on a conversation with somebody other than himself.

Finally, Ellis looked at her and smirked, "Who are you?"

"Who am *I*?" scrounged the receptionist tip tapping her finger on the security button. "That's my job. Who are *you*?"

"Who am I? Well, I used to work here."

"Well, I've been here for two years since we opened this office and I've never seen you."

Sobering up, Ellis explained, "No, I didn't work here, I used to work for *The Nubian*."

"Listen," said the receptionist, "either you worked here or you didn't; now, which one is it?"

"Um, er, can I get a lifeline?"

"A what? Listen I'm about to call security in three seconds if you don't..."

"Ellis! Ellis!"

Out of nowhere Ellis is tackled to the floor and kissed all over his face.

"Yo, lady, slow ya roll, I mean, shouldn't we have dinner first—or at least a drink?"

"Oh, Ellis, you ain't changed none."

Ellis stared at the woman who just tackled him; meanwhile, the receptionist stared at both of them, wondering if this was a tactic she could try on the delivery guy.

"Nicole? Nicole, that you?"

"Yeah, it's me, Ellis, where you been? I've been so worried about you. We sent flowers and everything, but after awhile it seemed like you were never going to wake up. It hasn't been the same here without you."

Her body was half the size it used to be, and she looked good!

So of course Ellis said, "Damn, Nicole, you, you look good! I mean, you look great! Only one question."

"Sure Ellis, anything."

"Could you take your knee out my liver? I plan on having a drink in the near future and I'm gonna need it-just a little."

"Oh, sure, Honey," smiled Nicole as she got up off the floor and pulled Ellis up to the disdainful stares and "un uh's," of the receptionist.

"Good to see you've come back from the land of the dead."

Dusting the lint off his linen shirt, Ellis smiled.

"Yeah, I figured if I could survive 20 years of KFC and carryouts, I could survive anything."

Nicole smiled galore, immediately, prompting wonder on Ellis' part, seeing that she has practically abandoned her rude-gal attitude made famous by former Chilean dictators, Israeli Security forces and Iraqi Presidential guards.

Nicole brushed herself off. Ellis watched, almost forgetting who she was.

Okay, okay, so she looks real good. It's still Nicole, so get over it, El thought to himself.

"So, El, come on in, and let me introduce you to some of the new folks. There have been a lot of changes here since you've been gone. You wouldn't believe some of these changes."

El just looked at Nicole, thinking, *Yeah, I would believe anything now.*

For Nicole was suddenly beautiful. It wasn't that she lost a lot of weight; it was more than that. She had lost the heavy attitude, the ill mentality. Damn. This shit was scaring him. If Nicole had changed that dramatically that quickly, then *he* might have to change, too? This was major shit for Ellis as it he worked it out in his mind.

Shit, she could change and that's great; be a better person—sure. Okay, yeah I was a smart-assed, sarcastic, wisecracking muthafuka. Yeah, I know, and as soon as I feel a hundred percent, I plan to return to being the same Negus I was before.

Nicole called a quick gathering of newspeople and announced Ellis to the cheers and hugs of his old and new peers. The experience was more than El could handle—too many hugs, kisses, handshakes—*hey, did somebody grab my ass?* His eyes began to swell up, until Nicole looked at him and smiled.

"Un, uh, are those tears, Ellis Rey?"

El disdainfully looked at Nicole, "Naw, ain't no tears; my allergies just acting up. Allergies, baby, El ain't going out like that. Fuck that sensitive shit." Holding on to his emotional detachment with the last bit of energy, El looked around and thought,

If somebody starts playing "Everything Must Change," by Billy Paul, I'm a dead duck.

Okay, thought Ellis, *breathe in and out, in and out.*

"Ellis, Ellis, Earth to El."

"Huh?"

Nicole's voice snatched Ellis out of his emotional vortex.

"Ellis, so when are you coming back to work for us? I mean, I never actually fired you," giggled Nicole.

"Yeah I know you never really did fire me. Then again, you could never keep promises."

"Yeaah, I know," smirked Nicole, "but that was then and now is now and now I'm living in the *now.* When you coming back?"

Ellis looked down at the floor and mumbled:

"I want to, but I still need a little time to get my shit together. You know it's still hard for me to walk right now. My legs are like Jello. Shit, I was walking down the block and everybody just assumed it was the Harlem Shake. Naw, it's just the shakes. But let me think about it for a second, and I'll let you know when I'll be back, 'cause you know I'm coming back now that we done moved up to the Eastside."

"Great!" said Nicole, "I can't wait to have you back," she whispered and while planting a huge hug and big kiss on Ellis' cheek.

"Great!"

ENLIGHTENMENT

"...Those who really seek the path to Enlightenment dictate terms to their mind. Then they proceed with strong determination. Even though they are abused by some and scorned by others, they go forward undisturbed. They do not become angry if they are beaten by fists or hit by stones, or gashed by swords.

Even if enemies cut their head from the body, the mind must not be disturbed. If they let their mind become darkened by the things they suffer, they are not following the teachings of Buddha. They must be determined, no matter what happens to them to remain steadfast, unmovable, ever radiating thoughts of compassion and good-will. Let abuse come, let misfortune come, and yet one should resolve to remain unmoved and tranquil in mind filled with Buddha's teaching.

For the sake of attaining Enlightenment, one should try to accomplish the impossible and one should endure the unendurable. One must give what he has to the last of it. If he is told that to gain Enlightenment he must limit his food to a single grain of rice a day, he will eat only that. Enlightenment leads him through the fire, he will go forward.

But one must not do these things for any ulterior purpose. One should not do them because it is the wise thing, the right thing to do. One should do them out of a spirit of compassion, as a mother does things for her little child, for her sick child, with no thought of her own strength or comfort.

**--The Way of Practical Attainment, from the
teachings of Buddha**

WALKING

The sky raged in a puzzling darkness, clouds floated haphazardly towards their objective. Ellis walked briskly, as brisk as possible considering his legs were not in full communication with his brain. But by the fourth block, he had developed a rhythm that lessened the stress of walking. For onlookers he appeared to be trapped in a Eighties style bop. All he needed was some suede pumas with thick laces and a D-hat.

His steps brought him to a cross-section with the light red. Ellis glanced at the other side of the street and moved toward it like Vince Carter seeing a hole in the full court pressure defense after being held dunk-less the whole game. He moved with purpose and poise and crossed the street like a vet, releasing a "Yes!" in exuberation. *Only two blocks left* he grinned slightly. Before he could continue his next step, his groove was interrupted.

"Excuse, buddy, do you know where you're going?"

"What?"

Frustrated at this intrusion, Ellis spouted off full blast,

"Yeah, mawfuka, I know where I'm going. Do *you* know where I'm going?"

Suddenly, Ellis noticed the shoes this guy is wearing are Metropolitan Police authorized. He looked up, smiling.

"Hey, officer."

The cop looked at him like a shark on a bleeding tuna.

"Yeah, Negus there is a problem, assume the position."

"The position? You mean point-guard, or forward? Because I normally play the two-guard, but if the coach asked me to, I'll even play center. You know on my Juco team we didn't have a lot of height."

"Huh?" responded the cop, after being caught off-guard by the sarcastic wizard of quipped. He paused for a second, then remembered that he hated them smart Negus, particularly those who had the nerve of thinking they was educated. Them that thought they had rights. The cop pushed Ellis up against the wall and pulled his arm behind his back and cuffed him.

He then pushed Ellis' arms up toward his shoulders to

the point where pain began seeping into Ellis' neck.

"This will teach you idiots a lesson. "What you think you was—Uptown? In Brook-NAM? Huh, thought you was in yo' Hood where you could get away with this type of shit?" asked Officer Riley O'Jerk in a pseudo-Blackened Long Island accent.

He continued his sermon.

"Being drunk in broad-daylight, waltzing down the street—that you folks problem, always complaining but don't know how to live civilized."

Ellis wanted to keep quiet but couldn't. He had a side of self that once unleashed couldn't be contained. It was like when some fool playing ball against him started talking shit, Ellis responded. That was like trying to put a tornado into a jar-just wasn't gonna happen.

"Yeah, you about as civilized as a Nazi. You bitches real tough firing 40 shots into a Negus like me's back. How you gonna be a cop and so afraid of Negus that a ninety year old woman gets shot by you fools talking 'bout you seen something look like a gun. Then allow some white farmer in a tractor to hold the whole damn city hostage for a week before you talk him out without firing a shot. You bastards is sick. That's the problem with you idiots in Blue, you think that we criminals waiting to happen, when you just violated my rights. Minding my own business trying to make it home and got to deal with some wannabe Rudy Ghouliani three credits short of a G.E.D., who ain't got shit else to do...."

Ellis continued to ramble through the roughhouse treatment, the constricting feeling of cold steel clamping tightly on his wrists, that the cop churned until pain etched its way into his shoulder, as a gathering crowd of passerbys stared at him like some circus act, until he fell asleep in the back of the squad car. Drifting into dreamland, lyrics begin to flow:

> *The brotha from another plane/ Sane in the membrane*
> *I rain fire and reign for Millennium*
> *We the Final One*
> *ratio equivalent to the sum*
> *Of 10 billion suns*
> *Amun/*

In unison/ with the one,
wickky, wickky two, three
Runnnnnnn, D=MC
Mind stimulated beyond the material/
Ethereal/ for real
Surreal/ kinetics
I connects the crunk/ like Uconn dunks/
well, er, actually all Blackmen can't jump/
Still we brings the funk/ like dos vegas in trunks/
We B
Old as the sea/ Still kicking PE
whether you agree/ or see me as an enemy/
It never matters
I sip cold duck/ then rise when U and I verse/
Put triple beam dubs on a hearse/
So dry you thirst/
But your DNA can't process FLUID/
Yeah I knew it/ do it
just 'cause I can/
Newbeing/ Supaman
who can't stand the flim-flam/
I be that I am/
'cause we be the shit/ Legit/ clenched fist
bring the panther back/
spray paint the whitehouse black/
still we lack the will to get off crack/
It be the year 21 and negus still tryna mack/
I stax the trax like amtrax/ prototype-antiwack/
The soul of Zodok rests within/ 2 Millennium ago we came
again
Knocking 3times/
VIP Pass and a grin
But still didn't get in/ Still they ask where I been
Nowhere but on the verge of us getting it On, and on, and on

"Jackson! Jackson! Wake the fuck up, criminal—yo' folks here to get you!" screamed Officer D'amdummy. Ellis awoke and groggily staggered toward the bars.

"Huh? What?"

"I said, get up, criminal; yo' folks are here."

Ellis looked at him. "Ya mother."

"What? What?" growled D'amdummy.

"Oh, nothing. Open up, biiitch," mumbled Ellis.

D'amdummy looked hard.

"Huh?"

Quickly, Sergeant William Bell stepped in.

"Mr. Jackson, excuse Officer D'aamdummy; he was raised by a pack of wolves. I'm sorry about the mix-up. I used to read your column all the time. Don't let this fool bother you."

Ellis smiled, "Thanks, officer."

Makeda and Uncle Breeze greet Ellis with much love that gives way to a 40-minute ride in complete silence. Makeda even refused Unk's request to put in his old Jazzy Five live tape from 1982, when they rocked the show with only one mike. Instead, Ellis and Makeda sat in silence, while Breeze hummed to himself, *Can you feel it/ Can you feel it/ my jazzy sensationuuuun, boop—Can you feel it/, Can ya feel it/, uh, uh, my jazzy sensationuuunm....*

TWO WEEKS PASS

Subtle music rises slowly through the room, interacting and deconstructing negative ions with positive vibrations. The smooth melodies contrasted with the rhythmic movements of Ellis. Moving his left hand up in the shape of a hawk's beak, he slid his right hand overtop the outstretched arm and brought it slowly toward his right. He then repeated the process with his right hand in a hawk's beak and slowly slid his left hand down the corridor of his arm towards his left, ending with his body leaning to his left and palm extended flatly.

In his rehabilitation process, Makeda decided to include Tai Chi, believing that by regenerating his life force energy, his recovery would go faster. For Ellis, it was more than a hard work. *Shit, I used to get loose at the club,* Ellis complained to himself, while considering turning his Tai Chi movements into some new dance that he could break out at the local spot. *Yeah, Yeah,* thought Ellis, *I could do that, probably get madd props. They'd be loving me, loving me, I'm luving it, bah, bah, da bah, bah, bah-naw, they might think I'm trying to pop or, worse, vogue?*

Every other day, Makeda would check his anti-oxidant levels using a Biophotonic scanner. As part of his rehabilitation, Ellis was to rise in the morning at six and began reading his Egyptian Yoga books. Makeda rationalized that if they were to stay together, Ellis had to up his consciousness to the point where they could hold conversations about something other than sports or music. Ellis agreed, if only because he knew it'd keep the discussion off marriage for a while. He read the heavy stuff for an hour and then began reading his sports magazines. He'd also go online to see what happened in the INBA while he was out.

His next two hours involved several sets of light weight lifting, and stretching. Followed by an hour of meditation followed by a meal of vegetable patties, rice, and Ezekiel bread. Makeda had based his schedule on some ancient Egyptian—or its correct name, Kemetic—concepts of time; she said Kemetic philosophy, which noted that the horoscope was based on the 24-hour period of the day, where certain energies and activities represented by Zodiacal signs must be performed in harmony with the appropriate time for these activities. She always said, "Just look at the name Horus, see 'horoscope,' 'hour'! It was about time. The same way that the Earth spins while rotating around the sun, the sun rotates around the galaxy and this galaxy is rotating around something else. It's all a wheel within a wheel within a spiral. Horus actual name was Heru."

She was worse than a 2nd grade teacher; or parent. He remembered all that she taught him, despite having no desire to.

Ellis' mind wandered over mountains before returning. He was becoming anxious by the second. The townhouse was caving in on him; there seemed to be no escape from boredom, meaninglessness. He had even lost his desire to make fun of things. Who woulda ever thunk it? He couldn't think, because thought led him to a depressed state. Ellis scurried around the apartment looking for something to drink—beer, vodka, rubbing alcohol, shit, somethin'.

As expected, Makeda had nothing; at least, nothing he

had access to. With Makeda's urging, Breeze set a combination lock to his liquor cabinet based on some 32-bit algorithm that was based on beats per minutes of his favorite break beat. Ellis had a better chance of making some homebrew than breaking into Breeze's stash.

Ellis sat and sat, getting angrier at the world. He felt trapped and fearful and he wasn't a fearful being, at least outwardly. What he hated more than anything else was the fact that at this moment in time he no longer felt in control of his destiny. This was a first for him. He always believed that making it out of the Projects had hardened him beyond reproach. After facing project life as a youth, he felt nothing could ever come close to shaking his foundation as a man, as a human being. He wanted to stop thinking, but couldn't. As his mind neared infinity's loop, his cerebral circuit breaker kicked in, slowing his metabolism, brainwaves and bringing in death's cousin—SLEEP.

BRRRRRING.....

'Who dis, um, who is it?" mumbled Ellis.

"El, Ellis, is that you? This is Nicole. What's going on? You okay? Hello," she continued, while Ellis was still stuck on "Nicole?" until it hit him.

"Oh, Boss Lady, what up, what's happening? How you feeling?"

Without giving Nicole her time to respond, Ellis raced on.

"Me? I'm just chilling, you know, chilling as usual. My lady got me doing this Tai Chi, you know, and it's helping me rehab, but you know The Kid, right? 'Member how nice I wuz on the court? You know, and now I can't even do a cross-under. Oh yeah, did you catch the game the other night? What's up with Johnson? I mean, you'd think for $20 million a year, he'd learn how to make a damn lay-up. How you going to be 6-10 and miss a lay-up? Shit, all you got to do is trip yourself and fall right into the rim. I mean, Damn."

Sensing Ellis catching his breath, Nicole dived into the conversation.

"Ellis! Hey! Can you slow down, baby? This ain't an audition for telemarketing. You know our audio autowrite can't follow Ebonic speech patterns that quick, my brotha."

Ellis finally realized that he's been going off and uses his reservoir of restraint to stay still and quiet. Well, for as long as he could.

"Hey, Boss Lady, sorry about the gab, but what's up?"

"Well, Ellis Rey, I've been thinking. We got to send a two writers and a photographer over to the continent to cover a story. You interested in being one of them?"

"Africa?" asked Ellis. "Hell, the only thing going on that I got any feeling for is the World Basketball Championships."

"Well," said Nicole, "that's what I'm talking about."

"*What?!?*" screamed Ellis. "You know I got to marry you now, right?"

Nicole smiled to herself. "Yeah, I know I chased you a little back in the day, but you won't owe me anything but a few good stories. Plus, your boy Yusef Black requested that you were sent over there. We wanted an exclusive with him, but the only way he'd give it to us if you were the one doing it. See, all those beers actually paid off."

"Bet. I'm with it," said an excited Ellis. "I'm with this! Mos' definitely."

COACH YUSEF BLACK

Ever the journalist, El immediately thought of updating himself on the tournament and Coach Black. He quickly punched into the 'Net and sees a story on his boy Yusef Black.

"Aaaah, this looks good.... 'Black Takes African Hoops to New Heights,' on The World Sports Network."

Ellis leaned forward and begins reading…

"It was this young-hearted coach who had the foresight to leave a championship team in New York and take the INBA expansion team in Sudan. The League was now a 70-team international venue, with revenues over $600 billion a year. It was also a year before the American teams placed age caps on coaches due to the 3 heart attacks and one suicide attempt by coaches over 55.

"Even with the coaching drama in the League, most thought U was crazy for leaving a phatt spot as general manager/coach of the New York Knicks, winners of back to back NBA titles, along with the 2nd-rated television show and a sporting goods line which made him one of the most wealthy and influential brothas in the sport, outside of Jordan. He was definitely eccentric; not too many knew or understood him, except maybe a few close friends. The few that he allowed into his sphere, knew he was special, in more than coaching."

Few people were aware of how bright this Negus was. Even fewer witnessed the mental skills, which NASA had first peeped during his childhood. To be sure, he was definitely one of the most perceptive individuals alive, and it had noting to do with Hoop. Anybody could recognize a 2-1-2 full court trap, or devise a pro-level defensive scheme that in actuality was a zone. But Yusef could tell folks things their parents didn't know about them after just meeting them. He was a serious debater, too. His skills were so advanced that he would embarrass professors in the classroom, acts that didn't make him too popular when grading time came around. Probably went down in history as the smartest C average student in the history of Howard University. This even hurt him more in embarrassing incompetent refs.

Ellis turned off his computer, after realizing that aside from the events of the past two years, he knew Yusef like a book. Kicking back he lay on the couch and turned on his favorite television show. "The Adventures of Melki" was high-level animation about a mixtape DJ named Melki, otherwise known as DJ Fluid.

The Adventures of Melki..........The Search for Ben Laden

WORDS ONSCREEN: The fictional adventures of Melki represent one of the various manifestations or alter egos of FLUID: The mental realm of hiphop. Melki, otherwise known as DJ Fluid, must make mixed-tapes to live. Trapped in the "NOW" and judged by the public, aka "Da Heads," he must constantly outdo his previous mix-tape or disappear into the dimensional void of "WUZ."
WORDS ONSCREEN: The Year 2008.
News Flash! "This live from TNN. Intelligence officials have come to the conclusion that Al Qaeda is no longer in Afghanistan. Reports indicate that every cave and crevice,

including the butt-cracks of every Afghani, Pakistani, and Iraqi, had been thoroughly searched, and nothing found could be described as dangerous, or linked to Osama Ben Laden. In response to the failure to find Bin Laden, President George II announced that he would personally lead the search for Bin Laden himself, accompanied by the FBI, Secret Service, CIA, and Joe the Pretzel guy to act as a decoy. The president indicated that their search would start in Hood City, America, in the Blinga-Bling Projects....

Brrrrrring! Brrrring! The telephone prompts Ellis to leave the television and return to real life.

"Hello?"

"Ellis?"

"Yeah, this is El."

"This Yusef!"

"U! Man, what up?"

"Yo, I know Nicole talked to you about coming over to the Blackland to cover the tournament and everything, right?"

"Yeah, sure, mos' definitely."

"Well," said Yusef, "I need another favor."

Ellis smiled, "Sure, man, anything for the brotha from another planet."

Yusef took a deep breath that made Ellis think of Jay for one second and wondered, *What the hell was coming down the pipe?*

"El, well you know my nephew Wardell, right?"

"You know we done hung out several times, U. What?"

"Well..." Yusef took another deep breath, as if he was asking a dead man to give up his last wish. He hated having to ask anyone for anything, even the few folks he considered friends. *Everybody loved yo' ass until you needed them, and the less you needed them the more they loved you,* was always U's rationalization.

"My sister-in-law... I... want him to travel with you over here. He contacted his mother and said that he wanted to return for a few weeks and spend some time with his family."

Ellis responded cautiously, trying hard not to show his

discomfort around the idea of Wardell traveling with him.

"Yeah, sure, U. Anything."

"Well, Ellis, it's not only that, but he has to stop off and pick up something important prior to arriving to Khartoum. His brother Menelik was supposed to do it, but you know his Mother believed that Wardell should do it, hoping that it would quell the beef between Wardell and his father. So she wants you to accompany Wardell to get this item. It'll only take a day or so and you guys can head back to Khartoum to cover the rest of the Tournament and chill out some. Don't worry, we'll cover all the expenses and some."

"Okay, U, you know you my man. So don't worry, I'll handle the business as needed. Just make sure yo' nephew don't start tripping; you know he a little ill."

Yusef breathed a sigh of relief. "Thanks El, you know I owe you big for this. It ain't really my thing, but I'm his uncle and I try to help the family whenever I can, so good luck—uh, I mean, see you soon. Peace."

"Peace."

Ellis immediately began to wonder, *What the hell did Yusef want Wardell to do?* He was not at all comfortable with this fool. Nor was he comfortable being responsible for anything or anyone beyond himself. *Shit, when you start getting responsible for other people is when your life gets fucked up. And when other people start depending on you is when your life gets fucked up more.* Ellis wanted no real part of this family drama. But deep down, he knew that if he was ever going to get his life going again—making some sense of this experience called life—he had to take this trip and handle things. This trip was his Lotto ticket, his big score. Shit, besides, if shit happened he could always blame it on Wardell. And if Wardell got too out of hand, he'd just have to whip his monkey-ass.

EXIT AMERIKA

Uncle Breeze and Makeda helped Ellis pack his gear and get ready for his flight to the Motherland to Cover the World Basketball Championships. Ellis purposely avoided telling them about the mission that he's been drafted into via Yusef—having to keep tabs on Wardell. That morning, Makeda informed Ellis that her consulting gig in New York was ending, and she'll have to return to DC. She wanted to spend her last few days with him, and maybe convince him to return with her. But things were heading down a totally different path altogether as her personal plans were pushed onto the back burner by Ellis' reentry into journalism.

The airport bustled with throes of travelers as the trio headed to the departing gate for BlackStar Airlines. BlackStar was a recent competitor to Pan Afrika Air, which had flights to every major city on the continent.

Uncle Breeze hugged Ellis.

"Yeah, baby, I know you gonna do yo' thing over there. I want you to be careful, you know me, Unk Breeze ain't followed Hoop in awhile. I mean when Vince Carter retired, that was it. I 'member back when I was a baby, and my pops used to take us down to Rucker Park, back in 1975 when they called him Dr. Funk—now that was Hoop," grinned Breeze, hanging on to Ellis with one arm.

Ellis grinned. "Now you know Vince Carter wasn't playing in no Rucker League back in 1975."

Breeze stepped back.

"What? C'mon, baby, I was there in 1975 and remembered seeing him play. As a matter of fact, he signed my T-shirt after the game."

Ellis laughed. "Unk, it was just a commercial."

Breeze frowned and brushed a piece of lint off his pants, and brushed clears a spec off his Air 2000s.

"Whatever's clever—be cool, baby. Hold it down for folks like me who ain't never been out of the city."

Ellis smiled. "Will do."

Giving Ellis and Makeda some privacy, Breeze took off to purchase some of the duty-free liquor; an old buddy of his worked the register there and owed him one. Ellis passionately embraced Makeda, who looked up with pleading in her eyes. With the look of a woman who was worried she'd might never see her man again. Worried that her future vision of them with children and a house growing old together might never occur.

Damn, why does he have to go?

"Ellis, take care of yourself, okay?"

Ellis grinned, "you know the K-I-D. I'm gonna handle

mines." Slipping her arm up under his and tugging tightly on his shoulder, Makeda looked into his eyes.

"Are you sure you are ready to travel like this? I mean, Ellis, I just don't feel right about this. When I left New York before, I almost lost you. I'm afraid I might not see you again. I'm not getting good vibes about this trip. Why don't you just tell *The Nubian* that you'll take the next story? You could move back to DC with me. It'll be great!"

Still embracing Makeda passionately, Ellis looked up and stared into empty space.

"Makeda, I know it's kinda speedy—this whole trip and things. But believe me, it's something I have to do. Don't worry, I'll be back. Remember: I grew up in the PJ's. Ain't too much gonna frazzle a Negus like me," declared Ellis, seemingly trying to convince himself more than his lady.

Loosing her embrace, Makeda steps away and holds onto Ellis hand. " I know, I know, this is something you have to do. Just return, don't forget you got somebody back here who loves you."

Ellis smiled, "Yeah, I know—Uncle Breeze."

Makeda frowned.

"Ellis, this is a serious moment. Can we just have a serious moment for once, no jokes? Why can't you just express your emotions to me? I need to know what you are feeling sometimes. That you are vulnerable."

Ellis stared into her eyes saying nothing, but attempting hard as hell to convey something more than love to Makeda using his eyes, his soul. Fuck it; he proceeded to use his mouth.

He pulled her close to him and kissed the sensitive spot on her neck. Brought his lips up around her ear and whispered, "I love you." Makeda's wet, thick lips embraced his as her sweet tongue enveloped his. He squeezed her tightly, tighter than he'd ever allowed himself to hold anyone and held on. At that one moment, they combined the total unabashed eroticism of full-fledged heated, sweaty passion into one small kiss.

Makeda looked into Ellis eyes, saying once more, "I love you, too, Ellis. So come back quick, and when you get back, I may have some special news for you," she smiled.

Ellis watched as Makeda and Uncle Breeze left the departure gate. He stared as they walked out, hoping a little that everything will be cool. He too had a feeling that something was wrong about this trip. Despite his intuition, he also knew that if he didn't go, he was doomed to a life offbeat, unfulfilled, what if? That's what he felt, as if someone had scratched the record of his life, and every time the hook came around it skipped a beat.

Ellis felt a tap on the shoulder and spun around. Staring him in the face, cheesing sinisterly from left to right, was Wardell.

"What up, El, you ready to do this?" said Wardell, like he, not El, was the O.G. Like he didn't know, or remember, that if Ellis and Jay hadn't taken this peon under their wings for a sec, he wouldn't know nothing 'bout nothing. *This idiot*, thought Ellis.

Ellis began a frown, then caught himself and grinned, "*Me*, Negus? *You* ready?"

Wardell pulled out a stick of gum and popped it into his mouth.

"Shit, baby, I thought you knew. A Negus like me's *always* ready."

MOTHERLAND 2020

The area was once called Nubia and Kush and before the split of the moon from the Earth, which we now know as Arabia from Africa, it had actually reached to the Indus Peninsula. This was the center of pyramids—even outnumbering those of Kemet. Ta-Seti or Qustul was the site of a censer depicting the royal symbol of Horus and the Crown, long before its appearance further north in Kemet. This was the Blackland, site of spiritual rebirth for the ancients and had given birth to Kemet. It was from Nubia that the great pharaohs of the 25th dynasty—Piankhi, Shabaka, and Taharka—arose to rid Kemet of the invaders, and to rebuild the temples and reestablish the domain of Amun.

Old Dongola, the former Christian capital that held off Muslims for nearly 700 years, was surrounded by the ancient Nubian-Kushite empires of Napata, with Kerma to the north and Meroe' further south, just above the junction of the Blue and White Nile which met at Khartoum. The travelers had stopped at Meroe' to enjoy the view of the old ruins before continuing north. As they stood among the tombs of kings and queens, the wind whipped sand into their faces like bullets. The view was incredible and extremely humbling. The sand dunes and mountains formed continuous pyramids, bursting forth from the sullen plains where you could see for 10 miles at a glance. They wondered: When their ancestors had built these grand civilizations did they know? Did they know that their seed would ostensibly become the wretched of the Earth?

OUTSIDE DONGOLA

Somewhere outside of Old Dongola, adjacent to the Nile as it flowed into Egypt, the visitors gazed at their surroundings. Green and white pastel colored one-story homes lined the street. New technology had been incorporated—a sensor stoplight. For the most part, animals had served as a major means of transportation; however, new 4X4s flat bed trucks were quickly supplanting them. It was amazing—only ten years ago, it remained an unimportant town in Sudan, practically covered by sand. Visitors always spoke of the attack of windblown sand when visiting the area, but that was no more. Sand was now suddenly being replaced by beautiful gardens and reemerging springs. The streets were small, but paved and expanding into at least four major roads interconnecting at the Central newly modernized marketplace, the "Souk."

It is said that the peacemakers shall inherit the Earth. Sudan had always been a mystical and historical place for the Ansaar Allah (or aiders of Allah, a term applied to the most devout believers who came to the aid of the prophet Mustafa Muhammad Al Amin, in his mission to promulgate the message of peace-Islam.) The first Ansaar were located in Arabia; however, according to the legend, Dongola had become the home of many shortly after the Prophet's death in 632 A.D.

After the death of the Seal of the Prophets, his followers were embroiled in a dispute on who would be Khalifat (successor). Muhammad had no male heirs, only his daughter Fatima who married the nephew of her father

Murymin Ali—one of the most staunch and bravest followers of the Prophet. Despite Ali being the son-in-law of the Prophet, it was Abu Bakr who became Khalifa. Ali and Fatima left Mecca and eventually settled in Ethiopia, and then Dongola. According to many, it was from his line that the Mahdi of Sudan Muhammad Ahmad (1845-88) came to rally the warring tribes under the Black, Red and Green banners to retake the land of the Blacks from the British and Turks. Wearing the white robes of righteousness along with the fearless thundering horsemen, the Ansaar defeated the Turks and British, who were at the height of their power. He established a short-lived nation with its headquarters in the twin cities of Omderman and Khartoum. Muhammad Ahmad was a tall Blackman who carried a staff—some called it the staff of Moses, others the Staff of Kings.

According to one legend, this staff was brought with the Ark of the Covenant to Ethiopia in the excursion of the noble sons of Israel and Menelik—the offspring of King Solomon and Makeda, the Queen of Sheba.

These members of the tribe of Judah formed a dynasty of 1000 years before their fall and reduction to strangers in their own land. Most religious scholars had never accepted the truth of the Kebra Negast, which meant "Glory of the Kings." In fact, most still referred to Christian Ethiopia as Abyssinia—as if it were in actuality a different place. The Europeans had searched for Prestor John, the mythical Christian King of Ethiopia, and found him to be a myth. However, with the miracle revelations uncovered beneath the ruins of Gondar, Ethiopia's connection to Judah was substantiated and the legend of the staff was revealed.

This staff supposedly had tremendous power—but only in the hands of the righteous. Scientists had theorized that only a genetic sequence particular to the descendents of the original kings could activate the power of the staff. Only those with a unique birthmark on their right arm were recognized as descendents of the royal blood. Word had it that this line of descendants began with Ra and continued through Narmer and his descendants. It had eventually rested in Ethiopia's control through Aaron's Line of Levitical priests since shortly before the fall of Israel to the Babylonians. Some scholars knew of the priests caring for the Ark of the Covenant, but they also had the responsibility of caring for the staff and ensuring that it remained in the line of kings called Negus. The name stood for "the righteous ones" and "the ones of peace."

It was not until the 19th century that some say the staff re-appeared under the banner of Muhammad Ahmad, the guide and reformer of Sudan. Others say that the whole story of the staff was merely a myth, just a legend. For most scholars and researchers, there was not enough evidence to verify the idea as anything other than conjecture or fantasy. The Mahdist state lasted a short time and the British returned to conquer the warriors and reestablish the Anglo-Egyptian Condominium, which would eventually be renamed Sudan—a word meaning "the Land of the Blacks."

The myth or legend of the staff continued. Some said that it would reappear again and, when it did, the land where it lay would see a resurrection of the spirits and minds of the people. They would seek the Creator of the Universe, and, as a result, a rebirthing of the land would ensue. There would arise a peace brought to the people solely by peace, not by swords, bloodshed, murder or wars. There would be born children who knew not war, who followed the teachings of the Most High that said "Thou Shall Not Kill." As opposed to men who used belief to murder, conquer, or divide. They argued that this was the true meaning of Islam, the Supreme Peace. The legend recalls that when the waters began to sprout and the lakes refilled, then the sign of things to come would be at hand.

THE TEACHER

"Peace," Ellis said as he and Wardell entered the home of Luqman, the Master Teacher. The strong smell of sandalwood and Frankincense floated within his abode-filling the air with an electric buzz.

Books in Arabic and manuscripts in Cuneiform and Medu Neter dominated his basically essential existence. Materially, he was poor and lacking; however, the value of his household lay in materials designed to uplift the soul and spiritual evolution. He was a sharp old charcoal-colored Nubian who was so deep that his presence provided the link between quantum physics, God, and the science of ancient Kemet.

As Ellis and Wardell entered his tent-covered backyard and made their way to their seats, twin Basenji blocked their path. They were reddish in color and appeared to be growling at Wardell. It was weird—not any normal dog sound. Basenji had been highly prized dogs, and the favorite of the Pharaohs. They were independent, somewhat small but fearless. They did not bark, and cleaned themselves like cats. As they tried to maneuver around them to the chairs in the back, the Master Teacher snapped his fingers twice and the Basenji sulked away slowly, but not after giving Wardell the up and down.

He sat teaching a group of youngsters. "You see," he said, simultaneously waving to his visitors, "ancient Kemet's society was built on mathematical principles also and the science of physics. There was no separation of science from life and life was in harmony with the Universe. Kemetians knew the secrets of Pi—not 3.24—which they understood and mastered. No, they were well aware of the more powerful formula for Phi, which is 3.106. They knew that when this number was multiplied, it created vibrations—sound—that transforms into energy at the right level.

Now, in terms of the Pyramids, some theorize that they were built from this type of energy and were left for the generations—you—in order that they might find their way home, among the stars in the constellation of Orion—you call it Heaven. At one time, all wooly haired people were Ethiopian—it's from the root word "ether" or "heavenly." The Greek sage Homer tells you about them in 'The Iliad.' He calls us 'the blameless Ethiopians.' Okay, I must end our session now, and we'll pick up where we left off next week." His class began to disperse.

"Would you like some dates?" asked his nephew, Askia, placing a bowl in front of us.

"No, no, thank you," said Ellis, attempting to avoid jumpstarting his nervous stomach.

"Please, have some dates," he pleaded. "I have some tea brewed." After a second of contemplation, both decided to eat, for fear of not offending their hosts.

"Sir, you understand why we are here," said Wardell.

"Yes," he said, " I have that which you seek, and you are the one worthy of transferring it to its rightful place. There are those who seek to meddle in our affairs, yet the Creator is merciful and the best of planners," he murmured, simultaneously signaling his nephew to bring more tea.

They sipped the hot taste of peppermint tea and chewed on hard dates, nervously awaiting this object that, for some reason, the two unlikeliest of characters had been chosen to transport.

His grandson returned with a long item covered in a white linen cloth with strips of blue.

"This is the staff of ancients," said the Master Teacher. His gray beard seemed to glow when the sun hit it. He spoke softly.

"It is the staff of power. As to its authenticity, I cannot tell you—only that it has been passed on for generations through a secret society that no man knows of except those who belong. And now you must take it to its final place, the place where the Earth has begun the process of rebirth. The place set aside for those of you who have returned from the wilderness back into the land of their ancestors, ending their oppression."

They nodded attentively.

"If the staff does not reach its intended destination, the end of this era will be forestalled and the righteous shall suffer. You have a great deal of work to do, and only yourselves to trust. Be wise, be strong and may the Creator's speed and grace be with you."

Gracious that the formalities were finally over, the dynamic duo hopped into the land cruiser. Ellis glanced at Wardell, who glanced back. It was like a scene out of a Western: you knew the rattlesnake was going to bite, you just didn't know when.

Attempting to defuse the energy, Ellis popped in an old YZ disc "Thinking of a Master Plan."

The music began kicking.

Oooh, Ooohu..Who's the man/ Who's the man with the Mamamammmamamaster plan…..

As their heads bopped, Ellis wasn't really feeling it. All he could hear were the words of the Old Man as the music became an afterthought. "You have a great deal of work to do and only yourselves to trust." It wasn't that Ellis was so worried about the work they had to do as he was worried about who he had to trust.

Oooh, Ooohu…Who's the man/Who's the man with the Mamamammamamaster plan…..

FUTURESHOT

It had only been a hot second since the NBA expanded to its international structure than the region of Sudan began fielding a team to compete on an international level. The team made immediate progress by offering dual citizenship to African Americans along with 40 acres and a jeep. The Sudanese knew American history—about the 40-acres-and-mule-Civil-War promise; however, they was all out of mules—besides, them Land-Troopers were worth a thousand mules and you could put rims on 'em. Plus, they had laser-disc players and booming systems. Brotha couldn't pick up no Honeyz on a damn mule. What line could you kick? "Aaah…The Benzi is in the shop? Naw. I'm just sportin' this 'till my cousin returns my camel?" Would it work if you put like a Gucci saddle and Nike straps on your camel?

The migration started slowly, but more and more brothas and sistas began to trickle in—integrating the old communities and forming new ones. Since the beginning of the millennium, over 150,000 Black folk had migrated to the land of their ancestors, a united African Union—Ghana, Tanzania, Mozambique, Angola. Not the least of who was Yusef Black, former coach of the New York Knicks, and who by all accounts represented the return of the native son—and that draft pick to be named later. Upon him rested all hope of bringing Sudan to the pinnacle of international Hoop competition. Now, in this once-forgotten nation, a thousand sportswriters and crews from 100 nations were crazy amped about the Basketball World Championships in Khartoum.

After kicking up some serious sand, Wardell and Ellis finally arrived at the tournament. They entered the arena, intensely scouring the packed, humid gym, squeezed to its 140,000-capacity limit. The African black, red, and green colors interconnected on the parquet floor and flowed up into the stands intermingling with fans dressed in the same colors. The sight, at first glance, caused an adjustment of the eyes, due to its brightness. When they did the wave, it was like watching an enormous black-red-and-green flag.

Ellis whispered to Wardell, "Do what you supposed to do, and we'll meet after the game." Wardell was supposed to deliver the staff to his father who would handle it from there. His father sat along with his mother, brother and sister directly behind the Sudanese bench.

Ellis made his way down to the floor, picked up his program and pre-game materials, and awaited the tip-off. He was already late and hated missing the pre-game meal. As he made his way to the floor, press pass swinging around the neck like a millstone, his mind drifted. *What the hell am I doing here? I ain't ready to be here. Out of all the Negus in the world, why did these people involve me in the extracurricular shit? I mean, why not one of those revolutionary type-brothas named Abdullah or something willing to do anything for the Revolution? Fuck dying for the Revolution, I ain't even trying to get shot for it. I might take a quick beat down, but that's about it.*

The game winded down to the final possession. Ten seconds left on the clock, the Nuba Giants down two, Toronto had the ball. Williams dribbled up court and kicked it out to Rush. Rush pulled up, pumped-n-faked. Staying with him every step, Hassan reached and tipped the ball out of bounds. "Toronto ball," screamed the referee. Seven seconds left on the clock. "Timeout!" yelled Yusef.

As the team huddled, Yusef scoured the circle of tired players and looked sternly at Hassan, his star player. Sweat dripped from Hassan's fro like a wet sponge. "Okay check it," said Yusef, "I want to force them into a bad shot, so let's overplay for a steal-nothing easy. We need you, big-boy!" Hassan merely nodded.

Hassan, after starting slowly, had been in a zone most of the fourth quarter, scoring 10 of the team's last 14 points to bring them back to within 2. He was what you might call a PTPer—kinda a cross between Jordan and Bob Mcadoo, could tear you up from the perimeter or beat you to the hole and dunk in ya face. Former Knicks star Walt "Clyde" Frazier always said in the fourth quarter you'd see the backs of a lot of uniforms; no one wanted the shot. But Hassan was pure hot-dog and he relished this shit.

Three seconds were left on the shot clock. Wells inbounded the ball to Rush, who pulled up from the key-miss! The rebound hung high above the rim. Hassan leaned his shoulder on his man and nudged him out of position, then extended his 40-inch vertical to the max, ripping the ball out of the air. He raced down the court, past Prasavic, whipped the ball behind his back, crossed-over Daniels—uh, oh—pulled up from three-point land. The shot drifted off his fingertips and hung in the air, almost an eternity as the shot clock reduced to zero. Floating like a jazz note, the ball finally cleared the front of the rim, barely grazing. The nets, nothing but the panties.

"It's good, It's good. It's good!"

A thousand miles away, in a dingy hotel outside of DC, one crusty old sportscaster in woman's underwear, screamed, "Yes! Yes! Yes!"

Ron Icky, the Toronto coach, can't believe it, begins raving and screaming at the refs.

"It's no good, no good! The clock expired!"

Referee Mel Wilson tried to ignore Ickey's raving and screaming by turning his back to the irate foaming at-the-mouth-coach. This only made the volatile coach angrier. He was a serious student of the Bobby Knight training videos. Too cheap to buy the whole series, he downloaded the free one on "How To Influence Referees And Still Be Friends," and refused to order any more. He was famous for throwing a TV monitor at the opposing team's mascot and for hurling a chair at the Laker dancers during the INBA Playoffs. More importantly, he was also famous for having the worst breath on four continents.

Wilson continued to ignore him, so Icky began screaming louder and louder.

"We need a review of the shot clock! We need a review! Listen, you god dam idiot! We need a review!" He was yelling barely an inch from referee Wilson's ear.

Enraged, but trying to keep his calm, the referee took a deep breath and turned around to face Icky.

"Listen, the damn shot was good. Fuck a review. If you need anything, you need a god damn breath mint, yuk mouth!"

Coach Icky lunged at the referee, only to be restrained by his assistants.

After languishing in a two-game shooting slump, which saw his scoring average drop from 34.3 to 25.2, the game's hero, Hassan, answered the call of his critics and evened the World Championship Shootout at 1 apiece for Sudan's Nuba Giants against the INBA's American divisional champion Toronto Raptors. His solid performance allowed a much-needed rest before Game 3 on Sunday. "Sorry," he said in Arabic, "No interviews," much to the disdain of the American sportswriters. As he headed towards the showers, he heard them whispering, "Prima Donna, definitely no Michael Jordan, couldn't hold Hakeem's jockstrap." He doesn't respond, but merely hums in his accentuated English, "Sometimes I dream that he is me…" and chuckled.

After the game's dramatic ending, Ellis looked over at where Wardell is supposed to be, but he's gone. Nowhere in sight, his brother, mother and father were still sitting and cheering as the seat where Wardell should be remained eerily empty. His absence stood out like Ewing's injury in the 1999 NBA Finals. *Did something happen? What's up with that kid? Maybe he just made the transition to his father and split. Damn! I need to get to Hassan for a comment and Yusef. Shit, this Wardell stuff ain't my problem.*

MISSING INAXUM

Moving quickly, Ellis raced down the hallway towards the NBA post-game press conference just in time to see U ascending the podium under a barrage of shouted questions.

"Coach Black, Black, Coach Black, what did you say at halftime to motivate Hassan?"

U looked slyly at the writer. "What did I say to Hassan? Nothing really, 'cept that he should forget about being on a cereal box with the type of performance he was having."

"Coach Black, Coach Black, how does this team compare with your Knicks teams?"

"Well, for one, nobody here carries a loaded pistol to the locker room. Secondly, the pre-game meals in New York put bacon in all of their food, collard greens, spinach, burgers, fruit salad—and I don't particularly like swine."

The crowd of journalists quieted down.

"Coach Black, I mean regarding basketball."

"I was joking," said U without a smile before continuing. "Yeah, for one thing, coaching here in the Motherland it's much easier. I mean we got some guys with big contracts, but the big contract mentality is not as bad, less stressful. And I don't have to worry about some two-bit agent telling a backup center he's worth a starting salary. The same backup center who might be worth a starting salary except he spends more time learning the girl's schedules at the strip club than learning how to make a turn around jump shot. More importantly, these guys are really hungry. They want the attention of the world. They want everybody to know that the Motherland will be the new Mecca for Hoop."

"Coach Black, did you take time to wash your ass this morning? 'Cause I know you getting kinda old."

"Huh?" said Yusef, as he stood up and stared into the crowd of reporters ready to open a can of whup-ass. He internally despised media, especially the way they treated him, but played the game like everybody else. As he stared at the back row of the group he noticed a somewhat familiar face and realized only one idiot would have the nerve to ask him some dumb shit like that.

"El, is that you? Ellis, is that you, Sun? Come on up here so I can smack you upside the head," said U with a slight grin.

El sauntered up to the podium, grinning from ear to ear. He almost had his normal walk back, but still looked like he was bopping.

"Yo, Sun, what up?" asked Ellis as he embraced U. "What's going on, Bruh? A brotha goes into a coma and you just jet back to the Motherland all quick 'n' shit. What's that about?"

U just smiled. "Man, we didn't know if yo' dumb ass was going to make it back to the land of the living. But, man there's so much to talk about. So much has happened that we got to discuss," said a nearly teary-eyed U, holding on to his emotions with the last bit of energy.

Meanwhile, the whole process baffled the other reporters. They simply viewed the reunion, dumbfounded. That is, until *Washington Pest* sportswriter Chunky LaRue opened his mouth.

"Coach Black, now that you've been reunited with your love child, can we get back to the press conference?"

U just looked at the reporter and calmly said, "Press conference over."

U then looked at his assistant. "And, oh yeah, scratch that fat bastard's name off the pre-game meal list."

As he exited the press conference, Yusef—the misplaced misfit, coach of the underdog Sudanese—was extremely relieved. For more reasons than one the American media had never given him credit for being able to coach. They said his assistant coaches and talented teams got him back-to-back rings. He always knew he could coach, but why, at age 59, did he feel the need to prove shit to them? He didn't want the critics to get to him the way they did Larry Holmes, who ended up fighting Michael Spinks when he could have retired as the only other undefeated fighter aside from Rocky Marciano. Still, nothing felt better than coming back to the Motherland and having the same fat-ass critics eat crow.

WARDELL IS HELL

While Ellis and Yusef made their way towards the Blue Nile Cafe, in the upper level of the stadium overlooking the junction of the Blue and White Nile, Wardell was on his way back to New York with a blue and white sash-covered object stashed in an elongated leather attaché case. It almost resembled an instrument-carrying case. He cleared customs quickly via diplomatic attaché status and boarded the 10-hour flight on luxury class. As scruple-less as possible, Wardell had simply accepted the dark side a long time ago. There was no Obi Wan Kenobi screaming, "stay away from the darkside." All he remembered was Michael Jackson singing *"Keep on/ 'Til the force stops/ don't stop till you get enough."* That was how he felt. "Don't stop till you get enough" of everything. He realized who and what he was and really didn't give a fuck. He knew there was going to be some heavy Karma for this shit. *In that case*, he thought, *might as well have another bottle of Cristal, since the*

Americans are paying for it. And he knew that eventually he'd pay too.

As the flight attendant passed, Wardell gently brushed against her behind and softly spoke, "Excuse me, can you bring me another Cristal? Also, I'd like some caviar and some of those expensive choc...lattes."

The tall blonde attendant merely smiled and nodded, paying no attention to the high level of lusty phermonic activity emanating from Wardell in her direction. He loved blonde hair and blue eyes—the bluer the better. *She'd look fabulous sunbathing on the yacht I plan to buy, once these fools pay me for the staff,* he smiled to himself.

THE BLUE NILE CAFE

The Blue Nile was circular-shaped. U and Ellis sat at a table that faced the Nile in the direction of Egypt. The constellations blinging in the sky were so low you could almost reach out and touch them.

"So El, glad to see you here. I told your girl Nicole that this was an event that you needed to be at. It has your name written all over it. Besides, so many times, brothas like you and me work hard and never get the recognition that we deserve. You know Hoop; fuck if you don't work for a big publication. We need to stop thinking that simply because mainstream society doesn't make us, doesn't mean that we ain't good at what we do. I mean people assume just 'cause this kid is on TV and you ain't, that he must ostensibly be better than you.

"Oob stens who?"

"Ostensibly—you know, like suppose."

"I know, U, I'm just fucken' with you," grinned Ellis.

U took a sip of his beer and leaned back. Smiling, he pointed at Ellis. "See, that's why you my boy. You don't take this shit too seriously. Everybody's a person to you. I hate when folks treat me like a celebrity or something."

U noticed that El seemed to be consumed by something. "El, you alright? Something' going on?"

Ellis leans forward. "U, I, I... you seen your nephew?"

U stared face down at the table and mumbled, "Wardell. Wardell, right? That mawfu..?"

"U, he was, we was, supposed to deliver something

important to your brother Musa, after the game. I know you and lot of people were depending on me, us, to do this thing. Man, it seemed far too important for somebody like me. But yo' nephew just disappeared and I'm worried 'cause I have no idea what he's up to. But you know him, U, and we can guess that shit is funky."

U glanced at the constellation of Orion while sipping his brew. He quickly signaled for the barmaid and the check. "El, where are you staying?"

"The Aten, Room 1111."

"Cool, go to your room and chill. I'll make a few calls and talk to some folks and hit you up in a few hours, alright?"

"Cool."

THE RAW

Because because/...I never ran from a man/...the first of what you call hardcore/ I guess hardcore's gritting your teeth and locking your jaw/...Flip the word around now raw spells war......" El sits back on bed listening to OC's "Word...Life." Thinking about everything and wondering where the hell he was and what the hell was going on.

He scanned the disc until he found his favorite cut "No Main Topic." The song was an anthem for his life; that seemed like some ménage of experiences and ordeals with no real meaning or overstanding. What was the point of being chosen to survive the Hood if his life would amount to nothing but a lot of missed opportunities? Surely he could do something right? Excel at something and move beyond the level of animalistic existence? At present he was just eating, drinking, and shitting. Surely, the Universe had more in store for him than *this*? Certainly, he was here for more than a continual string of half-successes? Maybe not; maybe it was his destiny to fail at the bigtime shit. Maybe that's why he didn't get to the NBA, why he wasn't working for *Sports Illustrated*, why he was of living with his uncle.

ROOM—Er, GUT—CHECK

Riiiingggg...

"El, this is Yusef. Check it—me and Musa will be by your room in 10-minutes. So that gives you enough time to take a shit and brush your teeth, not particularly in that order. Just don't go nowhere."

"Yeah, I'll be here," said Ellis, reclining on the bed surfing through 2,100 channels of mindless distractions. No sooner than when Ellis found something interesting on the tube—the final episode of "Jerry Springer," the one where he got beat down by a bunch of former guests—there's a knock on the door.

"Whoisit?"

"Yusef."

Ellis peeked the hole to be sure, and then quickly turned the channel before opening the door. He did not want folks to actually verify his idiot status if they knew he watched shit like "Springer."

Yusef walked in slowly with Musa right behind him. Suddenly they stood there together, both six three and broad shouldered. Ellis had an epiphany, "Damn! You guys look alike. Are you twins or sumthin'?"

Yusef grinned, in a *like-yeah-Negus-you-an-idiot* manner.

"Yeah, Musa and I are twins, but I am older by almost nine seconds. It's something that we keep as quiet as possible. He has his path to follow and I mine, and at times they both cross."

Ellis stood flabbergasted. *These guys are identical, except for the fact that Musa wears a full beard and U a Nubian trim.* U explained that he always wore either dark blue or brown and Musa always wore white linen, and cufi, normally with shades. This was amazing and a little more interesting than the "Springer" show.

"Let's get down to business," said Musa in a stern voice. "What has happened is partly my fault. This responsibility should have fell on my son Menelik. However, seeking any opportunity to bring my son, the "White Sheep," back into the Din, I agreed to his request to fulfill this obligation. It was simple enough, I figured. I had no idea that he was working against us, against me," Musa noted.

Yusef, seeing the pain of his twin, gently rubbed him on his shoulder. "It's not your fault, Mu. You, and me for that matter, simply tried to guide Wardell to the right way. But the boy got problems. And I'm'a kick his ass when we catch him.

You sure he your son?" Suddenly, Yusef caught himself, and closed his verbal barrage with "You've been a great father. We can't take responsibility for everything our children do, you and I both know that we could never blame the choices we made on our folks, so even though you hurting, give yourself some credit."

Musa, head down and with his breath barely escaping his larynx, slowly looked up and continued. "What we've found from our sources is that Wardell is on his way back to New York. It's clear that he's working as an operative of covert American Intelligence, who for obvious reasons believe that the staff is strategically valuable to their interests around the world."

Ellis now begins to feel overwhelmed—like a three-hundred-pound man suddenly realizing that the innertube he's floating on has a slow leak.

"Why would the government want the staff? I mean, it's just part of some myth, right?" asked U.

"Well, myth or not, someone has realized or believes that the staff might contain certain chemical properties related to some unimaginable energy source. I mean, I hadn't bought in it on myself totally, until this. It's clear that folks would love to capture and replicate the properties of the staff either for commercial or military or reasons or both," admitted Musa.

"Shit," said Ellis, as he stared out his hotel window, thinking pitifully, *Why me, Lord. Why me?*

"In any case," said Musa, "we've got you a ticket and full expense money to travel back to New York to get the staff. Wardell's flight is stopping over in London, and we've arranged for you to take a direct flight to DC You'll arrive a full 8 hours ahead of him, which should give you time to get to New York before him."

"What? Me? I mean he's your kid, right?" asked Ellis nervously.

Musa frowned slightly. "I cannot go myself, since I am sure to be detained by the American authorities, who have been trying to trump up some charges against me on mail fraud and tax evasion conspiracy. It's up to you, Ellis. This is what you have been chosen for. This is your destiny; there can be no other way. For whatever reason, you are the only one who can navigate New York in a manner that will not bring unwarranted attention. It's a matter of time, trust, and destiny."

Musa stood up and headed towards the door, quickly turning. "A taxi will be here in one half hour. You have until that time to make your decision."

Yusef stood to accompany his brother and, seeing the anguish on Ellis face, tried to comfort him.

"Ellis, this is up to you. It's your call, but never let fear of failure cost you greatness. In any case, I am still your friend. Peace."

ENTERING AMERIKA

Ellis lay curled up in the fetal position on the oversized bed wondering, *Why me?*

He had spent countless hours learning to manipulate whatever environment he'd been thrown into The Hood, college, and the "career" world, all without ever really buying in—never really belonging—never really taking any of it seriously.

He had attained the delicate subtleties necessary for the career of many a corporate CEO, despot, or politician, including the ability to do as little as possible actual work. While others struggled ruthlessly to attain the material items that John Q Public needed to see to be considered successful, El had simply skirted outside the lines, stepping in bounds to grab what was needed or wanted, then escaping back into his world. He was able to attain all the necessary, superficial items to indicate progress, but it never really mattered to him or held value. In this sense he was always old, old school and even if he fronted, he wanted to be remembered for doing something real as opposed to being remembered as some Negus that made dough.

At this moment in time, he knew there was no way around this shit. *This Karma bitch was a muther, and when I find her ass sipping bubbly in the VIP section of the club, I'm a put her in a LAPD chokehold, and finish up where they left off Rodney King. Nah, hoe, we can't just get along—it's judgment time. Heh Heh, yeah, yeah, it's Judgment time.*

By force of thought only, Ellis eased himself up with

the slight hope of finding himself. He was looking for something to pull from his stomach, something to grab onto—anything to get hyped about. Ellis Rey needed something to make him want to do this. Fuck it; if nothing else worked to give him his gusto, he could always turn to his old mistress, always there in times of need—Ms. Remy.

Quickly opening the room bar, Ellis poured two straight shots of Remy and downed them like a drunk after an "AA" meeting and a conversation with his wife on whether or not he still loved her. He turned on the music, dropped his sweat- soaked beige linen shirt onto the floor and headed for the showers.

The shower and the yak worked, like always—just for the moment. He knew he'd needed to find something in his spirit to carry him on once the intoxicants wore off. But that was something to think about later; plus, BlackStar Airlines served the best Cognac.

"I'm so fresh and so clean, clean/ So fresh and so clean, clean, so fresh and so clean clean /Ain't nobody dope as me…. " El sang to himself while throwing on his white linen shirt and matching white pants that flowed like water making him resemble the early Black Himyarites of Yemen. He packed one suitcase and sat quietly on his bed, staring out the window onto the solemn ageless Nile as he waited.

"Knock, Knock."

"Who is it?" asked a startled Ellis.

"I am Sulyiman, your driver. Can you hurry? We have just enough time to get you there and for me to get back and watch the game. I got a stack of chips on the Russians."

A bit perturbed, Ellis peeked through the hole and saw no one. He opened the door and still saw no one, 'til he looked down and saw a very short dark brotha with shades.

"Sulyiman?"

"Yeah, that de name—don't wear it out. 'Waaaasup?' I know you American brothas like dat shit, right? Come on, man, don't stand there staring; I know I'm short, I know the Black 'Mini Me." Fuck it, I was born short, you was born ugly. Grab yo' bag and lets get dis show on da road."

EMPTY SPACE

Reality sucker- punches me like a dope on the rope
While the crowd screams bomaye, bomaye
Instead of faltering, I swim upstream
Fake left/ then spin right like Black Jesus or Akeem
No dreams/ reality's enough for the moment/
I transpire and retire into dire straights
Only to respire and resurrect like Osiris
Though the universe never judges/
They try us
Then fry us
Just us and us alone will get us out of this shit
I spit in the wind and tackle backsliders
Slam Dunk the funk, like Shaq/ or young Isaiah Rider.
Then climb higher than Skywalker
Not a quick smooth talker nor stalker
My minds a money move/
Been schooling since a babe and still Negus want me to Prove/
I be real
Or better yet/ better than them
Hummm
Look at it from the back then hold it mid air like static
Eons pass within a few seconds and my mind eye travels through
your minds attic/
Radio organic compositions emerge from roots/
Governmental scientists destabilize DNA in cahoots
With otherworldly beings/
Simply mad 'cause I exist/
Tisk, tisk
Now ain't this some shit
The whole planet fucked
Just 'cause some be jealous.

THE AIRPORT RIDE

Ellis is whisked head down up Nuba Boulevard towards Pianki International Airport at breakneck speed, and Sulyiman is doing about 90 mph with his mouth.

"Ah man, I tell you, these new kidz out ain't got nothing on LL Cool J. Look! Look! Look! Behind you," screamed Sulyiman in excitement.

Ellis turned to see an old terricloth D-hat propped neatly in the back window.

"Damn!"

Giggling, Suliyman got excited.

"I know, I know, Kid. That shit's dope, right? They ain't really feeling it yet here in the Blackland, but I'm trying to make it happen, knowwhatimsaying? You know, like Common, I'm trying to resurrect the real elements. I even developed crazyphatt names for the five sections of the Omderman, named after the five boroughs of New York, on some 'Mr. Magic' type shit, you feeling me. We got …."

Suliyman continued to rattle on, while Ellis gazed out the window, lost in thought. He barely noticed all of the near-misses caused by Sulyiman decision to lean, despite his short frame. Ellis snoozed right after "Let me know when we arrive."

DELAYED

"'Scuse me, can I get another Cristal?" stuttered a high Wardell, more intoxicated off the idea of sipping Cris than the actual alcohol content. The flight attendant began to look better with each drink. *Maybe, I'll take her to the bathroom and do some work,* thought Wardell.

"'Scuse me, sweet thing, can I get another Cristal?"

The attendant, a bit frayed, walked past him quickly on her way to the cabin, then scurted past him again in the other direction. Wardell quickly reached out and grabbed her arm as if he was in the club and his bar tab gained him some additional privilege.

"'Scuse me, another Cristal, please."

She frowned with a look as if the tests were positive. "I'm sorry, Sir, but we only had four bottles of Cristal, and you've drank them all," she blurted out before quickly returning to the cabin. When there, she signaled to the sky marshall that they might have a terrorist situation emerging. The sky marshall nodded back at her and winked. He had spent two weeks training for his new position and would not feel comfortable until he was able to pump a few bullets into a suspect or possible suspect. If lucky, he would maybe be able to toss someone out the emergency chute, a new item that allowed immediate dangers, including terrorists, bombs, or flammable items to be thrust out of the plane without disturbing the cabin's pressure. Up to this point, his previous job had been way more fun, there at least could get all the leftover fries at closing time.

Pissed, Wardell leaned back before hearing over the intercom. "Folks, this is your captain. We will have to make a detour and will be landing in London to make some security checks and refuel. Please sit back and relax and we'll have you back on your way to New York within a few hours." The Captain flicked the cutoff switch for the intercom too lightly, unknowingly leaving it on. He leaned back looked at his copilot and took a swig of Iraqi scotch. "This is the second damn bomb threat we got this month. I hate flying to these damn terrorist havens—it's worse than Texas. Ain't these mawfukas got something better to do with their time, like race camels or drink beer? Or playing their favorite game 'Finding the Buried Shit In The Sand'?" he chuckled.

While the business section of the plane began planning the pilot's beatdown once they landed, Wardell remained in his own blinging universe.

What type of shit is this? No Cristal, flight delayed, rerouted. I know Jay Z didn't Big Pimp like this? I mean, how can I big-pimp without Cris? That's like a club with no VIP room-shit that's what made the world so beautiful-the shit that other people knew they could never have. This is some second-class shit. I wonder if I can get a refund? Contemplated Wardell as the attendant passed him again.

"Erum, you got any Moet?"

THE FLIGHT

BlackStar Air had a spotless record. Its aircrafts arrived and left on time. The company maintained an unblemished record for safety and comfort since the airline was first created by the merger of three African-owned airlines. It now provided direct flights to anywhere on the continent from Europe and the Americas. They were hoping to gain access to the Asian markets, which were expanding due to an incredible increase in tourists visiting Africa, as well as business ventures between Asian and African companies.

Maintaining a GNP growth rate of 7 percent for the past five years, things were on the lookup. It was indirectly due to the Congressional Black/Brown Alliance, which replaced both the CBC and the Hispanic Caucus in 2011. By consolidating their individual voting power in districts around the nation, the caucus was able to elect several members to the Senate based on what they termed the "First-World" agenda.

The key plank beneficial to Africa and South America simultaneously was the cutting back of funds for CIA covert operations and the passage of the Omnibus Small Arms Act, which prevented the US, as the No. 1 weapons producer, from selling weapons to nations identified by the Hague as being "warmongers." That—along with the African Mandela Plan (based on the post World War II Marshall Plan) and the West's plan for Poland, along with the cancellation of debt by G7 nations—changed the face of the continent. When the Occidental plague hit, it was like good and bad mushroomed into a second chance for Africa.

"Would you like something to drink, Sir?"

El looked up facing the beautiful Senegalese attendant. Her silky Black skin, thick lips, dimples, and a slight gap in her teeth, drew Ellis in as he stared at her pearly mouth. He loved staring at women's mouths, especially those with thick lips and a beautiful wide smile. It was inexcusably erotically inviting. Black women had the most beautiful of mouths.

His glance moved from her mouth to her slightly slanted eyes as his brain moved quickly telling his hormones to slow down. Seemingly, time overstood and slowed what appeared in Earthly terms as five seconds into an eternity to worship impeccable beauty. He was whipped already.

"Yeah, I would like a large cup of dandelion tea. Yeah, dandelion tea."

She smiled and returned shortly with his herbal tea and the most recent copy of *Afrikan Business* magazine. Her beauty made him lonely at a time when he needed someone to still his wavering resolve. Slowly he began to sip the dandelion. He knew he'd need a few more cups in order to gain the burst of chi necessary to move from this state of inertia and handle the shit he'd been handed.

You can do this, he silently began to repeat to himself.

You can do this.

Stay in the Now.

Now is Now. Don't worry and the past or future. Stay in the Now.

And right now he was on top of the World—literally.

Before his accident, Ellis was the king of self-motivation. His quest was finding something worthwhile to be motivated about. He learned that he could talk himself into anything, despite his fears. Normally, he could take the easy out—make the necessary joke—to put things in perspective. *It's all about perception,* he'd convince himself. *Look at the glass as half full, not half empty.* He kept his doubt at bay, knowing deep down that he simply wasn't the man he used to be, nor the man he thought he'd be. That guy was a professional ballplayer worth about half a bill. He wanted to believe that things always worked out, but he knew that took faith. Despite his intruding pessimism, he always attempted to hold onto a sincere belief that things would always work out—you know, the proverbial everything-happened-for- a-reason-type bullshit. But for a man who valued motion, physicality, physical ability—all ego-manifested attributes—being laid up for a few years drained his reserve of "faith," and demolished the ego-identity he'd spent a lifetime building. He'd heard all the bullshit before: "Suffering served to enhance us on our spiritual journey towards awareness and consciousness with the ALL." Yeah, that and a buck will get you a cup of coffee. Ellis realized that he was lost; no, he'd lost *it*. Whatever one might call it—the quintessence, "Fifth Element," the "Force," "Eye of the Tiger?" "Mojo?"—whatever it was, he didn't possess it any longer. His swagger was gone; he'd gone from a Negus spitting at the world to a man just trying to survive each day.

This was not simply a physical ailment on his part, but a crack in his armor. Somewhere, in between all the wise cracks and satirical humor, he had lost the ability to believe.

He believed in nothing. If put to the test, he knew very little of what he was committed enough to fight for. Was he willing to die for anything of value? He was like most Negus in the sense that he'd die over some BS, some dis, or some argument at a fast-food joint over nothing or over something his boy had said to some kidz. *But who wanted to die like that— over some meaningless shit that if you lived through, you'd never do again? How many Negus are sitting in prison right now, thinking that if they could relieve those seconds, that moment, that night would have walked away?*

Still, what did he believe in—*really* believe in?

He covered it well with the superficial positive affirmations, and strong support of people in need of affirmation, but his hope and faith in the Universe were gone. Maybe it was the fact that after viewing life as a list of vertical steps, he came to the realization that he was never going to be the conquering hero that he assumed was his destiny? Maybe he wished he could relate to someone in his family? Although he was one of four children, he had never had a big brother or a father. Maybe it was simply his failure to come to grips with his pervasive inability to trust people, his inability to learn from the past, or his inability to express himself emotionally? Shit, he was fucked up in ways immeasurable, and all of his pathologies had somehow decided to join forces against him at the worst possible moment.

That wasn't it.

He knew what it was, probably.

He just expected too much of people, too much from life. Expected them to be larger than life, unscathed by the trauma humans faced, he expected them to be like him. All this did was lead to disappointment, frustration and failed friendships when others couldn't master the territory, hold their liquor. Now he was what he hated—someone who couldn't master the territory, someone who for the first time in his life desperately needed someone to step in and help him without condemning him. But even if someone did step in, how would that stop him from condemning himself?

He wondered if hope had an email address?

Probably not—'cause it woulda been spammed by now.

A pager?

Shit, he had built up so many walls between himself and the Universe that if the Creator did want to communicate with him, she'd have to call upon Gabriel and the Stone City Band to get her message across.

He remembered a passage from the Bible that he read as a youth—well, not one that he read, but one his mother framed and sat over the kitchen entrance, as if that was her heaven, as if some how those words sewn together might prevent the evil of the world from entering that particular space:

"Who shall call upon the name of the Lord shall be saved."

I've been calling upon the name of the Lord since I was ten, when He gonna step up to the plate? I mean, I was supposed to be in the INBA, 'posed to have moved fam out of the Hood and bought Mom a house, 'posed to be happy.

Where does one turn when he has traveled the path, only to see its twists and turns before ending at a deep abyss separating him from Nirvana? Maybe he'd have to take the jump. He could no longer simply stand at the crossroads as his soul stared into the deep abyss. Vision gradually increasing enough to allow him to span through the multiple layers of darkness and see into Nirvana. He saw a figure standing— staring back at him. His vision zoomed in on a wooly-headed man anointed with a greenish sun-driven hue. As the glare decreased he saw his face and noticed that the figure staring right back at him *was him.*

How does one regain one's soul?

"We will be landing shortly," whispered the flight attendant, gently brushing Ellis on his shoulder. The intercom announced, "Please fasten your seat beats. We will be landing at Dullass International Airport in six minutes."

Ellis could hear the slow mechanical grind of the landing gear, exposing itself to the air. He sat up and locked in. As the attendant did a final walkthrough, he tapped her on the arm.

"Excuse me, is it too late for a drink?"

She smiled and leaned down, smelling of rose and musk, and whispered: "It is okay, you are not alone."

When he looked up, she was gone.

Instantaneously, the plane began to skip ever so slightly as its landing gear eased onto the ground in a perfect landing. As the plane rolled to its exit gate, the passengers applauded.

THE CAPITOL CON-NECT

Yo My Negus, Negus
Yo this shit is steep
I step into ya mental and your universe expands a thousand fold
Galactic I'm pretty young,
Though this continual physical manifestational shit is getting old,
Eventually cold
Too fucken valuable to be bought or sold
Caught on the other side of the SUN
A Malik
Still I shine
Like the souls of Blackfolks
Divine
Waking, walking into the light
I recite not to excite
Ignite like a Southeast Asian firefight
Rewrite the Nike commercial minus the hype
Tear off the Swoosh and replaced it with insight.
It's only right.
I've gotten every pair of Jordans,
And ain't never took flight
Words connect
Chew rocks like terrorsaurus rex
Complex
Or maybe just vexed
My words ponder
Then rain down like Malachi's holy text.
Nigger, Never
Niggaz never knew
Negus is Ethiopian for King.
As such calling someone the head nigga in charge would be
redundant
Like Krishna, Christos or Black Christ
I come like a thief in the night
Steal my way between your thighs
plant seeds like mustard that grow like tribes
of militant Jedi fed only on rice
Be I that nice?
Concise
no verbal heist.

I move inter-dimensionally
beyond the thrice
dimensional, demon-critical vortex of person, place, and thing,
Fuck a Bling Bling
Before light hits and you notice my whit
I transform the Blah to Chi and change into a book of destinies
To get paid like I-Ching
Or Yh King
Or should I say Negus.
Niggas no never
Negus should have know better
Men become mice when co-opted by cheddar
They be more trapped than Martin when he composed his
Birmingham letter
I said uh,
Maybe you shoulda
Read aaaaaa few more books
Instead U shook
Standing on the verge of Parkinson's
and only know the hook:
Big Pimpin spending G's, we talking big pimping...'cause we still
believe
that hay Sus
repeat in Ingles,
Ja Zeus,
Jesus is coming,
but he a virgin.
Come again?
Maybe we all getting jerked
Niggas,
no never,
but Negus be coming
Too late—we here

Walking towards the baggage terminal, Ellis noticed several shaded individuals dressed in FBDIE customary black suits, shoes, and briefcases. He noticed them watching him as he slowly attempted to orient himself to the airport. Plane rides always made him dizzy, clogged his sinuses. He recognized that he might be a little paranoid, so he said a mental *fuck it* and continued his trek to the baggage claim area.

This was the worst part of traveling: tracking down your bags and making your way out of the airport. Packs of angry, anxious, half-dazed people all suffering from post-flight meal acid reflux an mobile-phone-jonesitis. While peeping for his bags, Ellis thought he saw a somewhat familiar face. *Naw, couldn't be. Jay? Naw.* Everybody had a twin somewhere, but this kid looked exactly like him, 'cept he was dressed too nice. Congolese cut wool suit, and Tanzanian gators. The tie alone must have run $200. Jay didn't roll like that—*well, at least not the last time I saw him*, mused Ellis.

A woman with two huge suitcases packed tighter than the mass of a white dwarf and three raggedy children trailing her, walked by carving distance between herself and other airport patrons like a pulling guard. Distracted for a second, Ellis turned and Jay's twin was gone.

This shit was unnerving—like Duke winning an NCAA championship. With his bearings slowly returning, Ellis then noticed two suspicious characters by the newsstand. He avoided looking directly only by using his peripheral vision; it was a skill he had developed after countless hours of playing Hoop in addition to countless outings of sneaking peeks at other women while with Makeda.

Based on their inability to walk while chewing gum, Ellis immediately determined that they must be Federals. These guys were dressed down like civilians and it might have worked, 'cept for the fact that one of them had on a Bill O'Reilly T-shirt and a pair of red coach cons. Ellis remembered Unk Breeze telling him 'bout those sneakers while Ellis was growing up. "Nobody intentionally bought Coach Cons on the East Coast, Sun, only if they couldn't afford a pair of All-Stars."

Acting as if he doesn't see them, Ellis hurriedly walked

in the other direction towards his luggage. Walking quickly, he caught up to and bumped into the big lady, bags and kidz altogether.

Using her as a screen, Ellis cut in the other direction towards one of the departure gates. He blended in, stood silently and waited. It was an old trick that he learned growing up in the Projects, one of many designed to throw off pursuers whether it be kidz from other buildings, cops, or store detectives. Thirty-seconds passed before the two federal idiots passed by him in a rush.

Nervously, Ellis figured out his next move. *How the hell was he going to get to New York?* He felt a tap on the shoulder. Afraid to turn around, he swallowed air and turned slowly.

"Ellis?"

Standing before him is a six foot seven giant dressed as a limousine driver.

"Ellis, I think we should be leaving now. Your car is just outside. We should move quickly, I think your friends will be returning this way soon."

Without even the hint of some sarcastic rhetorical remark, Ellis got to steppin'.

Both jet—moving, it seemed, at another speed than everybody else at the airport. No it wasn't like another speed; it was like they were moving through space while everybody stood still. Ellis didn't even notice him grabbing his luggage and tossing it like a pebble into the trunk or even getting into the car. *My uncle told me about mixing light and dark liquer*, he thought, slowly returning to conscious reality as they drove beyond Dullass exit and hit 395-North.

"You, arum."

"It's Mali. That's my name, Ellis."

"Yeah, um, Mali, can I ask you a very small question?"

"Sure, Ellis, ask me anything, except whether or not I play ball—I refuse to answer that. Just 'cause a brotha's 6-7 I got to be in the INBA. I don't play ball, man, so don't ask me that. You know 'cause—"

"Yo, Malik," interrupted Ellis, hoping to catch him before he descended into a sobbing tirade of how his youth was destroyed by his experiences as a Catholic altar boy.

"I don't give a shit if you played ball or not. I just want

to know where the fuck we going."

"Oh man, I'm sorry. We're going to the Empire State, aka the Rotten Apple."

Relaxing a bit, Ellis leaned back against the plush leather seats, happy after the long-ass plane ride that he is able to fully stretch out his lanky 6-2 frame. The limo was old as hell, but it rode smoothly and was spotless. Ellis was so tight, he wondered about the ramifications of mixing a glocusamin chondritan cocktail with cognac. He pressed the mini-bar button and saw that the limo came well stacked with Yak, but no glocusamin in sight. *Oh well, I guess I'll just have to settle for the Yak.*

Aiding Ellis in his relaxed state, Malik threw on some Cannonball Adderly. As the horn section rips the smooth rhythms throughout the limo's 25 speakers, sleep slowly emerged from the shadows and engulfed Ellis. He welcomed it, too tired, too inebriated to fight.

BACK IN BLACK

John Shadow reclined comfortably while watching "Shaft's Big Score." He was a Blaxplotation-era freak. He had all the ill shit—"Coffy," "Super Fly," "Cleopatra Jones," "Black Caesar," "The Mack," "The Education of Sonny Carson," damn near everything. He could never quite understand why the Seventies flicks were called "Black explotation" flicks, while those made in the Nineties were not? Baffling, and he was not one to be baffled. Shit either landed on this side of the fence or the other—for John Shadow, won't no in-between shit.

It seemed to Shadow that we had it all wrong. During the so-called Seventies Blaxplotation flicks, we knew who the enemy was and what we was fighting for and against. In those films we could see Pam Grier bitch slap some redneck cracker responsible for trying to pump drugs into the community. Or like "Shaft in Africa," when one bad-to-the-bone brotha disrupted the whole modern-day African slave trade. *These guys were our heroes, fighting against crime and kicking ass against the folks we could never reach in real life,* Shadow rationalized, as he sat back taking puffs on his favorite Dominican brand Cohibas and sipped Belvadere. *Now in the Turn of the Century era,* he thought to himself, *we didn't know who the fuck we were supposed to be fighting against. We gave no answers to why the shit was happening in the Hood, around the world. Negus made films and told our stories like it hadn't already been done. We didn't have no heroes that fought the Power.* Shit, as a kid, Shadow actually believed in "New Jack City's" Cash Money Brothers. CMB were the ones that created crack and that Nino Brown was some modern-day Bumpy Johnson.

Not that he really gave a shit—it just baffled him. He was a brotha committed to doing the power-brokers dirt against his own and anybody who stood in their way regardless of color. For Shadow, being amenable to any issues relative to Blackfolks might get his ass capped. It would probably happen on a blustery fall day, where while he was walking a car would pull up and someone familiar would call out to him—like Skippy his old lacrosse buddy from college, or Justice Thomas?—they'd ask him to take a ride and that'd be all she wrote.

Regardless of Shadow's aversion to being in a perplexed state, he in turn baffled everybody else. He loved these flicks from the Seventies, and appeared, at least on surface, to love the Blackfolks in them. He always cheered for the hero to kick some white ass, unless, of course, he had company—which was practically never. Yet he hated Blackfolks now.

They used to be cool, I mean real cool ya dig, but now they just thugs was how he peeped it. He hated these so-called thugs and hated anybody who didn't hate thugs, or what he called the Black Culture Commoner. He looked at thugs with a serious distaste. *Anybody knew that the Africans weren't slaves when they came over here in chains—they had to be* made *into slaves—and some evolved into criminals and thugs. This was how they broke us. It wasn't a matter of Kunta changing his name to Toby; it was changing Kunta into a Toby.*

Now Negus embraced the animals we'd become like that's what it really meant to be Black. Oh, he hated them with a burning passion. This made his job easy, 'cause he didn't do anything to those folks in the movies, the heroes; his targets were just the "thugs." He was sure that if Shaft and Foxy Brown were still kicking it today, they'd seen things his way a long time ago after dealing with thugs.

For this approach he was well rewarded. Shadow was

the only Black in his luxury building with the best apartment on the 60th floor overlooking the World Trade Memorial that rose into the New York City skyline like modern gleaming obelisks. Glancing over, he admired—and then re-admired—all of his exotic and pricey trinkets with the latest gadgetry. He truly loved his infinity pool that appeared to stretch into the Gotham sky. *This was more than worth the price of my soul,* he mused. *More than enough,* as he sat smoking his expensive cigar, sipping Bel, friendless, alone. These times were the toughest for a man without a soul. Alone he sipped, gradually forcing from his mind the thought that he wished he had never been born. *Never been born—if I had my way, I wish I'd never been born.* The only thing he hated worse than thugs was himself. *Should have never been born*, he thought. *But since I'm here, all these mawfukas got to pay. Got to pay,* thought Shadow, tears swelling up. *Yeah, they got to pay; and, if they can't afford to pay? Well, then...they gotta pay.*

DA CAPITOL

Twenty minutes after leaving Dulles Airport and heading north, Malik half-heartedly agreed to Ellis' requests to stop off in the District to grab some grub. Well, truth be told, Ellis didn't really agree to stop off in DC, Shit, all he did was agree with Malik that they both were hungry and could go for some fish po'-boy style.

Malik was a big man. He was not a person ruled by things such as hunger or lust, but he had a premonition of things to come and knew that Ellis would fare much better in their mission with something solid in the belly. Plus, he knew this spot right off H Street where you could get a fat Po' Boy sammach of whiting along with some cakes. Hopefully, the spot would not be packed and they could get right in and out then hit New York Ave to the BW Parkway—a few minutes for some serious fish wasn't too much to ask, thought Malik.

Malik pulled the limo up slowly sliding in between a Lexus and Altima up onto the sidewalk just barely missing an older brotha coming out the fish store. Pissed, the pedestrian angrily glanced at Malik and thought about it, but like most—after seeing the size of the brotha—let it go. Besides, he wasn't going to take a chance on getting his ass kicked and dropping his fish. Those were two traumatic events that best be set apart by at least a few months.

The sky glistened like a freshly waxed whip. Crisp air made folks hustle. As the car came to a slow halt, Ellis regained consciousness.

Looking up he said, "Damn, what the fuck is going on, Malik? Is this Mardi Gras?"

"Naw, man, dis da fish store," grinned Malik. "You get madd fish for your money. C'mon, Ellis, lets get our grub on."

As Ellis eased out the limo, he noticed the line in the takeout fish spot flowed out the door. The line leaned back almost Mikejacksonish—like to figure, *Who's the brotha in the limo and his giant driver?* All El needed was some Blingtonium and a few ebonies on his arms to kick off the video scene.

After ten minutes of waiting, Malik finally made it to the front of the line.

"Yo, baby, let me get six whiting sammaches and three orders of fries."

Ellis moved to step out of the line, until Malik turned to Ellis. "What do you want?"

"Shit, I want one of your sammaches—I mean, sandwhiches."

Malik gritted, "Naw, Kid, you gots to get yo' own.'"

Ellis ordered one sandwich and the cashier slid him a bill for $40.

"I know I haven't been in DC in a while, man but $40 for one sandwich? Let me guess, the Homeland Security tax? No, naw, you guys must be using the Worldcom accounting method?" snapped Ellis.

The cashier stared, blanked face, except for a small twitch in his right eye. Ellis realized, *This kid is serious. Not only is this kid serious, but he's done some real bad shit, something real, real bad.*

"No, Sir," said the cashier.

"The big driver he said you gonna pay for both orders. That's $40."

Ellis grinned and glanced back looking out the door to see Malik working his way through his second sandwich.

"Okay, Okay," grinned Ellis, "I got it."

He walked out quickly moving backward like a defensive drill.

"Excuse me! Oh." Ellis quickly turned around to see whose foot he's stepped on.

"Excuse me, ma'am." Ellis suddenly noticed this fine-ass ,brown-skinned sista attached to thick and bowlegged thighs. Moving up her body her breasts swell like—like, well, like healthy melons. He noticed her thick pouty lips, and tight skirt.

Damn!

As Ellis stared at this beautiful Eboni dream, he remembered that he's seen her before; he knew her. She knew him too.

"Ellis, is that you? What you doing here in DC? Maya said you was going to be in Africa for a month!"

Quickly, Ellis' brain throws a fastball directly to his groin area, as he realized he's done mentally freaked Makeda's sister Nubia.

"Nubia, what—what are you doing here?"

"Well, I like fish. What *you* doing here?"

Ellis looked down and up quickly, "Well, just passing through on my way to New York. Makeda doesn't even know I'm back in the States. Something went down and I'm trying to deal with it now."

"You something, Ellis. You sure you ready for fatherhood?" said Nubia as she rolled her eyes and looked away towards her parked Burgundy Lexus, complete with "ALLMINE" personalized plates.

Ellis followed her eyes and saw a fine-looking figure sitting in the car. It was Makeda. *Shit! I'm not ready for this*, he thought to himself.

Then Ellis caught himself.

FATHERHOOD?

What the hell is Nubia talking 'bout?

Ellis looked back at Nubia. "So, what you talking about, 'fatherhood'?"

Nubia rolled her eyes again and turned away as if Ellis were some homeless person pestering her for some change.

Ellis was dazed. Sure as hell he wasn't ready for none

of this, but his dick was; when he saw Makeda in the car, his mind lost it, but his dick remembered all the good times and wanted to say hello. He had to get out of here before his erection reached full mast. Slowly, Ellis moved toward the car.

Makeda saw him coming and tried not to look at his direction, but she recognized him immediately. Her leg began to twitch frantically. She needed some weed—something to calm her down. *What's he doing in DC?* she thought to herself, at the same time, glancing at the driver-side mirror to make sure her face looked okay. She couldn't take it.

Ellis tapped on the window.

Onlookers gazed at the situation, wondering who this limo-riding fool was. The air was sweet like air from the southern hemisphere, from areas where the Earth was still alive. This scent that was warm and spicy; it was like that wherever Blackfolks be. The air seemed to blend with smell of the people.

Within a minute the environment began to change. Tension began rearing its head, sneaking a peak from the sewers seeing if it could kick off some shit. Tension peered the area with blood-red eyes and yuk-mouth grill. He knew where to find Negus at, and was an expert at starting some bullshit off bullshit. Oftentimes it could take something as simple as a prolonged glance, an inadvertent nudge, a misheard word, presumed diss, long-day, backache, headache, or low gas tank, or a light bill pending to turn the sky red with rage.

Pavement stained with blood would be the result, along with post-fight discussions that would carry over 'til the next conversation to the next 'til someone addressed the ill-legality that went down, either with the people involved in the first melee or anyone with a prolonged stare, inadvertent nudge, presumed diss. It didn't matter. Tension didn't give a shit. He was a one mean motherfucker, but tonight wasn't his night. "Shit, where the fuck is Jerry Springer when ya need him?" He growled as he slowly sunk his head back down the sewer hole, it was just a matter of time. "Just a matter of time for blood to be spilt and I eat," he grinned deviously.

Tension realized it wasn't his night, but whenever he

couldn't get things going, The FBDIE did its best to pick up the slack.

Few people realize the power of timing.

Being born at the right time could seal your fate up to the millisecond. Wars turned in a second. People lived and died in a second. Those who were able to master timing knew something that the ancients knew about the power of time. Everything had its time. Buried beneath the sands lay kingdoms that ruled the entire planet. Today, nations of poor sat and scrambled for crumbs on the same grounds where gold dust was once given freely to its inhabitants. Few realized that the first Portuguese ships arrived at a time in between the creation of the next great African Empire. Only if Ghana, Mali, or Songhay, had continued for just a little longer.

Time was important, but timing more so.

In the time it took for Ellis to walk to the car and tap on the window once, FBDIE agents had found his location. Not because they were that tight. No, they stumbled upon him, while attempting to find something to eat quick and cheap. They hit the jackpot and suddenly they had found their meal. Tension peeked again from its sewer hole. "Gonna eat tonight," it grinned.

Makeda stood outside the car.

"Ellis Jackson! What are you doing here? You're supposed to be in Africa covering the Tournament, right?"

Ellis blushed, unable to hold back his smile. Stuttering, he tried to make sense.

"Yeah, yeah, I know. I know I'm supposed to be there, but some slippery shit went down with Wardell and I had to jet back here 'incognegro' to take care of this shit for Yusef and his family."

Makeda frowned.

"What the hell are you talking about? I come down here to see my sister while you are away in Africa, and I run into you here? This is not making sense. I thought we trusted each other, Ellis! Why are you playing games with my life, my emotions?"

Ellis moved closer.

"Maya, I mean Makeda, what's going on? What your sister talking 'bout? I ain't ready for fatherhood! Something I need to know?"

Ellis moved even closer and took her small hands into his. Makeda looked deeply into his eyes.

"Ellis, I just found out, I'm pregnant. I was planning to tell you as soon as you got back, didn't want you to have more things on your mind while in Africa. But, thanks to Miss Loose Lips in there, you found out anyway."

Makeda looked away, water forming in her eyes, feeling that maybe they didn't have the relationship, the love for each other she thought they did. Ellis could see her sliding a door between him and her emotions that if ever closed, they would be over.

Silence ensued for what seemed like minutes.

Ellis smiled and kissed her on the cheek.

"I can't believe it. We gonna be parents. That means we have to get married," smiled Ellis as he hugged Makeda tightly. "Just trust me, Makeda. I can't explain everything right now; it'd just put you in danger. I got to handle this shit and I'll explain everything when it's over."

He began to stutter, "You, you, you got to understand, I mean overstand what's happening, I've got to do this serious thing. It's madd serious, and I'm not sure if I can do it or will make it back," quickly catching himself, he kills the doubt. "I mean, I'll make it back. I got to make it back now; it's just that I've got to handle this business first. I got to handle this first— no choice."

Makeda held his hand tighter and looked up with melting eyes. "Ellis, you always have a choice—you've just got to determine what is important for you. That's all we all have in this world is choice."

Ellis slowly looked up from the ground and stared into her eyes. At that moment, they finally reached the mental emotional sweet spot that lovers constantly physically squirmed in unison for a millennium to achieve. Ellis reached out and slowly touched her lips with his fingers. He moved them around her cheek, then drew her lips to his. Stars twinkled in their souls, transporting them for a quick second to a time and place that knew no time nor place—ecstasy.

FREEZE, NIGGA

Malik sat back in the limo, waiting on Ellis to do his thing, or at least until the fish was gone. He'd turned on the HDT headsets and watched music videos using PHD Technologies. PHD Technologies, which hiphop artists called "Playa Hating" Technologies, had made incredible advances in the area of real time video editing by using a unique freeze-frame system that could isolate video dancers from start to finish in video one-on-ones. What it did in practicality was to allow middle-aged men who didn't gave a shit about the artists to watch all the semi-naked women without bothering to have to watch the rappers emcee. It was amazing. All the ass-shaking hoochies you could watch without the bothersome hiphop artist clouding the picture. Although he normally avoided this type of entertainment, Malik, like everyone else on the planet, had his lower human tendencies that snuck back fighting for attention. They were showing a special edition of "Comicview," where the viewers were plugged into the dialogue between producers and cameramen during taping. To say it was interesting might be an understatement. It went sorta like this:

Camera 1*: Okay, I'm going in for a cleavage close-up for the hottie in row 2. Damn, she phatt.*

Camera 3*: Yo, Yo check me, I got this hottie with the big ass bending over in the front row.*

Camera 2*: Oh shit, you Negus ain't seeing what I'm seeing in Row 4. She got two midgets in a headlock, and one of them 'bout ready to break loose….*

Glancing between the video and back at Ellis from the rear view mirror every 7.6 seconds, Malik could see the changes in his environment as they developed. He was the type who often seemed aloof, unresponsive, or indecisive and all them other adjectives that society threw around when trying to figure out what motivated wooly-headed peoples. All of this, he was far from. Rather, more accurately, he was a 7th degree black belt in Wu Shu and a master of Akido, an artform that utilized his powerful electromagnetic energy as a means to deflect any aggression back on to the attacker. He had mastered several fields, including African, Asian and Native American herbalogy. He was on the verge of becoming a Sun of Righteousness, yet he was still tied too much to the world of material things—attached far more than he ever realized. Becoming a Sun of Righteousness moved far beyond the sphere of being a good Christian, Muslim, Buddhist or state sanctioned religions. Those belief systems were not that hard to master or become good at—at least on the surface. Becoming a Sun required individuals to give up all the internal bullshit that was acceptable in most religions as long as you put on the correct face. It wasn't about being perfect nor attending the right church, getting an education, or making money and giving to charity. It simply meant attaining the burning heart often associated with ancient portraits of masters, prophets and saints, where love for all ruled your every actions, where all the bullshit games humans played with each other for whatever self-justifiable reasons ended, where everyone was united, where there was no differentiation between all of the Universe's creations. It was akin to that scene from "The Matrix" where Neo began to see things in its true digital form. Most humans didn't understand that everything that we see just wasn't a reflection of the true image from the sun, but a reflection of ourselves that once you reached a certain level of consciousness became the difference between black-and-white TV and a high- def plasma screen. You came into the actual realization as opposed to those operating on some theoretical idea of things that they weren't totally sure of.

You learned, for instance, that all things originated from and would return to the same source. It was like water—regardless of the form it took, it retained the ability to return to its original form.

These individuals who attained that state could walk into a room and immediately change the vibrations of everyone there from negative to positive, even if only for a moment. A few of these individuals together could change the Universe. All beings from all galaxies knew this and were hugely disappointed that this present generation no longer overstood it. They thought you needed things outside of themselves to create.

Malik was an advanced being. But unknown to himself, he was still quite a bit away from reaching this coveted state of grace. As such, he could not understand why he been given this task that any peon could handle. Hopefully, if he stayed on point, he'd reach it during his next lifetime or the one after that.

Why he had been chosen to take Ellis to New York was not clear, but everything had its time and place and it would be revealed in due time. Nevertheless, he was a true soldier and his reputation was immaculate. He wasn't going to allow any nonsense to impact his credentials in that way. He was striving for perfection in the way some overzealous corporate employee pursued a top job, or the way some ballplayers focused on getting theirs rather than on winning.

As Malik peered through his right-side mirror, he saw FBDIE move into the scene. *These bastards don't quit*, he fumed to himself. *That's good, 'cause neither do I.* These agents amused him. *I think these mawfukas had to pass a non-rhythmic type of aptitude test to get hired. The rumor was that they could not have had an original thought in over three years or they would not have been hired. That was key. No thinking.*

"Freeze, Nigga!" Ellis, liplocked with Makeda, flinched. *What the fuck is going on?*

"Freeze, Nigga!" they repeated. "Now step back slowly or you will be taken down."

"'Taken down?'" repeated Ellis. "This some WWE type bullshit."

The agent speaks calmly, "No it's FBDIE, Negro. Now step back slowly."

Realizing the situation he was in, Ellis complied and slowly stepped back, wondering if this was it. He knew that FBDIE had smoked more brothas than the PG County Police. Suddenly while standing with his hands up, he heard two thumps. Two back-breaking thumps.

"Yo, El, man, let's go."

Still afraid to move, Ellis stayed put.

"Yo, El, man, let's move it, Sun."

Slowly Ellis looked back only to see both federals

crumpled on the cement, with Malik standing grinning.

"You know me; can't let you go out like that."

Ellis grinned for a second. "Yeah, man, I was about ready to handle dem cats."

Quickly he turned around and kissed Makeda again. "'You got to *jet*, and get your fish-eating sister. I'll contact you shortly."

"Ellis, Ellis what's going on? Who were those people?"

"I can't half-explain it now, but I love you and you and I got to go—Now, *go!*"

95 NORTH

"On the wheels of steel/ tell me how you feel/ dundundun dununu," blasted through the speakers while Malik handled the limo like a new Porshe. That Outkast shit was his driving music and it seemed that the volume as opposed to the gas pedal controlled his speed. Ellis merely peered out the window, mentally locked in his embrace of Makeda. Malik zoomed along 95 at breakneck speed through Baltimore and hit the Delaware Memorial Bridge in no time, skating through tollbooths on Quickpass and slid into Jersey quickfast.

Etched in Ellis mind were still major question marks. *Why him? Makeda pregnant?*

He began the backward trace of his existence of 32 years, attempting to find some hidden gem that would explain what was happening now. There was none.

PULL OVER

The New Jersey Turnpike rose to six lanes on either side, turning and swirling through the small state like Medusa's bounty. The Turnpike had long been a dangerous place for Blackfolks traveling north or south. Good thing the folks in the Underground Railroad didn't have to travel through it— no doubt they would've been pulled over along with those Blacks dat had deys papers.

Flowing along, Malik has changed up the beat to Ghostface's "Supreme Clientile." Half-awake, Ellis forgot for a moment that he's the chosen one and began to flow to the beat, already transforming the airspace with the car's cabin to nitro.

He started in his head and before he realized it, shit had expanded to the point where it was no longer containable within the mental.

Uh, uh, uh, uh….
"More than less, I impress
beyond existentialism-avoid the rest-
never slept
maybe manana
I spark ya mind with home grown habanas
Rolled tight
blindly rewrite prophecies with future insight
and out maneuver-agents of j edgar
or who ever
chooses to bite-
Beyond the clout, I give shouts
to ancestors
and sprout manifestos that showers the world's soul
one drop of this shit reverses mold
transforms death,
those in error sip and
gasp they last breathe
silence be kept
Some Push up to get buff
Still it's not enough
They stand lyrically on the rim of metaphysical annihilation
Frustration creates a bandwidth I can't get with
Infinity carries on as if I've never been here
What the Fuck do I care,
As long as she keeps it moving
If I fail, we catch hell
clock wizdom like we greedy
drop gems on the needy
No hype
 Recite
between sips of kava in Tahiti or noni
Gaze interrupted only
by her thick lips
fat hips-ass like Serena

The music ended abruptly.

Malik slowed down gradually. He quickly pulled over to the right side embankment, as streams of patriotic sherbet lit up the sky behind them. Ellis grimaced internally, keeping a straight-faced look that made anyone think he was serious and sober at all times. Even though this time he was serious and almost sober, once bodily reactions have been ingrained, they become automatic whether we realize it or not. In this case, it worked out in his favor. Slowly he began to tighten his butt cheeks, and begin his transformation to Bryan Gumble.

Ughrrr, Urghrr.

Slowly clearing the bass out of his voice, he wanted to be as non-threatening as possible. These Jersey kidz with badges were ruthless. Any type of indiscretion was met with Glock soup, once they began firing and re-loading and firing again a few more times for good measure. Ellis began increasing his focus—an old Jedi mind trick he mastered. Hell, one time, almost became one with J.C. Watts.

Inside he began smiling to himself and worry began to leave his mind as much as was possible when dealing the Jersey Gestapo. That is, until he glanced at Malik.

Immediately, Ellis realized that no matter how much real or imagined Caucasian DNA he was manifesting, this shit won't gon' work with Malik up there looking like a big ass dread-lock Green Hornet. At that point, he let his butt cheeks relax.

"GET OUT DA CAR! NOW! GET OUT THE CAR, GET NOW! OUT CAR, NOW, GET CAR, NIGGA, GET NOW, NIGGA, CAR!"

Two officers screamed at the same time, confusing the shit out of Ellis. Malik just sat there like he was half asleep. *One thing that really pissed me off,* thought Ellis, *was when these mawfukas start screaming at the same time. Don't they realize that shit just makes a situation get more potentially ugly?*

Within the span of the longest 20 seconds known to humans—outside of Dean Smith's four-corner offense, of course—Ellis was face down on the cold-ass highway.

While grass, gas sediments and cigarette butts introduced themselves to the left side of Ellis' face, he strained his neck slightly to see what was going on. All he could hear was the loud roar of vehicles passing them by doing 80 mph. He couldn't see Malik ease himself out of the car, while the stormtroopers stepped back slowly, Glocks pointed, fingers itchy. Before Ellis blinked quickly, he could see twin pairs of boots up a few feet from his face. Both troopers were on the ground out like a light.

Shit, this Negus needs his own theme music. I'm rolling with a fucken supa hero? Ellis wondered as he tried to stand up. Using his shoulders and forehead, he lifted himself off the ground. People always told him he was hardheaded; this time he finally agreed, and realized it was a blessing.

Malik handcuffed both troopers and carried their dead weight back to the police cars and locked them in the trunk.

Moving fluidly, they took off in the limo and didn't look back. Twenty minutes later, they were outside the Meadowlands heading towards the Lincoln Tunnel.

After five minutes or so of silence, Ellis, unable to control his curiosity, asked, "Did you kill them? I know you handle yo' business thorough, but man, we gonna catch madd flak for this. Shit man, I'm gonna have to leave the country and get some African name like Kwaku."

"Listen," said Malik in a slow and deliberate voice, "I didn't kill them, just disabled them. I shoulda, but I didn't."

"Damn," erupted Ellis, "You dangerous, Kid. How'd you take them down like that? I was just looking, you know, preparing to make my move and all I saw was you take one step towards them and that was it. They was out like Pro Keds."

Malik mused, wondering, *Is this kid on something, or is he genetically prone to hyperbole and wisecracks?* "It's called Akido."

"Akido? Shit, they should call it 'A'-kill-dem,'" smirked Ellis.

"No, it's Akido—a spiritualized Japanese fighting style that shows you how you can manipulate the energy within everyone's magnetic fields."

"Damn, Kid, you definitely got something under the dome there. Why in the hell you driving a limo?"

"I *don't* drive a limo," said Malik.

"Well you driving one *now*,'" quipped Ellis.

"No, I'm doing a task for some people that included

me driving a limo to New York. That's all."

"Okay, Okay, Kid, don't get all 'Oprah' on me, I'm just saying you kicked ass back there. Nawmean?"

"Well," said Malik, "I couldn't have done it without the inspiration of seeing you assed-out on the cement crying like a bitch."

Ellis laughed. "Ooh, oh, Damn, you had to go there, right? Catch a brotha down and out in his moment of weakness and smack him up. Alright, aaaiight, you got me. You caught me. You damn Buju-Baton-on-steroids-looking bastard."

Silence held for a quick five seconds and Ellis wondered whether Malik was about to pull the limo over and whip his ass.

If he does pull this car over, I'm running.

Malik finally broke the silence. "El, you one crazy mother. Be glad that I like you," he paused, "just enough to not pull this car over and whip yo' ass."

Both men fall out into a much-needed round of laughter that eased the stress of the moment. Ellis leaned back and relaxes as they exit the Turnpike and Malik tosses in his Dilated Peoples CD, *"If worst comes to worst my peoples come first/..dundundin dindindin, duddudin/ "If worst comes to worst my peoples come first..."*

As they bop to the music, the starry skyline of New York City slept in the background as if it was waiting for them to arrive. There was always a sense of excitement for Ellis, on any return to the City (or CI as many a Negus called it), especially once the skyline became visible at night. More importantly for Ellis, this was the first time he'd had a good laugh in what seemed like months, or, in reality, possibly years. This was the first time in a long time he again felt like Ellis, King Of Wise Cracks And One Upmanship. *A long time*, he thought, but his mojo had returned and could have come at a no better time than now.

BIG CITY OF DREAMS

Entering New York had a surreal feel to it. Malik drove smoothly and the limo rolled as if it were on panels of yellow-bricked glass. Amazing for the city of potholes, but if there were holes in the road neither Ellis nor Malik noticed. It was the quintessential calm before the storm—as if an endomorphic gaseous chemical had eased into the vehicle and overwhelmed them. They nodded to the music and floated as if engulfed by black liquid ether.

The sights and sounds of the city moved with them at their speed. Shielded from the normal noisiness of the city, time hung like a finger roll on the rim of eternity. It was like Einstein's Theory–everything was relative. Depending on at what rate you were vibrating on, your vibration rate actually determined how slow or fast time moved for you. For Ellis, it seemed that time was on the verge of stopping. Everything moved and flowed like where people, cars, clouds—night itself blended together into a scene of universality and duality had lost its meaning. Everything seemed connected and part of the same source. He had come into awareness of the state of NOW.

Suddenly, the pace picked up *Sccrrrrch!*

"What the—?"

Ellis erupted, as Malik swerved the car 180 degrees to avoid hitting this fool who stepped out into the street without looking. The quick turn and braking shifted the car forward and then back again like a pogo stick.

As Malik and Ellis settled down from an incident that their spines would eventually remind them of about twenty years from now, probably while they were in the midst of doing some old funk move like the Bizmark on the dance floor or while stretching prior to a game of streetball. But at this moment, they've got to address this idiot standing full frontal, screaming at the top of his lungs, "Hit me! Hit me, mawfuka! Hit me!"

Ellis got nervous while this kid erupted into a pedestrian psycho-maniac, foaming like Cujo in the latter stage of rabies. Sweat trickled down his brow, and Ellis could tell by the way his hand is shaking that he's got some unresolved childhood issues surrounding his father's failure to show him any approval. As a matter of fact, the way he's kicking the car, might indicate that he could have a problem articulating while angry…"

While Ellis amused himself with armchair pyscho-analysis, Malik's had enough of this shit ands 'bout ready to put an end to it. With one quick motion, Malik unbuckled his seatbelt and stepped out of the car, prepared to put this kid to sleep. Simultaneously, it hit Ellis: *I know this kid. I know him. I know him,* Ellis screamed in his mind, quickly stepping outside the car, as vehicles piled up behind them in a chorus of horns and obscenities that only New Yorkers could fully comprehend, appreciate or formulate.

"What? What? Oh, 'cause you some fucken giant Jesus- looking fool—I'm 'posed to get scared? Huh. Shit…it don't make no matter to me how big you are. The bigger they are the harder they fall," rambled on Mr. Foam-at-the-mouth.

Malik just stared at him, while seemingly steadying himself for some Klingonish-type deathblow to end this fool's misery.

"Jay! Yo Jay! It's me, El!" yelled Ellis.

Jay looked at Ellis and blinked like he could make El disappear. Blinked again.

Several decibels lower he uttered: "Uuh, El, Ellis, that you?"

"Yeah, Negus, it's me. What the hell you doing in the middle of the street? You lucky I recognized yo' ass, 'cause Malik was 'bout ready to put the serious smackdown!"

"Oh, what, El, you don' forgot already, Kid? Remember, this is Jay, Jay, Kid—'Daddy Kickass,' baby. You know how I do, Sun?"

Ellis smiled. "Yeah, I know you nice wit' the hands Negus, but Malik, man, he's just on a whole 'nother goddamm level. I'm trying to tell you. But fuck all this," said Ellis walking briskly at Jay and embracing him hard. "What the fuck up, cuzin?"

"What up, Kid? I haven't seen yo' ass in years and I run right smack into you. "

"You mean *almost* run me over, motherfucker. Tell Bob Marley over there you know I know that da 'Mari de juwana' 'sposed to improve cataracts, but it's fucken' up his judgment. You know I know, Kid."

Jay and Ellis hug and embrace like lifelong friends. They realized that each had already mentally attended the other's funeral and buried the body.

Malik turned and saw the traffic backed up. Drivers

were recklessly switching lanes to move past the limo. Malik motioned for Ellis to get in the car, but both Ellis and Jay continued talking. Seeing that time was slipping through their grasp, Malik more dramatically nudged the gentlemen in the right direction.

"Let's go, man! We got a hot situation that we need to address Ellis. We gots to motivate *immediately*!"

Ellis looked up at Malik. "You know what, Kid? You correct. We gots to move."

"Jay, hop in, man. We can drop you somewhere," said Ellis, while not missing the consternation on Malik's face.

"He's aiight. He's good people, Malik. Jay is straight-up M-O-P in a crunch. Trust me."

Jay hopped into the limo. "Damn, El, you living like dis? What you doing now to get all trumped like this? Yo, El, you got a bar in this skate? I know you got a bar in here," rambled Jay in a non-stop almost staccato monologue.

"Yeah," said Ellis. "Jay, just press that green button right there, and you'll be in Yak heaven."

Jay pressed immediately, barely able to withhold his enthusiasm, looking like fat kid on Slim Fast who mistakenly found the hidden stash of Hostess cakes.

"Damnnnn!" shouted Jay, seeing the rotating bar with every white liquor and VSOP in the universe.

Smiling, he looked up at Ellis.

"Cuzin, you definitely trumped on this one. Word is bond."

Jay cracked the VSOP, poured two shots and took one to the head. "So, Cuzin, where we going? I know you probably got some webs in the hotel waiting, right?"

"Naow man, this is all business—strict business. We heading to the airport to pick up Wardell."

"The airport? Wardell?" frowned Jay. That fucken idiot. I know he did something, El. What he do? He did something, right? What he do? Co-idiot. That's my man, dho. He still dress bad? Kid need some help with the gear. 'Member when he first came to the City? He was on some damn Craig Sager, Andre 3000-Menudo type, New Wave-old-school GQ shit. Yo, El, member that time he tried to get away with wearing his Church's Chicken uniform to the club? Talking 'bout, 'Fried chicken was an afrodisiac?' My man Wardell—he did pull a few phatt Honeyz that night, dho."

"You mean phatt or fat?" asked Ellis.

"Yo, truthfully, El, I can't recall it," said Jay. "But have no fear, Kid, I know everybody at the airport. My cousin and dem—you 'member Jabow with the ice pick, right? They wuz the first ones hired after they federalized security at the airports."

Jay downed his second shot and pouring another now in a state of yak-uberance while sounding like a real estate salesman trying to sell a piece of the Brooklyn Bridge.

"I know madd people, so just let me know what you need cuz—anything."

Ellis stared out the window into a wall of nothingness, his mind a thousand miles and light-years away, and mumbled.

"Yeah man, this time I'mma need the whole bag."

"Naw," mumbled Jay, "you just need Jesus."

"Yo, El," announces Malik. "We almost there. Time to put ya boots on."

THE AIRPORT PICK-UP

Tiny beads of sweat began the tedious journey from Wardell's scalp down his elongated face. His face was normally bigger than life, and appeared double the size of his body—almost as big as Jay Leno's. A skinny kid, his body still seemed to be trying to catch up to his face.

He blinked his left eye rapid-fire, dug into his blazer pocket like a man on borrowed time, pulled out a silk handkerchief and wiped his brow clean of sweat. The line of grumpy passengers moved in a slow ebb and flow. Wardell was a little worried about the full digital security scans or DSS. He had decided during his last dental visit to take the low-cost mercury fillings, as opposed to the composite ones. At the time people were unaware that many mercury filled mouthed passengers had experienced a low voltage shock when passing through the DSS at airports.

DSS was combined with full facial Recognition Identification. There were ways around the scans, but it took about a week to implement a full facial transfer using designer-based orthoprostetics. He carefully placed his leather attaché case on the luggage scan. He'd receive an intelligence-agency level clearance chip that prevented the full scanning of his baggage. All the attendants saw was a prompt screen indicating high-level clearance, which in their world translated to "If you value your job and life, please do not fuck with me."

As his turn came up, Wardell shook slightly after the full bodyscan. Dishelved, he stared through the Facial Identification Scanner, which quickly pulled up his data on the security attendant's screen. It gave his whole life history, including up to seven venereal diseases. Unfortunately for Wardell, his VD range far exceeded the machine's capabilities.

"Don't let the pussy go to waste," was his regular response when exchanging medical data chips with a possible sexual partner. "No disease means you ain't been around. How a woman know if a man can do them right if the man too clean?"

Logic was something that Wardell molded to his likening whenever possible. Hell, logically he should be back in Africa, building a new nation.

Yeah. Some kind of new nation. But no Rolex, no Cristal? No thank you, then; I like this old one much better.

After security scans were completed, Wardell skipped his way to the main terminal shuttle. He gazed out the shuttle windows at the city skyline in the background. The new Trade Center bounced the sun off them, causing Wardell to brace himself with his latest 2Grand Poelow shades.

He stood up straight in a blue single button wool suite. He dabbed on another heavy spraying of Clive Christians No.1 cologne that ran almost $2,000 a bottle. His brown suede shirt matched exactly with his brown leather attaché and Bruno Magli slip-ons. The only thing that stood out was his synthetic Aureilian Medallion that hung to his belly somewhat obstentatiously. Wardell had undergone some serious cracks about his style of dress when he first came to the states. Since that time he took great pains to ensure that he was among the best dressed; or more importantly, among the most expensively dressed folks in the world; or his world.

He'd do almost anything to ensure his gear was correct. Spare no expense. Not that he'd get a job—he did the fast food thing once to get his parents off his back—never again. But he'd beg his parents like a fat baby to increase his allowance, through, guilt trips, false health issues—well, some false health issues—and just about any means available. *Shit, what's the point of being rich, if you've got to work?*

Passing into the general terminal, Wardell completely ignored the M22 pointed in his direction by the FAA Guardsman on his 36th straight hour of grit-faced duty. Oblivious, Wardell dipped his head in a two-fingered salute and took one huge step towards the guardsman. He smiled and stuck out his hand as if he was greeting the president.

"God Bless America."

The guard just stared at him, then mumbled, "Fuck off."

Handshake or not, welcome or not, Wardell was back in Sin City and he planned to make the most of it. He moved briskly to the pay phone area to make his phone call and wait for the pickup. When this deal was done, there'd be no more calls to his parents for dough. Shit, he'd might even let them borrow some to build a school or maybe he'd be philanthropic and open up a Mickey D's over there. He was 'bout to get paid. The hard times of drinking normal champagne and having to take classes at a community college to keep the money coming were over.

As he reached the phone area, Wardell glanced at his Gold Breitling watch. When he looked up he saw this honey-brown, Gucci-suit-downed-Prada-wearing female, right out of fantasy dream number 245.

Daaaamn!

Wardell slowly became hypnotized by the jiggle of her ass, up and down, up and down, up and down. Moving past him, he smelled her perfumed that he calculated, *Must be in the high rent range.*

Dipping her Versace shades, she cut her eyes and winked. *Damn,* thought Wardell, *gots to get this.* "But yo, businesses first, got to get paid. I got time, business first, he kept saying to himself as he began humming Jay Z's *"I like girls, girls, girls, girls, Girls, I do adore/ Put your numba on the paper I really like to date ya and I hope you will endure...."*

PLAN B

SCREEEEECH! SCREECH! Screeech were the sounds filling the air as Malik pulled the limo up swiftly to the pick up section of the airport. Whatever ethereal groove they had been floating on when arriving in the CI had disappeared with the addition of Jay. Malik waved at the visibly shakened old man standing a few inches from his bumper. The old man shook himself into shape. He mechanically bent down and retrieved his glasses and stood up in time to see Malik wave his symbolic gesture of no harm, no foul. The old man promptly smiled, then gave him the finger, tipped his hat and walked off.

"Damn, Kid! Whatthahelltype of driving was that? You got to treat the car like a woman. You know whatemsaying?" Jay asked Malik. "Yo, smooth and easy, smooth and easy, just like the Yak, smooth, and easy, right, El? 'Cause you know how we do," sputtered Jay, while adding more doubt in El's mind about this whole thing than a Whiteman doing the cabbage patch for the first time. His mental state was gettin' ugly real quick.

Malik ignored Jay's incessant rambling, forcing Jay's ever-drifting mind to focus on something else. Normally Jay'd runoff at the mouth then sit bi-poloarish and sullen for the rest of the day. Today, he seemed as if his active side was in it for the long haul.

"Oh, Damn, El, did you see that Honey just walk by?"

Jumping to another subject, Jay continued like a man with a few minutes to tell his life story.

"Man, El, I was thinking, you know I was thinking, El? I think I could've shut Jordan down. He might've went for 20 or something, but hell no, I'da broke his damn elbow before letting him score forty or fiddy. You memba what I did to Wes that time? Memba! That Negus scored 39, but was carried out in a stretcher. Brother Jay don't play that shit, score on me at ya own risk."

Malik sat thinking as he looked for any sign of Wardell. He wondered what the hell he was doing here sitting in front of the passenger pickup area with these fools—*well, fool and a half.* Malik, unknown to El, Jay, or any except those like him, was a member of a secret brotherhood of mystics, healers, and warriors. They were a brotherhood several thousands of years old and had emerged around the time of the Pharaoh Khufu out of the Kamatic mystery schools. It was said that there was one of them in every tribe in Africa. The possessed the ability of telepathy, telekinesis and ethereal travel, as well as mastery of healing herbs. Some fools called them witchdoctors. They were doctors, but doctors of knowledge and the higher sciences spoken of in the Gnostic books.

Malik stared at the passengers exiting the terminal, being picked up by love ones and other relatives. He had long ago mastered the ability to recognize people based on the four given types, "Hot/Dry" or "Hot/Moist." Or "Cold/Dry" or Cold/Moist."

Western science didn't fully comprehend the process of metabolism, and the way each group of people and individuals processed energy. Malik had recently developed, through years of meditation, additional psychic abilities—including the ability to see a soul's karma. Karma composed many things. Some simply thought that it meant your destiny—what goes around comes around. But, it was also about our existence as beings manifesting on a physical level. What did our soul need to learn to evolve beyond this existence?

He stared at the grungy, unwashed homeless man, going begging from person to person. He looked deeper and saw that the man in his previous existence had been a rich man—extremely powerful. While he was overgenerous to his family and children, he'd been judgmental and stingy towards the poor. He didn't realize that we all were connected and dependent upon each other's good will. His life's lesson lay in overcoming his harsh judgment on his self and beginning to help others. It was his judgment of others that now made him judge himself so harshly. Once he forgave himself, his life would be transformed with abundance and the opportunity to give to all he was able to.

Glancing at the airport terminal, Malik's eyes traveled through the tall pristine glass, past hundreds of people. They centered on a tall, dark skinned man, dressed impeccably. He held a brown leather attaché case and spoke on the phone almost gleefully. Malik zoomed in closer and could perceive, although not actually hear, what the man was saying. Closer. Closer.

"Shadow, please."

"Yes, Sir, just a moment. May I ask who's calling?

"Tell him it's War."

"Excuse me, did you say 'War'? How would you spell that?"

"Listen bitch, if you want to keep your pissy little job and keep me from putting a foot up yo' ass, You'd better and quickly tell him it War. W. A. R."

Stuttering, the shocked receptionist answered nervously, "Right away, Sir."

The phone clicked over, "Wardell, my man, is it done?"

Smiling, Wardell answered, "Yes, it's done. I'm at the airport and I would like a pickup."

"Of course," said John Shadow, with a smile peering through his voice. "We'll send the limo. As a matter of fact, I'll meet you there myself. It'll be there in a few minutes. Hold Tight."

Grinning back, like he'd just stuck his finger in the change return and found a quarter, Wardell spoke softly.

"Will do. See you in a sec."

The job had been done. Now comes the payoff. Wardell, barely able to contain himself, held on just a little. Security didn't take too kindly to a tall Blackman skipping through the airport; the last brotha to do that was O.J., and everybody knew what happened to him.

Across town, Shadow, unlike Wardell, felt no need to contain his joy. As he stood looking out over the city, he suddenly broke free into an extended version of the Crip Dance. The Crip Dance was his secure party move. He'd tried that Uptown Shake move, but dislocated a shoulder and ruptured his bladder.

Buzzzzzz jumped his intercom.

"Sir, will you be needing anything?"

"Oh nothing," cooed Shadow. "Just have Brams bring

the limo around. As a matter of fact, take the rest of the day off."

Moving graciously, smiling and winking at every woman in sight, Wardell walked over to the counter and picked up a pack of cigarettes. He needed a smoke bad. *No time like the present,* he thought, as he walked out into the front entrance. He cautiously laid his attaché down and lit up a smoke. The second puff was the best. He inhaled and exhaled, feeling good about the world in general and excited about his prospects of truly being a Balla. Of course being a Balla, he'd have to conjure up a new name—*maybe War-Z? WDX? Naw, WDX sounded like some chemical that promised to clean everything. What about War Delly? Maybe he'd just take a name like Blunt. Um, now, that had potential. He could give it an aristocratic last name. Something sorta English or snobish, like Blunt Wellington, or Blunt L. Morganthau.*

Malik's eyes had followed Wardell the whole length. He continued to stare, as El and Jay rambled on about a plan to get Wardell, oblivious to the fact that he stood no more than ten feet away from them, smoking a cigarette like he was in ecstasy.

"Yo, El, I'm telling you. Let me go in and you know I just look for Wardell and when I see him, I tell him I'm with Mocha—you know that stripper he was always trying to get with, who wouldn't give him no play? You remember her, right? Yo, you remember that trick she used to do with the microphone and beer bottle? She was more talented than the average stripper, she coulda been on "The Apprentice"! But what I'm saying is that I go up to him, and tell him that, yeah, I'm just chilling and I'm with Mocha and she's waiting outside and was just talking about him. Saying she'd love to see him. Right, den, den we walk him out and I just put him in a headlock, slam him against the limo for old times sake and we out. Yo, I'm telling you El, this is it. Yo, just trust me, Cuzin. Trust me," said Jay.

Ellis shrugged. "Jay, I don't even half-recognize you. Man, we can't go in their half-baked. This is real, man; this ain't no corner store hustle. I got things to think about, I got a fam…" stopped Ellis in midstream.

Jay just stared mouth half-open. "Don't half-recognize me? Man, you tripping."

"Naw," said El. "You trippin'. You been trippin' since you got in the car. Before that, that's why we almost hit yo' ass."

"Fuck you, El. That's, that's, why yo' moms an enforcer for the Knicks. Everytime somebody gets hot for the other team she goes in and punches them in they shooting arm."

Ellis frowned while eying Jay.

"What? What? That's why yo' moms so dumb I asked her for hordouvres and she brought me uptown to the strip joint."

"Yeah, yeah, damn, El. Glad to see you still got it. You ain't all bourghied out. Just make sure you get some ointment for that shit, 'cause it's peeling." cracked Jay.

Ellis grinned, "Yeah, tell ya moms she can lick the—"

Jay joined in quickly—"sweat from my balls! Sweat from my balls!"

While Ellis and Jay broke mental bread again, renewing their bloodbrother bond, Malik continued to focus on Wardell's movement through the airport out onto the front entrance as he puffed on his second cancer stick.

Malik started the ignition and put the limo in drive. Jay and Ellis are finally shakened out of their stupor. Before they can speak, Malik ordered them

"Out of the car. Not on the passenger side, Negus— on my side. Just slide out. Our target is right across the street."

Ellis peeked up and saw Wardell across the street, puffing. He looked at Jay nervously.

"Yo, Malik is right. Wardell is right there. Let's go rush that bastard."

"No, I got it under control," interrupted Malik. "I know you never heard of the Chinese philosophy of Mei Mo— it's simply getting what you want by doing nothing. It's always better to work smarter than harder. Now, just ease out on my side and let me pick him up. When you see the hazards on, you know what time it is," whispered Malik.

"Cool," said Ellis quietly.

Even a rapidly sobering Jay agreed to ease out of the

limo and work the plan. This was the first time all three had agreed on anything at the same time. Jay immediately snapped to attention—like an internal light went on. His move prompted Ellis to once again remembered Jay's ability to recover in minutes from madd levels of intoxicants that would normally down a bull elephant and paralyze any normal man. They were like a veteran team that scabbed and bickered throughout the season—almost automatically pulling it together around playoff time. "All vets, no rookies in the camp," as Jay used to say.

Both quickly slide out the driver's side, bent down low, walking gradually with the slow moving limo as it eased front and direct to Wardell.

Wardell's head was spinning with ideas and potential partying. Sure, he felt a little guilt from selling out his parents, his whole continent, and—well, Blackfolks everywhere to be exact. *But what was life without guilt?* he rationalized. *Shit, you had no guilt means that you didn't PaaaaarTay.*

He dug into his inside jacket pocket and pulled out another cancer stick from his silver plated holder. Effortlessly, he reached into his lower jacket pocket and pulled out his lighter. Bending his head down slightly he lit up. As he took his first puff, he pulled his head back as if the motion helped the nicotine to enter his bloodstream quicker. He looked up and noticed a black limo rolling slowly towards the pickup curb.

Malik slowly rolled the car to a halt. Smiling, he glances over at Wardell and waved slightly. Wardell waved back, thinking, *These mothers are fast.* He took one last puff and flicked his cigarette to the ground. Wardell reached down and picked up his attaché case and steps towards the limo like a shoplifter heading towards the store's exit.

He stepped into the limo and leaned back. "So, where's Shadow?"

Malik smiled.

"Don't worry, we'll see him in a moment."

Simultaneously Malik put on the hazards. Wardell begins to feel slightly uneasy, and thirsty.

"Hey, is there something to drink in this tank?"

"Sure, look to your left and press the automated bar

button."

Before Wardell can make another statement, the door to his left opened and in stepped Ellis.

"So, what's up, Wardell? What brings you to New York?"

Wardell stuttered nervously, "I—I thought you were in Africa, I mean, you know."

Ellis' fake smile turned sour. "Yeah, I know—you damn greedy bastard."

Wardell gripped his attaché case and scooted to the other side of the limo. Before he could reach the door, it opened. In stepped Jay, grinning with a joy that only alcohol-breath could bring, "What up, you Cristal-sipping Biiiiitch!"

Malik pulled off, Blasting Gangstarr

"Dumdumdum, wickwwiciy Friends, Friends…

ESCAPING GOTHAM

Wardell looked straight ahead at the road, afraid to look right at Jay, or left at Ellis, who was probably the closest near-almost-friend he ever had.

Ellis hunched forward, elbows resting on his knees, watching the road. His excitement and nervousness mixed into anxiety.

"Malik, where do we go now? Africa?"

Malik looked up in the rearview mirror for a second.

"Yeah El, we go to Africa, but, as you probably figured, we won't be able to drive there."

Ellis smirked. "Ooh, you got jokes, huh, Peter Tosh?"

"No, seriously," said Malik, "We can't head south, 'cause folks are looking for us. We'll head north to New Heaven, where I have some peeps and we can get a flight outta there. I won't be traveling with you. Just to get you there is all I do."

As Malik and Ellis conversed, Jay looked at Wardell and snatched the attaché case.

"Gimme that, punk! Shoulda known somebody like you wasn't to be trusted. Yo, El, let's throw him out the car. I'll give you three-to one he rolls at least five times."

Wardell sat in silence and said nothing. Sweat begin to drip onto his Armani, causing him to feel flashes of pain each time a drop of sweat bruised his designer wear. He was less worried about the bodily harm from being thrown onto the highway at 80 mph as opposed to the damaged it'd do to his suit. *On second thought,* he mused, *if they toss me, it's gonna hurt.*

Fear of impending doom prompted Wardell to action.

"El, my main man," he uttered nervously. "I'm sorry things went this way. I didn't mean to bring you into this. Just between me and my family."

Jay poured a shot of Yak and took a sip while sneering at Wardell, whose mere presence caused him pain. "Yo, El, want me to slap the shit out of him?"

Ellis shook his head. "Naw, naw, man, that ain't gonna make no difference. "When the folks he working with find out he didn't deliver, he's going to catch the hell he deserves."

Wardell began to sweat profusely. "El, why it got to be like this? I'm just trying to get paid. I mean, you and Jay are to blame for me doing this anyway."

Jay poured another shot, "Yo, El, let me smack this mawfuka?"

Ellis simply shook his head no again. Wardell, seeing the safety of speaking, continued like a rat trapped in a corner.

"What I'm saying, El, is that when I came over here fresh from Africa, you kidz turned me onto the street life, the high life, thuggish-ruggish shit, the hustle, baaaby. You brothas took me down this road. Now, now don't get me wrong: I appreciate it, but don't blame me now for being a balla. When you and Jay talk about growing up and how you used to do things, baby, I hated that shit, 'cause I always felt left out. I just wanted to have my own stories to tell, my own respect, my own status, baby, that's all."

Ellis looked directly at Wardell, sweat beading off his face like ice-cold beer from a cooler.

"Respect. Respect. Wardell? Kid, you don't know what the hell that means. You just a snake man, a damn devil. Yacub ain't got shit on you, Sun. If me and Jay took you down this road mawfuka, the one thing you shoulda learned was loyalty. Loyalty means you don't betray your Fam, piss on the Negus that looked out for yo' ass when you didn't know no better. Negus ain't shit without loyalty. We looked out for you only because of your family, and you don't respect even them. You don't respect the love your family has for you. The type of love that allowed them to support yo' ass, even though you are breaking their hearts with all this selfish shit. Me an Jay did the shit we did 'cause we didn't have no family capable of giving us the shit you took for granted—like having a meal everyday. Man, you must be crazy. Naw, Kid, you definitely crazy. Just be thankful I don't let Jay toss you onto the damn highway. Be thankful that I still know what the fuck loyalty means, punk ass."

Scrambling mentally, Wardell tried again.

"I know, I know you right 'bout the loyalty thing, El, but what I'm saying—and Jay might want to hear this—is that I'm getting paid well for this delivery, Kid. Seven-figure-well, baby. You know that it's enough for everybody, even the driver to get some cake, Sun. It's all between us. Nobody in my family will know that you didn't get the staff back. It'll be our little secret. I mean, check it, I'm willing to split it 60-40. You decide who gets what on your team? No, No, I'm even willing to do half, 50-50, El. Now, you know that's strict. I know you could use the money; you certainly been through enough to appreciate it. Worked hard your whole life. This is your chance to get a slice, baby. C'mon, El," continued Wardell, getting more and more desperate as Malik zoomed through the Cross Bronx Expressway headed north.

Ellis said nothing. Just sat there silently staring ahead at the road. He wasn't gonna blow this, regardless of how much money Wardell threw at him. This was his chance. Awaking from a coma made him realize how much bullshit that he dealt with on a daily basis that he could live without. And how not important most of the things that people feel are important aren't when you facing death. His soul was at stake. He finally had a chance to grow up, be a man. Learn how to commit to something, and if he blew this he might not get another chance. Fear crept up on him and made him wonder if this is what Darth Vader felt before he crossed over to the dark side. He refused to go back to the old Ellis. That person was dead. Life was only a joke if you made it into one. He had finally come to the realization that he was valuable. Shit, we all were valuable, too valuable to be bought and sold. We was more than that, much more.

Ignoring Wardell, Ellis took a sip of yak and said, "Yo, Malik, throw on that Roots shit *"Never do, What they do/ What they do what they do.'* And yo, Blast it!"

THE ROAD TO HEAVEN

Two-thirds of the journey was over. Each person was in their own world of trials and tribulations tied to this mission. Each in search of something that only some wizard from Oz could give 'em.

Malik was attempting to jettison human desire and ascend to masterhood on a spiritual journey of the highest kind.

Jay sought redemption of sorts. He had hated Wardell because he had *been* Wardell. He'd already sold his soul for the cheddar and it ended with his family paying the cost for his greed. He needed to rectify some ill shit he'd done—shit that neither El, nor anyone else knew about—to his own peoples. He had to make amends to his family, and El was the only family he had left.

Wardell was on another mission altogether; he was moving fast and hard to separate himself from who and what he was—African. And Ellis—well, El was attempting to grow up and totally commit to completing something. He'd spent his whole life refusing to be involved or to commit to anything without a golden exit clause in the contract. He was tired of running, tired of the fear stalking him that kept him from getting too close to anyone because they'd only betray him in the end. El looked over at Wardell, who was either sleep or feigning sleep. Jay, unable to sleep, simply stared out the window as they passed into Connecticut.

Malik continued his driving, now switching up the

music to something more of his likening, "Cool and Calm," by Israel Vibrations.

Ellis' mind flashed back to him and Wardell's meeting with the Master Teacher in Sudan. He remembered the old Man's warning: "If you fail to complete this mission, the new age is forestalled and the righteous shall suffer." Tired of the strain of commitment, his mind drifted into a neo-consciousness. Not sleep, nor consciousness or even something in between. He went off the barometer into the realm of visions.

The air swirled, revealing its ethereal content broken down into molecule form. Man had sought to replicate this process ongoing in Ellis' mind through technology, but technology was a substitute for the mental-spiritual capacity inherent within us all. What the religious teachers of today failed miserably at was in teaching the truth known eons before the writing of any of the holy books of this day. That truth was that each person had the ability to ascend, to become anointed, become KRST, Kristos, a Christ. The only one (as in "da one") is the collective higher consciousness. Whether Ellis liked it or not, he was now accessing a higher consciousness. It was as if his DNA had been programmed to expand his consciousness at exactly this point in time.

Ellis stared into nothingness; he saw a moon covering the Sun. Air swirled and swirled into a ring upon a ring.

Ellis saw Wardell smiling with John Shadow—a malevolent being whose failure to learn from his past had cost his soul a thousand lifetimes away from the true light. Wardell handed the staff of ancients to Shadow, who smiled harder and harder, his mouth expanding to fill the sky. Inside Shadow's mouth, he saw millions upon millions of Africa's children dying from starvation, disease, war and rumors of war. He saw the souls of dead ancestors screaming. They screamed at the top of their lungs at a man sleeping. They prodded and banged their drums attempting to wake this man. Suddenly, the man awoke and sat up upright. He turned around and it was Ellis. He saw *himself.* The screaming began again.

WAAAAA!

WAAAAA!

WAAAAAAAAK!

WAAAAAKEUP!
WAKEUP!
WAKE THEM UP!

"Ellis! Ellis!" yelled Malik. "We got to pull over and get some gas."

Wardell, now awake, whispered out the corner of his mouth,

"Yes, I'd like to use the bathroom and freshen up."

Jay looked at him sourly "Yeah, I need to go break my bladder off. Plus I'll keep an eye on Tricky D right jere."

Malik moved like a panther. His height on some would cause immediate attention. Yet he was practically invisible. People looked right through him as if he did not exist. It was a different spin on Ralph Ellison's "'Invisible Man," and a talent that all Blackmen sought at times. Filling up the gas tank, he returned to the car and pulled out his energy elixir. It was some foul-smelling stuff, powerful enough to clean a car battery better than cola. It was a concoction of unknown herbs and root-remedies of which only a handful on the planet had an inkling. He got the formula from a Brazilian shaman in exchange for an original, never-published Pushkin manuscript written in Russian. The Shaman resided outside Bahia, said it was perfected after centuries of honing in the mountains of Tibet. He had got it from a Tibetan monk who told him he was over 300 years old, give or take a decade. Slowly consuming his elixir, Malik slumped back and removed a small book from his pocket with no title. Its only description read "Law and Application of Compensation."

THE LAWS OF RECOMPENSE

Everything flows out an in; everything has its tides; all things rise and fall; the pendulum-swing manifests in everything; the measure of the swing to the right, is the measure of the swing to the left; rhythm compensates.

--The Kyballion

Every fool knows the law of give and take. Everyone has heard the axiom of physics, which states that each action produces an equal reaction somewhere in the universe. This is applied not merely to the actions of individuals, but also the actions of groups. All are truly connected by strands of hair or steel. In reality, it is all the same. Everyone is connected. It can no more turn dark for seven weeks and not shine for seven following weeks, than can one swallow an elephant without eliminating the same in some manner or form. These are the laws of compensation. These laws act the same as rhythm—back and forth, back and forth. It is no different for individuals or groups of individuals classified as races or nations.

The law of compensation gives clarity to those walking in blindness. No group can oppress another person or group without the consent of its members. Likewise, no group can be oppressed without its own consent. Simultaneously—and the so-called races and nations must know this, for their elders were already aware—no oppression will go unreturned without the like intensity.

The souls of the "Great Nations" have already produced their own destruction and eventual oppression. The blood shed on slave ships, colonial plantations, townships, barrios, concentration camps, and ghettoes of physical and spiritual poverty are compensated with World Wars. The spread of dis ease and continual murder for profit too shall be compensated in unexpected dis ease, pestilence, and blood that the Earth will spew forth from its navel.

Every second, the Great Nation's karma is being filled every second. Only those aware see it. Others knowingly deny it, believing that one can traverse the laws through trickery. Regardless, it is the beginning of sorrows. A group can only oppress another group through the consent of its members—all are responsible. No group can be oppressed without its own consent.

The solution laying in wait is for the oppressor to reverse its karma, if it be at all possible? The time is already late and almost nigh. Only through appealing to the higher laws can compensation be avoided. What are the higher laws? Only ask what is right and you will know.

One only needs to consider what is best? And then do better.

Oppression is not merely the act of the oppressor, but the consent of the oppressed. Can the oppressed escape the karma of returning the savagery brought to their souls by the other? Can the oppressed avoid becoming the devils they hate? Can the oppressors children and children's children avoid the karma brought to them by the evil done on behalf of their ancestors? Only through our appeal to the higher laws can we change the future. Within us is the way. Only the laws that we choose to accept bind us. Impossibilities are within our daily grasp. Will we grasp freedom NOW or follow the dictates of compensation? No one can give freedom to none. Each person or group or nation must free themselves, or remain forever enslaved. Will we conquer or become our oppressor and oppress them as they have done us? If so, the cycle will continue.

SETTING THE TRAP

John Shadow was pissed. Steaming! He sat outside the airport pickup zone, wondering what the hell has happened to his client. This was supposed to go smoothly. He despised tardiness as much as he hated lack of preparation. "There's enough time to sleep when I'm dead," was his favorite saying.

To his security staff following him in another car, nothing could be determined by his blank stare. They had no idea that he was seething with so much anger that even demonic lower dimensional beings were scared to approach him for fear of being consumed.

Hate in its extreme had the same power as love; however, hate's power had a completely different affect. For Shadow's purpose, it was what stirred him to action. It was what allowed him to excel in a Whiteboyz game with no support system, no back. Shit, he had his own back and would be damned if he was going to let some street corner Negus stop his flow. He could digest competing against the Whiteboyz, since it was their game for the moment. But, he was too far ahead in the game to have to compete with some street corner Negus. *Who in the hell did they think they were fucken' with?*

As rain began to drizzle, Shadow flipped out a palm satellite device and enacted his program override code. The hand- held device immediately connected with the overhead orbiting satellite. FBDIE had developed the technology to patch into any satellite in the world for real-time digital photos. This was an unknown plank in the early century Patriotic Act, which granted them the power to access any means of communication in pursuit of possible terrorist acts. Of course, catching the mailman screwing a man's wife or regularly tuning into Playboy mansion volleyball games also fit the description.

Within seconds, Shadow's Palm device ran back the last two hours of photo transmissions for the airport pickup zone. He fast-forwarded the device until he saw Wardell step outside the airport hall to have a smoke. He fast-forwarded again. Then slowed the film down to less than normal speed.

"That's it!"

He focused the resolution higher and saw Wardell getting into an old black limo headed north. Focusing with a higher resolution he pulled up the license plate. It had DC tags and read "ANU21."

Thinking quicker than a ball player with a minute left on the SAT's, Shadow quickly typed the plate data into his Palm device then plugged into the NSA Supercomputer to find out who these bastards were.

"Shit! Nothing. These mothers are good," he angrily mused.

"Okay, Okay. Want to play games, right?"

Quickly accessing the intelligence data bank code name "Terrorsawus Rex," he ran a match scan for the plates in a 100-mile radius using the Terrorsawus delivery system, which forced all gas station owners to install digital photo transfers software. It took pictures of each license plate and then fed those numbers into a combined central data processing location. The site which utilized the latest Carnivore technology to track any alleged 'terrorists."

They had to get fuel sooner or later, smiled Shadow to himself, sweat trickling onto his wool suit. *Everybody needs fuel, especially a twenty-year old Lincoln. These bastards have no idea who they are fucken' with.* The program scanned 20,000 plates per second with foolproof accuracy. Shadow's Palm device began to hum *mmmmmmmmmmm, mmmmmmmmm, mmmmmmm...*

"Bingo!" screamed Shadow. "Got 'em."

He quickly typed in their last location and ran that through the system to interface with FBDIE's Security 4 Access satellite. Overriding some of his fellow FBDIE's security access codes that had up until this point allowed them to tune in to the Hefner Thong Volleyball Championships.

He'd of course have to pay for this with the usual horse shit in his locker, threatening phone calls for a week, and miniature cross burnings on his desk in the "Good Ole Boy" fashion. And that was just from the 't'tottler' receptionist with the low estrogen levels. He didn't mind; this took precedence. And success meant that he'd spend the rest of his career telling Whiteboyz why they'll never be as good as him, and ducking bullets.

Worth it? No contest, he thought.

After drifting away for a second, Shadow then latched the satellite interface into the local highway tracking devices that monitored plates every five miles. Once a pegged plate passed, the automated signal instructed the satellite to follow the vehicle and pinpoint its location to the tracker.

"I'm a Bad muther, shut yo' mouth, just talking 'bout Shaft," Shadow giggled to himself. Hell, he even had time to get a cup of coffee before accessing the secret government highway that ran parallel to I-95. This would actually allow him to make up two to three hours on them suckers. Shadow was as excited as a brotha without rhythm could get.

"Whose house? /Run's house! /Whose House? / Run's Houuuuuse!"

THE OTHER SUPER HIGHWAY

Most individuals live within their own world. Rarely, if ever, do they accessing the worlds of others, unless normally forced to or by some strange quirk their worlds became meshed. Worlds were simply dimensions that could be accessed on numerous levels. What existed in your world was as real as what existed in another's world, whether or not it appeared in a physical form. What the mind perceived it tended to believe. That being said, many a suicide victim actually believed that once they jumped off the building they would fly.

For high-level government intelligence, life meant that your world consisted of just about everyone else's world. However, only a misfortunate few would ever have access to your world.

Truthfully, though as the ancient Kemetic scribes discussed, "the universe is mental." The capacity for accessing these multi-worlds, or multi-verses, was within the reach of the former Godz of the planet. Not that the original Godz were superior or better than any other group on the planet; it was merely their purpose to preserve the history and knowledge of the Universe within their genetic code. This ability remained trapped within their DNA, until its programming went off, or was set off.

Technology in itself was the simple attempt to access and codify this inherent ability. Only the chosen few realized, or even wanted, to travel the road necessary to awaken these powers due to a psychic spell that the Godz remained under.

By simply keeping them believing that they were "only human," removing knowledge of their actual world, those who spun the spell trapped the Godz in a world created just for them. Mental awareness, like any other game, competition or sport, is determined by those able to dictate the way the game/competition is going to be played. The genius of creating a world to your liking is that no one but you could ever dominate or win. The ancestors were praying that the former Godz had enough sense to flip the script. But in order to do that, they first needed to figure of what style-game or competition best utilized their abilities. In simple terms, before they could win they had the figure out who the fuck they were.

Know thyself.

But they had no idea.

John Shadow was sure he knew who and what he was as he ordered his driver to head west out of Gotham. About 10 miles outside of the city, they accessed a hidden exit into a path through the woods. Five miles later, they were brought to a halt by a huge prison type wall with a canterking slow entrance gate. Shadow stepped out the car and entered his Omega Level Access Code.

As they passed through the gate, the gate then shut quickly, crashing steel upon steel. Twenty seconds later, they entered a huge three-lane tunnel drilled through the side of the mountains. They moved at above normal speed. But due to the aerodynamic structure of the tunnel, they actually moved much faster. In 20 minutes, they had traveled the distance that would normally take 40 minutes. Then another tunnel, one guarded by one soldier and his companion, a drone. The drone was human as well as a beast. It was created as part of a super-classified first strike tactical force normally sent into covert wars to buffer the forces of allies. Many had wrought terror into scores of Columbians, and in the Afghani mountains. They had committed numerous atrocities; and some even turned to cannibalism. The government had hoped that by altering the DNA with some less aggressive animals to breed a more domestic group of drones. The second batch of them were now patrolling underground cities and highways.

Shadow and his car moved slowly as the drone waved them to a halt, while his trainer looked on. *GRRRRRRR,* the beast growled, showing its teeth in an aggressive manner and quickly bringing the disapproval of his trainer who warned him.

"Take it easy. You'll never be allowed to mate as long as you show too much aggression. Now just ask them their business and run their security code and they'll be on their way."

Shadow stared out the windshield. He attempted to look unnerved, but it seemed that every time this drone turned his way, it growled. He didn't realize that part of the early training of the drones focused on analyzing dangerous situations and conditioned their aggression to increase due to the skin color of the of an individual. The darker you were, the more aggressive the drones were trained to become and Shadow was as Black as night—well, at least on the outside. Inside, he was whiter than Pat Sajak drinking milk at a Hamptons white party.

"Where are you going?" growled the drone in a manner reminiscent of Shadow's numerous infamous attempts to catch a taxi in any major city.

"Where you going?" it asked again, this time its electronic-aided voice getting deeper.

Its sharp fangs gristled white as if it was using some tooth whitening strips. Yellow eyes crunched together united by an overzealous unibrow. He eyed Shadow as if he were a freshly killed rack of lamb still dripping with blood. It startled Shadow. He didn't fear too many things, but he was afraid of dogs in the way some people feared math. As a youngster he saw a young child torn to shreds by a loose pitbull that escaped from his ganja-smoking master. They weren't supposed to have dogs in the Projects anyway. This was one of the major incidents that made him hate thugs. Despise them. Now this drone reminded him of his fear of dogs.

"Uh, oh, we are heading north. Do you need my security clearance?"

"Yes."

"Army, Zulu, Delta 441."

The trainer typed in the code and a small photo of

Shadow marked cleared appeared on his keypad. The drone then held the device to the window. Shadow nervously reached out, as a low growl emerged from the fang showing drone, and placed his thumb on the biometric scanner. *CLEARED.*

The trainer smiled and waved them through. "Sir," he whispered, "please stay on the highway north. There may be a few, er, drones running loose in the area. They have attacked a few personnel. Just to be on the safeside, especially with your, er, um tan. I suggest you hightail it out of here."

Shadow looked down, then up at the trainer. He smiled for a second and then frowned. "Thanks for the warning. We should be out of 'Middle Earth' in an hour tops. Tell Gandor peace."

As they pulled away he waved at the trainer and smiled at the drone, which politely showed his teeth and growled. *It didn't matter,* thought Shadow. *I'll be out of here in a minute and we'll set a trap for those bastards in New Heaven.*

NEW HEAVEN

Seven years ago, New Heaven had been created out of the city's wasteland. The home of Yale University, one of the richest universities in the world, New Haven was once the state's capital and an epicenter of wealth. Despite its superlative wealth, Yale was surrounded by one of the nation's poorest cities, with a majority population of African Americans and Latinos. It was to be the site of the first college for Blackfolks—that is, until Yale decided to squash it.

Once a vibrant city full of opportunity in manufacturing and construction, the city, like most in the nation, fell on hard times in the late 20th century. Seeing this as an opportunity, Yale decided to make a deal with the city that any street hustler could get with. *Ten get ya twenty, twenty get ya forty, Ooops! Try again.*

Knowing the financial constraints the city was under, the University with several billions in endowment, decided to purchase a portion of the city that surrounded the university and establish it as a separate township for its students, professors, and benefactors. Then-Yale President Bonz Skulls called it "The Final Solution." It was the culmination of years of strategy and the eradication of the contradictions that plagued the city since its birth.

Since the Seventies, the Ashmun Street housing projects, named after Yehudi Ashmun, a Jewish-American colonization society missionary who helped to settle Liberia, served as home to thousands of Negus, whose children used to rob Yale students and skate back into the high-rise buildings that held thousands of impoverished folk under lock and key. Yale had wanted to eradicate the contradiction. It was hard explaining to parents and alumni how their child got robbed in broad daylight off-campus again and again. Late in the century, after the murder of one of its coeds, Yale had become the first university to allow its campus police to carry handguns.

The deal was good for everyone, said Yale officials. New Heaven was to make New Haven a Heaven. The city was in debt and the deal brought them billions. Meanwhile, Yale had its own city within a city, separate and gated. Its crystal towers stretched into the sky like the raised hands of oppressed people groveling before God for mercy. They called it Varanasi—based on the Hindu "City of Light." Engineers were brought in from the far corners of the Earth to create an utterly new paradigm in urban retreat—er, um—educational landscape. It was beautiful. From the highway it looked like the grand city of OZ.

New Heaven didn't look too bad either. However, it was a different dynamic. Far from the somewhat sterile Varanasi, it breathed of life, movement, music and colors, its essence was more African. The billions gained from the deal allowed New Heaven to rebuild its entire city based on an African architectural style, reminiscent of Congolese artist Bodys Isek Kingelez and uniquely symbolized by its Triple Pyramid Center.

Spanning 30 city blocks in each direction, the Pyramid Center served as the pulse of its new downtown and the Mayor's office. Following on a path initiated by Imani Moore, the former mayor and current US ambassador to the African Union, they used the port of New Haven to establish trade with numerous African nations and transformed raw goods as well into goods sold worldwide. They established a technology partnership with the African Union that trained and exchanged students from the city and those from the mainland. It all started with a simple factory in Ghana that manufactured a herbal-based lotion, and an unique coconut oil hair grease that was distributed throughout a major grocery chain throughout the United States. This one seed led to the creation of products as simple as steam irons to eventually computer screens. From there, investors jumped to create African-controlled technology factories that mass-produced computer chips. It was a fusion of African, African American, Latino, and Western.

New Heaven replaced the Board of Alderman with the Council of Elders. Poverty and illiteracy had been eliminated. They had far exceeded the expectations placed on them when the deal was made. Most had expected that the city would implode upon itself into a major conflagration of Latino and Moors. But instead they shocked the world and began building a new future with untold optimism. The pundits had been silenced. The city renamed itself New Heaven. *Ten get ya twenty, twenty get ya forty. Damn! Go ahead try again.*

Those who still worked the service industries for the University were given weekly access passes or entrance. However, the petition to work in New Heaven was backlogged three years. Things had changed with the new opportunities available for residents of New Heaven. The Port was booming in trade, and the new Thebes Airport was acting as an international port serving every major city in Africa on direct flights. Now, the University had to compete with the city and wages and benefits shot up. Less and less were Latino and Negus willing to do slop work at the University. The big question at Yale now was who was gonna clean the buildings, manage their business and get toilet tissue? A university had to have toilet tissue, right?

THE ARRIVAL

Driving down Adam Clayton Powell Drive, which bordered New Heaven and the University City, John Shadow opened his sunroof to get a breathe of fresh air. He was a finisher and wanted to finish this shit. His stomach never quite rested 'til the deal was over. This often caused problems for him because when he became too nervous he began to fart incessantly.

Shadow was a man who had total control over his emotions, but something had to give in order to maintain the high level of self-control. That is the law. Nothing goes uncompensated for. Energy cannot be destroyed, only altered or channeled. This being the case, abstinence from any desire only made the desire more powerful. The more you fought it the more it began to build until it could be controlled no longer. Or if wise, the energy was channeled into a positive release or sublimation. If neither, then the same energy found its own expression. As such, he farted nasty farts—the kind that made your eyes water.

Initially, Shadow had developed a strategy of breathing to counter it, which worked for a while. But then each time he farted it got louder. Now when he busted one, it was like the speakers shaking from Schooly D's *"PSK making that cream/ People always saying what the hell does it mean"*-type audio.

Opening his sunroof was timely, although the escape of fumes did set off a few car alarms and caused dogs to bark in the extremely quiet neighborhood. Being near his old campus brought back memories of his years at Yale Law School, where he attended on one of the last active race-based scholarships. This was the place where he learned the value of disavowing his Blackness and decided to join the intelligence community.

Driving up to Dixwell Avenue, Shadow met two FBDIE agents there and switched into a less noticeable vehicle—an Accra, a limited edition luxury sedan imported from Ghana. With a deep blue exterior, it had crème-colored leather seats. Satellite accessible, it had two dataports that allowed him to plug into several information networks and a satellite—including the one that was currently tracking his prey. They had been picking up conversation for over 45 minutes and sat patiently awaiting their prey to arrive at their supposed safehouse. The estimated time of arrival was Six-minutes and thirty-three seconds. *Hummn*, thought Shadow, *time enough to have a smoke.* His stomach began bubbling again as he squirmed in his seat and once again opened the sunroof.

FINALLY, THE SAFEHOUSE

Heading off the Uhuru street exit into New Heaven,

Malik called Kima, his safehouse contact.

"Kima. Greetings, my sista," his voice smiled through the phone lines.

"Malik!" screamed Kima, exciting the both of them. He loved the way she always screamed his name, whenever he called or she saw him. Malik was not a man who needed a lot, but even he needed a place that was meant for him, no questions asked. Not that he demanded her to love him—he always reminded himself that he didn't need anything but air and water, and not too much of that. She loved him anyway, and he could feel the love evident in her voice.

After allowing Kima to tone down, Malik continued.

"We are in New Heaven and on the way. Eleven minutes and we'll be there for two days 'til our flight. Love." He gripped the phone tightly.

"Bye, Malik," purred Kima.

Overhearing the exchange, Ellis looked at Jay, who looked back smirking.

"Damn, Malik! You got her coming and you ain't even showed up yet," cracked Ellis.

"Yeah," said Jay, "Now *that's* my idea of foreplay!"

Malik looked back into the rearview mirror, seeing his grinning comrades. He almost broke into a smile; his right cheek began to curl slightly then fell off. Still, he smiled inside. He knew no one could take themselves too seriously around Jay and Ellis. That was impossible with these bastards.

His mind drifted back to Kima, which prompted a full-blown internal smile in more than one area of his body. Kima was about 5-2 with deep-bronzed buttery skin. Thick full lips surrounded her luscious inviting mouth. When she smiled it was if the whole universe lit up. Her eyes were slanted and hypnotic like the women of Burkina Faso. She was one of the most dynamic and intelligent women he'd ever come across. She wore here emotions not just on her sleeve, but all over her body. After being in her presence it was as if the world slowly moved back to the periphery and eventually disappeared to where it was just you and her and nothing or no one else existed or mattered.

They met during his travels around the world. Going to the Yucatan Peninsula to visit the Mayan ruins outside Tulum. He stayed at a small hotel on the ocean's edge about 40 minutes outside Cancun in a clean room furnished with only a bed and spring water. At night you could hear the ocean waves crashing against shore.

In his earlier, wild times, he traveled, exploring and researching with the aid of a silver flask of yak and Cuban cigars. He remembered first seeing her, while sitting on concrete bleachers in a basketball park adjacent to the water as young Mexicans played three on three.

It was night and you could smell the sweet scent of burning wood. It was the same smell in Africa and Brazil at night. It quickly reminded everyone of how these regions were once connected. She wore her hair naturally in two braids plaited down her back. Wearing white linen shorts and halter top tied in the back, her thick thighs curved slightly towards a small waist. She smelled of cocoa butter and Egyptian musk. When she walked past him, everyone else disappeared.

"Malik!" yelled Jay.

"Yo, how far?"

"Huh?"

Jay dropped his head to the right, mouth open.

"How far, man? When we arriving? I'm gettin' hungry as shit. Yo, O'girl, can she cook? Call her back and tell her to throw some stuff on so it'll be ready when we get there, Cuzin."

Malik looked up into the mirror.

"We'll be there in five minutes. Just hold tight," said Malik all the while thinking, *Just two more days 'til our flight and this mission will be complete. All of my assignments will have been successfully completed and I will have earned my way into the upper echelon of the mystic order. My job as a taxi driver for Frick and Frat will be over. Why didn't they give this simple mission to some initiate? I've already earned my stripes, proven myself time and time again. I need something worthy of my ability. This…this is definitely not it."*

THE FINAL ACT

Shadow's anticipation began to grow. His mouth watered incessantly for the taste of victory. Never one to get too far ahead of himself, he knew it was never over 'til it was over. He confidently lit his gingko biloba enhanced cigarette that allowed the nicotine to flow freely into the bloodstream, viewed by many as the tobacco industry's last hurrah. Shadow breathed in, *"phoooove,"* held it then exhaled, *"aaaaaah."* His favorite was gingko, ephedra, and huperzine. It stimulated his mental capacities to the maximum.

For Shadow, everything was used as an advantage. He rarely did anything for mere purposes of simple enjoyment. Every move he made was calculated into some sort of advantage or to cover any perceived weakness. Besides, the smoke industry now touted these "herbalized" cigarettes as "the best smoke around for the health-conscious smoker."

His two associates sat in the front seats and said nothing, merely glancing in syncopated fashion north, south, east and west via the car's mirrors. Shadow stepped out the car and leaned against it as he exhaled fumes into the environment. What was the point of smoking if you couldn't inadvertently spew your second hand smoke into some anonymous passersby?

He marveled at the citizens of New Heaven. They walked, jogged, and biked throughout the entire city. Despite technology available that could cart them from place to place, they retained the idea that fresh air and exercise were the best ways to health. Shadow stared as a small group of women jogged by with their ergomatic sneakers, lightweight hemp sweatsuits and natural hair. Their skin glistened with sweat that made them glow like mercury. They smiled graciously, slightly flirtatious.

Damnn! thought Shadow as he watched them pass him and followed their thick-shaking thighs. Shadow loved seeing ass shake. That was one thing about Black women he could never dislike—a phatt ass. He blamed this love of watching ass jiggled on his adolescent years, where he cracked the parental-watch code to watch years of BET's "Uncut." Video after video, ass upon ass—it was just too much for him.

These folks ain't like the regular Negus. Hell, even a brotha like me could get some play here.

He smiled, unconsciously long enough to almost forget who he was and why he was here. His frown returned with his fears. *They'd probably hate me, if they knew me. Probably just make fun of me, like they always do. Say I'm corny, or acting white.*

Lost in thought, Shadow barely heard the tap coming

from his vehicle. Quickly he tossed his cigarette at the "No Litter, Please" sign and re-entered the car.

"They're here," said one of the agents, barely moving his lips, while continuing to stare straight ahead.

"Okay, okay," whispered Shadow, "Stay cool. Let them get out the limo first and then we'll take our property."

The agent almost turned his head around, then deciding not to, spoke instead.

"Do we want to apprehend them also? Bring them in for questioning and reprogramming?"

Shadow stared ahead, mentally burning holes into the back of the agent's head. *Damn, he's close enough for me to bitch-slap him.*

"Are you being paid to think?"

The agent, slow to respond, finally whispered, "No."

Smiling, Shadow responded, "I thought so. From now on, keep your mouth shut and leave the thinking to me."

Truth be told, Shadow had actually developed some inkling of respect for his adversaries. He now saw they were a little more than streetcorner hustlers and, like him, had exceeded any expectations he had placed on them. They had actually moved beyond the level of "Thug Negus" and he could respect that. *But if they went through re-programming,* he thought, *the only thing left would be mental vegetation.*

Malik slowed the car to a halt in front of Kima's building, the Ali Towers. He excitedly anticipated the completion of his task. Two days and they'd be on a flight back to Africa. As excited as he was about the completion of his duties, he grew more excited about seeing Kima. She danced in his head like a seraphim in white flowing silk. She danced so much he was almost distracted to the point of danger.

A man with Malik's abilities could easily become overly dependent on them to the point of lowering his defenses. The Ego was ruthless bandit and in a millisecond could destroy decades of discipline and training, merely by allowing one to assume for a second that they had attained this growth due to being special or "da one" as opposed to overstanding that the Universe was working through them. Ego was the mistress of many a lost soul who dared to assume that their lower selves had given up the fight. Regardless of Ego's seductive murmurings, the battle between our lower and higher selves was an indispensable part of the universal ying and yang—and it was symbolized by Ra's daily battle against the serpent Apopis, whom he must defeat daily in order for the Sun to rise. The key for overstanding was that no side could be defeated; it could only be subdued, sublimated. As such, the Masters sought only balance. Without balance, the Universe could not exist.

Ellis slipped a stick of chewing gum into his mouth as if it were a placebo for nervousness. He opted out of the cognac mode.

Suck it up, Sun! he thought to himself.

The Ali towers rose 33 stories tall with green illuminated lights marking each level. Wardell and Jay simply stared with mouths open.

"Damn!" said Jay, "This how they doing it here? I got to gets me a lady down here like Malik and take some road trips, knowwhatemsaying?" he blurted out, slapping Wardell on the back of his head.

Wardell spinned angrily, staring at Jay, whose face upturned like a question mark.

"What?" screamed Jay at Wardell, attempting to egg him on, just to relieve frustration in a manner all too familiar to Ellis and Wardell.

"What? What, Biiiitch?!? I'll slap you sillier than Alan Keyes. Den, den I'll eat ya kidz for lunch," growled Jay, hunched up in Wardell's face like a baby Tyson.

Quietly and moving with slow contemplation like a man scrambling hard to explain to his girlfriend the phone number in his jacket, the lipstick on his collar and the naked girl standing in his living room, Wardell turned the other direction and sucked his teeth.

Jay had a mean streak in him that lay just below the surface; certain people could bring it into full blast and, at this point, Wardell was close to the finish line.

"Keep it down!" said Malik, rapidly redialing Kima's number. "I need to call Kima to let her know we're here. So, just hold your horses 'til then," said Malik, looking at the trio in his rear-view mirror.

"Kima."

"Malik!"

Her squeal sent a warm stream down Malik's spine. He wished it didn't. Normally people needed something he had, not the other way around. He was seeking detachment from this world—the Middle Path that was readily associated with Buddhists, but was the path of all spiritual masters.

Despite his advanced mental, spiritual, physiological development, he was still human—still a man, and reaching the level of Godz was a transformative process. Many believed it took several—even hundreds—of lifetimes to achieve that level, but for some it only took a single experience. Until that point, he was still human in the truest sense. And all humans needed something—something that stroked them in a manner that makes them feel loved and needed. Everyone needed someone to love and overstand him or her in a way that connected his or her souls.

Kima's spirit and sense of life made Malik able to enjoy every little thing. Even the way her voice smiled when she said his name. On his path towards spiritual mastery, he'd forgotten how to live in the NOW and enjoy life. He yearned for days of looking at his yard while his yet-to-be-born children played. He yearned to replace those lonely days of his with those of walking into the kitchen, with a scene of Kima's back to him, hair up, washing dishes. Her thick thighs, begging to be kissed softly. He'd call her name and she'd turn around smiling as he motioned for her to come sit on his lap.

Was that too much to ask for? he wondered.

Malik, focus, focus, he communicated to himself, overriding the Ego center and retuning his consciousness to the highest possible thoughts.

"Kima, we're right outside, across the street. Come down and meet us in the lobby. I know your building has a biometric scanner and if you get us in we can avoid the security data check at your front desk," said Malik.

"Okay, I'll meet you downstairs in five minutes. Positive Education Alters Corrupted Environments."

"Peace," added Malik.

Malik turned and faced the trio, warning them sternly,

like a camp counselor taking kidz outside the Hood for the first time.

"Now, this is a very special friend of mine—meaning that you will respect her and her place to the utmost. Is that clear?"

Everyone nodded, 'cept for Jay, who, of course, *had* to respond.

"Yeah, Yeah, Malik, we know that's yo' Honey-dip; we know you cutting that onion. You gets utmost respect, Sun. But don't act like we still felons, Kid. We was raised right—at least me and El. We know how to act and I'll make sure that if my shoes start humming too much, I'll put them on the balcony without being asked. And also, I'll make sure not to cut my toenails at the kitchen table without using a newspaper. Don't worry, Cuzin, we got you. Right, El?"

Ellis smirked, "Don't worry, Malik, Jay just fucken' wit' you. I'll make sure shit goes okay. Aaaight?"

Malik is once again dumbfounded. He wondered whether to simply laugh or pull out his Project Card. He just kept silent and hoped these fools had enough sense to not make him pull out his project card. 'cause, if they embarrassed him at Kima's, he was going to pull out a super-sized can of whup-ass.

THE HOUR OF DECISION

Malik grabbed his small book "The Laws of Compensation," and stuffed it into his back pocket. He wondered what would he have to give in return for Kima.

The backseat trio practically fell out of the car and shook themselves into shape.

Wardell tried hard to brush his sense of distress out of his suit like a suitor preparing to meet the parents for the first time. His whole persona was tied to how he felt he looked, for him the clothes always made him "the Man."

Ellis and Jay looked relieved for different reasons internally, but on the surface they were glad to be out of that funky car. Even Malik's incense couldn't do anything once Jay decided to take off his sneaks for the longest 90 seconds of the post-modern era. Passengers and driver eyes filled with water as their lives passed right in front of them. It was brutal—

worse than Chinese water torture or reading McWhore's "Self Sabotage."

The fresh air of New Heaven kicked them in the face and brought on a sense of relaxation that even Wardell could appreciate. They could hear the light sounds of jazz coming from an open concert several blocks away-the song seemed special—and for their ears only. Malik immediately recognized it: "Assinat" from Miles Davis' "Ascenseur Pour L'e'chafaud" album.

Looking both ways first, Malik led the trio across the street. Jay grabbed Wardell by the arm and walked him across. Neither noticed nor paid attention to the car parked several cars in front of them.

Looking through the rear view mirror, John Shadow tossed a mint in his mouth. He watched as the crew crossed the street.

"We want to let them walk up the stairs to the entrance and then apprehend our case."

The agent driving looked up in the rearview mirror at Shadow.

"Do we want to apprehend our contact?"

Shadow sucked on his mint, practically swallowing it.

"No, no, no! We don't need him, only the case. And in the process save ourselves a few million—Well, I save myself a few million," laughed Shadow. "Please don't think anymore or I'll be forced to shut your mouth permanently. You two distract the trio, and I will go after the gentleman with the case. Let's move now!" loudly whispered Shadow.

Standing in front of the towers, Malik saw Kima through the front door's glassy surface. He waved at her. Suddenly, the hairs on his neck stood up and, in one motion, he turned, pushing Ellis and Jay back towards the street.

"Let's go! Something is wrong. Let's move it back to the car—quick!"

Ellis and Jay don't question. They make a dash towards the car.

"Now!" ordered Shadow as he and the agents' jetted out the car, guns drawn, running hard towards the group.

"Freeze, mawfukas! Freeze! This is FBDIE!" yelled Shadow, gun drawn and pointed directly at Ellis, who is now holding the case. The other two agents, following his lead, direct their weapons at Malik, Wardell and Jay.

Jay and Ellis tensed up and don't move an inch. Malik stood dumbfounded, unbelieving that he didn't pick them up until it was too late. Wardell smiled, dropped his hands as if to thank God and excitedly walked towards Shadow.

"Freeze, bastard!" sneered Shadow.

Stupefied, Wardell stood between El, Jay and Malik and the FBDIE. Tears formed in his eyes as he pleaded.

"What's up, man? I came through for you didn't I? I just want my part of the deal, you know?"

Shadow barely blinked and spit on the ground. "That's your share, fool. This little junket of yours cost you your payment. So do a little crying and chalk it up to experience."

Wardell stepped closer to Shadow.

"C'mon, man, you gotta give me something, at least half. I ain't got nothing now. I sold out my family and my whole country—everybody. Where am I gonna go?"

Shadow flinched. "I'm warning you, stand back. You are not my problem anymore and I will not hesitate to bust a cap in you."

Tears dropping from Wardell's eyes brushed onto his lapels. He reached into his pocket for a handkerchief and both agents quickly moved the focus of their weapons off Malik and Jay and onto Wardell. Within a split second, Malik slid between the empty space, grabbed the gun of the federal nearest him with his right hand, and quickly disabled him by breaking his windpipe while simultaneously firing the weapon, shooting the other federal.

Everyone stood opened mouthed, except Shadow, who immediately shot Wardell in the chest and then quickly grabbed El from behind. Shadow's gun was pointed at El's head. The two agents and Wardell lay on the ground, crumpled and bleeding. Malik pointed his weapon at Shadow, who gripped El tighter, keeping his gun on El's temple.

"I guess this is what we call a Mexican standoff," chuckled Shadow. Malik's silence threatened Shadow, who continued his monologue.

"Well, maybe not. You see, Sir, I have no morals—none whatsoever. Either I get this case and go about my business or you kill me. Oh, well, of course, that is, after I kill your friend here. Now, being a betting man, which I am not, I would bet that your friend's life is more important to you than what's in this case. That I would be sure of," continued Shadow.

Feeling helpless, El searched his inner self for strength. He didn't want to die yet he didn't want to fail. *U and Musa had faith in him that he could actually deliver; he couldn't pull up short. But what about Makeda and their unborn child? He had to come through. Shit, no one had ever taken him serious enough for anything. If I die, what happens to Makeda? But if he gets the case, what happens to Africa?*

Now with the whole weight of the world on his shoulder Ellis realized what needed to happen. Africa needed the staff; lives of millions of people were way more important than his one life. Ellis was determined that he would not go down in history and the idiot who pulled up short on his jumper with a tick left on the clock.

His eyes began to water and he finally cleared the phlegm from his throat.

"Malik, shoot this bastard. It's crunch time baby, let's bring it home."

Shadow adjusted his grip tighter. "Shut up, fool, you know you ain't got the courage to die. I know, umm, Malik doesn't want your blood on his hands. Right, Malik?" said Shadow, smiling while seeking to shift the chess match back in his favor.

"Since this man here has shown enough courage to give his life away, I wonder how he feels about me shooting his friend over there," said Shadow, looking directly at Jay, who still hadn't moved.

"Malik, my man, I will give you and your friend here ten seconds to comply with my demands or the gentleman to your left—Jay, I believe?—will go to see his maker.

"Now, if Malik is smart, he will fire two rounds into the rear tire of the limo, place his weapon on the ground and sit patiently while I walk with Ellis to my car. Once inside, I'll let you go. Right, Malik?" said Shadow with a slight tinge of nervousness in his voice.

Malik stood silent for what seemed like forever. In a life- or-death situation, just like playoff basketball, ten seconds is a long time. *Maybe Ellis is right*, he thought. *He has to be sacrificed for the rest of us—for the continent—for the world. If Shadow kills him and I kill Shadow, we keep the staff and return it to Africa. My mission will be completed. One life for the life of many is not too much to ask, is it?"*

Malik's gun pointed at Shadow. Shadow pressed his gun to El's temple and placed his trigger finger a hairs-length from clicking.

Malik smiled and slowly lowered his gun towards the limo's rear tire and fired two quick shots. Then he placed the gun carefully on the ground. Shadow grinned, "Malik, my man. You've made the right decision. Ellis, you are a lucky man. Jay even luckier, very lucky, the Godz must like you—today."

Shadow maintained his hold on Ellis and began to walk backwards towards his parked car. Step by step, they inched further away from Malik, and a silent Jay. Malik watched as disappointment washed all over his face.

Ellis had summoned his deepest personal courage, but it wasn't enough; they had failed in their mission—choked in Game Seven. If the Universe had any sense, it would've cut them before the season started was the general sentiment. Well, except for Shadow, who was happier than a Black conservative draped in a flag while speaking at the GOP convention.

Shadow reached the car with glee, never once taking his eyes off Malik. *This guy was dangerous; maybe we can get him to work for us*, he thought. Looking at Malik's face, *Maybe not.*

Opening the car door, Shadow whispered to El:

"Well chum, looks like the end of the road. Never one to leave the party early, I must say it's been fun."

Shadow chuckled as he snatched the case from El, started his car and said, "Good job, you almost came close to beating me, which is.....um, well, impossible. Until next time, and WE OUT...haaaa, haaaaah haaaah," laughed Shadow as he drove away with El standing there, shaken to his core.

Ellis walked slowly back towards Jay and Malik.

"Yo, El, we did our best, don't sweat it, man—you didn't go out like no punk, nawmean?" declared Jay.

Eyes weary, head down, El looked up at Malik.

"Why didn't you shoot him? Why? I was ready to make the sacrifice. Why?"

Pulling a chew stick from his pocket, Malik bit down and looked away.

"Look El, me taking your life was not a decision that I am qualified to make. That's up to the Universe. Everything works according to the laws of compensation, so don't sweat it. Something stopped me from pulling the trigger—and believe me, I wanted to. I guess you alive for a reason."

Jay looked around at the damage and spotted a car across the street with its window slightly cracked. Quickly, he went to work and in a matter of seconds hotwired it and pulled up next to Malik and El.

"Yo, man, I don't mean to spoil this episode of 'Real World Reunion,' but we best be going before Five-O show up, feel me?"

Neither Malik nor El saw any logic in arguing. They quickly climbed into the car. Jay did a 180-degree turn and sped off. Standing in front of the building, Kima caught a glimpse of Malik as they drove off. He looked, but didn't wave. She waved anyway as the trio gets ghost.

POST-THEN: JUNE 2022

Along the Georgia coast, Ellis and Makeda are resting in the back yard deck of their home grilling fish and playing with their twins Anu and Kenyatta. Ellis is showing them a docudrama about Richard Wright when the front door bell chimes in.

"I'll get it, Honey," chirped Makeda, quickly flipping red snapper over on the grill. She walked around the side to see a mail truck parked outside and mailman on the porch with letter in hand.

"Ellis Rey's residence?"

"Yes. I'll sign for it," Makeda said quickly.

For Makeda, getting mail was almost as exciting as going shopping. She hurriedly sprinted around the side of the house to the back, almost tripping in the process.

"Ellis, it's for you and it's from Sudan."

Ellis looks up from the computer screen.

"Sudan?"

"Yes, Sudan!" exclaims Makeda, smiling like a child. "Open it; I can't wait."

Ellis just stares at his wife, amazed as always at her sincere exuberance, which was just the opposite of his melatonin persona. He held the envelope up to the sunlight and looked at it from several directions.

"Are you going to open it?" Makeda chirped again.

"Okay, Okay," said Ellis quickly admiring the stamp of the pharaoh Piankhi. Ellis slowly opened the letter, careful not to tear it. He was the type who saved all his personal letters, articles, photos and other items in such a miserly way a curator would be impressed. Unfolding the letter, it read...

Ellis,

One hopes to find you in excellent health and spirits. I know the experience of being a parent can be most rewarding—don't worry how I know—everything gets back to me in some way or form. I know we lost contact after the staff experience, but I simply wanted to share some things with you that the Old Teacher shared with me that may make sense of your journey during the past year.

The continent is still doing fine, as a matter of fact we are having a bumper crop year all over the continent and fertile ground is sprouting up all over the place. The journey for the staff was simply part of our souls' evolution as a people, not more important than us. The rebirth of Africa in reality had nothing to do with the staff—in fact, when the FBDIE had it tested by NASA they found it simply to be a piece of wood from Africa. What happened to that fellow Shadow was a pretty ugly sight, I am told.

Not to make this too long, but what the Old Teacher imparted to me was and is simple and powerful. Our power is not some mythical object or belief that a messiah is coming. Our power is the consciousness of the people—not anything else. That consciousness is responsible for the resurrection of the people and the land.

It is through this group consciousness that we bring to life what is needed—your scientists may call it a spiritual form of nanotechnology. There was no magic-balm, or magical wood able to begin the process of rebirth that magic—or, as some people call it, God Force. It is already a part of us. All we need to do is to bring it into existence.

In other words, we don't need to wait for God or a Messiah to return because they have never left and are already within us. It is like the sayings of Yshua (The Book of John) 11:34-38. *"Is it not written in your law, I said, ye are gods? If he called them gods, unto whom the word of God came, and the scripture cannot be broken."*

It is the same as in Luke 17:6, *"And the Lord said, If ye had faith as a grain of mustard seed, ye might say unto this sycamine tree, Be thou plucked up by the root, and be thou planted in the sea; and it would obey you."*

This "overstanding" began long before the holy books emerged and your people must now overstand who they are and the God Force is within them. Neither you nor I need wait for anything to bring into existence that which we seek.

The time that we have always sought is NOW.
Please hug Makeda and the little ones for me.
Your Brother,
Yusef Black

Ellis folded up the letter, slipped it back into the envelope, and stared into the eyes of his two infants.

"Well, what was the letter about?" asked Makeda.

"Oh, it was just Yusef," said Ellis shrugging her off.

Undaunted, Makeda continued to attempt to pull bits out of Ellis.

"Well what did he want? What did he say? Are we going to Sudan?"

Ellis leaned back and looked skyward. "Oh nothing, just that it's time."

Makeda shrugged her shoulders and pouted, "Time

for what? Aaww, you're no fun at all," she said, grabbing him in a playful headlock.

"That's why you love me so much, huh?" cracked Ellis.

"Yep," added Makeda. "But it ain't the only reason," she added in her sexiest voice.

"Okay now, " giggled Ellis. "Don't start nothing you can't finish."

Giggling back, Makeda responded, "Well, don't start none," as Ellis joins in, "won't be none!"

CODA

"One of the consequences of quantum mechanics, hitting at the very essence of the 'common-sense' Newtonian model, was the elimination of the dichotomy between subjective and objective. In quantum theory, the properties of an electron or photon do not exist until they are perceived and measured. Thus, what a photon is going to be—wave or particle—depends entirely on how and when it is measured; it comes into existence as one or the other only by virtue of being measured!

"If the most neutral, unencumbered experiment imaginable could be designed, the results of the reaction would still be altered by the very act of observing it!

"This means that the perceiver and the thing perceived are indissolubly linked; absolute objectivity is impossible.

"Moreover, from the quantum point of view, things exist because they are perceived...."

--From *The Star of Deep Beginnings* by Dr. Charles Finch III

www.ingramcontent.com/pod-product-compliance
Lightning Source LLC
Chambersburg PA
CBHW070622100726
47907CB00007B/1825